FLESH AND METAL

FLESH AND METAL

JOHN EARLY

CARROLL & GRAF PUBLISHERS, INC.

NEW YORK

Copyright © 1998 by John Early

First Carroll & Graf edition 1998

Carroll & Graf Publishers, Inc.
19 West 21st Street
New York, NY 10010

Library of Congress Cataloging-in-Publication data is available.
ISBN: 0-7867-0511-6

Manufactured in the United States of America

1

*J*ane. In the years before Jake Warner's life assumed the posture of flat Dakota prairies, he often conjured the name, and the peace it afforded let him go on thinking that, as long as he had her, there was no one he needed to convince, that such a single talisman would endure forever. Later, when he allowed her memory to return, he permitted small shards of their marriage to enter, like how, at the outer edge of the daybed along the rear wall of the screened porch, he had rolled away from her and disentangled his legs from the light blanket wound snugly around them. How, through the screens fronting the lake, he had surveyed the tops of trees hooded by white clouds along the far shore, their leaves newly illumined by the rising sun to his left. How, in that safe silence, the early July air had moved coolly into the porch with the sounds of birds.

Jake swung his legs over and sat along the daybed's side, stiff from sleeping through the night in a bed he was not accustomed to. He stood, naked, among his clothes and hers on the floor, chilled after having lain next to her under the blanket. He remembered how the night before they had sat in separate chairs watching the last light, smelling the dew collecting in the grass; how, when it had grown dark, he had suggested the daybed and two beers; how it hadn't been long before they made love; and how, too tired and too content to go into the house and their bedroom, they had slept to the rhythm of the mild waves breaking along the rocks and sand.

Jake turned to her from the lake, whose calm surface he could now see. She had not awakened but moved into the middle of the small space they had shared, turning toward him almost fully on her back. Before she had fallen asleep she must have been chilled, for he saw she had put on his white T-shirt. Jake's eyes followed the white neck opening as it lay wrinkled above her breasts, whose rise he took until the small protrusion of a nipple. Around her neck, a silver-chained half of the engraved oval pendant they had shared since marrying, the halves when joined composing their mutual desire for elongated love, "so much a long communion tends to make us what we are." Jake felt his half slight against his chest. Her brown hair obscured her eyes and forehead, Jake descending along the line of her nose and remembering how he had brushed his lips along hers and how his hands had been on that brown skin, his mouth. He bent, reached to touch her face but refrained, thinking he might wake her. And before he left her to shower and dress and drive into the city, the light and the air moving and the gentle rise and fall of her breathing and the white cotton against tan skin and over swellings and the memory of their lovemaking and his whispered poem looking down on her again: "as long as neither angels in heaven above nor demons down under the sea ever dissever my soul from yours." *Jane.*

∎

Four years after her husband stuck his hand out a pickup's window to point at a pheasant, and then watched the meat and bone of that hand fly away into the gray October sky, Beverly Mortonson stepped into a sun-filled bakery in Mitchell, South Dakota, and saw Jake Warner, the lawyer she believed had screwed her and her husband Tom out of a lot of money, sitting in a booth reading a newspaper. She had little desire to sit across from him and speak of the past, but once she had seen his face she felt she had no choice, thinking *it's the last thing I need to get beyond it forever.* She had tried very hard to manage Tom's memory, to grieve as she had been instructed and move on, but *sometimes it's a smell, like wet new grass that takes you to an old yard where you lived when you first got married. Sometimes color, sometimes just the outline of a stranger's face that reminds you of someone you last saw in a coffin.*

She had driven from her farm a few miles outside of town. When she recognized Jake in the corner booth she stood in jeans and a sweatshirt covered with grain dust and *my hair looks like shit*, but she dismissed that as less than what she had to say. She walked resolutely over the worn linoleum toward him, holding her purse against her stomach with both arms like it might keep her safe from what she thought about whenever something flashed Tom's face to her.

Jake sat reading intently, about halfway through a long chocolate roll and a green ceramic cup of coffee. He looked up when he realized someone had stopped at his elbow, was facing him.

The woman cleared her throat and "You're Jake Warner, right?" her words more an accusation than a question.

Jake put on his usual smile and "Yes, but I'm sorry, I don't recognize you."

"Beverly Mortonson, Tom's wife," offering her hand. Jake remembered the name, then put it with a case from two or three years before. After the particulars came back to him he lost a little of his smile, remembering as well as she what had passed between them. He glanced around the cafe looking for Tom. He shoved his coffee cup and the small plate with the roll to one side and "Of course, of course," sliding out of the booth and standing. "Where's Tom? How is he?" as if the three of them were old classmates or friends.

She told him very calmly, "Tom died about a year ago."

Jake blinked in surprise but did not hesitate with "I'm deeply sorry. Honestly." Then sympathetically, "Accident?"

"He'd been sick for quite a while. During the trial even. Cancer."

Jake searched his memory for images of Tom, thinking maybe he could see physical clues that he'd missed then and "I remember him not looking all that well, but I didn't know it was so serious. He was such a solid man." *About my height,* Jake thought, *just under six feet, but powerful, especially in his upper body. Thick, strong hands.*

As Jake recalled shaking hands with Tom Mortonson his wife remembered how Tom used to touch her, how he felt on top of her in bed, but then she told herself *don't think about that.*

Beverly Mortonson resolute and "Mind if I sit? I got something to say." Jake motioned for her to take the red-vinyled bench opposite him. She kept her purse to her stomach as she slid in and *he knows what I am going to say won't be pleasant.*

She took a long breath and "Ever since we had that claim with you, and lost that trial, I wanted to tell you what a shit you are. So when I saw you over here I told myself that I wouldn't feel right knowing I had a chance and didn't."

Jake, ignoring her words and their tone, said smoothly "Look, I'm sorry that whole mess had to come between us. I know we could've gotten along a lot better under different circumstances. It wasn't a good way to get to know you and Tom."

"We'd a been a lot better off if we'd never met you."

"True," he agreed. "And if not for the accident, you wouldn't have. Bad luck, I guess," smiling.

She stared impassively and *bad luck—Christ, I'm not letting him off with that.*

She hardened her voice and "It's what happened after the accident . . . that could've been different. Tom got used to his hand being gone. But we never did understand what happened with the insurance. You could've made Tom and I a lot happier that last year or two. But you're all such miserable assholes. God it pisses me off the way you treated us. You and that fucking insurance company. You—" Her purse couldn't stop the tears, which surprised her when they ran suddenly. But just as quickly she checked them, refusing to be a pathetic woman in front of the man she felt herself hating. She took a tissue from her purse and wiped her nose, dabbed at her cheeks where the quick tears had passed.

"I didn't mean to cry when I came over here," Jake wanting to comfort her and "don't worry about it."

They were silent for what seemed like minutes, staring at the gray Formica marred by scratches from uncountable plates and cups and silverware. She decided to leave and began to slide out of the booth because she believed she had said all that required saying. But Jake stopped her; he couldn't leave what she said alone, couldn't accept it because *it's not the truth* and "Stay a minute, let me explain myself again, why the company took the position that it did."

She sat back and "You've *explained* that crap before. I didn't come over here to have a courtroom drama about it. I came to call you an asshole and I've done that." *I haven't been this angry in a year,* she thought. *I'm quiet since Tom died. There isn't much to say about being lonely.*

In Jake's speech the unmistakable tone that it was important for her to understand, like he was giving a child some very important instructions and "Just listen, will you? I've never talked to just you. Will you listen?"

She glared at him and "It won't make any difference."

He had full control of the details of their case now and "Yes it will. You see, the thing that bothered me about that deal with Tom and you was that you took it so personally against me. You seemed to blame *me* for everything that happened."

"Why wouldn't we? You wouldn't pay us what we wanted, what you owed."

"But we *didn't* owe you anything. Still, that isn't what I'm saying right now. It was as if you blamed *me* for Tom losing his hand. Like it was *me* who blew it off. And if there's one thing that's true, that no one can argue about, it's that I didn't pull the trigger. Gary Myers did that. When you looked at me, like you're looking right now, it seemed as if you believed I held the gun. I couldn't—I can't—understand that."

The woman sat unsoftened and "You owed and you would-n't pay. You're a lawyer, that's your job. What the hell else were we supposed to think of you?"

"What do you mean *I* owed you?"

"You, the insurance company, it's all the same thing. You owed us for Tom's hand."

"Wrong. Gary owed you. He's the one that aimed that gun and pulled the trigger." She listened, thinking *always the explanations, the only things you get from lawyers and insurance people. They got nothing else to give.*

She practically shouted, "That was an accident. Gary didn't mean it. They were hunting and he made a mistake. He would change it if he could. But you, you meant everything you did, and you wouldn't change it now for anything. Bastard. Measure everything with your checkbook. You knew how bad Gary felt. That's payment enough from him. He still calls almost every day, and it isn't just words he gives me. He'll live with what he did the rest of his life. But you . . . "

"It may surprise you, Mrs. Mortonson, but I have feelings myself. I didn't particularly enjoy denying you what you thought you had coming, but that was the only position I could take. I can't go around passing out money to people just because I feel sorry for them. Legally I was correct, the company was correct. They hired me to look into their liability. I did that and proceeded according to the law. Somebody owed you, yes, but it wasn't me." He looked at her like he thought that ought to clear things up, like his words had served as dispensations of incontrovertible truth.

"To hell with that *legal* shit," she said. "Just like goddamned insurance policies, only you people can understand them. You write them so you can twist them any way you want. The agent smiles and takes your money and then when you need some of it back, then nobody's smiling. They're *talking*." She suddenly hated words, wanted to get rid of Jake and all that he had spoken. Back to where Tom was sleeping next to her.

Jake believing inviolably in right and wrong and "That just isn't true. Why do you think they have insurance commissioners? And courts? Judge Conroy said we took the correct position. There's no way we can just interpret a policy any way we please. They're contracts, they stipulate specific things."

"Why wouldn't a judge agree with you? You're all in bed together."

Jake sat incredulous that anyone could hold such an opinion and "That just isn't right. If anything, judges favor the public against insurance companies." He parted his hands, palms up, showing her that what she needed to see was right there, plainly visible on the tabletop.

"Just an accident, I suppose, that judges usually say you're right?" She sensed she didn't know what she was talking about, but she knew she would go on so as not to give Jake any peace.

"But they *don't*. In fact, more often than not they side with the insured, or claimants like you," his face and words taking on the urgency of a preacher's.

"No doubt."

He pleaded with her, "They *do*, I know what I'm talking about," ignoring her anger and *she's softening, she'll believe.*

But she spat out "You don't know shit. You can talk smooth as you want, but that doesn't change that Tom didn't get a damn penny for all his suffering. You proud of that?"

Jake remembered when he was young, remembered Mark and what not speaking can do. He had to go on talking and "It isn't a matter of pride, for heaven's sake. The point is that you felt you were owed some money for the loss of Tom's hand. And you were. Why people equate money with the loss of a limb I don't know, but that's the way it is. Tom *did* have some money coming. But not from me, not from Gary's insurance carrier. Why don't you go talk to Gary Myers, tell him what you're telling me?"

"*He* didn't owe us anything."

"*He's* the one you sued. *He's* the one shot Tom's hand off. I don't even own a gun."

"We sued him to get at you. Gary's only mistake was getting mixed up with you bastards. Gary was a friend."

"But who, if not the person that injured you, owed you money, then?"

Her anger flowered and "Jesus, how many times do I have to say it? *You.* But you lied and twisted the words and got out of it," thinking *it's sickening, like we're children arguing over who's going to sit in the front seat.*

Jake felt as if his whole life depended on her nodding and saying *Yes, now I get it, you're forgiven.*

"Listen to your own logic, Mrs. Mort—"

"Don't tell me what I'm saying. I can hear." She glanced at the knife near his plate and *I ought to grab that fucking thing and run it along his throat. See how he likes his talking then.*

Jake ignored the direction of her stare and "I wonder if you can. Will you drop your hatred for one minute? What you're telling me is that the man who blew your husband's hand off didn't owe you or Tom anything, and that I, as representative of the insurance company that carried Gary's automobile insurance, did owe you, and that the whole thing was my fault. I wasn't within a hundred miles of Tom when Gary's gun went off. Why do you hate *me?* Just because his auto insurance didn't cover what he did doesn't mean I—I mean the company— weaseled out on what they owed. You *must* understand." He smacked his hand against the table, the loud noise rattling the silverware and causing the five or six others in the bakery to turn. "*I* didn't wrong you. Please."

She saw in his need that she had a way to hurt him and "Fry in hell."

Jake couldn't let it go, get up and walk away, understand his present speech could not make up for old mistakes, so he continued with "I am, right now." He waited, thinking, then "A legal trial determined that my company wasn't obligated to pay on Gary's behalf. The automobile insurance did not apply. Do you pay bills you don't owe?"

"So the whole system screwed us."

"It wasn't my fault Gary didn't have any other kind of insurance."

"You fucking lawyers are all the same."

Jake suddenly smiled and "No, there are a lot of insurance people who can't hardly spell their name. Not every one is smooth and sophisticated like me." She waited, wondering if he thought he'd been funny. Jake looked half sick but *words can make me well* and "Anyway, we insured Gary's pickup and—"

"Jesus yes and I know that on that policy there was liability coverage for anything he might do to injure someone. He injured Tom. End of case. Write out the check."

A waitress came over and put his bill on the table between them.

Jake decided he would talk until the end of time if that's what it took to convince her. "But don't you see? He had to injure Tom with the car. It makes perfect *sense*. He didn't necessarily have to be driving the car, he could have opened the door into Tom, or slammed the trunk lid on . . . well, on his hand, let's say, but the car in some way had to be the instrument of the injury. The *instrument*. The policy clearly states that."

She knew better than he what had happened and "Pickups don't have trunks. They were *riding* in the truck. Hunting. They saw pheasants, stopped, got out. Tom and Gary were both *touching* the truck when it happened" *Why don't I just leave?*

Jake nodded and "True, but what caused Tom's hand to be blown off had nothing to do with the car. It was Gary's shotgun, not his car, that injured Tom. It was Gary's use of the gun, not his use of the car. And we insured him only for the car. It's all quite clear. All you have to do is listen."

"It was the car," she shot back at him. "Gary was leaning on it."

"No, the gun. Personal liability, not auto. The court said the auto policy did not apply," suddenly thinking that a man had slid into the booth beside her, someone else who wanted explanations. But Jake wouldn't look at him.

"Why the hell did you offer us a settlement that first time, then?" She remembered clearly that night he'd come out to the house with a check.

"I was wrong. I—"

"Excuse me, did you say you were wrong?"

"About that offer, yes. I almost made a ten-thousand-dollar mistake. I didn't realize we didn't owe the claim."

"So you think ten thousand is enough for a hand?"

"Of course not," he said. "A hand . . . a hand is a living part of you." He held his hand in front of him and waved it over his plate like some fool might and "How can you pay money for a body part?" He was fighting his memory and his fear, almost stuttering.

"You said you'd pay that first night, then you wouldn't. What do you call that?"

"I would have filled in that check for ten grand right there. You should have taken it. But you and Tom laughed, practically threw me out."

"A hand is worth more than ten grand."

"Not legally."

"Fuck you, legal or however."

"What I mean is that in the past, in trials where the person suing has lost a hand, ten thousand has been an average verdict against the party found liable. So that's what I offered" and *I'm in control here, I am.*

"Christ," she said, "if you were in a band I bet you could play more tunes than anybody else in the world," then "You would have gone higher?"

"Some. Not much. Tom worked with his hands, but he wasn't a doctor or someone whose livelihood completely depended on having two good hands. His job at the grain elevator, he could have gone on with that. But before making another offer I had to obtain authorization from the company's main office in

Denver. When I sent the report in some new supervisor looked
it over and thought maybe we didn't owe it. He gave us some
court cases for precedent. I was embarrassed, him doing my job
for me, and doing it better. I pursued it. As it turned out, he was
right; the auto coverage didn't apply to the matter between Tom
and Gary."

"So Tom got one less hand and no money and we couldn't get
any from Gary even if we wanted. He didn't have shit. You bastards got stacks of it, why don't you share?"

"That's a myth. You should read corporate reports sometime."

"Yeah, I'll do that."

"Really, I'll send you one. You'll see these companies don't
have such deep pockets."

"They had ten grand more than we did."

"But see—"

She had suddenly come to the end of it and "Christ, what am
I sitting here for? Tom's dead. I'm alone. What a goddamn wonderful life." She turned to the wall and began crying.

Jake pushed a napkin toward her and "I wish you'd believe
how sorry I am about Tom. That's why I'm explaining all this.
So you'd know I really care." *Now he sounds like a greeting
card,* she thought.

"We were fine till you came along, now you tell me you *care.*
How nice. How fucking nice."

"Tom lost his hand before you met me."

"You had a chance to be decent, but what did you do? Went
to court."

"I didn't make you unhappy. I really didn't. The gun and the
cancer you can blame for that."

"How you treated him, Tom couldn't deal with that. He did-
n't trust anyone after you. I thought he was getting better, I
believed he would live. Then you. Then he was dead."

"So Tom's *death* was my fault too?"

She wanted so badly to hurt him and "Yes."

Jake threw up his arms and shook his head at the ceiling. "I can't . . ." like he wasn't talking to her but to someone in one of the apartments above the bakery, someone in the sky outside.

She looked not at the sky but at him and "Tom wouldn't have been sick if he hadn't been so depressed. I've read about how your mental health affects your physical health. And you shot that all to hell with Tom."

Jake lowered his eyes to hers again and "Cancer isn't a state of mind, a side effect of depression."

"Oh, you're a doctor now, too. Tom kept it inside him for a year, then it just went wild and they couldn't stop it. His hair fell out and he couldn't work. He had too much to worry about. If we'd had that money it would have been a lot better for him. But he spent the last months worrying about me and the farm. I'll probably have to sell it next year."

"You didn't have any life insurance?"

"No. Want to sell me some?"

Jake nearly desperate and "I would have made it better if I could have. Mark, you've got to believe me."

"Mark? Who's Mark?"

"What did I say?"

"You called me Mark."

"No."

"All right, believe what you want. But killing people isn't a good way to make them better."

"God, I did not kill your husband. I did not kill your husband. I did not."

"Keep on, you might convince yourself."

"There's no way you'll ever understand this, is there?"

"None," she said, adding an emphatic "Fuck you."

Help me Jane. And with those words Jake convinced himself that his speech, as it had always but once, had finally reached Beverly Mortonson, and when he saw this he imagined he had slid out from his side of the booth and in beside her. He had not given in to her anger, her despair, but had somehow gotten around them. He had put his left arm around her shoulders as she sat sobbing quietly, and they had then talked as friends. Jake believed that at some point in their new speech she had said "Now I get it. You're forgiven," and her face had lost whatever strain had troubled it. In this glossy illusion Jake sat satisfied, kneeling at the altar of right and wrong with an offering plate full of words and *I believe, I believe.*

■

A week later Susan Wheeler rigid in a high-backed spindle chair watching her son ten feet away side-sleeping on a matching blue-fabricked couch, the boy even in sleep stiff like his mother, not as he used to sleep before an iron-shod hoof in a sloping pasture shot up deadly through humid air and the heavy scent of knee-high grass and forever rearranged his face and life. She has removed all photographs of that previous face, pictures of him smiling, laughing, the face balanced and even. His new face, with its reconstructed half, would be forever *wrong*. Her face has altered too, for it allows itself since that afternoon only the memory of smiling. She remembers how they used to be, she together with her boy.

Across the carpet, watching the woman and her son, Jake sits, their lawyer come to the house again as he has a dozen times through the three years since the boy startled the horse. Jake has brought finally a rectangular paper draft and a two-page release form to settle the matter between the boy and the man who owned the horse. Not once, despite his having inquired long into its size, weight, breed, and temperament, has Jake ever wondered what became of the horse. Triangulated about the shadowed room the three of them arranged in a silence that Jacob Warner refuses to acknowledge, different from the woman who acknowledges the side-turned face that no longer resembles the son she bore.

The woman sharing with Jake a desire to fill the silence and

"I'm glad his father didn't have to see him like this. They looked so much alike. I'm just happy he didn't have to suffer through this with us." Immediately acknowledging the absurdity in her own words and *I speak only to make sound and it doesn't matter what I say.*

Jake desiring to reaffirm his enduring belief that all error finds correction in speech, turning as he often has to poems loved and memorized long before he learned the law and denied the heavy-hoofed nature of life and "You and Michael have suffered a lot. But try . . . 'to strive, to seek, to find, and not to yield.' That's Tennyson. 'Ulysses.' I often think of those lines when I feel like events are overwhelming me." But then unexpectedly, like a hoof, *she requires of me more than poetry.*

She fixes him with a stare. "And strive for what, Mr. Warner? Seek what? Knowing what I know, how will I not yield?" In her eyes across the room and in the tenor of her voice suddenly Jake sees and hears another's but as always refuses to allow that other presence in his memory. He feels the need to say something more to her but cannot find the words, cannot for once call them up; the premonition of a coming silence fills the cavity near his heart and renders him speechless. Trying to think only of the woman and the boy and *two years settling this, two years, a good check now to take care of them.* Other thoughts he will not allow, of Michael's face disappearing, of what it must have been like when the huge brown horse, spurred by God knows what, shuddered and shot its rear hoof out, its sharp heavy hoof. What it must have been like later for Michael to come out of darkness into that big open summer field with the horse still close by cropping grass languidly unaware and the world the same only half his face smashed in and one eye gone, the blood of what he had been a half hour before in his mouth with pieces of his teeth. The T-shirted back of another boy, turning.

Some minutes pass, then the woman not caring but "Did you bring the check?"

Jake remembering the certainty of numbers and "Yes," reaching into his thin briefcase and extracting a manila folder which he spreads open on his lap. Recalling other shelved files back at the office, thick legal folders filled with words nearly beyond measure, medical reports and summaries of visits and negotiations. Form after form after form filled out dutifully, words that have led to this resolution; he pages, locates the yellow check, takes it between his forefinger and thumb, lifts it like a trophy and "Right here." He glances at the black numbers marking it and *three hundred fifty thousand dollars less my third*. He rises from the chair, walks to her and deposits the paper in her shaking upturned palms. She stares, revolves it front to back.

Jake smiling, official, and "I'll need you to sign this release. It's exactly as we discussed. This money is exclusive of some future reconstructive surgery costs, which you know all about. Take your time, read it through."

The woman shaking her head and "I don't need . . . I trust you." Pausing, then "Do you have a pen?" Jake reaching into his pocket and holding forth a cheap ballpoint, watching as she scratches out her name. Automatically and meaninglessly he speaks words with good intentions but hollow as rotting, fallen tree trunks, "You'll be all right now."

Then, for the second time ever, *those aren't the right sounds.*

He shivers, takes the release and steps back to his chair, fights what's coming by turning and smiling and *thank God this is over*, but when his eyes find the woman she is risen and walking toward the boy, holding out the check before her like a chalice. She pauses over the shallow-breathing form and to Jake "We'll be all right now?"

Jake wary of her question but "Yes."

The woman bends slowly at the waist, places the check over the boy's face, the paper and its attendant shadow covering the asymmetric undulations. She straightens, moves her hands in shallow circles before her, mouths something like an incantation. Jake sees her face tighten as a long-ignored supplicant's might in a last prayer. She bends again, takes the check from the boy's face. She and Jake see the unnatural bones and skin unaltered.

Inquisitor again, she swivels to Jake and "We'll be all right now?"

Jake involuntarily wordless, the woman watching, thinking *even he might begin to get it now, even he has no words.* She bends and kisses the boy so tenderly Jake feels tears but stops them.

Jake shakes his head to clear it, ignores the evidence that he has brought them nothing at all, that after the horse and the pasture and that summer afternoon there would not be anything he *could* bring; half smiling, trying to convince himself and "Well, I guess that's the end of it," but simultaneously seeing her head twist slightly, like a horse's coming up the pasture and seeing him for the first time.

■

Jake left the woman and the sleeping boy and drove through the warm streets toward his office, one room among many on the second floor of an old, four-story stone building in downtown Mitchell. A city of twelve thousand known for little else but as the home of the world-famous Corn Palace, where Bob Hope had once performed during the annual city celebration in the fall; fashioned on one of the building's sides had been an appropriately nosed portrait of him entirely of ears of corn. A typical Plains city with one short Main Street and white frame houses, little more than an hour's drive west of the Minnesota border, almost that same distance north of Nebraska. It lies along the James River between a small lake to the north and Interstate 90. Each humid summer, thousands of travelers go past it on their way to places interesting in a way that Mitchell is not, to fish the Missouri River, to find, awestruck, the majesty of the Black Hills and Badlands rising from the plains. Sometimes the colorful billboards big with enthusiasm con tourists onto the Mitchell exit to see "the world's only Corn Palace," a brick building with bushels of corn affixed to its exterior walls and strange, mosque-like turrets on its roof. Inside are basketball tournaments and concerts and souvenirs.

Jake drove into his parking slot at the rear of the building, glancing at his 3:30 watch and *I thought it was later.* He sat looking at the black-lettered sign announcing his ownership of the stall and deciding whether to go in and take the elevator up to the office, denying that anything was wrong and *I've no more appointments today.* He did not consider how he had never before left work early—had never felt the need—or that doing so now would admit that the check on the boy's face and his own lack of speech were warrants that what was to come would not be the same as what had passed before in his thirty-five years.

He partnered with two other men, both older, in the alpha-betical Anderson, Klein, and Warner. Randall I. Anderson and Stephen M. Klein had begun the firm more than thirty years before after graduating as classmates from the law school at the University of South Dakota in Vermillion. A two-man opera-tion suited them until 1975, ten years before Jake took a check to the woman with a strange boy on her couch. They had won a multi-million-dollar liability suit brought by a Mitchell man's wife against a large hospital in Omaha. Her husband had undergone surgery to remove a brain tumor, the surgeon taking the tumor but neglecting to remove a small sponge. An infec-tion developed and the man lived as a vegetable for nearly two years before dying, accumulating huge medical expenses and producing in his wife immeasurable anguish. After that case, Anderson and Klein had found a flood of the wronged and injured at their door, and they decided to add one additional lit-igator. They turned to their alma mater and found Jacob Warner, not the top graduate of his class but close enough. Moreover, he was from Sioux Falls. They weren't about to hire someone out-of-state; they wanted a homegrown boy, and they took Jake. Plus, his good-looking wife was from Parkston, a small town twenty miles south of Mitchell. Her parents farmed there. Jane taught school, the two of them were respectable and God-fearing—what more could be required to satisfy iconoclastic farmers and small-town citizens? They watched him carefully for three years and then agreed that he was as smart and as honest as any other young lawyer in the state, and that he could carry on the good name of their firm after they retired. They made him a partner, and he made himself and them a lot of money. People liked Jacob Warner because he wrote well and always seemed to have the right words; when he spoke they were comforted.

Jake shifted his Lincoln into reverse and backed out of the stall. He rolled out of the lot and through town, north a few miles on the highway until he came to Lake Mitchell. He and Jane had lived on the north shore two years in a big informal house fifty yards back from the water. Along the dock was a lift holding a ski boat, and pulled up onto the fine-sand beach was a small aluminum fishing boat; both had come with the property but neither saw very much use. Jake did not fish, other than now and then to entertain a client or a friend. Jane skied some, but they did not spend much time on the water. Rather, when the season permitted they sat in the big-screened front porch, reading or listening to music, Jake working on briefs and Jane grading papers or planning lessons. She taught fourth grade at the school several blocks north of Jake's office.

They had married three years before Jake began with Anderson and Klein. They had first met in Vermillion as English majors, she a year ahead of him and drawn to teaching. But even then Jake had begun to believe that the law worked more precisely than poetry, could be comprehended more readily. That no matter what anyone said about it, it would always stay firm and make sense. Three hundred people had come to the wedding in the big white-enameled Hope and Peace Lutheran Church in Parkston, Jake's small group of family and high school friends from Sioux Falls overwhelmed by Jane's far-flung aunts and uncles and cousins.

Jake parked the Lincoln on the gravel drive in front of the attached double garage, noting that Jane's car was not there. He walked back out to the mailbox, grabbed a handful of envelopes, then went down to the basement where he changed into work clothes. Then he walked out to the shop he had built immediately after moving. It was a big wood-framed structure with dark brown siding to match the house's. Three stalls wide and one and a half deep, filled with the tools of Jake's other passion, metalworking. More precisely, the metal of fenders and hoods and doors. Summers as an undergraduate he had worked for a school bus company in Sioux Falls, repairing and repainting the buses, readying them for the next school year, in doing so discovering his talents for shaping metal and flowing enamel from a spray gun. Later he had worked two summers in a body shop owned by a law-school classmate's father who, disgusted with modern plastic fillers, still worked with lead whenever he could. From him Jake learned quickly how to tin, to move the lead into seams or slight depressions, how to file and form. Jake's hands were gifted with metal and paint, his mouth and mind with words.

Only one vehicle now occupied the shop, a 1940 Ford Deluxe Coupe. He'd owned it a dozen years. Jane had found it one autumn when he was still in law school and she was teaching in Centerville, a small town twenty miles north of Vermillion. Law studies took all his time and she supported him; they lived in an apartment above a bar several blocks from campus. A farmer not far down the highway from Centerville had parked the '40 at the end of his drive with for-sale signs in the glaucomous side windows. Jake and Jane drove out one Sunday. Since he was a kid building models he had wanted a '40 coupe. This one ran, barely, a cloud of blue oil smoke filling the air behind it and the flathead making noises engines aren't supposed to make. It was rusty but complete, and, at five hundred dollars, cheap. Jake borrowed money from his father and bought it, stored it in the corner of the implement shed on Jane's parents' farm. He dreamed of being financially secure enough to build a shop, of working the car's metal back to where it had been when new. He had patience, waited, believed in the future.

Jake preferred old cars nearly original or restored, not overly customized or hot-rodded. Sometimes sitting in class or staring at a textbook his mind wandered like a child's and he pictured what the coupe would look like after he had finished its restoration. He would take the rust and creases out of the body, weld patches in the floor, repaint it black. Update the brakes, bolt in a slightly dropped front axle but leave the rest of the running gear intact; he would retain and rebuild the flathead and the manual transmission. He knew where he could get material for the interior much like that which had been stitched thirty-five years before. Big wide whitewall tires around red rims, the chrome hubcaps and trim rings gleaming.

He had waited twelve years—through graduation and beginning with Anderson and Klein, through weekends weighted by a heavy caseload, through the sporadic restoration of two other cars—until he was sure he had the money, the tools, and the talent to make the car exactly as he wanted it to be. Only a month before *I've waited long enough.* He had the coupe towed up from the farm and into the shop. Still he put off beginning, almost too happy to finally have the chance to begin. But now he turned to it to quiet the voice that had begun whispering to the hooves sliding through the pasture grass.

■

It was nearly six o'clock before Jane returned to the house. She could not find Jake on the porch, as she usually did, so went out to his shop. She had been waiting for him to begin work on the coupe and felt some excitement thinking that today he must be out there at last, at least disassembling it, celebrating the end of the Wheeler case. But she found him beneath the bright fluorescent lights sitting on a stool near the workbench, one elbow resting on its wooden surface. The shop's interior, above the faint odors of lacquer thinner and oil, still smelled of new wood. He did not appear to notice that she had entered. She followed his eyes; he was staring at the coupe, but she saw no tools out and nothing had been taken off the car. She sensed that something had happened to him and thought that maybe something had gone wrong with settling the Wheelers' claim, that maybe the insurance company had backed out or the mother had changed her mind at the very last and refused to sign; such things had happened before. She stood for some moments watching him as if seeing someone for the first time and then mildly "Jake?"

She saw that the question brought him back from some other place, he turning to her and smiling but she mildly disturbed, thinking *he had to work to find that smile.* She kept her eyes on him and "You all right, hon?"

Jake shifting on the stool and nonchalantly, like a child getting caught, "Sure."

"Everything go all right with the Wheelers?"

"Sure" again.

"You got the check, the release . . . you're done?"

Jake trying to take control once again, confident and "All done."

She persisted with "You look a little off your feed for someone who just made more than a hundred thousand dollars. Problems?"

"No."

"When I walked in you were staring at the car. I'm not sure I've ever seen you look like that. What were you thinking?"

Jake lying and "I was just imagining what it's going to look like." He slid from the stool, put his hands on her waist and "Just thinking, that's all."

"About how it's going to look and nothing else?"

"Nothing else." They had been married long enough that she

could tell in his eyes that he was not telling her everything but she dismissed it with *the boy, he's thinking of Michael Wheeler and how he looks. He's thinking of her, the mother.*

"You're right," he said, "I should be happy. Hell, a little more than happy. I've had a pretty damn good year already and it's only July. If I didn't bill another dollar it would still be a most excellent 1985," smiling. Poetry again and "'Spend all you have for loveliness. Buy it and never count the cost.'"

"I should know that one, you've quoted it before, but I can't place it."

"Sara Teasdale." She thought he lightened then, fully returned to her and the shop and "I know where we can get some lovely steaks. Why don't we go buy them and not 'count the cost.' My God, Jake, we don't have to count. Who ever would have believed you'd be doing this well?"

Jake put his hand lightly to the side of her face and she felt his fingers the way she had felt them the first time. He ran them along her lips and "*We*, woman, who'd have thought *we'd* be doing this well?"

Jake locked up the shop, went into the house to change into jeans and a cotton shirt. Jane put on a casual dress. When they came back out to where the cars were parked he wanted to take hers. He'd given it to her two years before, on their anniversary, a '61 Chevy bubbletop that he'd bought up in Huron. He had spent two years on the body and paint, working in the double garage of the house they'd owned in town, had farmed out the mechanicals and interior to local people he'd gotten to know. White enamel with red trim and red interior, thin whitewalls and full wheelcovers. Bumpers and trim rechromed or polished. He often stopped to look at the way the light played off its long surfaces and *I did that, me,* believing in the power of restoration, of making things right. Jane loved the way it looked but had not particularly enjoyed driving it, at least at first. She remembered all the big old farm cars and pickups her father had owned, how they embarrassed her when she first began driving to school and more than a few of her classmates laughed when they saw her turning into the parking lot. But the more she drove the Chevy the more she liked it; she'd had a little Toyota for several years and the big heavy car took the bumps out of the road better and she got used to how it handled. The previous summer she had asked Jake to install air-conditioning.

They drove into the city, found friends at a restaurant, and the night was pleasant in the way most of their nights now were, and how, she believed, they would thereafter be. But two nights later she found him in the shop again, and the night after that, and the next as well. This by itself did not alarm her, for he went through periods where he spent a lot of time working with his hands, needing that physical contact. But on none of these nights were there tools out; she heard no familiar sounds of the air compressor or hammering; she didn't know what he did out there, perhaps just sat on the stool. She knew only what he didn't do, for one morning she went out and looked—nothing on the coupe had been disturbed.

When he came home from the office a week after that she stopped him just inside the door and "Jake, what's wrong?" He put her off with "I've been really busy at the office," but she knew he lied. And her concern moved toward worry.

■

For three weeks his behavior at home swung between two or three days out in the shop after work and living as he had before he took the check to the Wheelers, cooking dinner with her, sitting close to her on the porch, talking and laughing. But Jane's worry did not abate, for he had never acted this erratically. During the periods in the shop he was hardly ever in the house with her other than to eat and sleep. They did not make love, nor did they even when he seemed his old self. At night lying next to him she could feel as if tangible a wall between them that hadn't been there before, composed of fear or anger, she couldn't tell which. She would reach across and his skin would soften and bear her touch and she could feel him relax. And a few times he touched her face or her arm but went no further. She began to imagine that he was having an affair or doubting his life with her—it was clear he was doubting something—and she could not bear his periods of silence. He would lie or sit next to her and his voice would touch her as it always had, but the next day he would turn mute, uttering only a few cursory descriptions of his hours in the office, though it seemed an effort for him to do even that.

She told him she thought he was working too hard and that they should get away for a weekend, and he agreed. They took the Lincoln to Sioux Falls on a Saturday. In the afternoon they walked around Tuthill Park along the south edge of the city, where he had biked hundreds of times, even in the winter with his sled. He showed her again where he'd had a paper route, and the hobby shop where he worked in high school, things she'd known before. He seemed to want contact with the past, and they visited the playground next to the grade school he'd gone to; they went to a different spot along the river where he'd fished with friends near the old Cherry Rock bridge, but they found the old riveted I-beams and wood torn down and a new span of concrete half completed. They ate and wanted to go to a movie, but the one they chose was sold out and it was too late for any other. They went back to the motel and had a few drinks in the bar, then back to the room where, to her surprise, he seemed eager to make love. He was very active, searching her body as if needing something, and in the morning he woke her with his kisses and his hands and made love to her again and she felt almost completely restored. Whatever had bothered him would fall away, she believed.

Just past noon they walked across the wide blacktop parking lot between the motel and the mall and went slowly along the concourses as the after-church crowds grew. He seemed content and talkative and she held his arm. She sensed that the lights and the colors and the sounds of people talking set him at ease. They had been walking almost an hour and were ready to leave when Jake stopped short. Jane had been looking at a window display and when he stopped suddenly she turned and looked ahead. Toward them came a man in an electric wheelchair, moving steadily. She saw Jake staring at the man as if terrified, and the man raise his eyes to Jake's. She saw that they recognized each other, that the other man wanted to speak. But Jake held the man's gaze for only a couple of seconds, then spun away quickly toward an exit. Jane looked back at the man, who now had turned his gaze to her. He seemed about Jake's age. His eyes shone hard and dark, and she did not like looking into them. She followed Jake, who had disappeared in the crowd.

She found him outside leaning against the facade of the mall. He'd clenched his fists and set his face rigid and she knew he was back where he had been that day after the Wheelers. She tried to search his face and eyes but he turned away from her. She put her hand on his shoulder and found it tensed, hard. She lifted the same hand to his cheek and "Jake, who was that?"

He didn't speak, Jane refusing to accept his silence and "Jake, I think you better tell me who that was. And what the hell is going on with you."

He hesitated, then "Someone I used to know," but he did not continue, Jane waiting and finally "That's not good enough, Jake. Who exactly?" She saw that he was terrified but he finally managed "Mark Neld."

"Go on."

"I knew him in high school. We were friends, used to hang around together almost every weekend."

"What happened to him? Why is he in that wheelchair?", but Jake didn't answer.

"How long's it been since you've seen him?"

"Since . . . June, 1968."

"Well, you certainly had a nice reunion back there. Let's go back in and find him," but Jake just shook his head and would not move or speak, as if there were something he just could not admit. Jane got angry and *maybe he's screwing the guy's sister.* She left him, ashamed of what she had thought, went to the car and waited. It was twenty minutes before he got in the Lincoln next to her. On the highway home she was astonished to see him crying, because he had never done so in her presence. But he simply would not speak. She sat with her arms folded, holding herself, staring, ignoring the lack of logic and *he doesn't love me anymore.*

■

She had to keep him out of that shop, make him come with her. She backed the Chevy near the walk-in door and called to him. He came out and they spoke. Then, Jake through years of long nights alone remembering the last time he had seen her and what he had said to her in the minutes before her passing. Jake trying feebly not to but *unthinking I bent to the car's open window unaware that my stupid words would not be the last I would ever say to the woman whose face is forever window-opening picture-framed but the last from me she would ever hear. Unthinking I bent. She did not lie on stiff white sheets in a hospital bed dying from a disease we had known for a year. I did not await her final breath, her eyes' last plaintive glance. She was merely leaving for the afternoon. So it is possible for me to tell myself that because nothing sang to me of what was passing or to come I spoke in ignorance and my words therefore carried no true meaning and cannot be held against me.*

Such words uttered as easily as he had lived before he listened to Susan Wheeler and was unable to reply, before he saw some-one from years before confront him in a wheelchair and force him wordless, before Jane steered the car along the street away from him, in the beginning Jake mouthing the sounds often, but in time no longer believing or even speaking them; for years he waited like a clumped barren field for rain that refused to fall;

he sought inactively the dignity of a man who had made the last mistake that required of him apology.

■

Jake had bent to the car's open window "No, I want to work in the garage. That front fender, I want to begin."

"Begin tomorrow," Jane had said, raising her eyes to him, they and her inflection unmistakably that he should step around the car and climb in the other door and go with her. Her hands gripped the wheel tightly, unusual for the driver of a vehicle not moving.

"No," Jake had said unconvincingly, the slightness of it allowing her to realize that he knew he should do what she wanted. But he could not, he too failing to understand why. The only thing clear was that he did not want to go and therefore could not, wanted by beginning on the car to show her he was past the Wheeler boy and the man in the mall, *I will show her.* Jake believed he needed one more afternoon in a place shared by no others' breath. The garage. Labor with metal, physical and demanding. Space where he could choose the exact right wrench and turn with his hands and wrists a nut reluctant or acquiescent. Threads cut precisely and fenders arcing logically, *fitting.* He would do that this afternoon and then speak to her when she came back from Parkston. He would explain everything, as he always had, to himself and to her. Watching her and *it will be all right now.*

"Mom and Dad want to see you," Jane had said. Then lightly, "that dumb old car can wait a day," Jake remembering *I understood that her words came from anger I caused but I pushed her away. I thought Old but not dumb. Jesus just leave me alone for a while. Please, my thoughts angrier than my speech which came flat like the level horizon.*

"We'll come back for a late movie. We haven't been to the movies for a long time." The bright-hot afternoon light fell through trees of a summer unusually warm. The exhausted bristly grass spotting the yard had stopped growing. Jake heard some kind of bird from one of the trees, but he did not hear *her*. He needed at that moment only the car's metal.

"No," Jake had said. "I want to be alone this afternoon." He saw that she misunderstood what he had been going through. He knew he should speak it right then, but he did not. He stupidly let the silence draw out, then saw the saddest look on her face that he had ever seen and then anger and her "Goddamn it, Jake." He began to speak but she backed the length of the short driveway, then wheeled up the road toward the highway. Jake heard the tires reverse over the gravel, then roll out onto concrete. He thought of street-cracks tar-repaired and pebbles in the gutter. He heard the power steering pump as she spun the steering wheel. He heard the car roll past him through sandy dust near the curb thinking *the muffler already going bad*, the extent of his mind's working. The breeze brought him her engine's exhalations. He stood ashamed for his neglect of her, but he did not turn to watch her go thinking later *I did not turn*.

■

Memory, your powerful speech. Plain and simple. The last things I said to her were "No" and "I want to be alone." The last thing I did was not look after her as she left. For a time I justified "How could I have known?" but after a few months that stopped being adequate.

■

The intersection of South Dakota State Highways 44 and 37 in the bright July light of a Saturday afternoon. The quiet slow summer air shattered for some seconds by the sound that rubber makes on concrete when it cannot prevent what is about to happen, and the sound of metal rending and glass shattering. An old white car on its side in the ditch with a woman's body somewhere off from it whose eyes cannot read what is stamped now in the stretched metal of one door: the brand of the tire that hit it, the size and rating numbers. And a two-tone 1957 DeSoto back by the intersection with its front and passenger side compressed as fully as the recollection of lives its passengers had experienced the moment before impact. Two stop signs immobile in the still air.

Three people dead.

A man and a woman married fifty-two years and driving the last car they ever bought new, who had been eyeing death for a decade; and one who believed that the only thing dying was her husband's love for her. The sounds then of other cars stopping, doors slamming, feet running. Later the shriek of sirens and silent departures. And finally two wreckers, the commencement of forgetting for all but one.

■

For ten years Jake remembered bending to the open window. And not watching her go. *I could have fixed what was wrong, like turning perfect a brake drum out of round, restoring the curve of a fender shiny new.* And the first night, three months later, how the feeling came to him that he wanted to go back and change what he had done, then the overwhelming first-time-ever feeling that what he had acted out was not now a rightable thing and never would be. No surgery, no signed release, no words could right it. No faith. And he quit living, put himself on idle, and the numbers on the odometer inside him stopped turning over.

■

That afternoon light through which Jake bent to Jane's open window, to the metal he had with his own hands made beautiful: July 17, 1985, the signifier of how three times Jake's speech had failed him. And beyond that day a man who chose not to speak, constantly motionless from a threatened journey back to words and silences whose inversion had made hers the last of his betrayals.

2

Past the humping green-shingled wooden Quonset named Jimtown Body and Frame in Jamestown, North Dakota, a man drove his pickup; Thomas Gifford, new manager of the Western Inn downtown, recently transferred from Casper, Wyoming. He had purchased an acreage seven miles south of the city, and his usual route did not take him past Jimtown's hail-damaged T-lock shingles and flaking white enamel gone yellow. But on that Tuesday road construction detoured him several blocks through the early summer morning light, and one of the streets ran along the side of the body shop where men in the '40s and '50s had straightened frames but no longer; the fading sign nailed above the front door had hung there long enough to remember. Morning traffic strung back slow from the makeshift four-way stop at the usually open intersection ahead, so Gifford had to wait. He listened to a tinny AM station, hummed a country song. He had not yet lost, and probably never would, the sense that he would rather be back in Casper where he had lived for eight years. There the land wasn't so damnably flat.

The traffic did not move and Gifford's eyes wandered out the side windows. He examined the cars inside the body shop's chain-link fence, newer models except for an older El Camino, an orange GTO, and a couple of bare race-car frames. *Sprints*, he thought. Wise civic leaders had decreed years earlier that a fence such as that surrounding the rear of Jimtown must have vertical metal slats to keep the wrecks from irritating the city's eyes, though as Gifford took in the scene he could not imagine what, exactly, would constitute a visual offense in this particular neighborhood filled with old houses and dirt driveways and cars older and more wrecked than Jimtown's. Barbed wire had been strung along the top of the fence to discourage vandals. As Gifford moved forward he came to where some of the metal slats had been blown or torn away and he saw more clearly through the opening into the yard. Against the back wall of the shop Gifford thought he saw a 1940 Ford Coupe. The curves of such a car, to those who know them well, are unmistakable. Roof curves like a woman's drew Gifford's attention; he had been looking for something like a hot rod, some old car to deliver him from middle age, return him to high school days cruising the streets of Iowa City. The move from Casper to Jamestown had brought him a bonus and a raise. His wife, who hadn't worked for years, had taken a job with a bank down the street from the motel, and suddenly they were earning considerably more than they ever had. Their only child, a daughter, was in southern Texas studying to be a teacher, and nearly self-sufficient. It was time, Gifford thought often, to do something for himself.

He edged his truck forward, impatient, eyeing a second opening in the fence slats a couple of car-lengths down. When he reached it he looked right again and *a '40 coupe all right.* He could not mistake the split rear windows, the slope of the trunk lid, the v'ed taillights. His place south of town had a big outbuilding where he could work on it. Tools wouldn't be a problem. He had played around with cars before he married and he heard their call now strong as he might a woman's who wanted more than mere flirtation. Gifford looking and *why is there nothing covering it? Valuable piece of tin to keep outside.*

His quick glimpse told him that the coupe looked pretty complete and pretty straight. Around it tall grasses and weeds rose up from the gravel, even a small sunflower beginning behind it. The coupe sat like a plant itself, unmoving, as if rooted. Gifford made a note to come back and ask.

■

Jake had for ten years thought about little but his work at the
body shop. He did mostly body work, painting now and then
but only when the job was simple, when the car needed only one
solid color. Tim did the newer metallic acrylics and urethanes
that Jake did not understand or want to; he had tried them, but
they had turned out unacceptably thick in places, thin in others,
never an even, consistent metallic. When he had first learned to
paint, in his friend Rod's garage in Sioux Falls, and later at the
school bus garage those summers in college, he shot straight
enamel thinned carefully and strained. A couple of times straight
lacquer. But it had always been the enamel he loved. The buses'
yellow enamel.

Jake had run parts at the school district's bus repair shop,
part-time during the school year and full-time summers, saving
for college. The three mechanics who worked there hated summers because of the heat and because it was the season for body
work required by a year of Dakota-winter wreckage and corro-
sion. They wanted grease and wrenches and not a summer
replacing riveted aluminum panels and filling creases with
Bondo and sanding and masking and spraying yellow enamel.
Precisely the work Jake had found he loved. They wanted the
right gap and the timing of spark inside cylinders precisely
round, precise metal flat between manifolds and blocks.

Jake now seldom allowed his mind to return to the work that
he had done in Mitchell; he cared only about the work he did in
the present, and sometimes about how he had come to love that
work. That summer he worked the buses it was Don's turn for
body work. Don hated it worse than Doug or Warren. Don
loved transmissions, repairing the old automatics in the GMC's
and the clutches in the Fords. Don had a gift for getting others
to do the work he didn't want, and by July during Jake's first
summer he had him going full-time on drilling out the old rivets
in a smashed or rotted side panel. Fitting new aluminum.

Hammering fat new rivets. Sanding new metal, laying on thick gray primer. Sanding again. Tacking sanding dust. Don didn't think twice about grease or transmission fluid on his hands but he hated that sanding dust on his skin and in his eyes and the yellow paint overspray in his hair and ears.

But Jake loved making old bodies new again. At least new looking. Shaping filler to restore a curve. Spraying heavy enamel from the hissing Binks gun, watching it collect on flat or curved surfaces, in ridges around the rivets. He had learned fast the perfect point of balance between where the paint has built thick enough so that the color shines deep and firm and the point where it gathers too heavy and gravity draws it down in ugly runs. Lessons Jake never forgot. That light first coat, feeling the humidity and heat in the air and knowing how long to wait until the next coat, often thinking *Jesus, that yellow enamel so smooth because of me and shiny, color so fine in the right angled light I could cry.*

The morning Gifford had driven by and seen his coupe, Jake had to paint an old woman's Bel Air, a '65 four-door. Elroy, who owned Jimtown, had written the estimate a month before. She had turned too sharply into a parking space at the store, she said, creased the right front fender against a pickup bumper sharp and angled, Jake thinking *I saw her when she brought it in two days ago. She's too old to drive. She will ruin that car. Eighty-two years old she told me, proud. Fifty-two when she and her husband bought the car new and two years later he was dead. She talked like she was the only one who could know something like how that feels.* But Jake had kept quiet.

And refused as best he could any memory of Jane. *Only the car in front of me, here, now*, he would think. He had worked the Bel Air's thin metal as best he could and built up the low spots with filler where he could not get the metal straight. Masked and papered all but the fender, sprayed primer and let it sit, roughed the primer with 180 grit sandpaper. Something for the color to hold to, Jake thinking *deep Chevy red unfaded because she garaged it, had it waxed and kept it off the North Dakota winter roads.* Elroy had tried to talk her into painting the whole car but she had looked at him the way people often look at Elroy, like he either has no sense or is a mean-dumb sonofabitch.

Jake walked into a place where no past could find him, the paint booth where the Bel Air sat ready, a quart of acrylic enamel on the bench by the spray gun, the exhaust fans on. He slid on the overalls hooked behind the door and fitted the aspirator mask over his face and the goggles over his eyes. Fitted his cap, worked the can lid loose and poured red liquid through the strainer into the paint gun bottom and measured out the thinner, stirred it into the red back and forth, slow and even. Long enough to mix it good. Jake had always been able to feel the changes in resistance that come through the wooden stir-stick. He knew when the paint was ready, fastened the metal cup back onto the spray gun and snapped the air hose's coupler onto it. Set it on the bench holder and tacked the surface another time.

He watched the act itself as if detached from it. First coat took only seconds. Only one fender, and he wished Elroy had got her to do the whole car. He feathered the first coat so thin the surface dulled with stickiness. Two sideways steps from back to front, one around by the big grille to get inside the headlight opening, the air hose trailing from his left hand as he gripped the gun with his right and forefingered the trigger. He didn't wait long for the first coat to set up. Dry day. Bent to it again and pulled the air hose through his hand for more play and watched as his arm and hand pooled the red on the metal just on the edge of beauty and *red and black the best colors because they move opaque perfect over the primer.* He didn't think about his movements, just watched, disembodied and *I am not me inside that booth, inside the goggles and mask. I am not me. Or that is the only place I am me. Red moving like water but not water, slower and thicker, heavier, so you feel the weight with your eyes.*

Jake loved how paint was a single thing inside the canister

and how air drew it through the gun and blew it apart, how it then gathered again to what it had been, reassembled on the metal.

He waited again and then laid on the final coat, attending to the lipped wheel opening and the curve of the fender's upper line and the graceful convexity top to bottom and *where we find beauty, not in any context but in the thing itself, in the moment of the thing.*

He uncoupled the air hose, cleaned the gun. Set the can on the shelves, though he believed *we will never need that color again.* He thought ahead to buffing out the fender the next day and waxing it and running his fingers along the lines restored and the scent of good wax filling his nostrils and he began to consider how the cool red would be like Jane's skin beneath his fingers but then *no, only this metal and paint for what they are.*

■

Mid-afternoon Gifford walked through the hot air into Jimtown's office, a small square-linoleumed room filled with repair manuals stacked on rickety chairs and file cabinets and one tinny metal desk. A single eight-foot fluorescent fixture illuminated a fine film of indeterminate dust on every surface, Gifford thinking *body filler* and the smell of it taking him back to high school shop class. A large rough-haired thick-snouted dog lay curled in a corner by the desk, and as Gifford entered it lifted one mean and dark eye to him but did not move, as if daylight precluded any interest in strangers. No one else was in the room. A sign screwed to the shop door held hand-markered words: "No Customers! This means you!", the "you" underlined three times with bold strokes, Gifford thinking *friendly.* He leaned a thigh against the dusty desk and waited. Occasionally, the pneumatic hammer of an air-driven tool or the metal-on-concrete of a fumbled wrench punctured an air that seemed to Gifford increasingly filled with the smell of paint thinner. He

remembered cleaning brushes in an old red coffee can in his
father's basement.

Gifford had only a half hour before a staff meeting at the
hotel, so after five minutes his growing impatience urged him to
leave, but then the steel shop door swung open as an older man,
maybe sixty, limped through. He wore thick-creased dusty shop
pants whose fabric had been dyed a color like the brown found
on folding chairs in church basements, and a white shirt with
paint spots and cigarette burns and his name embroidered in red
letters over the pocket: "Elroy." A white plastic protector and
several pencils filled the pocket. Elroy clung to a clipboard holding several sheets of estimate forms. He didn't appear to notice
his customer, and even when he did he failed to ask if Gifford
had waited long or apologize or even say hello. He lowered himself into the groaning desk chair, glanced in Gifford's direction
and uttered a flat "Can I help you?" Gifford thinking *must have
been a marketing major.*

"Hello, I'm Tom Gifford. I manage the Western Inn on the
north end of Main."

"I guess I know where it is," Elroy said. He limply shook the
strong hand that Gifford offered him.

"Yes, I suppose you would," Gifford said. "I drove past here
this morning, been in town about three months is all and I don't
drive by here but the detour took me this way. Well, I drove by
and I noticed the coupe out back. Thought I'd ask about it."

Elroy didn't answer right away. Then, "Ask *what* about it?"

"Is it for sale?"

"I don't know."

"It's not yours, then?"

"I guess if it was mine I'd know if it was for sale."

"You probably would." Tom Gifford stood calmly looking at
Elroy, having been good with such people ever since the day he
realized not everybody in the world had to like him. Assholes.
You dealt with them as you would your own and then you
moved on to something more likable.

"Do you know who owns it?" Gifford asked thinking as he did *he will say yes but not give a name and then I will have to ask him for a name. He won't give it to me without me asking, the way assholes do.*

"Yes," then the expected pause.

"Who?"

"Jake."

"Where might I find him?"

"Shop" in a final terseness.

Gifford, remembering the sign, at first wanted to ask if it were all right for him to go into the shop, but then he just went thinking *fuck him.* He stepped past the dog, who swished its tail once, turned the slippery metal doorknob and stepped into the shop where it was dead quiet now. He found a typical arrangement, wide center lane with cars dispersed to either side and in one corner a partitioned paint booth. Gifford couldn't remember the shop sounds stopping. The smells he had first inhaled in the office were now exaggerated, stronger in the inactivity of a place usually working. He checked his watch, which indicated three o'clock exactly. He guessed they were outside taking the afternoon break. He saw a side door and took it.

Beyond the door he found a grassy, breeze-moved vacant lot touched by bright sunshine. To his left Gifford saw three men uniformed like Elroy reclining on the grass against the peeled cracked side of the Quonset. He faced them. The man closest nodded "Hey there" and seemed to Gifford a thousand times friendlier than Elroy.

"Hi. Looking for Jake Warner."

"Here." The middle man stood, brushed flakes of something from his hand before taking Gifford's. Gifford saw that Jake had been eating a candy bar and sipping from an insulated plastic coffee mug. Gifford noted how Jake, thin with bristly brown hair, stood an inch or two below his own six-two, and that his skin color suggested he did not spend too many hours outdoors, thinking *not a fisherman. Probably every night in the garage.*

"I'm Tom Gifford. I manage the Western Inn." He did not indicate the hotel's location this time.

Jake nodding and "Sure."

"I've seen you there," the first man speaking again, a short, heavy-chested figure with thick forearms and fingers whose sun-darkened skin stood apart from Jake's. "Tim Kinneady's my name." He grinned wide and they shook. "We have a drink there sometimes after work. Sometimes." He winked at the third man, who hadn't gotten up, Gifford thinking of him *more the Elroy type*. Gifford could not make out his embroidered name.

"How do you like the place?" Gifford said, a man forever working the crowd, marketing.

"Beer's cold. Free food. Works for me," Kinneady said laughing.

"You're a good man, then." Gifford turned back to Jake. "Elroy tells me that's your '40 coupe out back."

"Yes, it is."

"Here we go again," said the third man, unmoving against the Quonset. "Here we go again," Kinneady echoed, laughing loud, free, infectious.

Jake said, "I hope, Mr. Gifford, you're a man who can suffer fools." He glanced at Kinneady and the other man. "Don't pay them any attention. Yeah, it's my coupe."

Kinneady and the other spoke in unison, as if having practiced: "No."

"They're acting this way," Jake said, "because a lot of guys come around here asking me if it's for sale, and I always answer the same: no."

"The only way to get that car is to shoot this sorry stupid bastard and buy it at the estate sale," the third man said. "Though it wouldn't be much of a sale. That Ford and a couple of pieces of furniture about all he owns." Gifford could read Kinneady clearly, that he was loud and good-natured and up front, but this other man, it was difficult to tell if he were serious. Jake didn't look at him the same way he looked at Kinneady. But Gifford wasn't going to worry over it too much and decided these men were having a kind of conversation that men in body shops have with each other quite often. And since he had practiced long at judging men and what men said, he knew that when Jake said the coupe wasn't for sale, that is exactly what he meant. Pursuing the matter would be pointless.

Still Gifford interested and "Well, thought I'd ask. Mind if I look at it anyway?"

Jake bent to the grass for a blue-covered notebook that Gifford hadn't noticed before and "Sure, go ahead. I'll walk back with you. You seem like better company than what I've been associating with these last few minutes."

"Fuck you," Kinneady said laughing.

They re-entered the shop and then out the open overhead door that emptied into the fenced rear area. The coupe lay, seemingly forgotten, hard by the door. Its flat tires hunched it low to the earth. As Gifford walked around it he noticed that every piece, as far as he could tell, was still on the car, bone-stock complete. But tall weeds and grass and the sunflower rose up along its perimeter; this was the north side of the building where full sun reached only in summer. Otherwise there was nothing to dry the dew among the grasses. Gifford noted patches of rust along the bottoms of the fenders where the running boards attached. Such desolation made him half ill, half angry.

"How long's it been sitting here?"

"Nine, ten years now," Gifford wincing at Jake's answer.

"You haven't moved it once?"

"No."

"Shouldn't you cover it with something?"

"Probably."

"Going to rust sitting out here."

"I imagine the floor's pretty bad right now." Gifford could not comprehend Jake's words, untinged by emotion or regret. Such a vehicle was worth several thousand dollars, maybe more.

You just didn't find complete old Fords sitting around anymore, Gifford thinking *goddamn him.*

"What do you plan to do with it?"

"Restore it."

"When?"

"When it gets bad enough that I have to."

"Jake, this coupe's too nice for this. At least it used to be."

"He's heard that sermon before." Kinneady spoke, having stepped unheard from the shop.

Jake lowering his eyes to the ground and quietly "Same could be said for a lot of things, people, too. Still, things get done to them eventually." Then, "I'm not sure if I'll do it, ever."

Gifford didn't know what to make of that and "you're sure it's not for sale?"

"I'm sure."

Gifford knew that there were other cars for him to buy, maybe he'd even get one already finished, and clearly something was going on between this one and its careless owner. Still, it baffled him that somebody who worked in a body shop would let a '40 coupe just sit outside and rot away. Didn't make sense at all.

"Well, thanks Jake. Just thought I'd check."

"Sure, no problem."

"Did you forget you had a job?" This time it was Elroy, suggesting Jake and Kinneady return to work.

Jake grinning and "I did. Thanks for reminding me," Kinneady adding "Fuck you, Elroy."

"Sorry," Gifford said, and then left Jake and the other wrecks and went to his meeting.

■

"**Allow me, my** good fellow, to enlighten you concerning how negotiating with me unfolds." Dan Gippart swiveled his dark leather desk chair back and forth slowly, metronomically; the leather made an expensive wrinkling sound. Though the chair and his body arced constantly, Gippart's dark intense eyes stayed focused on the man across the desk, who occupied a stiff, sparsely padded chair Gippart reserved for those he didn't care much for, which included almost everyone. Through his fifth-floor window—glass that made up the entire wall—Gippart could look south through taller buildings and glimpse the Mississippi river as it swung through downtown St. Paul. He desired a better view than the one he currently had, but it would have to suffice for now. The river at that point was neither as wide nor as deep as Gippart's arrogance; brown, irrepressible Mississippi water could run into its immense vessel for an hour and not fill it. On the door to his office hung a polished brass plate: "Mr. Daniel Gippart, Senior Vice President—Claims." Each morning Gippart stood a moment, fondled with his eyes the brassy shine of the plate, let seep into his core the status of the position he had held for two years.

The man listening to Gippart's leather and watching his motion was Craig Jonason, a St. Paul lawyer for thirty-one years currently representing sixteen-year-old Lori Hanson; two years before, her legs had been badly burned while visiting her best friend Anne Kurdy, the daughter of Dr. Anthony Kurdy. Dr. Kurdy as a hobby did metal sculpture, cutting and welding scavenged and new metal into abstract forms. He had constructed on his acreage just outside the city limits a studio, above which he had added a playroom for his two daughters, who had outgrown it over the years but still used it occasionally. One fall Saturday when Lori and Anne were upstairs, Dr. Kurdy finished his welding and went into the house for lunch. Something started the studio on fire, and Lori didn't make it out without diminishing, according to her lawyer, her value as a woman. The insurance company for which Dan Gippart worked, IncAmPride—shortened from Incorporated American Pride—had issued property and liability policies to Dr. Kurdy covering his professional and personal liability, his three homes and all their furnishings, his four cars, two boats, jewelry, gun collection, and paintings. Jonason and Gippart were meeting to perhaps conclude the claim, the documentation of which filled two thick folders on the desk and one heavy briefcase laying softly on the thick carpet by Jonason's hard chair. Jonason had moments before suggested, for the girl's disfigurement and her pain now and everlasting, in addition to the mother's and the father's, a figure of seven hundred thousand dollars, exclusive of Lori's future medical expenses.

Gippart habitually swiveled his chair when others spoke, as if to suggest an impatient desire to move on to something relevant, like what *he* had to say. He let Jonason's words disintegrate in the air, and when he began his response he halted his movement and trained his eyes like some predator driven by angry hunger. "See, Craig-o, you people—and, to be fair, others in positions similar to mine—look at negotiation as a game. Let's call them traditionalists. You come in high, I respond low, we work from there. We haggle." Gippart calmly modulated his words. "Not me. I determine what I'm comfortable with—and don't doubt *my* professional comfort has much to do with any check we cut you—and I spell it out so even lawyers can understand and that's as high as I'm going unless a jury tells me I have to, and that doesn't happen very often. My way saves us much precious time and keeps us from thinking that only the other guy is an incredible asshole, when the fact is we both are."

"I see." Jonason guessed that he, at sixty-three, was maybe two decades older than Gippart, of whose reputation he was aware—other lawyers were never more serious than when they spoke of Gippart. Over thirty-five years of law Jonason had seen countless men and women who threw up cold initial granite walls and then retreated when battle commenced. But Jonason did not sense the possibility of retreat in Gippart's words, his inflections, his reputation—Jonason had no reason to doubt that Gippart meant exactly what he said. No one had ever called him Craig-o. And Gippart's eyes, dark and mean. There were people now and then one knew to fear; Jonason felt sure one sat across from him.

"So here's what makes me comfortable," Gippart went on, "like I'm lying back in a big old recliner with a beer and the remote and I'm watching football or some skin flick, maybe both, picture-in-a-picture. You with me?"

Jonason nodded.

"Two hundred grand," pausing, then "Ooh, it feels good just to say it." He smiled, a short, good-looking man with a tan and close-cropped black hair. Standing or sitting, he always looked compressed, a steel spring ready to uncoil.

Jonason attempted to master his surprise, tried not to let it turn into open disgust. He hadn't expected that Gippart would toss him seven hundred thousand, but something near it. He hadn't expected Gippart to begin at anything less than half a million. Two hundred thousand seemed absurdly low, especially with its no-negotiation preface.

"You're suggesting that a check for that amount will cause this matter to go away?"

"You catch on quick." Gippart knew he could go as high as half a million and raise no corporate eyebrows; the company's claims committee, made up of three other Vice Presidents and Gippart, a group that oversaw all large liabilities, had authorized that much. No doubt Gippart could exceed the half million, though he'd have to get authority again, which he hated. He hated the others on the goddamn committee, who thought they knew what claims handling was all about. To Gippart, they didn't know shit.

Jonason peered into the deep wells above the desk. "I must respectfully suggest the unacceptability of that figure."

"*You* must, but maybe not your clients. Two hundred large is lots of cold hard. Hell of a lot. Maybe not to you lawyer-types, but to the average guy, he's rich."

"You've seen the pictures of the girl, of course." Jonason imagined a jury examining the glossy, colorful, 8x10 fourteen-

year-old, smiling and strikingly good-looking, her legs
unabashedly beautiful, and then watching her limp awkwardly
across the courtroom toward them, the same girl from two years
before from the waist up but whose legs were now bent and
scarred and twisted. Looking into her eyes and seeing what the
knowledge had done to her. Jonason shaking his head and *he's
got to be kidding*.

"Sure, I've seen them."

"And you think the difference is worth two hundred thousand dollars? She was an awfully happy, pretty girl. To a significant degree, she isn't anymore. You've got the doctor's reports,
the pictures, the psychologist's reports."

"Doesn't have anything to do with my view of the subtle vari-
ances in her appearance or her abused little teenage psyche. It
has to do with what I'm comfortable taking out of my wallet
and putting in yours."

"The way the girl looks should have some influence on you,
because it certainly will to a jury."

"See, there you go, not listening to me. All right. Maybe,
maybe not. *That's* the game, isn't it? You and me on different
teams, but the jury there too, refereeing. Sometimes they call it
close, other times they let a lot of shit go. Picture yourself hollering for a technical, but the game's over. And I don't mean to
brag—well, yes I do—but I win more than I lose. In fact, I'm
leading the league."

Jonason didn't respond.

Gippart went on. "See, I know this isn't a question of liability. Our guy started the fire. Accidentally, sure, and he's feeling
guilty as hell, but still he started it. And I suppose you could go
on and on suggesting it might have been better had poor little
Lori been killed. Then she wouldn't have to *live* with those legs.
Maybe so. But shit happens. *This* happened. No one can make
it un-happen. Where do we go now? I've had my guy following
little Lori around. And from what I see, it don't look like she's
doing so bad. She's got plenty of friends still, even a boyfriend.

Some hot little junior-high-schooler willing to do her because he feels sorry, maybe. Years from now Lori'll be sitting at a bar wearing slacks, some guy hitting on her, and she'll say 'Let me tell you what happened to me one time,' and the guy'll be so hot to see those legs and pretty soon they're in bed together just like there never was a fire. Shit happens to us all, but this shit won't stop her from getting laid, and that's what it's all about, right? Isn't that in the Bible, that shit happens? The difference here being that Lori's going to get paid for hers. Besides, we cover all future medicals. Remember that."

Jonason sitting as if paralyzed and *Jesus Christ*. He still enjoyed his office work, and most of his court cases. But times like—people like—this, well, he thought more often of retirement. There were more Gipparts than he cared to admit, more than there used to be. Too many people ego-mean and conscienceless who turned the air cold when they entered a room. All he could manage was "You've had her followed?"

"Sure." Gippart pulled a different folder from his desk, from which he took two videocassettes and a sheaf of still pictures. There was a thick written report as well. "This is where we live now," he said. "I mean, look at O. J. You can do something real bad and not have to pay. Here I'm *willing* to pay. Consider yourself fortunate."

Jonason refused to look. "It's not enough."

"Better ask the client, Craig-o."

"I will. But I know what they'll say."

"No. You *think* you know. But maybe you don't. I got a hunch."

Jonason waited a few moments, then "That's it? Two hundred thousand or we go to court?"

"For an old guy your hearing's still pretty good."

Jonason, who had taken nothing from his briefcase, stood and sighed. "I will communicate your offer." He left the office without shaking hands, something he could not recall doing before. And when he was gone, Gippart said out loud, "Fucking right you will, you fucking leech. Fucking right." He felt a stirring in his lap and smiled.

■

Wally Reno, lean and colored like a greyhound, worked exclusively for and under the direct supervision of Dan Gippart, though no IncAmPride employee roster listed him, nor had one ever. He was an independent contractor whom Gippart paid in cash. Since they had hooked up, Reno had paid no income taxes. Reno was a kind of trained dog, pantingly loyal to the last pulse of his blood because there had been but one man ever who threw quality cuts of meat over the fence and kept his water dish full. Reno frequently got choicer cuts, bigger portions, for performing particularly well, and he knew this food didn't come from IncAmPride's usual supply. It came somehow from Gippart himself. Reno didn't know exactly how, and he didn't presume to ask.

They had met in South Dakota, working opposite sides of a car crash investigation, Gippart for Sun State Insurance and Reno for a company based in Chicago. Gippart had approached Reno with a plan to make some money. Never having been much in the way of honest, Reno went along, then they parted ways. Reno worked nearly two more years handling hail storms, fires, crashes, windstorms, haggling and fighting with people he detested. He decided to quit, to look up Dan Gippart, whom he found in St. Paul. They formed a partnership; Gippart would be the suit-wearing office man—a role Reno despised—and Reno would be his "assistant," working in the field. They had operated this way for several years.

At five-thirty Reno scratched on the closed rear door of Gippart's office; Gippart worked late more often than not. Gippart hollered that he should come in, and when Reno padded lightly onto the carpet he found his boss back-tipped in his chair watching the late afternoon sun deepen and begin to shadow the buildings and the river beyond them.

"Drink?" Gippart asked without turning to Reno. He held a short, smooth glass third-filled with whiskey.

"I know where it is." Reno extracted a glass for himself from the desk's bottom drawer and then pulled a brown-bottled liquor from the low file cabinet. "You know company policy stipulates no alcohol on the premises."

"Oh dear, I must have forgotten. Guess you better fire me."

"You're fired."

"Thanks. I hate this fucking job anyway."

"I love hate."

"You're a right-thinker, then." Gippart sipped from his glass as Reno long-swallowed. "Been kind of dull around here lately. Hope something comes up worthy of our abilities. Big car crash, maybe, lots of people killed."

"Young people, prime of life."

"Exactly. Earnings of a lifetime extinguished in a moment of our insured's stupidity. A nice young doctor and his wife and two kids mangled inside their van. Thin tan people with shiny teeth and perfect hair. Give us a challenge, for Christ sake. Something where the lawyer asks for millions."

"Fucking millions," Reno laughed, wiping a small bit of drool from his mouth.

"Not this piddly 'my-legs-got-burned-real-bad' shit. Jonason was in today. Wants seven hundred."

"Probably worth it."

"Are *your* kid's legs worth that much? *Your* ugly little bastard?" Reno had been married once about ten years before; it had lasted four months, by which time his wife was pregnant. He had lived alone since, his latest place an apartment a mile from IncAmPride. In his daughter's short life, Reno had seen her exactly three times.

Reno not giving Gippart's question a second thought and "Wouldn't be able to tell you. Don't really know what they look like."

"Well, if she looks anything like *you* . . . "

Reno laughing and "I'll bet they don't take it."

"A twenty?"

Reno extracted a smooth bill from his wallet and slapped it on the desk. Gippart reached into the desk's center drawer, took out a twenty of his own and an envelope: "He'll call back day after tomorrow, take the offer. I can guaran-ass-tee it." He placed the two bills in the envelope, handling the money reverently. Gippart stood and went to the window, where Reno joined him.

"Isn't that one of our people?" Reno pointed to a woman crossing the street below them, wearing a short-skirted suit.

"That's Sheila, you moron," Gippart answered. "She left just before you showed up."

"Has she lost some weight? She's looking good. Nice ass."

"Yes, it is. Reason number one I hired her. That and she doesn't take shit from anyone but me."

Laughing, Reno nodded. "Day after tomorrow you think?"

Gippart raised his nearly empty glass in a toast to the skyline and repeated the word he had learned from his father long ago, as the older man sat on the porch firing at squirrels and birds with a .22 pistol: "Guaran-ass-teed."

■

At 9:15 two mornings after Gifford had examined Jake's '40 coupe, a sheriff's car with South Dakota plates panted into the Jimtown Body and Frame lot, its hood and tires hot from nearly three hours of hard driving. Its roof-mounted lights had flashed until it had reached the Jamestown city limits. A single deputy emerged and walked into the office looking for a Mr. Jacob Warner. Elroy, who must have had some history with the law, was even less polite than he had been to Gifford; he refused to allow the deputy into the shop and only grudgingly brought Jake into the office. The deputy asked if they could have some privacy, and Elroy said that they certainly could if they cared to get their asses outside because there weren't too many people in the parking lot at the moment. The deputy stared at Elroy and then took Jake out front, where they stood by his car, the tired engine clicking and cooling.

Taller and heavier than Jake, he waited some moments before speaking, then "First, I need to make sure you're Jacob Warner, so I'm not wasting my time." His words came fast and flat, almost angry.

Jake uncertain and "What's this all about?" He didn't care for the deputy's stoic officiousness.

The deputy remained emotionless, terse: "*Do* you have identification?"

Jake extracted his brown leather wallet from a buttoned rear pocket, pulled from it a North Dakota driver's license. The deputy eyed it carefully before returning it. Jake, apprehensive though aware of no reason why he should be, stood holding the wallet and the license without sliding the one back in the other, and neither in his pocket.

"Sheriff Frederick down in Mitchell wants to see you," the deputy announced. Jake judged the voice to be the kind found in unintelligent but forthright men who refuse to consider too closely the nature of their convictions or duties but will act on them until forever.

"Mitchell, South Dakota?" Jake asked, bewildered.

"You used to live there."

"Yes, but a long time ago. Ten years." Jake lying and "I don't know the sheriff in Mitchell. I never did," thinking *what would Andy Frederick want with me?*

"He knows *you*. He wants to talk."

"Then why didn't he come himself?"

"He's in the hospital. Dying." Saying it seemed to strengthen the deputy's resolve. Jake felt the man's determination; this was not some kind of joke or mistake.

"I do not understand what the dying sheriff of Davidson County wants with me. You must have me confused with someone else."

"No. You're the man."

"What man? Are you suggesting I've broken some law?"

"I'm not *suggesting* anything. I'm *telling* you that Sheriff Frederick wants to see you. What he wants, I get. We haven't got much time. You need to get in the car right now. I'll drive you straight to the hospital."

"The hell you will. That's four hours away."

"Not the way I drive. And then I'll bring you back."

"You know I don't have to go with you."

"I strongly suggest you do."

"Why?"

"Sheriff Frederick, he said it was a matter of life and death."

"You've got the wrong person."

"No. You used to live in Mitchell and ten years ago your wife died in a car accident south of town. The sheriff says he needs to talk to you about that."

Jake's breath stopping a moment and *why would a man walk into where I work and start talking about a man I knew only on the witness stand and an accident I have been trying to forget?* Jake had long ago reached the point where he could, when he remembered Jane, separate her from the places where he had known and loved her, especially from the Chevy which he used to imagine smoking and mangled but no more. Jake wanted nothing to do with the specifics of his past, only Jane's image floating unmoored in his memory.

"I have to work," he said.

"I'll take care of that."

"You don't know Elroy."

"Elroy doesn't know me, either."

"I'm not going with you."

"Yes, you are. When Sheriff gives me orders, I carry them out. If he says go get a certain man because it's the most important thing in the world, you better believe I'll go get him. He hasn't got long. I will put handcuffs on you if I have to, and damn the lawsuit. Let's go."

The deputy, his size and strength commensurate with his devotion, took the helpless Jake firmly by the arm, opened the rear door, and shoved him in. Jake did not resist, had not for a long time resisted being directed by circumstances. Then the deputy reentered the shop while Jake waited; he checked the handle and found he could not open the door. A wire mesh prevented him from crawling into the front seat. Five minutes passed before the deputy returned, somewhat red in the face. They drove south out of Jamestown on Highway 281; a mile beyond the city limits the deputy turned on the cruiser's flashing emergency lights and stepped it up near a hundred.

This was the only conversation they engaged in for nearly three hours, and it occurred early: "What did you tell Elroy?"

"You were taking the rest of the day off."

"That was all right with him?"

"Eventually, it was."

Jake did not speak the rest of the frantic trip.

■

They steamed up on Mitchell from the north at just past one o'clock, Jake thinking *I could get on the whole rest of my life without ever seeing that house, that lake, that shop again.* Images came to him, how he and Jane had walked the sand beach along the lake they would be passing in a moment, what they had done in the bedroom and porch of the house, what had and had not passed between them that last warm afternoon. *I do not wish to be in this city*, though he believed that if he did not go past the house, as he had not in years, or even if he went by the water only, those old scenes would not alter his dreams and *I can block the rest. And I will not go south on the highway she took because I never have, I will not look at where she died*; except for the funeral, when his mother and father drove him along another road, he had not been south of Mitchell.

■

The deputy did not take him to those places that shamed or saddened him, but to the hospital in the heart of the city. After a slow elevator ascension they found the sheriff's third-floor room, dim with the curtains closed almost all the way like an eye near eternal sleep. They walked in on a man alone in the single metal-framed bed. An older woman, not a nurse, bent over him with her head turned as if to hear him better, and though they saw his lips moving they heard nothing as they entered except the clanging of a food cart along the polished hallway and a bell toning from somewhere near, summoning a nurse.

The woman straightened when she heard them enter and then faced them. "Thank God" she said, then "They've come, Andrew." She offered Jake a drawn and pale face, and eyes suggesting that whatever had gone wrong had done so because of him. She walked abruptly past him though the door and off down the corridor. The deputy stepped quietly to the bed, removed his hat, stood for a moment, then motioned Jake to replace him. Jake stationary and *how did I get here?* The deputy came to him and placed his large hand in the middle of Jake's back and suggested wordlessly that he move toward the bed. Then he stood off from the scene.

The man on the bed lay on his back elongated and stiff below a single white sheet. Jake remembered times when Sheriff Frederick had been a witness, how he had interrogated him. Sometimes their exchanges had been friendly, sometimes not. Now that meant nothing; now Jake silently examined him, stretched thin, emaciated but for a mound of belly that ballooned the sheet between his chest and legs. His left arm, away from Jake, cocked across the belly, the other paralleled his side atop the crisp white. The withered brown arms against the starchy cotton appeared as small branches blown from a tree in winter. Jake smelled faint urine mixed with medication, noted the catheter exiting the sheet on the bed's far side. A tube snaked from an IV bag into the straight arm. Sheriff Frederick's eyes seemed eagerly open, blinking as if a bright light had assaulted them, though his breath rasped and rumbled through his throat so that Jake, clearing his own, expected him to cough.

The sheriff did not, could not, turn his head, so rolled his eyes toward Jake, who felt from them what he felt in his own whenever he remembered what he hadn't said. After a few seconds, with great effort Frederick moved his left arm from his belly and pointed a knobby wrinkled finger to a wheeled table tray some feet from the bed. He moved his eyes left right left right until even that seemed beyond his strength. Sweat came on his forehead below silver hair swept back. The deputy knew what the eyes meant. He positioned the cart over Frederick, where it might be were Frederick eating. Then he stepped away again. What was left of the man in the bed grasped a white-corded control and pushed a button; the bed with its hidden but not silent magic began to raise his upper half. When he had been lifted to where he could see the top of the tray, he let off the button, Jake thinking *if I took this sheet off him he would float up. It can't be long.*

Jake's eyes followed Frederick's to the tray. On it sat two small, die-cast metal cars, one blue, the other yellow. Jake had seen such models advertised by various mints in car magazines; he knew they weren't cheap, sometimes costing two hundred dollars or more. Jake as a kid had constructed hundreds of plastic models, so the metal cars, to him the most interesting things in the room, intrigued him, and he looked closer. The blue was a 1957 Bel Air convertible, the yellow a 1965 Mustang. They appeared highly detailed and beautifully constructed, but grotesquely out of place in an antiseptic room where people came to die.

With great effort Frederick reached for the cars; he seemed surprised when each hand grasped one, Jake thinking *his hands don't do what he wants them to much now.* Frederick then rolled the cars slowly together, the Mustang grille-first into the side of the Chevy; the position, Jake realized, of a classic inter-section collision. Images of the DeSoto and Jane's Chevy came to him. He wanted to leave the room, but didn't.

Frederick rolled the two cars together a second time, then his eyes darkened. He shifted the angle of the Mustang and began to rub it along the door of the Chevy. Jake guessed there must have been some rough edge of metal along the Mustang's front bumper, some casting not removed before plating and assembly, for the bumper began to scratch the paint on the Chevy's door. Jake shivered at even that slight sound of scratching, at the sight of the blue paint flaking off the door's metal; controlling his desire only with great effort, he wanted to take the cars from the sheriff but did not.

Frederick kept scratching until what little energy he had left was exhausted, then he released the cars. His face and body seemed to fall away, to shrink back into the bed and pillow, but Jake did not notice, for he continued to stare at the cars; Jake's gaze narrowed to the ugly surface of metal that moments before had been a perfect gloss of egg-shell blue and *no man ought to be allowed to do that*. The deputy, who seemed upset as well, pulled the tray away, and he and Jake stood silently, each to one side. Mrs. Frederick re-entered the room, and within a minute Sheriff Andrew Frederick, without the aid of metal and rubber, collided quietly with death.

■

Jake finally learned the deputy's name. Frederick's wife had whispered "Thank you, Deputy Siverson" as she emerged from her husband's room fifteen minutes after Siverson and Jake had left her alone there. She had been crying, her make-up run below her eyes, but was not now. The three of them went into a large waiting room and sat, Siverson and the sheriff's wife on a small couch facing Jake in a single chair, Jake thinking *now they will explain this to me* and "I'm sorry about your husband."

"Thanks." She seemed as limply relieved as the body back in the room. "He's been getting worse for three months, cancer. Two days ago he got bad and we thought he was just disoriented when he started talking about you, asking for you. He asked Duane"—she nodded at the deputy—"if he could borrow two cars from his collection." She turned to Siverson fully. "You must have what, Duane, twenty of those cars?"

"Thirty-six now."

"He'd roll them together, back and forth, until he got too weak. I knew he had been thinking about something, seriously, for several months. He had made a list a few weeks ago, kept it in his wallet like he was going shopping. I finally saw it last week. At the top was 'things to do,' like he was fixing something and on his way to the hardware store. Your name was at the top."

"Why?" Jake asked. "I knew your husband only professionally."

"In what capacity?"

"I was a lawyer here in Mitchell, a long time ago."

Her surprise evident and "I thought you'd be somebody he'd arrested years ago, somebody he didn't feel had been treated right," pausing, then "No?"

"No."

"You and Andy had no fights, no grudges?", Jake telling her "No." She turned from Jake to Siverson as if he might have an answer, Jake thinking *it must be Siverson. He knows.*

But Siverson told them he did not. "The only thing is that Andy told me to find this man, to bring him to the hospital. I did that." He nodded in affirmation. No one was going to suggest he hadn't done his job.

Mrs. Frederick going on and "He'd crossed off the other three things on his list, so what you did wiped his slate clean. Thank you for that." Siverson nodded once more. She turned back to Jake. "Well, I guess it can't be as much of a mystery as it might seem. Before you came he asked me to get a file out of

his suitcase, and when you came, to give it to you." She fished
a thin manila folder from her large purse, pushed it toward
Jake like it was the last thing on her own list that needed to be
done.

Jake grasped it with hands still marked by body filler and
paint dust, noted the penciled title on the folder tab:
"Warner/Jenson." He knew what it contained but had no desire
to open it. He had left a lot of things closed for a lot of years,
and this was no place to begin the openings.

Jake pretending and "What's in it?"

"I have no idea."

"Deputy?"

Siverson shook his head.

Jake continuing his feigned innocence and "What was that
business with the cars?" Thinking about it now nearly brought
laughter.

Frederick's wife shrugged and "I couldn't tell." Siverson
remained silent.

"So Siverson here drives about two hundred and fifty miles to
get me, takes me back to see a dying man I haven't even thought
about in a decade, I go to the hospital where this man just before
he dies grips two toy cars. Then you give me this file, and you
don't have any idea what's going on?"

"I thought *you* would. I don't understand."

Jake lying and "Neither do I. It's been so long since I've lived
here," then *not long enough*.

"But you did once?"

"I told you, yes. Eleven years almost."

"Open the file," Siverson commanded. Jake had tried to
ignore it as it lay in his lap. He reluctantly flopped it open and
confirmed that it was the sheriff's investigation into the accident
that killed Jane, Jake thinking *I do not wish to read this. But he
was trying to tell me something.* He closed the folder quickly.

"This is about my wife's accident," he said, staring at the
floor.

"When was that?" Mrs. Frederick asked. It had become clear Siverson was incapable of unrequired speech. Jake began to think more highly of him, that if he ever needed a subordinate, Siverson, with his pet-like devotion, was the sort he would want.

"1985. Down by Parkston. She was killed."

"I'm sorry."

Surprisingly, as if suggesting Jake examine the file more closely, Siverson said, "Must be something in there that would explain this." Jake nodded at him dumbly, but he did not page into the file, afraid still, thinking *I will not go any farther south of Mitchell than I have already been.* Finally he said, "I'm sure you're tired of this. I'll look at it when I get home."

Siverson straightened his back and "Maybe you should look now."

Jake met his gaze and "No."

They sat in silence until Frederick's wife said "I've people to call, children and grandchildren to gather."

Siverson told her, "I'll take Mr. Warner home, check in with you when I get back." Jake felt numb as they shot through dusky South Dakota hours, lights flashing and the car less heavy as it now and then crested a small hill. Otherwise the land was flat and empty, the sort of landscape Jake preferred.

Siverson dropped Jake at the body shop, and just before Jake got out, Siverson said, "Take a look at that file."

"What do you know about it?" Jake asked. Again, they hadn't talked on the trip back, even though Siverson allowed him to ride in front. Idle conversation, or even serious, had not occurred to Jake at twice the speed limit on the narrow gravel-shouldered two-lane highway, his right foot poised on an imaginary brake.

"Look at the file," Siverson said, then he rocketed off into the soft dusk. Jake watched as the changing light swallowed him. He got into his own car without going into the closed shop, and as he drove home he tried again to pretend that what had just happened really hadn't.

■

Jake carefully placed the file on the cheap metal-and-Formica kitchen table when he reached his two-bedroom basement apartment. He had lived in the ordinary frame building for nine years, a mile from the shop. There were two floors above him, twelve apartments in all filled with elderly couples and young ones with children. Jake was the only bachelor, and over the years he had made not even a casual acquaintance with anyone else in the building. Jake, because he considered all seasons but summer too harsh for any car worth its salt, drove a late-seventies Plymouth Volare, white with a rust-colored vinyl roof. He cared so little for the car that he had changed its oil but once and had not had it tuned in his seven years of ownership. He had not added many miles to the 78,000 the odometer showed when he bought it. He seldom traveled beyond the city limits. Though his apartment came with a garage, he left the Volare outside in all weather; others in the building considered it as much a fixture as the light poles by the parking lot, or the storage shed.

Jake flicked on the television but soon found himself staring off somewhere beyond the baseball game, his mind whirling and numb with strange images and sounds. He called Tim Kinneady and agreed to meet him at a bar north of the city. They talked over beer and shot two games of pool on the warped, brown-felted quarter table. Jake related the events of the day, but heard them himself as so odd that even he had nothing to say beyond them. Kinneady spoke little, thought Jake ought to get drunk and think things over tomorrow. Jake drove home at eleven thirty, nervous and dissatisfied.

Though it was late, he called a woman friend, as the phone rang unable to think why he had dialed her number or to fix on how she might help him. He told himself he neither wanted nor needed help, but he let it ring anyway.

He had known Luella Alger for three years, since meeting her after work one Friday in the Gas Light bar. Kinneady, at that time the only other employee who could stand working for Elroy, had talked Jake into Happy Hour, though drinking after work was something Jake disliked because it usually made him tired and sad by seven o'clock, and then he wasn't much good the rest of the night. He usually ate, read, watched television, bored but unable to find energy for anything else.

Luella Alger owned and managed Alger's, a struggling family clothing store in the old business district downtown, inherited from her father when he died, a store that had been in the Alger family for five generations but which had limped along or lost money for years while Luella's father drank himself to death. The new mall by the interstate had siphoned customers from the dark brick buildings downtown, some of which had stood since the twenties. The store needed a face-lift—some of the other downtown businesses were modernizing their exteriors—and complete revamping inside. Luella knew exactly what she wanted to do, what new fixtures and displays and brands she wanted to try, but couldn't get a loan.

Her mother had died of cancer thirty years before, leaving Luella ten and alone with her father and his increasing whiskey. She had been married twice, only the latter producing offspring, an eighteen-year-old daughter who had finished high school the previous spring and worked full time at the store. Luella often said of her, "She's deciding," then rolled her eyes in mock exasperation.

When Kinneady had introduced them, Jake didn't realize she was sitting in a wheelchair. The first sentence she spoke to Jake was a command to pronounce her last name Alyer, the g not hard but soft like a y: "You say somebody's first name—Al— and then you're like you're from Mississippi—yer. Alyer. If you hear it before you see it you're okay. Now you say it." Like a gradeschooler being instructed by his teacher, Jake had mouthed it slowly, got it right the first time. Luella had reached across the small round table, patted him on the head laughing, snatched a pencil from his pocket and drawn a star on a napkin. When she touched his hair Jake remembered what it had been like to feel a woman's hands, so rather than politely ignore her, as he usually did anyone he didn't know, he kept on talking. She left before he did, and he stared as she rolled rather than walked toward the exit.

"What are you gawking at?" Kinneady had asked.

"I didn't know she was paralyzed."

"She's not."

"What, she uses the wheelchair to pick up guys?"

"Believe me, if it worked, I'd be sitting in one right now. She had an accident several years ago, the day after her father's funeral. He had this old Ford sedan, an automatic, and she drove it home that night, got out to open the garage door and the damn thing slipped into gear and nailed her just as she was turning back. Right hip, thigh, knee. Drove her into this big workbench at the end of the garage. Long time in the hospital, long time in therapy. Sometimes its easier for her to use the chair than to walk. And regular chairs give her pain. The wheelchair has a certain angle, certain padding. She tells me she can still fuck all right."

"Jesus, Tim!"

"Well, it's important. At least to *some* of us."

"You might phrase it more delicately: she can yet engage in physical relations."

"Jesus, *Jake*!"

Over a period of months after that first meeting they saw each other several times, slept together once, then Luella broke it off. She didn't care for his lethargy. He had no opinions, at least none he offered. If they saw a movie, all she could draw from him were clipped sentences that said nothing beyond that he had liked it or hadn't. While she wandered freely between opinion's poles, he never got excited. He never berated anyone from work, never criticized Elroy. Though sleeping with him had been enjoyable, Luella felt that even sex had failed to penetrate his stoic facade, one, she sensed, he did not have the courage to look beyond. He had been brief in talking about his past, and Luella understood that losing a spouse could be devastating—she had lost two, though "only" to divorce. She could not comprehend that he had been a lawyer but had quit to work in a body shop. She wanted to dig into him deeper but refused to be his therapist, the woman who might straighten him out. "Get a life," she would bluntly offer, or "grieve, goddamn it, or something. Somebody needs to slap some sense into you, some nurturer with a mothering instinct. But it ain't me, babe. No no no it ain't me babe." Jake failed to comprehend the allusion. She continued to call him now and then, and he her, to talk; he listened well, didn't trample her speech like too many other men. He had made love to her one other time after she had announced over the phone one late Saturday night how desperately horny she was.

When Jake called her that Friday, his relation of what had happened went slowly, as if he were trying not to speak it but at last could not help himself. It was the first time since Jane's death that he had reached for someone, and he did so with the longest sequence of sentences she had ever heard him utter. "Ooh, a mystery," she said with the cheeriness that often grated on Jake's impassivity and just as often attracted him. "I'll be over in the morning."

■

Over coffee she paged through the file, Jake still reluctant beside her. The night before there had been something new in his voice, a hint of need, but now he sat quiet again, impassive. Luella usually refused his coffee, for even that, to her, was weak. Luella had expected a thick sheaf of papers, a mountain of inscrutable detail, but there was not much inside the folder. Sheriff Frederick had been the investigating officer at the scene that afternoon, had diagrammed the intersection and sketched where the vehicles had come from, where they had met, and where they had come to rest. His diagram was essentially as child-like as the cars he had moved the day before. His drawing indicated the old man had T-boned the Monarch as if a target had been painted on the door. There were no skid marks prior to impact. Jane's Chevy had, according to Frederick, come to rest tangled in a barb wire fence on the southwest corner of the intersection, 113 feet from the point of impact. The other vehicle, driven by Leonard Jenson, having come from the east, after impact had traveled 98 feet, stopping along the north side of Highway 44. He had also written out a very brief description of how the cars had torn the air and three lives in two. A controlled intersection, two wrecked cars, three people dead, not a mark on the road. There really hadn't been much to say.

Mounted with tape on separate sheets were several pictures of each vehicle and the intersection. Jake refused to look at them, thinking for the ten-thousandth time *I will not*. Luella peered at the still-glossy but yellowing Polaroids in silence. Something mean in her wanted Jake to look: "There aren't any pictures of *her*, Jake." When he failed to answer she peered at him across the table, saw him staring off beyond her somewhere. "Look," she said again. "Maybe they're what's important."

"Important about what?"

"Jesus, Jake, about yesterday."

"I will not look at those pictures," he insisted with an intensity she seldom heard. She did not pursue it. Instead she examined more closely the first page of Frederick's report:

MOTOR VEHICLE CRASH REPORT
Department of Transportation, Drivers License & Traffic Safety
SFN 2355 (Rev. 2-96)

AGENCY

CRASH DATE (M/D/Y)	TIME (24 HR)	OFFICER NO	OFFICER NAME		AGENCY NAME
07 / 17 / 75	10:45 AM	137	Andrew Frederick		Dav. Co. Sheriff

POLICE NOTIFIED (M/D/Y)	TIME (24 HR)	EMERGENCY UNIT RESPONDING		EMERGENCY UNIT NO	AGENCY REPORT NO
07 / 17 / 75	11 AM	31		31	797

LOCATION

COUNTY	CO CODE	CITY CODE	CITY	RURAL / URBAN	FUNC CLASS
Dav.	6			RURAL	

HIGHWAY	HUNDREDTHS MI / KM	FROM REFERENCE POINT	TOWARD REFERENCE POINT

TOWNSHIP	RANGE	ROUTE	HUNDREDTHS MILES / KILOMETERS	FROM NODE	TOWARD NODE

	(STREET NAME)		(STREET NAME)	NODE
ON	Hwy 44	AT INTERSECTION WITH	Hwy 37	
OR	FT/M FROM	(INTERSECTING STREET) NODE	TOWARD (INTERSECTING STREET)	NODE

UNIT 1 / STRIKING UNIT

OPERATOR NAME (LAST, FIRST, MI)		OWNER NAME if not operator (LAST, FIRST, MI)	
Jenson, Leonard M.			

ADDRESS	PHONE	ADDRESS if different from operator	PHONE
RR2 P	726-1911		

CITY	STATE	ZIP	CITY	STATE	ZIP
Parkston	SD				

DAMAGE AMOUNT	OPERATOR LICENSE NO	ST ISS	DOB (M/D/Y)	PLATE NO	STATE	MAKE	YEAR
$1,000	040756	SD	11,15,98	113798	SD	DeSoto	59

INSURANCE CODE USE ONLY	POLICY NO	INSURANCE COMPANY NAME (NOT AGENT)
	73145011500S	Great Lakes

INSURED BY	CARD ISS.	SPD LMT	DVR NO	VIN (OUT-OF-STATE VEHICLES ONLY)	RETESTING
☒ OWNER ☐ DRIVER	☒ YES	55			☐ YES *

UNIT 2 / OTHER UNIT

OPERATOR NAME (LAST, FIRST, MI)		OWNER NAME if not operator (LAST, FIRST, MI)	
WARNER, Jane L.		Warner, Jacob N.	

ADDRESS	PHONE	ADDRESS if different from operator	PHONE
415 McCarty St.	341-2112		

CITY	STATE	ZIP	CITY	STATE	ZIP
Mitchell	SD				

DAMAGE AMOUNT	OPERATOR LICENSE NO	ST ISS	DOB (M/D/Y)	PLATE NO	STATE	MAKE	YEAR
$6,000	122349	SD	10,17,50	705931	SD	Chevy	61

INSURANCE CODE USE ONLY	POLICY NO	INSURANCE COMPANY NAME (NOT AGENT)
	00015MM211	Sun State

INSURED BY	CARD ISS.	SPD LMT	DVR NO	VIN (OUT-OF-STATE VEHICLES ONLY)	RETESTING
☒ OWNER ☐ DRIVER	☒ YES	55			☐ YES *

TRUCK / BUS ONLY

COMPLETE THE TRUCK AND BUS INFORMATION SECTION FOR ALL ACCIDENTS INVOLVING TRUCKS WITH AT LEAST TWO AXLES AND SIX TIRES OR MORE AND BUSES DESIGNED TO TRANSPORT 16 OR MORE PASSENGERS INCLUDING THE DRIVER. INCLUDED ARE PICKUPS WITH DUAL WHEELS AND ALL PICKUPS TOWING TRAILERS OF ALL TYPES. (IF MORE THAN ONE TRUCK IS INVOLVED, USE AN EXTRA FORM, ATTACHED TO THE ORIGINAL). **UNIT NO.**

CARRIER NAME	CARRIER'S IDENTIFICATION NO. (USDOT OR ICCMC)	IS CARRIER INTERSTATE?
		☐ YES ☐ NO

CARRIER'S ADDRESS	PHONE	SOURCE OF CARRIER NAME ☐ DRIVER ☐ LOG BOOK ☐ SIDE OF VEHICLE ☐ SHIPPING PAPERS OR TRIP MANIFEST (BUS)

CITY	STATE	ZIP	GROSS VEHICLE WEIGHT RATING ___ LBS.	AXLES ON VEHICLE (INCLUDING TRAILER)

HAZARDOUS MATERIALS PLACARD? ☐ YES ☐ NO	HAZ. MAT. 4-DIGIT NO.	HAZ. MAT. 1-DIGIT NO	WAS HAZARDOUS CARGO FROM VEHICLE RELEASED? (DO NOT COUNT FUEL FROM FUEL TANK) ☐ YES ☐ NO

HAZARDOUS MATERIAL NAME	ESTIMATE TOTAL LENGTH (FEET / METER) FROM FRONT BUMPER TO END OF LAST TRAILER

OTHER

PROP. DAMAGE $	ACTION SEQUENCE, CITATIONS, AND DAMAGE	VEHICLE 1	VEHMVT	CONFAC	CONFAC	CITATN	EVAACT	DVRCON	DAMAGE	EXTDEF	TOWED
		VEHICLE 2									

UNIT	SEAT	AGE	SEX	ADI	AT	DT	SAFETY EQUIP.	AIR BAG	INJ.	EJC. EXT.	OWN. NOT.	OCCUPANT, WITNESS, PROPERTY OWNER NAME, ADDRESS, PHONE, PROPERTY DESCRIPTION
1	F	87	M						F			
2	F	35	F						F			
1	F	87	F						F			
Witness												Don Brown RR Parkston

NOTE: IF MORE THAN TWO UNITS (OR SIX OCCUPANT / WITNESSES) ARE INVOLVED, USE AN EXTRA FORM, ATTACHED TO THE ORIGINAL.
* DESCRIBE OR EXPLAIN IN NARRATIVE.   ** EXPLAIN IN REQUEST FOR RE-EXAM FORM.

DIAGRAM WHAT HAPPENED:

INDICATE NORTH BY DRAWING ARROW THROUGH CIRCLE

DRAW OUTLINE OF ROADWAY AT PLACE OF CRASH ⟶ [1] ▷

NUMBER EACH VEHICLE AND SHOW
DIRECTION OF TRAVEL BY ARROW

USE SOLID LINE TO SHOW PATH BEFORE ACCIDENT:
⟶ [1] ▷ ◁ [2] ⟵
- - -▶ [2] ▷

SHOW PEDESTRIAN BY: X
SHOW RAILROAD BY: ┼┼┼┼┼┼┼┼
SHOW UTILITY POLES BY: Φ
SHOW MOTORCYCLE BY: ○─○
SHOW ANIMAL BY: Ω

No skid marks until impact

Stop Sign

98'

113'

#37

#44

Stop sign

OFFICER'S NARRATIVE: OBSERVATIONS AND ASTERISK ITEMS. (PLEASE PRINT)

Vehicle #2 Southbound on Hwy 37 failed to stop
at intersection with Hwy 44. Was struck broadside by
vehicle #1, westbound on 44. Driver and passenger of
#1 dead at scene. Driver of #2 dead at scene.

DATE OF REPORT: 10-17-85   SIGNATURE(S): Andrew Fredarick

She didn't see anything unusual, so turned the report over and scanned the diagram and terse, handwritten account. Frederick had labeled the old couple's car #1, Jane's Chevy #2. From beginning to end the account was done with sloppy handwriting, but without erasures or cross-outs.

"How was that intersection marked?" Luella asked.

Jake pointing at the paper as if irritated and "The east/west highway ran straight through. North/south you had to stop. Like it says in the report. Here," his finger thumping on the paper.

Luella felt an uneasiness wedge itself between her and Jake and "I know what it says, I just wanted to see if you remembered it that way. Stop signs, not yield signs?"

"Yes, like it says in the report," Jake nearly angry and *read the goddamn report.*

"That means Jane either went through the stop sign or stopped and then pulled out in front of the other car."

"I guess."

"Jake, you asked me over here. Now you act like this is a pain."

"It is."

"Then why . . . Christ, Jake."

"Sorry."

Luella resumed looking at the report, and after a minute or so "She never stopped. Look." Her finger, tipped with a red nail, led him to an entry indicating the speed of both vehicles was "approximately sixty miles per hour at the time of impact."

"She'd driven that road about a thousand times," Jake said, apostrophizing *why didn't you stop the one time you should have?*

"Maybe that's why, she'd done it too often." Luella paused, then "Maybe she had something on her mind." She saw how Jake turned his face away, how in the instant before he did his skin seemed to darken. "Could have been anything," she added.

They came across pages that indicated the sheriff had been interviewed by the insurance adjusters from both companies.

"What was the nature of the settlement?" Luella asked.

Jake hesitated. "I don't know. The adjuster called me about the car. I had it insured for an agreed value, seven or eight thousand, I think. I guess I got a check for it."

"You guess? You must have been a hell of a lawyer."

Jake flat refusing to go back and "Yeah, I guess."

"Well, what I meant was, how much did the Jensons' children get."

"How do you know they had children?"

"Every farmer in every state in the union has children. It's the law."

Jake didn't respond and Luella went on with "Somebody must have gotten something from your insurance."

"I couldn't say," Jake thinking *it never really crossed my mind to ask.*

"What did your agent tell you?"

"Never a word about it. I guess I sort of gave everybody the idea that it wasn't my favorite topic for conversation."

"You guess a lot," Jake not responding. They sat. Luella drank her coffee reluctantly. She found herself as lethargic as Jake, which reminded her of the primary reason she had stopped seeing him regularly. But staring at him, she realized how much she liked him anyway. "This doesn't say much," she told him, patting the papers spread out on the table. "And it sure as hell doesn't tell us why that sheriff had those cars. Was he trying to say something about the accident?"

Jake shook his head and "How would I know?"

"Jake, why did you call me if you don't want to talk about what happened?" Jake silent and afraid.

Finally he muttered "It happened after Jane left home. She would have been going south to her parents. The address of the old couple, they lived east of the intersection, so they would have been going the way Frederick said." After a moment, "Unless they were going home."

"But then the impact would have been on the other side," Jake thinking *yes it would.*

"Autopsies?"

"Not that I know of." They paged again through the meager file, and did in fact find brief coroner's reports, which revealed to Luella nothing significant, listing the causes of death only as "blunt trauma." Jake refused to read them.

The phone rang, Jake surprised to find it was Deputy Siverson. "You find anything in that file?" Siverson asked.

"Nothing."

"Read it again," Siverson said, then hung up, Jake thinking *that unnerving goddamn son of a bitch Siverson things happen way too fast.* And way too intensely for a man who outside of work didn't move much and said even less, who would admit only vague recollections of the years he spent working hard, speaking, and loving a woman. Jake and Luella went back over the pages in the file, word by word, didn't finish until after noon. They found nothing strange. Then Luella was needed at the store and Jake spent the rest of the afternoon alone; he ate supper alone and spent the night sitting at his kitchen table staring at the file which, having been closed earlier when Luella left, remained unopened.

■

Monday he went back to replacing a quarter panel on a 1986 Ford Tempo. In beginning to fit the panel the previous week he couldn't align the trunk and bumper and taillights properly; whenever he looked at the car from the rear something appeared canted, improperly aligned, though he couldn't tell what. Elroy called such a condition "off-whacked." Such a lack of fit was the only situation that could anger Jake, and he would work and fit and bend and realign until any tiny thing that hadn't looked right finally did; outside the body shop nothing moved him that way.

In the office Jake passed Elroy at his desk; Elroy said nothing to him, as Jake had expected. Jake did not ask what had passed between Siverson and his boss, and Elroy did not volunteer. Jake picked up his old routine as he would a wrench and considered a future that included little beyond replacing fenders and bumpers, straightening door and quarter panels, occasionally painting what he had finished reconstructing. He walked out to look at the coupe, but did so only to make sure it was still unmoving there, as it had been since his first day working for Elroy—he had asked if he could store it somewhere inside the fence and Elroy had assented. Jake had towed the coupe in, parked it next to the building, and had not so much as touched it since. He glanced at it that Monday thinking *I drove this car but have not sat in it, have hardly put a hand to it, since she was gone, the fender I set to work on that afternoon but never started, not even dreamed of the shiny black I imagined. Why?* But he could not answer and left the coupe in its old stasis inside the fence.

Each night that week Jake sat alone in his apartment but did not open the file again. He sat in the living room with the television off and the air conditioner humming and did not move for hours, thinking or trying to think about the next day's requirements. Whenever his thinking turned him around, asked, like Siverson, that he go back, his lethargy increased, Jake thinking *I ought to get up and cook or I ought to read* but he would continue to sit. Each night late. He would fall asleep on the sofa, wake up well past midnight sore and crooked from the awkward way his body lay, and summon all his strength to stumble into the bedroom. Mornings he had no difficulty; as long as someone or something else demanded his energy, he could move. But each night, too, he could not ignore a lost part of him that wanted to know what Frederick had meant with the cars, some old voice that wanted to ask questions and get answers.

■

The following Saturday morning, as Jake lay face-up on his bed following intricacies in the white-spackled ceiling, the phone disturbed him. He reached a heavy arm across the bed, lifted and dragged the receiver to his ear. Siverson's voice again, Jake thinking after the first syllable *goddamn it leave me alone just leave me the hell alone,* angry for the words and the memory driving with them.

"You read that file again?"

"Yes, deputy, I did."

"And?"

"And nothing."

"Nothing that would explain what Sheriff did?"

Jake felt the stirrings of more than mild anger. "Siverson, what are you all about? Just say what you know. What am I supposed to find in that file?"

"I've never looked in it. Sheriff told me not to. He said 'Warner will find what happened there.'"

"And I did. My wife ran a stop sign and got killed. Simple. What the goddamn file says." Jake tried to push the rising anger back. "Look, I'm sorry, I just don't understand any of this."

"Some of it must be gone then."

Jake impatiently "Some of *what?*"

"The file."

"Why do you say that? Damn you, *what* is so important?"

"Sheriff said if you read the file you'd find how your wife's accident went down, but what you're telling me isn't what happened." Jake lay silent thinking *Jesus Christ just tell me.* Then Siverson reserved and officious like a judge and "Call the man who reported it."

■

When Luella called mid-morning Jake still lay in bed. He mentioned Siverson calling, what the deputy had told him to do with the man listed on the report as having called the sheriff after the accident.

Luella intrigued and "So you called him, right? What did he say?"

Jake mildly "No."

"He said no?"

"No, I didn't call him."

"Why not?" Jake not answering.

"What's his name?"

"I didn't look it up."

"You are a real bulldog when you get a lead, Jake. My god, slow down," Jake not responding to her sarcasm.

Luella came over, and when Jake let her in she went to the kitchen table and opened the file, found Don Brown's name. She dialed directory assistance but they had no Don Brown listing in Parkston or Mitchell. She asked for any Brown near there but was told she needed a first name. Irritated, she asked for Mike Brown but was told there was none. She asked for Steve Brown and scribbled the number on a yellowing newspaper she scooped from the floor. Jake watched her flurry of activity impassively, listened as she dialed the number and interrogated whoever answered until she was satisfied that the person had never known the man who may have watched Jane die. Before she hung up she got the number of yet another man named Brown, from whom she learned that Don Brown had been dead three years. When Jake heard this he was almost relieved.

But she tracked down Siverson and when he answered she put the phone to Jake's ear and commanded him to speak, Jake unwilling but "Don Brown is dead, Siverson. Any other bright ideas?"

"Yup. Check the highway department." Then he disconnected himself from Jake's life again.

■

Wednesday at ten Luella snatched him from Elroy and Jimtown and led him like she might a child out to her car. She actually took him by the arm, which neither embarrassed nor irritated him. She continued to be more interested than Jake in the aftermath of Jane's accident, Frederick's deathbed strangeness. It had taken her three days to convince him that they ought to drive to Mitchell and do what Siverson suggested. Even though Jake finally agreed, he said he had to finish a car on Wednesday morning and maybe it would take the whole day and maybe they'd have to wait till Thursday. But Luella had ordered him to be finished by ten, and to her surprise, he was.

They ate a quick lunch in Aberdeen, then continued south toward Mitchell. Jake, to Luella's surprise, remembered most of the county buildings and directed her to the low brick building that had for nearly forty years housed the county highway department, located several miles south from Jake and Jane's lake house and the street upon whose concrete Jake had heard her last tires turning.

Before they got out of Luella's car Jake asked her, "Just what are we supposed to say in there?"

"Ask what kind of records they keep."

Jake reluctant and "Records of what? We don't even know what we're looking for."

"See what sort of records they keep, then go from there. Use your imagination," though at times she doubted he had one. "Siverson must believe there's something here."

Inside, a woman who looked far older than the cracking, dingy building told them that the county maintained three types of records: personnel, work orders, and financial. Upon entering the small, bright office, Jake had first seen her in an indolent posture at the lone desk sipping slow coffee from a lipstick-smeared white mug and reading a newspaper. But her responses to his mild inquisitions were crisp—they could review the work orders; the others were confidential. Then she asked them the nature of their interest, and Jake told her it had something to do with his wife's accident, something he wanted to clear up.

"I remember that accident," she said in a voice he found kind.

Luella hoping for another source and "You worked here then?"

"I worked for the county, but not here. I was at the court-house, in the auditor's office. Been with highway about five years. I'll retire in another twelve months," Jake hearing in her voice a yearning for that time. "Yes, I remember people talking about it. I'm sure sorry that happened to you," the woman eyeing Luella.

"Thanks."

"Well, walk back with me to the storeroom and we'll find that file. Every year has a separate folder." They followed her through a narrow hallway to a large room filled with file cabinets. She led them to a metal cabinet with four tall drawers. Its olive-drab paint suggested army surplus. The woman seemed to know exactly where to look. She pulled open the top drawer, which moved crankily on old metal rollers.

"1975 you said?"

"Yes."

Inside the drawer were thick envelopes of the kind whose flaps are secured by thin cords wrapped around thick paper buttons. She found 1980 and picked backwards with her fingers, but she didn't find anything with 1975 written on it. The sequence of road-repair history skipped from 1976 to 1974. She looked in every drawer in the cabinet, and in the one next to it which held similar records. Jake and Luella checked as well. They determined that somehow a year had been lost, Luella muttering as she looked at Jake, "a lot more than a year."

Before they left, the woman, whose name they failed to ask for, took Jake's number and said she'd call if the file turned up. "Just call me Hillary Clinton," she hollered after as they passed through the wooden door to the parking lot. Luella told Jake to drive to the courthouse, where they found Siverson walking along a granite-floored hallway; he asked them to step outside so they could talk privately. A tall tree shaded them from the warm sun as they told him about the missing records.

Their information didn't seem to impress him and "Missing, huh?"

"Yes," Jake told him.

"Well, I'm not surprised."

"Siverson, you *told* me to look there. Now you tell me you're not surprised that there's nothing to look for. I don't get it."

Siverson drew a long breath and ran his right hand across his face. He looked tired. He turned his eyes until they met Jake's squarely and "I'm going to tell you this once, and once only, and I'll never say it again, even if it means going back from the gates of heaven." He paused, then "All right if she hears?" pointing at Luella.

"Sure."

Siverson glaring hard at Jake and "I promised Sheriff I wouldn't repeat, ever, to no one, what he told me. He didn't want me mixed up in it. But I'll break that promise a little, maybe just bend it. He must have thought something was in that accident-report file that isn't." Jake and Luella waited, silent. After a few seconds Siverson went on. "The official report, that's there, isn't it?"

"What do you mean?"

"I mean, is the official accident report form there, filled out?"

"Yes."

Siverson paused yet again before responding. Jake could almost hear him thinking. "It's official, but it's a lie. Your wife wasn't going south, and the other car wasn't going west. Sheriff told me this a year ago, not long after he found out he had cancer. We were fishing and he just started telling me, like he was confessing to a priest. I didn't know what to say."

"He told you the report's account wasn't accurate?"

"Your wife was going east, the other car south."

Jake shaking his head and "That doesn't make any sense. Why would Jane be going east? She'd left Mitchell and gone south on the highway."

"There was a detour that week, mile north of the intersection. You had to take the mile road west, then south, then back east to the intersection. I thought you'd find that in the highway records. Your wife had come back east and was going to turn south."

Now it was Jake pausing, considering, then "But how could the other car come from the north through the detour?"

"The old man drove around the barricades. It was Saturday and no one working, they'd just put up signs and flashers on sawhorses. Sheriff found the old man's tire tracks where they shouldn't have been—he drove around the barricades then south right through the stop sign. Don Brown saw it. Not the accident, but the old man going south on the highway."

"Jane wasn't at fault."

"That's what Sheriff said. Said it looked like she was hardly moving, maybe saw him coming and tried to stop. He said he just made up the diagram."

"I don't get it. Why would he alter the report?"

"Money."

"Whose?"

"Your insurance company's. Sheriff said there was this hot-shot young adjuster working this area for your company. Out of Sioux Falls. Sheriff said he was ambitious as hell. Sheriff didn't like him, but the Monday after the accident he come to Sheriff and talked him into this little scheme. Sheriff was going through some bad times, and he agreed. I'm ashamed to say it, but he did. I admired that man more than any other, but I guess he was human."

"What scheme?"

"That's all I'm saying. You'll have to figure it out." Siverson then planted a thick finger on Jake's chest and his loyal eyes narrowed. "Understand this," Siverson said, "what you just heard from me, I never said it. If *God* asks me, I'll deny it. Andy Frederick was like a dad to me, and I will never again say anything against him. You're on your own now." He jabbed his finger twice into Jake's chest, hard enough so that Jake fell back a step and "Understood?" Jake nodding. Siverson left them on the courthouse lawn.

As they reached the highway Jake turned to Luella and "No sheriff, no witness, no records, no deputy. Will you leave this alone now?" But he saw the incredulous look on her face and knew that she wouldn't.

And then his old lawyer voice with *Neither will I*, but fighting his desire to know and *I do not want to go back.*

■

Four days later, Sunday morning, Jake and Luella, Luella driving, in her Explorer rolling south yet again along 281, the same route, but at half the speed, that Jake and Siverson had taken sixteen days before; four days since Luella and Jake had gone to Mitchell. Silence between them now aggressive and loud, Luella remembering their drive back late Wednesday, their talk. She had listened to Jake hopeful, thinking *Well, he'll have to do something now, finally he'll have to get off his ass and do something.* Halfway home she had asked him what his plans were now.

"I don't know," he had said. "I don't know there is much I can do." Though Luella had not known him before Jane died, she believed there had to have been more to him than his mild passive speech, that something deep within him, if touched, would resurrect the man who had warmed Jacob Warner's body before he had assumed his current futility.

Luella silent looking at him, wanting to take her nails and rake his face, elicit from him some acknowledgment of pain. She wondered why he had even bothered to call her that first night after Siverson had brought him back with the file, if all he wanted was someone to witness his paralysis.

"Say that again," she had said.

"Say what again?" he had asked, seemingly having forgotten his own words in the few seconds that had passed.

"Jesus Christ, Jake, you ought to do *something. Most* people would." His blank evasive eyes wandered past her. "For instance," she offered in a sarcasm usually reserved for her ex-husbands, "a person, some wild ballsy type, would contact the insurance company, check out Siverson's story. Find the adjuster, see what could be done about exposing him."

"What did he do?"

"Jake, didn't you hear Siverson?" She grabbed his earlobe like a teacher might a child's and "Dammit, Jake, where are you? What the hell happened to make you like this?" Jake only sullen, almost pouting, mumbling "What could anybody do now? That was a long time ago."

"Jake, somebody made money off Jane dying."

"You don't know that. And I mean it. What could anyone do? What could *I* do? We've no evidence."

"Jake, you got hammered ten years ago, but not castrated. I mean, Jesus." She wanted to tell him to stop wallowing in what-ever shit had been thrown at him, but somehow she knew that Jane dying was the biggest part but not all of the problem.

"Maybe I did," Jake muttered, hearing the pathetic sound of words formed by his own mouth and remembering a time when his speech came differently and thinking *maybe I did*.

They rode home in silence. When they reached Jake's apartment she went in with him. She watched him sit listlessly at the table, made a decision and "You told me a few years ago you hadn't gone to that intersection after the accident. Not ever since. That you'd never seen the car. You won't even look at pictures of it. That Jane's parents still had the car, kept it in a shed locked up like some mausoleum. They still have it?"

"Far as I know," Jake thinking *not this*.

"A distance which doesn't take too long to cover. Call them."

"Call who?"

"Jane's parents. Ask them if they still have the car."

"Why?"

"Just do it," Jake not moving. "Like today. Like now," she commanded. Still Jake still, refusing both her and his own voice. But then assenting to them both by looking through the address book near his phone and dialing the number and putting the receiver to his ear. Jane's father answering and Jake asking about the car and making up an explanation why he was asking and Luella not needing to tell him to say they were coming on Sunday to see the car, Jake saying it and hanging up and then the two of them in the Explorer driving south.

■

Jake south of Mitchell wants to go another way and Luella, driving, her right hip throbbing, refuses. They come to the intersection, drive a hundred feet beyond and stop. The day still and bright with little traffic. Luella parks on the down-sloped ditch filled with brittle thick grass and thistles and they walk silently, making over again what had happened and the sounds of tires and metal and the smells of burned rubber and antifreeze leaking and oil spilling out, but not the smell of blood, not that smell, Jake thinking *beneath this dirt there is glass still, her blood*. Luella watching Jake and seeing in his eyes the same vacancy as before and thinking *maybe he's beyond any help maybe this is what happens sometimes and you can't fix it*, but still not believing it entirely, something salvageable in him, and then the two of them back in the car over the few miles to the farm outside Parkston.

■

"Hi, Pete," Jake sheepish when he sees them because it has been a long time, like a dog caught after chewing something wrong and knowing it.

"Jake." They seem pleased enough to see him, though his distance over the years has distanced them. They don't know him. Kathy, well into her seventies, looks much older than the last time, Jake not thinking it has been over two years since he saw her. They had stayed in touch by phone or letter, Christmas and birthday cards, now and then meeting in Aberdeen for an after-noon.

Luella limping but refusing the wheelchair, they go into the house, one-story wide and flat, a hundred yards from the old two-story steep-pitched house they lived in for thirty years together farming. A scene like a hundred others on the Upper Plains, the rotting and the recent juxtaposed. Jake notes the farm remains nearly the same as when he first saw it, the barn and machine shed duller now and two new metal buildings and grain bins. Pete and Kathy in recent years renting their land to Jane's brother, Jake remembering how much he liked Ken. They had fished, played cards, talked, Ken's place five miles east and north, toward Alexandria, though all the equipment kept at Pete and Kathy's. Jake had noticed a newer green tractor, big and eight-wheeled, as they passed beneath the elm-tree arches and into the yard.

Jake expects Ken to greet him too, but he is absent. Kathy brings them coffee and they sit uneasy. Pete, never a man of idle talk, comes to the point: "You called about the car, Jake."

"Yes."

"Why?" Jake remembers telling him over the phone, but now he cannot recall the reasons he might have given. He pauses, looks at Luella. Then honest: "Luella thinks it might do me some good." He says nothing of Siverson, the file, Frederick.

Pete surprised and "Some *good*?"

"Jake seems to have been a bit numb this last decade," Luella says with just a shadow of the sarcasm Jake knows. Pete turns, as if acknowledging her for the first time, Jake wondering if he's angry.

But "I guess the same with us," he says. "After the funeral, Ken and me we went up to the filling station and put it on the trailer and brought it back here. It was important to me to do that. I didn't know why then, but I do now. Had to gather up all the pieces that got broke and bring them back. We brought Jane back. And then the car."

"What do you mean you brought Jane back?" Luella asks.

"For the funeral."

"She's buried *here*?" Jake has never mentioned the family plot in a tree-shrouded field corner three-quarters of a mile from where they sit, Jake looking in that direction and thinking *she's right over there*, almost reaching out his hand. Pete explains the buried, the parents grandparents uncles aunts.

"I don't like other people having my things," he says, firmly, Luella hearing and seeing that he doesn't. "I don't mean people are things I own. You know what I mean." Jake nods.

"That little shed beyond the trees north, we put the car there and chained the door shut and no one's been inside since. Mice, rats, cats, I imagine. But none of *us*." He circles his arms grabbing nothing.

"I didn't know that," Jake says. They sat in silence for a time, the moment building, some kind of acknowledgment in the air.

"Well," Pete says, standing and patting the arms of his chair as if he's been waiting a long time to walk, "maybe it would do us some good, too. Mother?"

"I'll stay here," Kathy whispers, Jake thinking *she looks so much like Jane, I never saw before.*

"I thought maybe you would."

■

The key for the lock that secured the now-corroded chain had long been lost, so Pete walked back to the machine shed and returned with a heavy chain cutter which severed two sides of a link as easily, Jake thinking, *as the thing that halved us, her and me.* The chain-ends clattered against splintering wooden doors. Pete lifted the latch and pulled on one door but couldn't move it; though the yard was meticulously mowed, bunches of thick grass and weeds held the lower door-edge in place. Jake helped him pull but they couldn't move it.

Pete fetched a spade and began to clear away the built-up dirt and roots.

"Jake," Luella said, nodding toward Pete.

"What?"

"Maybe something *you* could do?"

"Oh." Jake shook his head as a boxer might after a punch. "Pete, let me." He took the spade and in a few moments had cleared the impediments. Pete swung one side of the door open, then the other, rusty hinges shrieking in surprise. They stood back. Though the sun lit the air brightly, it backlit the opening and could not penetrate the dark yawning maw.

"We'll need light," Pete said. But then he searched the air and they followed his gaze to wires that ran from a pole to the little building. "I forgot, this place has juice. Or it did." He stepped inside and reached for a remembered switch. They listened to the old circuit close, saw the single unshaded bulb ignite. "I'll be damned," Pete said. They filled the doorway.

■

A clear bulb and the light therefrom harsh and cold like the inside air, the cool dampness of eternally shaded places, fecund and spoiling at the same time, muted light filled with dust motes even in the absence of things to disturb the dust. Light cold and hard as metal, as jagged as the edges of rusty rendings. Ten years before on a day like this two men had pushed the car front-first inside. Now the three began at the car's rear, a step inside the door, then worked along the passenger side, Luella dragging her leg and Jake head down seeing only the old white enamel, dusty and cobwebbed and mouse-droppinged. Numb, a buzzing in his brain. Nothing filling his heart but its own expanding empti- ness. At first that side seemed oddly untouched, until they saw how its slab side bulged unnaturally, suggestive of what had happened opposite. Shuffling slowly like three judges reviewing evidence. Then the front, the rectangular flat metal grille bent but not terribly, the driver's side headlamp bezel wrinkled on its outside curve. The front from where Luella and Jack went on, leaving Jake who hesitated, his eyes lowered to the sheetmetal beneath the window line, thinking *I do not wish to see what's inside,* even though the windshield held the residue of ten years and would not admit his gaze.

Old sounds began to return to him, his words and then these very tires on the gravel and then turning on the street away from him and the power steering pump and the muffler maybe going bad. Though he knew they were the same, Jake could not connect this curved disrupted dirty thing with what had left his driveway.

"Jake." Luella commanded him, Jake obeying, stepping to where she faced squarely the violenced side. Jake's breath stopping at the rending, the door caved in two feet and the glass shattered so that the two side windows stared like empty sockets covered only by spider webs, in one of which hung a dried fly. He stood for several minutes, the other two stepping back, and then bent to the window again, again hearing himself, and seeing now only the bent seat and wrenched steering wheel. When his eyes found the silver pendant hanging from the rearview mirror he went cold and *she took it off.* Not wanting to believe and *no, someone else found it and hung it there. No, she didn't take it off.*

Luella following his eyes and "that's just like yours, Jake, the other half," Jake's hand reflexively to the past chained around his neck, whispering "almost" and "together they make lines of a poem."

Luella demanding and "What *do* they say, Jake? Speak it."

Jake quivering, holding out his own and "So much a long communion," then pointing at Jane's and "tends to make us what we are." He could barely breathe but "lines from Byron. We . . . we intended a long communion."

And then he saw the blood. Not everywhere but enough, Jake thinking *now it is going to come, now that not once since has come.*

Then the absence of detail and only the singular wholeness of

a wreck so violent and death-causing that once again Jake
forced it to become unreal and without meaning. But one last
detail for him to carry from the shed. Luella taking his head in
her hands and swiveling his eyes back and down to the door,
forcing him to kneel and to see what was stamped in the door's
metal skin. The print from the DeSoto's front wheel and tire
where it wrenched sideways at the very end of senility and surprise and imprinted itself in the sheetmetal, the wheel cover
stamped perfectly circled and the tire's Goodyear and even the
smaller letters and numbers with such force that all of them on
the sidewall reversed in the metal: P235/75R15. Luella's hands
holding his head steady and Jake looking, and then Luella:
"Don't you want to know? Someone made money off of this,
and it wasn't you. Don't you at least want your money back?"

"What do you mean?" Pete asked bewildered, but neither
answered. Jake stood. They stared at the monument and themselves reflected in the dusty shine of old paint refracted at a
thousand angles, at what too many years or mistake and sometimes stupidity can accomplish. Jake—before his long-pent grief
burst and ran—as trained, estimated the car as he might himself:
total loss, even the salvage worthless now so old.

And having finally made that calculation, Jake understanding
her, thinking *Maybe she's right. Maybe anger will make sadness
less sad. Maybe it will.* Then *not sadness. Shame, the misunder-
standing.* He considered his ten years of backwashed limbo neither death nor life, then a spark among the running tears and
maybe I can be the living once again.

3

Jake and Luella gone from Pete and Kathy after two hours, declining supper as the afternoon and their appetite for memory waned. Jake nervous, anxious to leave, them driving the dusty length of gravel and under the elm-arches after whispered good-byes, Jake accepting Pete's thick-fingered farmer's grip and enfolding Kathy in arms then-reminded of her daughter's body. Luella driving again, Jake directing her through three turns to the field-corner graveyard where they pulled off on its narrow, dusty approach. No fences, Luella expecting one of old iron spike-tipped, or one of rotting wood, but nothing between the corn reaching heavenward and bones gone down. Corn, a narrow border of tall bunched grass enlivened by yellow flowers, then the graves. A single elm in the northwest corner, mild wind disturbing its leaves, the tree misshapen since losing two secondary but large limbs. Luella noted where wind or age had taken them off.

She counted seven granite markers of similar size, two feet high perhaps and three wide, eight smaller set into and level with land covered by recently but roughly mowed grass. Her eyes following again the descension from corn, the taller bunched and rustling grass, the dead's lawn. Here and there beside a marker flowers, some in urns and some in beds of dry, unweeded soil. The cemetery, private like nothing else with space yet for three times again the monumented rectangles, looked tended by people occupied with other, living things.

Jake stepping to Jane's flowerless stone, Luella standing back

and watching, Jake on his knees, his shoulders slightly taller
than the granite's top-curved edge. And then his arms out and
hands grasping that edge, him looking like a grave father stern
with a child or one consoling. Still as rock he remained for minutes, and then she heard him speaking, too far distant to receive
the words clearly. And then silence, Jake patting the ground
open-palmed three times and finally rising, and a last look out
the car window and then the road back to the highway and
Mitchell.

When they reached the two-lane pavement Luella asked him
what he had said, ashamed for seeking into grief private in a
way only survivors understand, but jealous of her and wanting
to know.

"I was . . . ," Jake began but did not go on. A moment later
"She and I . . . ," but that beginning went unfinished too. He
glanced at her and she knew that he would not speak. When
their eyes met Luella realized that the flat and shallow man
beside her, who fixed cars and lived lonely, had begun again,
perhaps to seek what he had been before that day, Luella ignorant of that previous Jake and uncertain of the depth of his
desire to return.

■

They took a motel room in Mitchell, Luella assuming because
Jake did not want to drive back to Jamestown after the long and
exhausting day. At first Jake had directed her into the gravel lot
of a run-down wood-framed place on the edge of the city, but
Luella had objected and demanded at least the Family Inn, for
which she had seen billboards close to the city.

"You cheap bastard," she had goaded in the lot of the first
motel, noting discolored white paint flaking off the siding and
curled brown shingles missing in places. "Is this what you think
of when you think of taking me to a motel? This looks like the
body shop," Jake turning to her laughing, a sound she seldom

heard from him. His laugh, which seemed tenuous as a nervous child's, pleased her.

"I am a cheap bastard, aren't I?" Jake laughing stronger.

"Are you all right?" Luella asked. "You seem almost . . . happy." He did not respond, directed her to what he remembered as the nicest motel in town.

"I would like to sit in the hot tub before we eat," Jake announced, having noticed a large one near the pool they passed after checking in. He and Jane had enjoyed a primitive, homemade whirlpool when they honeymooned. Worn out by their lovemaking, they would take coffee and towels and soak out the stiffness in what looked suspiciously like a big tank of the sort farmers use to water livestock, Jake remembering her saying "Well, not *all* the stiffness." Bursts of the past fired by chlorine, Jake recalling eating in a Chinese restaurant for the first time, later dancing to a loud band, thinking *in some other lifetime.*

"So would I, but I didn't bring a suit," Luella said. They had packed hurriedly that morning, unsure if they would stay overnight. Luella had one suitcase and a make-up kit, Jake a canvas duffel bag.

"Actually," Luella went on, "I don't even own a suit."

Jake uncomprehending and "Why not?"

"My leg, stupid." She had never allowed him to see the smashed-up part of her, and during their first lovemaking, when his hand had gone there, she had moved it higher up.

"Oh. Sorry."

"It's all right. You go ahead," Jake realizing *I don't have a suit, either.*

"I suppose it's too late to buy anything in this bustling metropolis. The motel doesn't have a shop," Jake thinking *ten years and I have come back to Mitchell, gone nowhere,* then telling her "I'll just wear my boxers." Luella watched as he undid his duffel's drawstring and pawed Neanderthal through the bag. "Men," she muttered, Jake not hearing. Then, "You go on and enjoy yourself, I'll stay here and watch television or stare at the wall, maybe floss," Jake catching her frustrated inflection.

He turned to her and "Look, I've got an extra pair of boxers and a T-shirt. Wear those. The shorts will cover your leg at least some," Luella at first wanting to say no but then considering the proposition and deciding there was no reason she shouldn't.

"Walk on my right."

"Why?"

"Hide my leg."

"Good Lord, you've got a towel around it now."

"Walk on my right, damn it," Jake obeying.

They passed across a portion of the stone-tiled lobby and then through a door into the pool area, only Jake's forearms tanned and the rest of him startling white, Luella as pale, Jake anxious and hoping the water wouldn't be full of children or, if so, that the hot tub wouldn't be crowded. Three children splashed noisily in the pool, and a low, water-stained ceiling kept the air heavy-odored with chlorine. Only a man and a woman occupied the blue foam-covered and bubbling water, Jake, because of their glazed expressions, guessing them the three children's parents. Jake nodded at the man as he reached the edge of the sunken tub, but neither said anything. Anxious to step down, he tossed his towel on a nearby chair, but Luella stopped him, pulled him by the arm back whispering "I can't."

"Can't what?"

"Go down those steps. My leg doesn't bend very well."

Jake suggesting "Hold my hand," but Luella resisting and "I'm embarrassed," Jake seeing near terror in her eyes and taken back thinking *I can see how she feels, hear her like I heard Jane, my senses coming back, a start.* Then *do not turn away this time.*

Jake bending to her and "I can fix this," lifting her startled from the wet floor toward the hot tub, Luella through clenched teeth "Jake!" But he stepped confidently down three steps and set her into the water, turning to the man and winking

"Newlyweds" and grinning wide, Luella wondering at his play and pleased because *neither of two previous asshole husbands would have.* As she slid down into the warmth she watched the man across from her as his eyes contemplated her breasts. She had not considered what her front would look like once Jake's T-shirt got wet; she stayed low in the water until the other couple went to gather their children.

"Let me see your leg." They had come back to the room, Jake showering first and returning towel-covered and unfolding tired into the single king-size bed. Jake had gotten the room, Luella surprised but not bothered to see it had only the one bed. Luella had showered and come back in the light of a single lamp, robed. His desire took her off guard, men other than her doctor not usually requesting it, and she thought *I have too long been a patient.*

"Excuse me?"

"Let me see your leg."

"I'm not that easy," she joked, stalling him. The two times they had made love they had coupled in the dark of her bedroom and Jake had touched her everywhere but on her shattered, badly mended flank, Jake now asking again, Luella being more direct this time: "No."

"Why?"

"Not a body part I'm proud of."

"At least let me touch. Turn the light off, get in bed with me."

"No."

Jake asking once again but Luella turning, pawing the switch, extinguishing the light.

"I feel like that car inside at Pete and Kathy's," she said, Jake not responding. She hesitated, then stepped to the bed and lay down beside him on top of the blankets, pulling the robe tightly about her and saying softly "outside, not inside," Jake assenting.

Jake's palm and fingers followed the misshapen bones and the scarred flesh from her pelvis to just above her knee. Lumps of scar tissue and bones joined together in ways different from the smooth curve of flesh that had eased her life before a car's transmission slipped from neutral into drive. Jake's fingers found a square-edged something high up on the leg bone and "What's this?" running and pressing fingertips along the edges.

"A plate," Jake not responding. "Six inches long, six screws to hold the worst break," Jake's fingers still following. "I'm screwed together."

"Does it have to stay there always?" Jake thinking of a car frame out of sight, straightened, plated, welded.

"Doctor said it could come out, but I'm afraid of letting him."

A continued searching with his fingers, then "Why?"

"Because the operation would have me bedridden a week, and because I think the bone might break again without the support. Doctor said the bone's as strong as ever, but I don't feel that confident. Must be psychological," Jake thinking *people feel that way about their cars, that once they get hit they're never the same even if all new parts, once something goes wrong you never trust it again.*

"Is it all right to leave it in?"

"Yes," Jake leaving the plate and running his hand again along her leg-length, Luella telling him "You're the first one who's done that," Jake thinking *the place on a '37 Ford where the top comes down to meet the trunk, the out-curve of the top falling to a shallow seam and then to the trunk and then falling away to the bumper,* his palm flowing along her and *flesh and metal, flesh and metal.*

Then his hand down to the robe's lower edge and her knee's skin, then between fabric and skin and beginning back up the leg where she had told him not to go. She didn't object, letting herself fall finally as far as she could beneath the blessing of his hand and not caring about imperfect flesh, that something had smashed it up and made it ugly, that it was something better left to darkness. And Jake's hand there for minutes and then in other places not destroyed and then his body on hers and inside her until neither body nor light made any difference.

And the next morning stepping awkwardly naked from the shower beside him where he stood brushing his teeth and watching his eyes in the mirror fall to the lighted leg and staring and her thinking for the first time nearly unashamed *this is me* and then in her mind kneeling and speaking to a gravestone of her own and ready, she felt, to rise with him, but *a journey's beginning is always more confident and easier than its ending.* Wanting to believe that together they had found the last circle and a guide, rising.

■

When he and Jane were living young in Mitchell, Jake had purchased insurance from Carl Slobidnik, an agent representing a company in Sioux Falls; Jake's father had purchased all his insurance from Slobidnik for almost fifteen years before Jake even began driving. When Jake had moved north to Jamestown, he'd transferred his insurance, what little he required for his few possessions and old car, to a local agent; he wanted no contact with anything involving Jane's accident. Jake now remembered that Slobidnik hadn't been an independent agent, but worked for one company selling auto, property, and life insurance. At first he couldn't remember the company's name, but then it came to him: Sun State.

"That name can't be right," Luella said, sitting on the motel bed.

"No?"

"South Dakota? Sun State? Oxymoronic. Should be a company in Florida selling to old folks—'Sun State for the Sun Years,'" Jake not disagreeing. He remembered the Sun State building, two stories of pale brick on a corner a few miles from where he had lived. He had no idea if it still existed, but called directory assistance and got the number. A chirpy receptionist answered, asked how she could help, Jake asking "Can I talk to Mr. Slobidnik, please?"

"I'm sorry, who?"

"Mr. Slobidnik."

"No one by that name works here. You must have the wrong number."

"I used to buy insurance from him, years ago. He's probably retired," the receptionist with a voice sounding sixteen responding with a now-unenthusiastic "Probably."

"Don't mean to take up too much of your time, but is there someone there who's been with the company a long time that might remember? I really would like to get in touch with him."

"I'll transfer you."

"Thanks."

In a moment "This is Jack Kindler."

"Yes, Mr. Kindler, my name is Jake Warner. Years ago I did business with a Carl Slobidnik. The receptionist tells me there's no one there now by that name, but maybe you remember him." Luella sat on the bed wondering at Jake's words; she had not heard him string so many together in a tone nearly firm and confident.

"Sure, I worked with Carl for years. He was an agent, me an underwriter. Fine man."

"Does he still live in Sioux Falls?"

"No. He died, oh, six or seven years ago, just before he was scheduled to retire."

"Sorry to hear it. I haven't lived in this area for a long time. I liked Mr. Slobidnik a lot."

"Everybody did."

"Listen, the reason I wanted to talk to him is I'm trying to find out some details of a claim I had, way back. I thought he might remember."

"I'm sure he would have. Remembered everything. Great mind for detail. But why don't you check with claims? They might still have a file. In fact, I'd be surprised if they didn't. I'll transfer you."

"Thanks for your help."

"No problem."

Two rings and a woman answered, not nearly so young-sounding as the receptionist, Jake explaining what he wanted. She asked for a policy number, laughed when Jake told her in what year the claim had occurred. She noted Jake's first and last name, said she would check the basement storage when she had time, probably but not certainly before noon. She sounded fairly sure they'd have the file. Jake told her he would call back after lunch.

■

They made love again, Jake thinking afterward of an old Chrysler he fixed for one of Kinneady's friends. The car, a big four-door with about a thousand pounds of bumpers and chrome trim, had not one dent in it except for the passenger side rear fender, which had been mangled in some kind of accident on the first owner's farm. They couldn't locate a replacement fender, and Kinneady asked Jake to fix it. It was beyond metal-working, so a lot of plastic filler would be involved, and Kinneady hated the mixing and filing and sanding, the smell. His approach to any dent, shallow or deep, was simple: remove the damaged panel and put on a new one. Jake favored keeping the old metal no matter how distorted, restoring the original curves with plastic if their contours could not be otherwise restored. He had not returned to the old way with lead, had a vague desire to some day go back to the tinning and filing he had been so good at. For now, plastic was better because it was easier.

By the time he had finished, nearly every square inch of the big fender had some filler on it. But there was not a ripple or sanding mark or air hole to indicate that what lay beneath the surface was anything but original, never-damaged metal. Kinneady painted the whole car enamel black, and Jake's fender ran beneath the light as smooth and graceful as the hood or trunk. Jake had spent more than twenty hours hammering the bent metal into reasonable shape, applying the filler, shaping it with a rough file called a cheese-grater, sanding, primering, sanding, sanding more, then sanding again, the grit numbers progressively finer. Jake could tell curves with his hands better than with his eyes. "Good hands," Luella had told him just before drifting into sleep, Jake feeling his own fingertips rough from sandpaper but sensitive to the slightest undulations. As she slept Jake had pulled back the sheet and stared at her broken side.

After lunch Jake called the woman at Sun State. She identified herself as Sharon, told him she had a file, then asked him two questions to make sure it was the correct one: "What sort of claim was it?"

"Car accident."

"When—the exact date—did this accident happen?"

"July 17, 1985."

"That's the file I have."

"I assume it's thick."

"About two inches."

"Would it be possible for me to look at it?"

"I don't see why not. I'll keep it here on my desk. Ask for me at Claims, in the basement."

"Thanks. I'm in Mitchell right now. Be there in two hours."

In the car east Luella sensed Jake's mounting interest in Sun State's file, in the business of Sheriff Andy Frederick and the anonymous adjuster. She recalled how reluctant he had been to examine the file given by Mrs. Frederick, thinking *a stationary body tends to stay that way until something moves it, and now something has moved him.* She had wanted him to be moved, but watching and listening to him now, she grew uneasy. She had prodded him to face the past though she did not fully know what it held or the nature of his immobility. Not for him to change the past, merely to stare it down. She had wanted him to expunge his grief by finally looking at the scene and the car. But since the farm he had changed, almost too quickly, a man emerging from a three-fourths coma. His eyes seemed brighter and his speech edged. She suddenly felt that getting his attention as she had, demanding that he see the place where Jane had died and the car, might lead to worse things, though she could not think of what. She was simply uneasy. She wanted him to keep moving but would have preferred knowing at what point he would stop again. He had seemed so casual about missing work, where before she could not imagine him taking a day off; he had phoned Elroy right at eight o'clock, telling him he would be gone that day and maybe the next one as well. And the way he had touched her the night before, yearning, seeking, not the reserved lover of before. More than just the car was moving, Luella in a way pleased but thinking of other men, unwilling to trust and *to where? For how long?*

Luella asked, and as they rolled toward Sioux Falls he told her of growing up there, in a small house on Dakota Avenue on the same block as a grade school. A cute little boy, popular and his teachers' pet. An only child seeking friends at school and throughout the neighborhood, playing army with them, cowboys and Indians, then leaving behind horses and guns for cars. Building models, reading early issues of *Hot Rod* and *Car Craft*, riding his bike to the dealerships downtown to see the new models in the fall and to take home glossy literature describing them. And books, he loved books, but not as much as cars, he said, apologetically.

Halfway between Mitchell and Sioux Falls Jake went quiet in contemplation of what his child's life had been, thinking *why should I apologize for what I loved?* He remembered going to see a car on Western Avenue between 22nd and 26th streets thirty-five years before, when he was ten. On that street he discovered true beauty for the first time, became aware of what endures.

It was a red Ford coupe, a '40 like his that waited still behind the body shop, a hot rod with gold wheels and a gold and chrome hemi engine. Jake and his friend Rod had heard about it at school, biked nearly two miles from home hoping on that early summer day they would see it. As they rounded the corner they found it parked. They stopped a hundred feet away, that red and gold and chrome so beautiful they were frightened, each in a boy's shallow conception of heaven. Slowly they pedaled closer, the coupe like an animal sleeping by the curb, down-slanting raked, tires bigger in back, fat whitewalls, the paint so shiny red it might still have been wet. The body and trim all stock but low and red-mean and they left their bikes on the sidewalk and sat down and stared, hardly able to breathe.

As he and Luella drove Jake remembered it so real that *whatever you could learn about a line curve-moving and flowing out of other lines was there and I learned the lines better than any catechism or school lesson. I did not know it, but I understood that metal had flesh. That metal had flesh.*

Later the owner, a young man lean and white-shirted with black and shiny back-combed hair, came from the house behind them full of pride and "Hi boys, want to look under the hood?" They nodded wide-eyed and he raised the pointed sloping halved metal up and they peered with the sunlight at a big hemi, gold-blocked with huge chrome valve covers, red spark plug wires going in and a big chrome air cleaner and polished brass radiator top.

"I'd give you a ride, boys, but I'm late," the young man said. Then he got in, the hemi coughing to life and rumbling through two long pipes out the back with the amplified purring of a big cat and Jake didn't care what noise it made or how it moved away from the curb, only how it looked standing still and forever and *I see it now and I am looking for it again. I have read poems and stories so beautiful I cried. I have read arguments so clear they shimmered. I have seen paintings, heard music so beautiful that I shook but I am not ashamed to say that red coupe, banished from my mind until now, that red coupe, there was no beauty ever like it,* Luella wondering where he had gone in his head, waiting for him to return.

■

Jack Kindler was on the second tee at the Minnehaha Country Club course, playing with his usual foursome, when the name of the man who had called him earlier that morning flashed up through a mind years-layered and softened by the ease of forgetfulness, his recollection of danger instantly restored when the name rose to the surface of cognition like a bubble from a sunken steamer, Kindler remembering and shivering *Jacob Warner, Jesus Christ Jacob Warner.*

Quickly he mounted his cart, his partner's clubs still secured, and drove back toward the clubhouse, skirting the dog-legged first hole and drawing stares from the foursome trudging up the fairway and the three men waiting on the tee. Without waiting for it to stop rolling, he leapt from the cart just past the starter's small white house, leaving two sets of expensive clubs. He ran through the pro shop, up the stairs to the dining room, then out to the parking lot. His spikes clacked on the blacktop as he ran, and when turning the corner of another parked car he slipped and fell, banging his 65-year-old knee against the small stones littering the lot. He tore his slacks and scraped the knee; tiny pebbles embedded themselves under his pale skin. Distance back to the office two miles and light-years long, and he reached it just after one.

Immediately he went to Claims, where decades before he had been an adjuster and then Manager. He had hated claims, where whining people always wanted more than they had coming. He had felt the company owed him something for those terrible years before he moved into Marketing, and he had found a way to get it.

Sharon had been back from lunch only a few minutes when

she saw him come through the door that led from the hallway
into the large open room on the building's lower level. She
scanned Jack Kindler like she would a newly submitted Notice
of Loss, Kindler by then sweating as well as bleeding from the
knee. She seldom saw him anywhere in the building, and never
in Claims, which didn't bother her because she had never much
cared for him. He'd been drunk at a New Year's Eve party, had
kissed her far too passionately at midnight, had tried to put his
hands where they shouldn't be. To her he was old-boy and lazy,
and little he did could justify a salary she guessed to be four or
five times her own.

Kindler breathless and "I know this looks weird, Sharon, but
I can explain. I was just playing golf when I remembered the call
I got this morning, which I transferred down here," Sharon
thinking *the Monday afternoon Marketing Meeting?* "I told that
man I couldn't help him at all, couldn't remember anything
about the claim he was asking about"—he stopped to catch his
breath and wipe a forearm across his chin, where more than a
little perspiration had gathered—"but now I *do* remember. I *can*
help him. Did he leave a number? Where can I reach him?"

"Just hang around and you'll see him. He should be in soon."

"He's coming *here?*" Sharon surprised by his loud response
and the way his face looked, frightened.

Sharon patted the rubber-banded manila thickness off to her
side and "Yes, to look at the file."

"Oh, wonderful, just . . . wonderful," Kindler said with trans-
parently phony enthusiasm. "I'll get to see him, then. Here, I'll
take the file. Yes, I'll take it. When he comes, send him up."
Kindler scooped the file quickly with eager hands. "Yes, send
him up."

"Okay," Sharon said, thinking *management!* and then *screw
you.*

At 1:42 the intercom buzzer on Jack Kindler's phone startled
him, and he drew in a deep breath when his secretary told him

Jake Warner had arrived. She mentioned that he did not have an appointment, but Kindler instructed her to show him in. As Jake and Luella passed the receptionist's desk Luella whispered to him "Be confident." When they entered, Kindler stood but remained behind the desk to hide his knee. "Mr. Warner," he said, smiling wide in a way he had not been required to for many years, his job secure.

"This is my friend Luella Alger," Jake said. Kindler took her hand, saying "Nice to meet you. Please sit down." They lowered themselves into two fabric and wood chairs that faced his desk.

"Sharon downstairs told us she had found the file regarding my wife's accident," Jake said, "and that you had it."

"Yes," Kindler smiled, Jake looking at a man clearly nervous and wearing a shirt half-sweated through. He hadn't seen a goofier smile in years, not since Elroy had come on to a woman needing an estimate.

"What makes you want to see the file now, after all this time?" Kindler said. "If you don't mind my asking?"

"Not at all. It was a pretty traumatic experience for me, as you can imagine," Kindler nodding too quickly. "I didn't pay much attention to the claim, in fact I was grateful for the way it was handled, not involving me much. But a couple of weeks ago I was talking to a friend, an insurance agent in Jamestown, North Dakota, where I live—do you know Bob Ring?"

"Not familiar with the name."

"Well, anyway, Bob asked me about what had happened—I don't remember how it came up—and then about the settlement, and I had to tell him I didn't know anything about how it was settled, and that sort of surprised him. Sort of surprised me, too, since I usually like to stay on top of things," Luella pleased with Jake's invention and *part of what Jane saw in him*. "So, it's no big deal, I just wanted to find out. You understand."

"Sure, sure," Kindler said, leaning back in his chair. Then he quickly bent forward and moved the file closer to him. "And let

me just say how sorry I am to know you lost your wife that way.
Sure."

Jake pointing and "That the file there?"

"Yes, yes it is," Jake thinking *why are you repeating everything?* and sensing that Kindler wasn't going to let him anywhere near it.

"Can I look at it?"

Kindler coughing and "I'm afraid you can't, you can't" Jake
thinking *you are afraid.*

"Oh? Why not?"

"Well, you see, it's the law."

Jake never having heard of such a statute and "What law
would that be?"

"The state insurance law. I mean, one of them. Insurers are
requested—I mean prevented—from disclosing the details of a
claim when it involves them. Anytime it involves them."

Jake realizing *he doesn't remember I was a lawyer* and
"When the claim involves the insurance company?"

"No," Kindler laughing lightly but not convincingly, "I mean
another party, a third party. When it's a liability claim."

"But Sharon indicated my reviewing it wouldn't be a problem. I've driven all the way from Mitchell."

"I guess she didn't understand what you wanted."

"I guess not."

Luella sensed that Jake was just going to drop his inquiry so
she leaned forward and "Have you looked at the file?"

Kindler clearing his throat again and "No," Luella thinking
then how would you know it was liability? That Jane died? She
edged forward further and "Then how—," but Jake put his
hand on her arm and stopped her. She gave him a look usually
reserved for her second husband's lawyer, but sensed through his
touch that he didn't want her to pursue her question.

"Well," Jake went on, "can't you just *tell* me? I don't actually have to *look* at the file. Why don't you just take a peek and
relay the information?"

"*Any* divulgence of information is prohibited. Any." Kindler made an odd gesture with his right hand, as if chopping something.

"So there's no way I can find out anything about that file?"

"No. No."

"My goodness, it's right there. So close. Just couldn't look through it a moment? I just want to know how it all turned out. It's important to me."

"Sorry."

Jake silent, then "Well, the law's the law, I guess." He stood, took Luella by the arm and pulled her up. He thrust his hand toward Kindler. "I appreciate your help and your candor, Mr. Kindler, and I sure wouldn't want you to violate any laws. I guess I'll just have to forget the whole thing. Dumb idea anyway, I suppose. Thanks."

"I think forgetting it would be best. I can assure you were represented as well as anybody could be," Jake thinking *I bet.*

Luella glaring and "Why did you stop me like that? Pissed me off."

"I stopped you because I wanted to leave him the impression that we weren't all that concerned about finding out, that looking at the file was just kind of a whim. That I wasn't going to push him."

Though she heard confidence in his voice again she told him, "Which, apparently, you aren't. Typical Jake."

"Don't say that. I was acting."

"You mean the last ten years?"

"No, at the end there with Kindler. I was angry. They took my money and now this bastard telling me I can't look at my own goddamn file. He's clearly got something to do with Frederick and the adjuster. Hell, maybe he *is* the adjuster, the guy who hooked up with Frederick. A man who's worked so long in the insurance business shouldn't be that nervous about telling somebody no. Probably does it twenty times a day."

"He pitted out that shirt big-time, repeated everything."

"Exactly. Think about it. There were three people necessary for such a scam—sheriff, adjuster, claim manager. Wait, I'll bet Kindler was the manager. He's too old to have been a 'hotshot young adjuster' ten years ago. Sheriff alters the official police report, the adjuster falsifies the file, the claim manager okays the large check. I bet Kindler's name is on that check. They split it up somehow."

"It's fine to let Kindler think your showing up wasn't important, but we still don't have the file."

"Well, maybe we can get it another way. I'd like to know who got my money, whose name is on that check," Luella turning to him, liking the way his eyes seemed more focused, his voice edged with questioning rather than acceptance.

■

In the middle of that afternoon Dan Gippart returned from an executive meeting to find Wally Reno in his office, standing where the sun couldn't warm him and staring out the window; his presence surprised Gippart because Reno seldom came into his office before 4:30. They nodded greetings without speaking, Gippart setting a folder on his desk and waiting for Reno, who in a moment began "Got here about thirty minutes ago to check if anything new had developed with Miller. I looked for the file on your desk, saw that message." He pointed to the shiny mahogany surface. There were several blue message slips stacked in a space between files.

Gathering them up, Gippart asked "The one on top?"

"Yeah." Gippart read the name, then recognized it. "Jack Kindler. I'll be damned. Haven't talked to him since I quit Sun State eight years ago."

"Your old boss at Sun State who helped us out."

Gippart smiling and "that was one of the first times I, we, ever fucked somebody over big-time. I wonder what that bastard wants."

"If you don't mind, I'll stick around and find fucking out," Reno said, seemingly on edge, concerned.

"Not at all," Gippart dialing and switching to his speaker phone. One ring and "Sun State, may I help you?"

"Yes, darling, you may. This is Dan Gippart returning Mr. Kindler's call. Could you get him for me?"

"Certainly."

Moments of silence and then Kindler's voice filling the room with nervous words. "Dan, glad you called right back. I'll bet you can't guess who stopped to see me today."

Gippart turned to Reno and whispered "I never did like this son-of-a-bitch," it not crossing his mind that he had never really liked anyone. Then to Kindler, "You're right, Jack, I can't. Tell me."

"Jacob Warner," Reno recognizing the name and turning to Gippart, who seemed unmoved by Kindler's announcement and "Social call?"

"Hardly. He wants to look at the file."

"Let him."

"Let him? Are you nuts?" Gippart shaking his head, whispering to Reno "asshole."

"What would he find that he wouldn't ordinarily find in an honest file?"

Kindler hesitant and "I don't know, but maybe something."

"There's bigger questions, Jack. *Why* is he looking, and why *now*?"

"He said he was bothered that he didn't know anything about how the claim was settled, wanted details."

"Seems a bit odd, but not so unusual. How did he act?"

"Friendly enough. Didn't make any demands. At the end he said he'd just forget the whole thing. I told him that was best."

"You mean he's not coming back?"

"I don't think he will. I told him it was against the law for me to divulge any information about the claim or its settlement."

"And he didn't push you?"

"Not at all. Apologetic about taking my time, thanked me for seeing him, then he left. He was with a woman."

"What woman?"

"I don't know. Maybe his second wife. He introduced us, but I can't remember."

"You can't remember."

"No," not that it mattered to Gippart, who merely wanted to make Kindler feel like he'd done something wrong.

"You don't think he'll be back," Gippart said flatly.

"Didn't say he would be. Didn't seem like he was concerned about it. Almost relieved."

"I trust your judgment. You won't see him again."

"What if I do?"

"Then let him see the file. We covered our asses completely on that deal. He couldn't find anything even if he suspected. Even if he *knew*."

"I'm not so sure."

"What exactly makes you nervous?" Kindler unable to answer.

"Trust me, Jack. If he comes back, let him see the file, then call me. Have a nice day." Gippart leaned across and pressed the connection closed before Kindler could respond. He looked up at Reno, who faced him stroking his chin.

Gippart smiling and "You look worried."

"Not really," Reno said, "but it's damn odd that bastard Warner would all of a sudden worry about an accident that happened ten fucking years ago." Reno considering how his ex-wife kept asking for child support even after she had remarried and "The past has a way of fucking you up sometimes."

Gippart pondered Reno's words and "True, it is odd. Maybe something triggered a memory for old Warner. Maybe he's seeing a shrink and recovering memory. Maybe he had a wet dream about his dead wife. Who knows? Maybe I'll call my old pal Frederick one of these days."

■

"So, Jake, how we going to get what's in that file?" They were having coffee in a long, greasy restaurant where Jake used to eat late weekend nights when he was in high school. Jake kept glancing down the street to where the old State Theater stood. He did not tell her an old girlfriend had worked there, or about what the two of them did after he picked her up on Saturday nights when she got off.

"Don't know. What I do know is that Kindler's lying about not having to give me the information. Freedom of information, the consumer's right to information a company might have regarding him. We could call the insurance commissioner."

Luella wanting to move now and "I suppose, but that would take time."

"Sure, but he'd have authority."

"Why do you assume it's a he?"

Jake sighing and "Even if he or she says we can have access, you can bet Kindler won't give it up easily. That file could mean losing his job, maybe, and I'd be surprised if he didn't misplace it now that it's been disinterred. 'Oops, filing error, we just can't locate it.' I imagine it's gone already."

Luella chiding him and "You used to be so non-committal, now you think the worst of people," Jake thinking *no, just of myself, but no more.*

Luella smiling and "Let's bribe Sharon, then," Jake considering it a good suggestion, telling her "I might be—have been—negative but at least I'm not devious."

"You have no idea."

"I've got no money with me."

"We'll use my cash card. Find a machine, get a hundred bucks."

"Better get more than that. She's going out on a limb."

"Okay, but what do we want?" Luella went on. "The whole file? Theft?"

"Really, all she has to do is look at it, give us certain information."

"What time is it?" Jake checking his watch and "Just past four."

"I would guess she quits at four-thirty. We'll get the money, follow her home," the sudden intrigue lifting their spirits again.

An ATM half a mile north of Sun State along Minnesota Avenue spat ten crisp twenties into Luella's hand. They reached the Sun State lot exit at twenty-two minutes after four, parked across the street and waited. At 4:30 people began spilling from the low brick building, Luella seeing Sharon first and excitedly pointing "there she is."

They followed her compact car through thick rush-hour traffic south along Minnesota Avenue, turning east at 33rd Street for about a mile. Sharon turned south again at an intersection whose northeast corner was occupied by a fenced cemetery. After two blocks she pulled into the basketball-poled driveway of an upscale two-story house in a neighborhood of others just like it, Jake thinking *two hundred won't be enough*, then marking the bikes and rollerblades and basketballs and thinking *it takes money for kids, maybe she'll accept*. Sharon was shouldering her purse and closing her door when Luella pulled in behind her.

"Hi, Sharon," Jake said, emerging from the Explorer. "Remember us?"

She didn't appear to, Jake adding, "we talked to you this afternoon about looking at a claim file. Called from Mitchell. When we came you didn't have it. Jack Kindler had taken it." Kindler's name brought her recognition and "Yes, I remember."

"Kindler won't let me look at the file."

"Why?"

"Says its illegal. Private, company information."

"I've never heard of such a thing."

"He's lying, but I don't want to spend the rest of my life trying to get him to give me access to the file, and I'm wondering if you could help me out." Sharon invited them into a basement family room strewn with toys and video games.

Sharon suspicious and "Exactly how could I could help?"

Jake hoped for her sympathy, played to it. "My wife died in that accident. I have some questions about how the case was handled."

"I glanced at the file. I'm sorry."

"Thanks."

"And you want me to steal it?"

Luella wanting to do more than sit mute and "No, just to look at it. Would take you two minutes, tops," Jake noting Sharon's uncertainty. He stood, took the twenties from his pocket and placed them on a coffee table before her. "I need three things: how much the check was for, who it was made out to, and the adjuster's name."

"How much money is that?" Sharon directing their eyes to the twenties

"Two hundred."

"Not enough," Jake feeling stupid for beginning with all he had and asking, "What *would* be enough?"

"Five hundred," Jake relieved and liking her directness as he did Luella's and "Take this now, you'll get the rest when you give me the information," Jake hearing his voice as from a cheap movie and wanting suddenly to laugh.

Sharon reached and swiped the money from the table's polished surface. "Where will you be?"

"Is the High-Rise motel downtown still in business?

"Yes."

"We'll stay there till noon tomorrow."

Sharon quietly thinking, then "I'll go in early, see what I can find. Jack big-shot doesn't come in till eight, usually. Unless he's playing golf. Then it's noon."

"Call us one way or another. We'd like to know if the file has been 'lost,'" Luella told her, and then they left.

Later, in the motel, Jake lay thinking of when he and Jane took a brief, hurried honeymoon in Omaha, the colors different but the room the same. The furniture chromed metal tubing and bad leatherette, the carpet mottled green and brown and yellow, ugly as old linoleum. In the dark that first night her head against his chest as they stood beside the bed, her body sweet soap clean and hair black shiny from the bathroom's pale light. Her breasts against his ribs as she raised her head to him saying "I've got an idea" and leading him to the bed and he turning her still standing and circling her with his arms and taking her breasts in his hands and lowering his face to where her hair fell alongside her neck, his hardening length against her back and her reaching up and back and holding his head. Her body beneath him, over him, and then from beyond thought some quivering on his fingertips and palms come from searching the memory-length of her young skin.

Luella turned from sitting on the bed reading the hotel services guide and saw his hard length straining against his jeans and then his eyes through the glass and out into the darkening sky, then "You're not thinking of me, are you?" Jake turning and "No."

"Jane?"

"Our honeymoon. The room was like this."

"Where?"

"Omaha," Luella knowing she should not but "You romantic stud. Anywhere near the stockyards?"

Jake surprised her, turned laughing and "Yes, it was."

"You're joking."

"Honest, it was. We'd never been to Omaha, didn't know the location of the motel when we made reservations," Jake winking and "besides, we didn't spend much time out of the room."

"You want to talk about it?"

"The sex we had on our honeymoon?" Luella narrowing her eyes and "Yes, Jake, give me all the intimate details. I get so turned on listening to a man talk about making love to another woman. Jesus."

Jake told her that his memories weren't something he needed

to discuss but later, after eating, Jake sat opposite her in the restaurant twelve stories up and stared over the city through soft-reflecting glass and began to speak of other things. "There was a girl in the youth group at our church. Don't remember her name. She was crippled, in a wheelchair," then embarrassed remembering Luella who had taken her chair into the restaurant and remained in it eating because she had walked too much that day, Luella asking "What about this girl?"

"Well, I guess it's not a story particularly matched to the occasion, like me telling a blind person a joke about being blind."

"You were going to tell me a crippled *joke*?"

"No."

"Then tell. I'm interested in the church part, didn't know you're religious."

"Was."

"Well, tell about the girl."

"She was . . . I don't know what she was. She couldn't get out of the wheelchair without help and she couldn't talk plainly. Cerebral palsy, I suppose. But she laughed a lot. Too loudly, maybe. Wore these thick glasses. Not pretty. I never paid much attention to her, though I did talk to her now and then on Sunday nights when we met." He stopped, the lights of the city spread out below them.

"And?"

"And one night in the spring, when I was a senior, she had someone push her chair across the social hall in the basement of the church and she asked me if I would take her to the prom at the Crippled Children's School."

"Oh, Jake. What did you do?" Jake shaking his head quietly, unable to go on, Luella not pressing him and seeing him set his jaw as if against something, as a man might knowing the onset of pain, refusing it. "If we could see beyond our words, or our silence," he said, "if only we could."

Then desperate for the laughter he had rekindled in the last day, trying to move toward it and "I remember this guy at the bus company the summer I worked there," Luella thinking that she had heard little about Jake's past until recent days and *over forty years of it before I met him.* "He had just graduated from the local tech school in diesel mechanics, hired because one of the regular guys was in the hospital and wouldn't be back for maybe two months, so they hired this guy, Dan, to take his place. He didn't last long in the shop. Ron told me the guy was just plain stupid and didn't hardly know which end of a wrench to hold, so they booted him out of the shop, assigned him to body work with me," Jake smiling.

"The first day he's helping me I'm just finishing a bus, painted it the day before and now I'm peeling the masking tape and paper off and need only to paint a black stripe below the windows. I hand Dan a roll of tape and watch him, and I swear he couldn't tape straight if his life depended on it. His line looked like he was drunk," Luella laughing with him.

"So I get him started on a different project, a bus with the door-side caved in between the wheels. You have to drill out all the rivets to lift the old panel off so you can get at the beams beneath and straighten them. I get Dan a drill and tell him to take out the rivets. He can't keep the bit on the rivet. He sets it on one, presses hard, starts the drill and it spins off wildly, chewing up the paint and metal on the heavy strip where the panel mounts. So I get him a center punch and a hammer and tell him to punch the rivets first and the bit won't spin off. This is a trained mechanic, allegedly, and he can't figure that out. I watch him for a while and he's doing okay, so I go back to masking.

"We leave for lunch and afterward he gets back at it and by two he's got all the rivets out and I think this is going to work out. Then I help him pull the long panel off and I see what he's done. He's drilled every rivet, apparently, until the drill goes in up the to chuck, about three inches."

"He was just being thorough," Luella offered.

"Trouble was, he'd drilled holes through every interior panel and in several places into the seats. He's pulling this fluffy stuff out from the rivet holes and it never occurs to him that it might not be something that *should* be coming out. No one would see the holes in the seats, but we had to replace all the interior panels.

"And one more," Luella thinking *what did he talk about before?* and amazed at him going on, liking the desire he had to speak. "We had to park all the buses inside, and there wasn't a whole lot of room, so we'd stack them two deep end to end. You'd back one up against the wall and then another one up to the first. So you'd get someone to help you, the guy not driving indicating with his arms how close you were getting. Well, Dan's helping me and he's got his arms spread exactly like he should and he's watching intently the space between the buses getting smaller and bringing his arms closer together and I'm watching him, and just after I caved in the front of the bus behind me he yells 'stop!'" Jake laughing hard now remembering and Luella watching him fascinated, thinking *I don't remember him having more than one drink before, maybe this is what he becomes.*

When he calmed she asked "Jake, why are you telling me this?"

His answer, he felt, was more honest than he had been in a long time: "Because I didn't want to think about the girl in the wheelchair who had the guts to ask me to her prom. I keep unpleasant thoughts away. It's what I do. Or at least it was."

Later, Luella beside Jake in the bed feeling him staring upward, and then his words quietly to the ceiling and to her, "I won't keep this buried anymore. I lied. I told the crippled girl I'd made some other promise, a different prom date, I think. I don't remember the specifics of my lie or what happened the rest of the night. But I remember lying, how the light left her face when I told her no," Jake turning and holding Luella strong the first time not sexual as if wanting to speak of forgiveness but refraining and hoping he would sleep before other pieces of his memory broke loose and floated through his veins.

But yet again, early morning and Luella sleeping, another

mooring loosed, lines from a poetry-love he had forgotten, speaking to the dark as if to himself, the titleless, authorless lines *And many a man is making friends with death even as I speak, for lack of love alone* and laying his hand on her shoulder tender in the way of quiet rime with *not me anymore.*

Jake awoke from his dream sweating, rose from next to Luella and went to his duffel bag in the dark. He rummaged through his clothes until he found his notebook, which he took to the small, round table in the corner of the room. He switched on the lamp, hoping not to wake Luella. He opened the notebook, paged through it for a few moments, then began to write swiftly thinking *I've never written this one,* unconvincingly *maybe it will leave me if I write.*

My feet tread thin carpet like that in an office-building hallway but as I draw forward slowly I see no walls or ceiling, touch none. There is only the light in the distance, bright but hazy edged, compelling me.

I move forward for a long time. As I near the light's foggy edges I begin to fear it, as if I know what it illuminates. As the light widens it grows dimmer and I stare. In its center a long, disappearing row of tables, each thick-topped and heavy legged.

I move inside the ring of light, suck in a sudden breath when I see on the first table a woman, naked, outstretched stiff. The smooth granite table top extends a foot beyond her head and feet, an equal distance to the sides beyond her arms. I feel the cold of stone along her back as if it were me lying in her place.

Her body appeared whole when I first looked, but the longer I gaze it changes and I see that her left leg below the knee is gone, her left arm at the elbow. Her left side seems pushed in. The ends of the limbs show a rusty red, caked perhaps with dried blood. I refuse her face. I step close and touch the stone she lies upon. Cold as I imagined.

Finally I brave the head. Jane. The left side of that face where my fingers went is bent in. Touched now only by blood.

Her eyes open and her stone-held body begins to stir. I move quickly backwards, out of the light and far enough into the shadows so that she cannot see me.

She stares upward as if surprised. Blinks. Moves the fingers of her remaining hand as if testing its presence. Bends the arm at the elbow, the hand rising, fingers contracting and straightening in rhythmic alteration. Extends her toes, angles her good leg. Presently she raises the arm of which part is missing, looks at it without emotion. Raises the gone leg and stares. Lowers it and returns to stillness as if in contemplation.

Suddenly, she raises into a sitting position, swivels her head as if looking for me. I feel safe outside the light. She cocks her head, listening, then looks directly at me. She swings the good leg over the stone and faces me, the other leg now dripping blood.

Her voice Jesus her voice resonates through the light and commands me to enter. I go because I have to. Her stare is merciless, hard, like it never was. "Closer," she orders. I take two steps, then stop, refusing her, trembling, twenty feet away. With all the strength I have I will myself to go no further.

She raises her half-arm, blood flowing from it now, too, and points. "It was you, Jake," she says in a voice inconsistent with my memory. She turns and points to the table behind hers. I see a man lying there whom I didn't see before. He raises, too. I see his face. I wake to sweat flowing on me wet like guilt.

Jake closed the notebook and sat until his trembling stopped. He did not know Luella had been watching him, and she pretended to be asleep as he crawled back in beside her.

Well before eight the phone on the light table beside the bed rang loudly, banging Jake out of sleep. Disoriented, he searched the darkness, saw only the outline of light around the curtains, remembered the strange place of his sleeping, thought *Siverson calling again to ask if I've read the report.*

He shook his head to clear it and fumbled the phone from its cold plastic cradle and "Jake Warner."

"Sharon Melville. I have what you asked for."

Jake instantly aware and "Let me get a pencil. Hang on."

"No hurry. There's no one down here yet," Jake opening a drawer beneath the phone and finding green and white hotel stationery and a pen. "All right," he said, eager to write.

"The check was for $75,000, made out to Madelaine Nuegebauer. And—"

"Wait. How do you spell Nuegebauer?" Sharon telling him and Jake printing the letters carefully. When he had the name marked out clearly he asked her "Who was she, some relative?"

"You didn't ask me that," Jake kicking himself and telling her to go on.

"The adjuster who handled it was Dan Gippart."

"He still work there?"

"No, not since I've been here eight years."

"Who signed the check?" Sharon pausing momentarily before telling him "I didn't look."

Jake anticipating her and "I didn't ask. Where was the file?"

"I looked for it on Kindler's desk, then in it. Desk wasn't locked," as if that justified her action. "Nowhere in his office. Then on his secretary's. Found it in her refiling basket. Apparently he was going to have it put back where it came from," Jake puzzled for a second, then *they aren't afraid of the file, nothing in it, but why then not let me see it?*

"What about the rest of my money?" another condition occurring to Jake.

"I'll drive by your place, put it in your mailbox."

"All right. I'll trust you."

"On one other condition, that if anyone ever asks if you told me this stuff, ever, you tell them no."

"Like in court or something? I won't lie in court."

"No, but if someone asks you at work, anytime you're not under oath."

"I'll agree to that, but only if the money's there. Otherwise my mouth will be unpredictable."

"Understood. The money will be there. And thanks."

■

In his bedroom Wally Reno spent the hour prior to meeting Lori Hanson's father working himself into a controlled fury, putting on a face much like a boxer might by punching himself in the head before a bout. Or a football player who butts his flesh-covered and helmeted skull against a wall or someone else's, dressing himself with an attitude as he dresses himself with pads. Practiced in both, Reno knew that mental violence requires the same preparation as physical. Reno chanted his mantra, "those fuckers," referring to Lori's parents and to Jonason their lawyer and to all the other stupid bastards in the world who could not distinguish what was good for them from what wasn't. Ever since junior high football, the world for Wally Reno had been Us and Them. He pasted a false mustache on his dry upper lip and slid thick dark glasses over his eyes as he chanted; positioned a strange hat on his head until he looked something like Humphrey Bogart on a case. When he had achieved a sufficient level of disgust for his opponent, he left for a kind of battle he had never lost, really the only thing he was good at.

A week before, Jonason had phoned Gippart and announced in a voice Gippart did not care for that the two hundred thousand offer was not acceptable. Gippart realized he had lost the twenty dollar bet with Reno, and once again that certain people in the universe did not see things the way he did. Like the deeply religious, he got angry. Within fifteen minutes he had summoned Reno and, fixing him with a malevolent glare whose intensity no pleasantness can hope to match, exhaled a biting "I'd really appreciate it if you could find the time to have a short chat with

Mr. Hanson. I believe he's confused about the nature of our offer, and unaware of the consequences that not taking it might bring."

"He and I will converse on the matter," Reno had said. Reno knew where Carl Hanson worked, and the next morning phoned him. "Mr. Hanson, I have information regarding your daughter's insurance claim that might help to conclude the matter," his voice light, breezy.

"Who is this?" Carl Hanson had said, skeptical of talking to someone who had in no way identified himself.

"Gosh, that's not terribly important. I—"

"Who do you work for?" Hanson sensing in Reno's tone that it wasn't for Jonason.

"Again, that particular detail is immaterial. The important thing is that you'd like to get Lori's matter concluded, and I have information that can help accomplish that noble goal. Can we meet for lunch?"

"You work for the insurance company?"

"Mr. Hanson, pay attention. Stay on task. Can we meet for lunch? You will find it most informative."

"I don't know you, don't understand how you can help me."

"You will, one way or the other."

Carl Hanson eventually agreed to a 12:30 meeting at one of the restaurants along the I-494 strip, chosen by Reno because its jostling lunch crowd was too noisy and hurried to notice much, and when he entered the restaurant he found the mustachioed and dark-glassed Reno waving to him from a dimly lit corner booth. He took the bench seat opposite, not removing his stare from Reno. A harried waitress tossed him a plastic-covered menu.

Reno, without offering his hand, said cheerily, "Mr. Hanson, so good of you to come. Will you order something? It's on me." Reno himself had only a heavy mug of coffee before him.

"Just coffee," Reno pouring from the insulated server and pushing the tray of cream and sugar toward Hanson, who did not take from it.

"I ought to know who you are before going any further," Hanson said.

"Don't need to discuss that. You'll never know who I am. Ever," Reno taking a long drink from his thick mug.

Feeling tangible danger coming across the table, Hanson asked, "What the hell is this?" For seventeen years Carl Hanson had worked as a salesman, then sales manager, for a sprawling automobile dealership not far from the restaurant. He was not an evasive man. He had long been accustomed to directness with people, the best way he knew to do business. He was short and thick-muscled, had never backed away from a fight. Reno did not frighten him, yet.

"What the hell this is," Reno offered, "is me suggesting to you that turning down the insurance company's offer is not in your best interest."

"I understood you to say you could help me."

"You understood correctly."

"So you *are* employed by them."

"*They* don't sign my checks," Reno said, despite his other failings not one to lie.

"This is very strange, and a conversation I'm not willing to pursue." Hanson rose from the bench and began to slide out into the aisle, but Reno leaned and grasped his forearm with a grip intense enough to arouse Hanson's anger.

"I'd really like you to stay," Reno indicating with his eyes that Hanson should take his seat again. Not understanding why, Hanson did so.

"*This* would make me happy, Carl," the use of his first name disconcerting Hanson. "Call Jonason—" Hanson thinking *he knows the names!*—"this afternoon and tell him you've reconsidered. Tell him you want to accept the offer."

"But we haven't reconsidered."

"Not yet, at least."

"Two hundred thousand for what Lori's gone through? For what her mother and I have suffered? That offer's a joke."

"See, this isn't a discussion about what's right and wrong, serious or funny. It's a discussion about what you should do this afternoon. Let's focus on that."

"The claim's worth three, four times your offer."

"Not *my* offer. Still, you're probably right. But focus, Carl, focus. We're not talking what Lori's legs are worth. Though, as long as you've brought up monetary values, I have a free bonus for you, a one-time offer. Not available in stores. Pay attention here. If you call Jonason today, you'll get a ten-percent bonus. Think of it, twenty grand just for calling today! Such a deal."

Carl Hanson had been a negotiator a long time, but with selling cars there wasn't much of a down side if he or the customer refused an offer. Either the dealership's sale wasn't consummated or the customer didn't get the car. He sensed that with Reno, however, walking away wouldn't be so innocent. "And what do I get if I don't?"

"Behind door number two lies a great deal of unpleasantness."

"A court fight? Lori can handle it. So can my wife and I."

"Nope, not talking courts here," Reno's voice beginning to gain an edge, an inflection, that caused Hanson some apprehension.

"So what *do* you mean by unpleasantness?"

"Let me just say that I know where you live."

Hanson trying to remain calm and "A lot of people do."

"Not a lot who would hurt you."

"Hurt me? Are you telling me that if I don't accept the two hundred thousand—"

"Don't forget the bonus."

"—you'll do me physical harm?"

Reno calmly reached into his sport coat's inside pocket and withdrew a business-size envelope. He placed the envelope on the table, withdrew eight pictures, laid them in front of Hanson, who gathered them up, reviewed them slowly. The first five were of Nancy Hanson. The top one showed his wife coming out of a grocery store, Hanson recognizing it as one not far from their house. The second showed her getting out of their car in their driveway. What startled Hanson was that the photo had been taken from inside their home. Picture three showed her in the kitchen, picture four in the living room, picture five in the bedroom, Hanson understanding and thinking *inside my home.*

Carl Hanson looked up from the photos to the smiling face of Wally Reno. He examined Reno's eyes. As he did so, Reno's smile disappeared.

"Keep all the photos you want," Reno said, "we'll make more," sliding from the booth and walking away in no particular hurry, his voice not trailing off. "Anytime I want her—and I'm starting to get a real bad hankering right now, pardner—I can have her."

Any parent can tell the difference between a child simply misbehaving and one mean by nature. And most men can tell the difference between a person possessing semblances of reason and one bereft of it. When to fear, when not to. As both parent and man, Carl Hanson understood—with the kind of understanding only sudden quiet terror can produce—with whom he had just talked.

■

Used to ride my bike here in the summers. My friend Rod and I." They stood in a sun-colored rising mist on a steel walking bridge built over the Sioux River at the base of the falls in the northern part of the city. The head of the falls lay south from where they stood, a quarter mile away. The water fell not in a single descent but progressively over and through ancient granite, tumbling wider and flattening before a final pinching by the rocks just beyond the bridge. To their left lay the crumbled remains of an old mill, to their right a city park. Behind, the meat packing plant where Jake's father had worked until he retired, Jake thinking *he retired the same weekend I graduated and then a month later he collapsed in the yard and died. Mom ten years later.*

"How far from here to where you lived?"

"Couple miles, I guess, maybe three."

"And your mom and dad let you come here without supervision?" Luella taking in the sheer faces and sharp corners of stone and the swirling water thinking *my mom wouldn't have let me within a mile of a place like this, my dad wouldn't have cared.*

Jake shrugging and "I guess. We didn't think about it being unsafe. We'd get on our bikes and ride all over the city, on our own. I don't think half the time we even told our parents we were going."

"I envy that freedom. I was always on a leash. Mom had a seizure if a bee flew too close to me in the back yard. Overly protective. Maybe that's why Dad drank."

Jake surveying patches of sun-warmed rock and "It must be dry this year. I remember more water, roaring down through here where the channel narrows and the spray floating up so heavy it would soak us. On sunny days we'd angle ourselves right and watch rainbows in the mist. Throw stones. Jump across the breaks in the rocks."

"And neither of you ever fell in?"

"Never. Like I say, we didn't even think about it. We were kids."

"Where's Rod now?"

Jake modulating his voice and "I don't know."

"He was one of your best friends?" Jake nodding and "Grade school, junior high, high school."

"And you don't know where he is now," Jake shaking his head.

"Doesn't that seem odd to you?" but Jake did not add his voice to the water's.

Luella withdrew her arm from his, turned and stepped across the bridge's narrow planks. Jake remained motionless, staring, hearing his child's voice come across years and above the falling water. Luella leaned forward, her forearms on the railing. Not far downstream the falls ended and the river curved away. She noticed a small stick in the current as it plunged over the last drop, then reappeared farther on. She marked bubbles on the water's surface and considered the swift current and *how long do they last, and where?*

They walked the falls another hour, then bought flowers at a greenhouse and went to visit the side-by-side graves of Jake's mother and father.

■

Sally Corner, dispatcher for the Davison County Sheriff's Department, taking one call out of many, announcing who she is and for whom she works.

A man asking cheerily, "Can I speak with Sheriff Frederick?"

Sally bluntly, "Sheriff Frederick passed away a few weeks ago," thinking *I've explained why and how too often, no more.*

A pause, then "I'm sorry to hear that. Very sorry."

"Who's calling?"

"Doesn't matter. We weren't close." Wally Reno broke the connection.

■

"Pete, it's Jake."

"Jake," Pete pausing because he had not heard from Jake in a year and now three times in two weeks. "You want me to get Kathy on the phone, too?"

"Yeah. Got a question maybe either of you can help me with." Jake heard Pete's deep voice bellow and momentarily Kathy picked up one of their other phones. "Hi Jake," her voice shaded like Jane's and Jake's breath catching.

"Did you guys know the old couple that died with Jane?"

"No," Pete said, "other than I knew where they farmed. I think I maybe met him once, but I'm not sure. Why?" Pete wondering at Jake's interest that maybe should have been evident years before.

Jake attempting nonchalance, to off-handedly embellish the same lie he'd told Kindler and "Seeing the car, I don't know. I'm thinking about things I never thought of. Someone asked me last week how the claim was settled and I didn't know and then it seemed like I really wanted to. All of a sudden I'm hungry for details. I know it must seem strange," neither Pete nor Kathy answering.

"Did they have any children?"

Pete answering and "I don't know one way or the other. Kathy?"

"No, I couldn't say," her voice static-crackling, Jake guessing because she spoke on their old cordless phone.

"Any relatives you know of?"

"No," Pete said, then Kathy with "I think they had family in Emery. I don't know why I say that, but I seem to remember hearing it after the accident. Something in the paper maybe about relatives in Emery," Jake thinking surprised *Jesus yes the paper* and wondering why he hadn't simply looked there first.

"Well, I'm sorry to drag this stuff up again, to bother you with it."

"No bother, Jake." Pete pausing, then "Is something going on?"

"I'm not sure what you mean."

"It's just strange, that's all. Your coming down here to look at the car and now these questions. Something we should know?" Jake thinking he ought to tell them but deciding against it, mumbling that he was merely getting himself together finally and then hanging up, thinking *later but not now.*

Two weekends later they drove south again, Highway 281 shouldering a nothingness that moved them beyond boredom. The Mitchell library had all of the *Mitchell Daily Republic*'s issues before 1993 on microfilm. A young woman at the main desk assisted them in locating the right drawer in one of the reference rooms. Jake had used microfilm in accomplishing legal research but hadn't been in a library for years and could not follow the directions taped to the table where the microfilm reader rested. Luella watched him fumble with the spools and "You can rebuild an entire automobile so that you can't tell it from new, but you can't work a simple machine like this."

"That seems a fair assessment of the situation, yes."

Luella mounted the spools and scrolled through issues and pages. Sunday's paper from July 18, 1975, carried a brief report of the accident on page three, Jake guessing the paper wasn't staffed well on weekends, so no pictures and not much information. But the Monday edition's front page held a photo of the old DeSoto, taken at the gas station where it had been towed, Jake looking at it closely for almost a minute, amazed at the size of the front bumper, which looked like it weighed by itself more than half of his Volare, thinking *if you saw a bumper like that you'd know it was death come calling.*

Page four of Monday's edition held the obituaries. The Jensons were first, and in the final paragraph Jake and Luella read "The Jensons are survived by two sons, Marvin, of St. Paul, and Howard, of Watertown, SD, and one daughter, Madelaine Nuegebauer, of Emery, SD," Jake wondering why, if there were three children, the check was made out only to Madelaine.

As he followed Luella from the library, the smell of books filled him, their rough or smooth-papered pages coming imagined back to his hands, and he wanted to find who had written "many a man is making friends with death" and to simply then hold the book, but thinking *miles to go.*

A few minutes on the highway brought them to Emery, where they asked about Madelaine Nuegebauer at the only gas station in town, a newer Texaco out of place on the corner among old buildings long past their youth. A young attendant told them he knew of no one by that name, but they asked for a phone book and found her listed. The young man gave them directions for the address shown, only three and a half blocks away. It was a small, old house no one had cared for in years, between a new four-plex and an older two-story stucco that had been maintained well, Jake thinking of a Faulkner story he could no longer name. On both sides of the old house were tall wooden fences, the neighbors apparently preferring not to look at the eyesore next to them.

It wasn't unlike the house Jake had grown up in, and he guessed it no more than twenty by twenty, that inside would be two tiny bedrooms, an absurdly small bathroom and kitchen. A living room with space for two chairs and a television only. Shelves filled with knickknacks and dusty photographs. In the kitchen art-foam butterflies and old linoleum. It was wood-framed with thin, lap siding of cracked boards, its roof low-pitched and blue-shingled. The dirty white paint only partially covering the siding had been hit by hail recently; large flakes of it lay on the weed-filled grass near the foundation. The asphalt shingles were warped and brittle, missing in large chunks where hail had sharded them. Between the four-plex's fence and the house ran a gravel driveway, Jake remembering one like it at their first house in Mitchell, but no garage, the two lanes of gravel overgrown unused for many seasons. The only things flourishing were the low leafy bushes to either side of the small front porch and a purple-flowered clematis that had worked its way up a tall lattice attached to the siding, then to the rain gutters and on ascending to the chimney, where it could climb no more.

"Nobody lives here," Jake said as they walked a crumbling cement path between grass a foot tall. But someone did. Jake knocked softly on the splintered wooden storm door because it looked like it might collapse were he to rap harder. The metal screen hung loose on two sides in the lower light. Almost immediately a woman about their age pulled open the heavy inner door, stared through the screen and challenged them with a sullen "Yeah?" Jake, surprised, did not speak, so Luella, used to such customers, calmly "Does Madelaine Nuegebauer live here?"

"Yeah," this time not a question.

"Could we see her?"

"You selling something?"

"No."

"What do you want, then?"

"Talk. Are *you* Madelaine?"

"I'm her daughter, Betty Klemke," Jake hoping Madelaine Nuegebauer would be lucid enough to remember.

Jake said, "Can we come in?"

"Not until you tell me what you want to talk about," Jake gathering himself and explaining that they'd come to talk about the accident, the daughter finally giving way and Jake pulling open the sprung door and stepping in behind Luella. Inside, the rooms stood orderly but smelled of decomposing newspapers and the exhalations of old age. A wall of photographs but only one bank of shelves, upon which stood glass-blown characters, mostly swans of varying sizes. The daughter asked them to sit on the couch and said she'd get her mother. The floor creaked beneath her as she went, though she was not heavy. Dust rose from the swirling avocado carpet. As they waited Jake noticed water stains on the low, claustrophobic ceiling. Soon the daughter returned with an old woman, the daughter helping her as she moved her walker across the floor. An odor of lilacs entered with them, and then the old woman lowered herself onto a stiff, hard-backed chair.

The daughter bent and looked at her mother directly, speaking loudly and "These people want to ask you some questions," the mother smiling vacantly and nodding her head.

Betty Klemke turned to Jake and Luella and "She won't be much help" in a tone of resigned exasperation. "She'll be seventy-two next month. She's been like this since she had a stroke twelve years ago."

Jake peered at Madelaine Nuegebauer, tried to imagine her getting and signing a big check, could not and *they took all of it.* "Mrs. Nuegebauer," he shouted, "do you remember the accident when your parents were killed?" Luella thinking *yes, make small talk to ease into it, Jake.*

The old woman kept on smiling and nodding and then offered a soft "yes."

"Do you remember getting a check from an insurance company to settle the claim?"

"Yes," she said, pointing at the roof, "for the hail," Jake understanding that the only connection Madelaine Nuegebauer could make with insurance was hail.

"No, I mean a check because your mother and father got killed?"

"Yes," she said again, and again pointed up. "Going to put . . . new roof."

Luella noticed that the daughter seemed nervous, thinking *she got the roof-check, not her mother. That money's gone.*

"What sort of check do you mean?" Betty Klemke blurted, suddenly very interested.

Before Jake could try to explain, the daughter asked again, insistent, "Was my mother supposed to get money?"

"No."

"Then what check are you asking about?"

Jake fumbling and "She was supposed to get money for the funerals, that's what I meant. That was all. The accident," Jake testing, "was your parents' fault, as you remember," thinking *they played both sides, made each side think the accident was their fault. Both companies paid.*

"Yes," Betty Klemke said, only slightly quieter.

"I remember my agent telling me at the time that my company was going to pay for the funerals, and I just wanted to make sure, now that I'm actually here, that that was done."

"If the accident was Grandpa's fault, why would your company pay for the funerals?" Jake thinking *this woman is no fool,* then telling her, "My policy had a special rider on it that would do that," Luella thinking *that sounds as lame as my leg.*

Jake wanting to cover his tracks further and "I don't know anything about insurance. I'm just relying on what my agent told me. Would that sort of coverage be unusual?"

"Did you get the funerals paid for, Mom?" Betty Klemke asked, Madelaine Nuegebauer smiling, nodding. The daughter turned from her, disgusted. "She's no help."

"No, I can see that she isn't, and I'm very sorry to have bothered you. As I said, I never paid much attention to the claim when it was being handled. My wife got killed and I wasn't in very good shape. Lately I've been thinking about it, contacting those involved. Since my agent's dead, I've had to piece it together."

"Weird," the daughter said.

"I guess it seems that way."

Outside, as they began to drive away, Luella said, "I don't have a good feeling about the daughter."

"Me either. But she'd remember if her mother had ever gotten $75,000. She seemed honestly surprised when I mentioned a check." Sighing and "God I must have sounded lame in there. She probably didn't buy a word of it. I wonder if she'll check about the funerals."

"What could she check, who paid for them? I guess it wouldn't be too tough to find records like that."

"And she seems just the type to do it, a scavenger, the scent of money drawing her like rotting flesh." Pausing, then "One thing we can be sure of, the old woman never got the money," Jake pointing at the house resting precariously on its foundation.

Luella sad for the old woman and "She didn't even get a roof."

■

At dinner that evening, Betty Klemke sat across from her husband. Their three teenagers had quickly eaten their steaming

chicken and potatoes and dispersed to activities their mother
knew nothing about. Her husband, Bill Klemke, owned one of
the largest hog operations in the state, exactly three miles south
and two east of Madelaine Nuegebauer's decomposing house.
Opposed to that house was Klemke's farm with its long shiny
metal buildings and picturesque old barn, traditional red with
white shingles. The barn, seventy-three years old, stood as
square as the other buildings. Trimmed lawns and carefully
edged roads portioned out the property. Everything looked as if
it had been recently washed. New pickups and in the well-swept
garage a Lincoln for his wife of twenty years, upon whom Bill
Klemke relied for much of his money management. She was pro-
ficient with money, a financial mind detail-oriented paired with
his strong back and long-winded capacity for physical labor. She
had grown up poor, and guarded their money like the green bills
were children. She had only this philosophy: make sure more
comes in than goes out. As she sat across from her husband,
chewing slowly, she asked aloud, "Why would they pay for the
funerals when it was Mom and Dad's fault?"

"What's that?" her husband asked.

"Nothing, nothing," she replied, hardly ever involving him in
matters that she could take care of herself. She kept turning it
over in her mind: *why pay for something you didn't owe?* ultimately finding the proposition incomprehensible.

The next day she phoned her insurance agent, inquiring about
funeral coverage.

■

Along a dim hallway on the second floor of Jamestown's oldest
office building Jake found a solid wooden door upon which was
mounted a very contemporary multi-colored holographic which
read "Carson's Investigations." The letters seemed to move and
sparkle as Jake approached. The new sign on the old door didn't
seem right to him, and he thought of the latest billet-aluminum

wheels on old cars otherwise nearly stock. Jake had gotten the address from the yellow pages; this was apparently the only private investigator in Jamestown.

Despite a more conventional "Come On In!" sign screwed beneath the holograph, Jake knocked, hesitant. From inside a young man's voice rang out and told him enthusiastically to enter. Jake twisted the old metal handle and the door popped open of its own accord, as if it had been straining against its hinges. Inside Jake found a small room, the extent of the office, two large double-hung windows across from the door. A close-cropped young man stood from behind the desk and "You must be Jake Warner."

"Yes," Jake guessing the young man before him must have been in high school when Jane looked to her left and saw a DeSoto's bumper coming. Jake took his hand and found the grip strong. The rest of him seemed coiled and eager, as if he had played football all his life.

"John Carson," he announced. "Please sit down," Jake taking one of two wooden chairs.

Carson leaning forward and "You called about having me find someone."

"Yes. His name is Dan Gippart," Carson asking him to spell it and then a lot of other questions that Jake answered as best he could. Carson explained how little and how much the search could cost, given how easily things might go. Carson had him sign a contract that required a hundred-dollar deposit. He never asked the reason for Jake's search. Their intercourse took all of twenty minutes.

Jake left and returned to work, more than a little surprised when, just as he came into his apartment about five-thirty, he answered the phone and heard John Carson give him the name of Dan Gippart's employer: IncAmPride, a large insurance company in St. Paul.

"That was pretty quick," Jake told him.

"I'd hoped it would drag out a while so I could bill you more, but your Mr. Gippart falls in the categories of 'employed' and 'not trying to hide.' When that happens, it doesn't usually take very long. This kind of work is a lot electronic now."

Jake almost disappointed because things in his life didn't usually move so quickly and "Yeah, I figured a couple of weeks at least."

"I wish, but the bill I'll send you isn't much. The hundred covers about half."

"Thanks for your help."

"Thank you. Keep me in mind if you need anything else," Jake wondering *do you sell lives?*

■

She had called his apartment the previous two evenings, but Jake hadn't answered; she could not remember ever calling him anytime after work and not getting him. The morning after the second night she called Elroy and "Can I talk to Jake?"

Elroy typically impolite and "Sure, if you can find him."

"He's not working?"

"I guess I'd know where to find him if he was."

Luella had met Elroy a few times, had heard others talk about him, so she expected his orneriness. "How long since you've seen him?" she asked.

"This is the third day he ain't showed," Elroy sounding angry but then his voice softening and "Not like Jake to miss work, with or without letting me know. I take it you haven't spoke to him either."

"No," Luella worried and "I'm going over and check his place."

Elroy interested in anybody's sex life and "You got a key?"

"No, Elroy, I don't. I'll get the manager to let me in."

"Let me know," again from Elroy's voice the cantankerousness gone.

Luella left the store knowing it wouldn't be difficult to get into Jake's apartment. She had known Marilyn Bennett, the wife of the building manager, for years; Marilyn shopped often in Luella's store. Luella found her home in their upstairs apartment, not surprised that Marilyn hardly knew Jake. She agreed to let Luella in after hearing her concerns about Jake. On their way downstairs they passed his mailbox but had no way to check its contents.

Jake's door swung open on rooms half-lit by the sun, and the two women, apprehensive, stayed together as they walked. But the rooms were empty of human life and gave no evidence he had been there recently. Luella, picturing her own cluttered rooms, was surprised at how few things Jake possessed. She believed that if she picked up the few magazines and books in the living room the place would resemble a furnished apartment no one had moved into yet. A thin layer of dust lay over every flat, shiny surface.

Marilyn Bennett said she had an appointment to show one of the other apartments in the building and left Luella alone. Given this opportunity Luella slowly explored the small apartment but found there was almost nothing to search. In the living room were one chair, one sofa, two lamps, and a television. In the bedroom one bed and one chest. In the kitchen one table and two chairs. No desk with drawers filled with mysterious papers, no closets with intriguing boxes on high shelves, Luella thinking *his place as boring as him*. His few clothes were hung neatly in the small bedroom closet; only underwear and socks filled the drawers of the single chest; the upper cabinets in the kitchen held a few glasses, bowls, and plates, the lower drawers mismatched silverware. A lot of unfilled space. She could not even identify a *smell* in the rooms, and the light from the curtained windows seemed neither bright nor dim.

On the kitchen table, beneath a newspaper four days old, she found the spiral notebook she had sometimes seen him carrying. It reminded her of the kind she'd used in high school. She slid it out and saw its wrinkled blue cover marked with paint smears and even a greasy fingerprint. It gave off a faint odor of the body shop. Luella moving to put it back and *I've no business looking at this* but then opening the front cover. On the first page was a single word, Jane, written in a clumsy hand. She guessed it had been written a while ago, for the blue ink was faded. The second, third, and fourth pages revealed the same word, then came two where every ruled line, margin to margin, held her name. Then one with her name single again, centered. On several other pages was another name, Mark, written neither as large nor as often as Jane's. Since she had never heard Jake use that name, Luella wondered who Mark was. She was going to close the notebook because she did not care to learn more about Jake's apparent obsession with his dead wife, but decided to page on till the end. The pages marked with words filled just more than half of those available, the ones beyond that blank until, on the final pages, she came across the account of his dream regarding Jane on the stone. Still standing, she read it through twice.

Afterward, she lowered herself onto the chair and *thanks for sharing, Jake.* After a while she stood again, slid the notebook back under the paper and walked out of the apartment. She drove slowly back to work angry with him for his exclusion of her from whatever he was doing, her anger then working into fear because of what she had read; fear for what lay behind the facade that Jacob Warner gave to the world. And then loneliness, because few of her days in the last month had passed without her seeing him, and she missed him and could not stop thinking of his touch.

■

Gippart and Reno drifted toward Charlie's, a watering hole twenty stories up on the top floor of a hotel close to IncAmPride. Wednesday afternoon, 5:00 p.m., early for them to be gone from the office, on the sidewalk a strong current of workers running beside them and the two men slower at the current's edge and falling off into the hotel lobby and then the bar's muted light. They took stools at the long shiny dark-wood bar, rested their feet on the scratched rail below. They ordered Jack Daniels on the rocks, Gippart telling Reno "You ought to pay for these out of that twenty you won."

Reno removed his wallet, withdrew a twenty and "this is the exact one. Ought to frame it." A man took the stool next to Gippart. Reno flattened the twenty on the bar, saying "the Lord giveth, the Lord taketh away."

"I like that comparison."

"Didn't know you were so goddamn religious."

"I do indeed worship the Lord."

"You mean the Lord's goddamn *power*."

"Well, yes." They raised already-sweating glasses, tilt-clinking rim to rim and drinking like men experienced in satisfaction.

"I should ask you what you said to young Lori's parental units."

"You sure as shit shouldn't."

"I'd really like to know. Purely a scientific interest, how an action begets a reaction. You seem so eloquent in those situations."

"I am. But no fucking way you need to know."

"When Jonason called back and said they wouldn't take the two hundred grand, I wanted to ask him to reconsider. Wanted to say 'look, I think you'd better ask again, because this is what's going to happen if you don't. There'll be a man, a man you wouldn't like very much, show up at your clients' house. He will say certain things to them, things they will like even less than the appalling man who says them. They will be afraid.' You really want to make it so Jonason *knows*."

"Somehow I think the prick does."

"And you want to have heard that conversation when precious little Lori's mom and pop called Jonason with a change of heart. You want to know if old Jonason heard that exquisite inflection of fear in their words, fear now instead of righteous indignation over the inadequacy of our initial offer. Now suddenly they oblige, say for twenty thousand more we'll settle, because you were kind enough to suggest that amount would make the claim and the appalling man go away. You want to have heard that conversation."

"The Lord is omniscient, and could have," Reno told him.

"The good Lord does indeed have the advantage of me there."

Next to them, holding a half-emptied scotch, Jake sat circling his glass so that the cubes swirled. After they had returned from Madelaine Nuegebauer's he had done nothing but work and sit in his apartment as he used to. He saw Luella more frequently and was finding out that he needed her. He could not explain why one morning he had awakened ashamed of his nothingness, determined to carry further what they had begun. He had gone to the detective and driven late into the night to St. Paul. Had located Dan Gippart easily and spent two days hovering uncertain around the IncAmPride building.

The bar was the first chance he had to get close to him. Jake listened to Gippart and Reno a half hour more, finally thinking *you can learn to hate someone awfully fast. To hate the man with him, too, the hatred renewing you, teaching the thing you must do.* Looking a last time at Gippart and for reasons he couldn't articulate *I must do unto him,* continuing to believe that it was possible for him to reassume the motions of a life long abandoned.

4

As metal can select a certain slant of light and drive it toward suitable agents, the remaining cars' side glass and windshields cast the lowering sun's intense illumination onto the Eagan, Minnesota, high school's west face. Painted and ornamented hoods, chromed bumpers and trim, glared at the brick and glass and threw the redirected light of four o'clock in that direction and found, upon their enthusiastic emergence, Tammy Chorske and two friends, who then broke like enamel and ran along the November sidewalk's bright surface. Their blond sheeny curls too reflected the late afternoon sun, but seemed, compared to enduring paint and chrome, empty of color. Tammy and Sonja Bjornson and Kathy Dahl skipped to the parking lot where they clambered into Tammy's shiny sleek and sun-roofed red Pontiac and became a trio of chirping, eager birds. Tammy's mother usually drove the Pontiac to work but twice a week allowed her daughter. The girls were bound for Tammy's house so that she could shed her sweaty cheerleader outfit. "Home first!" she had told her friends. "I am majorly pitted and there's no way—no freaking *way*—I'm using that grody locker room and those grody showers." After Tammy changed they planned a journey to the Mall of America where they would "chill," mimicking a black vernacular come from a life whose only connection to theirs was citizenship.

"Jam time!" Tammy squeaked, sliding a new rap disc into the player above the leathered console shift lever, heavy-bottomed music and an angry black vocalist filling the otherwise white interior with "Motherfuckers gonna take what I give 'em." The bass vibrated the door panels. Able coincidentally to absorb loud music, think clearly and converse, Sonja and Kathy reviewed briefly the contents of the day's final class.

Sonja slapping open palms along her jeaned thighs and "We discussed an essay by Sid Hartha?"

Kathy mimicking the effeminate tenor of their teacher's voice and "How gay! But I thought he had just one name, like Bono or Slash!" as the music ran "all the pigs want is to lay us niggers down."

Sonja disgusted and "Like I wouldn't know? First name Sid, last name Hartha?"

Tammy mocking wide-eyed and "Oh tell me what it is about! The deep meanings!"

Kathy mimicking again after "bitches and ho's, bitches and ho's" and "This weird Indian dude who wanders around with nothing but a loin cloth for a while, then gets rich and does drugs and this whore, then becomes a ferryman?"

"Loin cloths are cool!"

"Ferrymen are cool!" Tammy exclaimed, then "we studied sarcasm in poetry class. It's like when you say something and then you say *Not!?*"

"Now listen, young scholars, this book is all about experiencing life, being individuals, suffering in order to find salvation!" after "dissn' stops with bullets."

"I move we experience life at the mall and bag the suffering!"

"Seconded?!"

Assailed by images and information ubiquitous as their music, these thoroughly educated young women had been pumped full of unearned self-esteem and understood, to the depth of a single coat of paint, the consequences of certain pairings: sperm and egg, AIDS and the immune system, alcohol and brain, fatty diet and hips. But not, as they skimmed the lot's smoothly asphalted surface, flesh and metal.

Tammy snapping her fingers and "That locker room is a fucking joke! Dissn' us, like cheerleaders don't deserve better?"

"And cheerteam too!"

"It's like no one *cares*!"

"Everything in that fucking school is a joke!"

"Everything in life is a fucking joke, girls!"

Tammy cranked the volume higher as they rolled through chilly November air, the already-falling sun reddening to their right. They put on sunglasses, popped their gum to the beat of rap insistent as the athletes they dated. After three songs Tammy barreled up to a t-intersection from which a left turn and six blocks would bring them to her house. She began her turn and glanced to her left but not in the opposite direction, where a woman with three children in a station wagon closed, a middle-aged mother frazzled from an afternoon of her four-year-old's non-stop chatter, returning home from the grade school where she had just picked up her daughter and a friend they watched until five-thirty, when the other girl's mother came from work. The woman's son went mornings to a nearby church preschool. All three children sat, belted and quiet, in the rear seat.

Tammy arced one-handed through her turn with a global awareness that ended just beyond the passenger-side door. The woman in the station wagon at the last moment slammed on her brakes and stopped no more than two feet short of rearranging the painted metal-skin beyond which Kathy Dahl sat drumming her hands on her knees in time with the music, and maybe Kathy Dahl herself. The brief screams of her tires on the asphalt echoed through Tammy's Pontiac but did not disturb the girls.

The woman turned first to the children in back, each wide-eyed but unhurt. Tammy at the last instant had been unable to avoid seeing the other car coming and had braked suddenly too. When she realized her car had not been struck, knowing how angry her parents would be if she had an accident with it, she began to drive away. The woman, throwing her door open in anger and emerging with her white walking shoes squishing on the asphalt, stood open-mouthed as the red car accelerated down the street. She slid back into her seat and pressed her palm hard against the horn and started after them, accelerating as abruptly as she had braked. At a stop sign for a busy through-street two blocks away the Pontiac halted, momentarily behind it the station wagon. The woman threw her door open again and ran enraged to Tammy's door and began pounding on the glass. Tammy blankly acknowledged the woman's earthly existence for the first time but refused to lower the window. She found the woman's antics unusual, then entertaining. The woman screamed, pulled on the locked door handle. Finally she kicked at the plastic trim on the door's lower edge, cracking it.

Tammy looked at the woman impassively, then curled her fingers into catclaws and scraped them against the inside glass. The music still thumped from the speakers, so the woman could not hear her mimicking the sound a cat might make in warning. As they drove away Sonja lowered her rear window, but only to yell "Bitch!"

Then "God, what's her problem?"

Then three cat sounds above the music.

The woman from the station wagon, shaking with anger, did not think to get Tammy's license number, and the shackles of heavy traffic bound her at the stop sign so long she did not see where the red car went. She turned to the wary children, frightened at a world far beyond her control and "that girl will kill someone," then for emphasis "*kill* someone."

■

Returning to her desk after placing new-reserve files on her boss's desk, Sheila Voigt heard Dan Gippart begin to laugh. She saw him smile often—a smile her father, who worked thirty years pouring cement in southern Minnesota, had always referred to as a "shit-eatin' management grin," the sort bet-winners give losers—but she seldom heard him laugh outright; the sound both intrigued and pleased her and, though slight, the notion came to her that Gippart might be a more pleasant human than she had previously believed. The depth of his laugh, come belly deep, made it seem honest, a word that for vague reasons Sheila did not normally associate with him. When the laughter continued, intensifying, she found herself drawn and went into his office hoping to share in whatever had caused it. As she did so she did not think that it was the first time since she'd been hired—nearly two years—that she had entered his office unbidden.

Gippart, seated at his desk as she had left him moments before, glanced up as Sheila stepped in timidly; his door stood always partially open, but falsely as he disliked interruption. She saw that he held a claim folder and that his laughter had produced tears which had run down his face and neck onto his white collar. The folders she had handed him were for large claims he needed to review for establishment of a reserve fund, money set aside now to cover whatever potential IncAmPride liability he determined. Sheila called them simply "bad" files, big fires or deaths or serious malpractice, though she knew there wasn't of the latter any other kind but serious. She stepped only half way through the door and "Are you all right?"

Gippart drew a tissue from a desk drawer, dabbed at his eyes and cheeks trying but not entirely succeeding to stop the involuntary after shocks of his laugh. Finally he managed "I'm fine . . . fine," waving away with his hand any concern.

"Mind if I ask what's so funny?"

"No, not at all. Come in. Close the door," as Sheila did so "Goddamn I should be quieter with it open. I bet they heard me all the way down the hall. Think I'm a goddamn lunatic," Sheila thinking *too late to stop that.*

"Sit down, sit down," Gippart said, pointing to a chair. They did not usually make small talk. He looked her over as she moved cautiously over the carpet, lowered herself and crossed her legs, Gippart admiring them and thinking *damn fine* and noting the shadow where her short skirt crossed one thigh to the other. He rated high his decision to hire her. Sheila had not been the most qualified candidate but had scored highest on his personal "visual impact" scale—he and Reno had worked it out one night—the top rung of which he had identified as "Fucking A."

He shifted forward, leaned his elbows on the desk and "This new file, the guy over in Wisconsin who got electrocuted," laughing again, it growing once more uncontrollable. Sheila waited. She never examined the details of a file; that wasn't her job. Her only obligation was to determine if all the necessary information boxes had been filled in, if they hadn't to call the branch office where the claim had originated, then to prepare a folder and to establish a file number. From that point on, to manage correspondence regarding it.

"Electrocuted?" she said uncertain, half-stammering, feeling it a dumb question.

Gippart eager and "This guy—what's his name," paging into the file, "Conrad Schmitz. What a name, could have been one of the stooges, he trots down to the local store for a new TV antenna—probably never heard of cable—carts it home, runs it up his ladder onto the roof. Check the pictures," shoving three pages of mounted photographs toward her and Sheila leaning, her blouse falling open on further shadow, taking them, examining as Gippart's eyes followed the curves of her breasts as they disappeared inside her jacket. The pictures, initially, were views of a lightly-pitched roof, closing in finally on a four-legged mounting device attached with bolts to sheathing below light-colored shingles. Sheila guessed that the antenna would have mounted in the short tube in the middle of the four legs. The photographer had then moved to ground level shots, where now she noted the proximity of the house to a multi-wire power line. She saw that from the house's slightly bowed rain gutter a person could reach out and touch the nearest wire.

Gippart explaining and "So old Conrad the Magnificent bolts the mount to the roof, assembles the antenna and lifts it up, all by his lonesome, but finds it hard to hold straight because it's so tall and heavy and it begins to tip. Toward the power line there.

Does Conrad let go? No, Conrad does not. He's thinking, big macho guy that he no doubt was, that he can stop it falling, so he's got hold of it with a death-grip with his big pollack hands and then it lays onto the line and now old Con *can't* let go. The electrical form of life-termination now has seized him. According to the medical examiner you couldn't really determine if Connie was dead when he rolled off the roof or if the fall killed him," Gippart fallen back now into an erratic chuckle and Sheila wondering *why is he laughing?* She smiled at Gippart in order not to betray her mounting disgust.

"Jesus, what a hoot," Gippart went on. "And it gets funnier. The poor widow and the kids, they got nothing now, no income, so they figure somebody owes them something and they get a lawyer and now's when everybody stops laughing. They sue the power company. Fine. Let them. But the fucking lawyer includes the manufacturer of the antenna and the store that sold it, too. We got liability coverage with the seller. Like they should have told him on his way out the door 'hey remember to look around you fucking moron, see if there's any big wires around with juice, because you know what happens when you touch one? There's a big buzzing sound, though you don't hear it. And the smell is awful,'" Gippart laughing again and thinking of Reno. "This is your brain, this is your brain on a thousand volts."

Sheila remembering her husband and "How old was he?"

"Old enough to know better," Gippart told her. "Christ, a damn three-year-old knows enough to stay out of power lines," then finding the age and "Thirty-four," Sheila thinking *I would have been gone a year if that were me.* And she considered, as she did more often in the last year, the payments some must make for a small mistake, a lapse in judgment.

Gippart shaking his head and "That'll be my new phrase— pulling a Connie. The Conrad awards. The Connies. Well, I wager we get ourselves removed from the lawsuit. Deleted, like Con. Judge'll be laughing hard as me."

Sheila didn't know what to say, stood, turned for the door,

just before reaching it Gippart offering "You lost some weight, your ass looks good," Sheila feeling his eyes on her backside, low, thinking *finally it's come.* Even early in her first interview she had sensed Gippart was the sort of man who wouldn't hesitate to comment on her appearance. That he had not done so until now surprised her because frequently he gave off a predatorial sexuality. She had frequently considered what she would say when such a remark came, pretending she would be firm, turn and face him squarely, make it clear she wouldn't allow such speech but mindful always that she was a single parent with two children and that there was a reason her position paid at least five thousand more than any other like it in the city, honest enough to know it wasn't only because she was good at her job. Mindful too that consideration of such moments is always easier than their reality, like the birth of children, that when they arrive actual and squalling, resolve for most fades.

Afraid of him and without turning "Thanks."

"You look mighty good from where I sit," Gippart said, Sheila speechless then through the door to her desk, ashamed because she had lacked courage. For minutes she sat trembling both at him and her own cowardice, startled finally by her intercom buzzer.

"Did I embarrass you?" Gippart asked.

"No," thinking what she could not speak.

"You look damn good from the front, too," he said. "Damn good," and then his voice shrinking back into its hole and Sheila turning to her work, her fingers trembling.

Sheila's night to meet other women after work for a single drink, the one school night she allowed her ten- and twelve-year-old daughters to walk directly home from school rather than to a friend's house where the other four days they stayed until she retrieved them on her way home from work. Sheila feared the drivers that sped along the busy street a block from where they lived. She feared the men she read about too often in the paper.

She had agreed to this once-a-week arrangement only this year, so they had been in the rhythm of it for nearly three months, not enough time for her to feel completely comfortable. She didn't care to leave them alone but knew they were old enough now, had shown a willingness to be responsible for short periods. They needed time by themselves, she needed a place that wasn't work or home, for too long the only locations that defined her. She needed friends.

Each Wednesday Sheila walked to a nearby bar, stayed until six. She would reach home by six-thirty, on several occasions to find dinner ready, which pleased her greatly. Besides, she called the house every thirty minutes to check on them, hearing each time an exasperated "We're not boys, Mother. We are capable of acting like adults." Tonight Sheila hesitated as she left her office—the girls had been mouthy and uncooperative the previous few days; maybe she ought to drive straight home and by so doing let them know she wasn't pleased with their behavior. But the chance to talk to adults outside of work drew her, and she walked the usual route to Mick's, a nominally Irish pub a block from the office and across from the ramp where she parked.

They were a group of four—Darla from Marketing and Cindy and Lorna from Accounting—of which none could precisely define her attraction to the others or how they had first come to meet on a regular basis. They covered the parent and work-experience spectrums from twenty-six to sixty-three; their children ranged in age from two to thirty-five. Each had at least one child, though Lorna's five boys were grown and gone. In her early sixties, she looked forward to a couple more years at IncAmPride, then lots of time at their summer home on Gull Lake near Brainerd. Her husband brokered investments, had accumulated sizable bank and stock accounts, never spectacularly but always steadily. Darla was twenty-six, with two- and three-year-olds, who said little about her home life. They had never persuaded Cindy to divulge her exact age, but since her girls were sixteen and eighteen, they guessed her at least forty. They had never met outside their after-hours group except at the company Christmas party; yet, if asked, each might have responded that the group was as important to her life as any other single thing.

Sheila didn't see the others as she shouldered through the milling crowd of happy-hour drinkers. The smell of beer and smoke and free chicken-wings greeted her. She smiled at the poster behind the bar that offered a seven-course Irish dinner—a boiled potato and a six-pack. She had never indulged much in after-work drinking, but then she hadn't begun working until after she had the responsibility of children. She had married at twenty-two, just after college, found herself widowed at twenty-seven when her husband, Orie, drove his motorcycle off a curvy highway near the Wisconsin Dells. They'd had a small life insurance policy, but not much. He had left her little except for two daughters and a tall stack of medical bills. She smiled at Travis the young bartender and he waved as she searched for a table. He reached for her usual non-alcoholic beer—two months earlier she had had one drink too many and thought the girls looked at her oddly after she had reached home—and set it on the bar.

Sheila claimed a table in the dim heavy air not far from the solitary pool table and waited. Wally Reno watched her from his tall stool at the bar. She had glimpsed him only a few times with Gippart in his office, and because he wore dark glasses now she did not recognize him.

"I'd sue the bastard. At the *very* least report him to Personnel," Lorna shouted over the din of the crowd, Sheila thinking *yes, you would, because you've nothing to lose. You've somewhere else to go.* "Have some balls, girl."

Cindy amused and "Lorna, do all Scandinavians have that kind of mouth?"

Lorna laughing and "We're all so hip."

"Did he touch you?" Darla asked.

"What?" Sheila leaning across the table.

"Did he touch you?"

"No."

"Then *don't* say anything. Your job is more important. What he says, unless it gets real bad, won't hurt you. Let it ride," Sheila understanding that was exactly what she would do. She would refuse to give up the highest level in IncAmPride's Secretary category and thirty thousand a year because somebody had said she looked good, and they all knew that office politics and power wouldn't give a damn about who was right and who was wrong, only about who could survive. Sheila going so far as trying to consider Gippart's remarks as compliments, because in such a light they didn't appear so ugly. Stupidly justifying *he is a man, after all.*

"I'm with Darla," Cindy said. "Long as he doesn't put his hands on you."

"He's truly slimy, isn't he?" Lorna asked.

Sheila surprised that Lorna even knew him and "Why do you say so?"

"Can't define it. Something about the great Mr. Gippart. Few years ago his regular gal was sick, I filled in three or four days. The guy gave me the creeps," Sheila not telling them that Dan Gippart frightened her indefinably but more efficiently than any movie or lightning-filled night ever had.

"What exactly did he do?" Darla asked Lorna.

"Nothing specific, nothing I could explain. Never did figure it out. But my time in that office was like a movie where the dog senses something and his hair goes up."

Sheila laughing and "So you're comparing yourself to a dog."

"One of the finer breeds, of course. Perhaps the best."

"Somebody take this down. A collar or leash for Lorna's Christmas gift."

"I thought we decided to forego presents this year. We spent way too much last year."

"Fine, fine. I'll get you a *cheap* collar."

Darla didn't want to let the Gippart discussion drift away like the cigar smoke coming from someone at the bar. "I never told anyone, in fact I agreed not to, but last year I filed a sexual harassment complaint with Personnel." The others raised eyebrows in surprise.

"No kidding?" Lorna asked. "Against who?"

"I shouldn't say. Part of the resolution was that I wouldn't mention names or particulars to any other employee."

"Oh bullshit," Lorna said. "Spill your guts. We promise not to snitch."

"Carl."

"No shit? Carl?"

"Carl." Darla was the youngest of five women who worked for Carl Anderson, Vice President of Marketing. Her office adjoined his, just as Sheila's adjoined Gippart's.

"What'd he do?"

"He'd come in two or three times a day when I was at my desk, lean over so his face was side-by-side with mine. Always had some good excuse, some paperwork he needed me to examine while he was examining me. He'd actually get his nose in my hair. If I was standing up he'd brush his hand against my hip, his arm against my breast."

"I don't think I'd mind that much if it was Carl," Cindy said. She'd made it clear for years that she held her husband at a level of contempt others might reserve for child molesters, and no longer allowed him to touch her. She seemed constantly horny.

"Cindy, we don't need that."

"Well, you have to get sex someplace."

Darla dismissing Cindy's words and "He never verbally harassed me, but I think I would have preferred that. Finally it got so I was thinking about his little games all the time. Couldn't sleep some nights. After work one day I asked him to stop but he pretended he had no idea what I was talking about. The next morning he started in again. Since I've thought about it, I wonder if he really didn't know, still doesn't, that what he was doing was inappropriate. It's just the way he is around women. But I wasn't going to have him touching me. So I went to Personnel."

"How did they respond?"

"Pretty well. Didn't treat me like some emotionally disturbed, over reactive type. Overall they handled it well. Carl hasn't come near me since."

They sat silent for some moments, then Sheila said "It takes guts to do what you did."

"I guess it does. But you know you're not alone. We're here to support you."

"Thanks. Talking like this helps."

"Just don't encourage him. Wear baggy dresses, long skirts."

"And hide these gorgeous legs?"

"Yes."

Cindy winking and "Save them for Travis over there," Sheila blushing.

Their talk turned to children, husbands, church, went on for another half hour, Sheila removing herself from it after Darla talked of what she and her husband had done for their anniversary, Sheila lonely, thinking *just a touch now, someone's hands, not even sex, just hands on me, some warmth next to me in bed,* remembering. She slept alone in the brass bed she and Orie had bought two years after their wedding, its shiny surface as bright as ever, lasting on impassively as her flesh aged and yearned.

She tried again to smile sexily at Travis as she walked out, past Reno perched like a carrion-hunter waiting. He shoved his stool back, began to circle.

He knew which parking ramp she used, that each Wednesday she went to Mick's to meet three other women from IncAmPride. He found himself uninterested in the others, though the young one looked good and maybe in the future he would get around to her. About Sheila he was mildly curious, but he knew that his deeper interests usually began that way. He had stopped to talk to Gippart about a file but he was gone and the afternoon had turned long and boring; he had, as usual, no

plans for the night, and to check his boredom he decided to follow her home. His technique was to go a little further each
week; at first he had merely watched her leave the office. Then
he had followed her to the pub. Then out of the pub to the
ramp. This time he would follow her home.

He had parked on the ramp's lower level knowing she was
higher up. He let her walk a block ahead, got in his car and
waited. In less than a minute she rolled past. He lined up behind
her and three others in front of her at the toll booth, cutting off
a man in a big white car whose horn reverberated off the concrete, Reno thinking *fuck you you rich prick*. He guessed she
would have a monthly pass to show, that she wasn't stupid and
would save money that way. But then he wondered, thinking
always the worst of anyone, did she need to save money or did
she have some rich bastard husband like the guy behind him,
some sugar daddy? Most of the good-looking ones did, he
believed. He didn't actually know about Sheila, had never asked
Gippart.

He watched her wave her pass at the attendant, tossed a
couple of bills at the old man when his turn came, then followed her out of St. Paul on 35E. They drove several miles
until they reached 494 where they went west until Cedar, then
south into Bloomington. Reno followed her a few miles
beyond the sprawling Mall of America which he contemplated
with disgust picturing all the cute little yuppie people spending
money they hadn't really earned. He thought of little else until
they reached her home. Her house was small, the yard not
appearing to have been kept well. Maybe her husband was
some poor working slob who didn't deserve a good-looking
woman. She left her car outside the garage which appeared, its
opening back-lit by a weak bulb, filled with a lawnmower and
bikes and garbage cans. He rolled past and stopped a few
houses down; when she had disappeared through the front
door, he turned around and pulled up to the curb opposite,
where he sat for nearly ten minutes considering. He didn't feel

comfortable staying longer; in these times pussy parents feared for their children, did not like strangers in unfamiliar cars. He pretended to page through a newspaper months old, turning frequently to her house. He saw shadows pass across the covered windows but could not guess how many were inside. He noted two different bikes, guessed at least two children. No other car came. Maybe the old man worked late. Reno wondered if the husband would be getting any that night, pictured an anonymous man on top of Sheila, thrusting, her tight legs bent high and wrapped around him and thought *son of a bitch, maybe I'll come back sometime. Maybe.*

■

"Elroy, I'll be gone a while," Jake speaking in Jimtown's office after lunch.

"Can't keep away from your girlfriend?"

"Not that I can't. Don't want to," Jake said, Elroy shaking his head and spitting into the wastebasket to his left and "You've got enough money you can take off an afternoon just to diddle your woman?"

"Jesus, Elroy, she's not *my woman*," Jake wanting to laugh and then realizing he wouldn't exactly mind if he and Luella woke up together each morning, her side plated and lumpy alongside his. "You want me to whistle some tunes from the fifties?" he said, Elroy spitting again.

"Anyway, not what I meant by a while."

"Afternoon not long enough for you two lovebirds?"

"I meant three, four months, maybe more."

"That is some serious fucking, Jake," Jake wondering how he could think so much of such a pig of a man *but I do.* He had liked Elroy from the first.

"I'll be out of town."

"You will, huh?"

"Yes."

"You say that like I'll be so pleased I'll maybe offer to help you move. Like I'll wait pining for you to haul your ass back. Like you'll have a job when you do."

"I'd like that, yes. The part about me having a job."

"Where out of town?"

"Can't say."

"Can't or won't?"

"Won't."

"Something you got that needs doing?"

"Need is about right, yes," Elroy understanding by the tenor of Jake's words that it was but not willing to let him go free without worrying him some more.

"Who's supposed to do your work?"

"I'll work another two weeks. Give you enough time to find someone."

"Temporary?"

"If you tell him it's temporary he won't mind. Then if he's better than me he can stay and I'll go," Elroy thinking *ain't no one better*. Jake had not sought to, but had built for Jimtown a reputation.

"You been wanting to add someone anyway," Elroy grudgingly nodding, "so I'm doing you a favor by forcing a decision."

Elroy pausing and "Golly I hadn't considered it that way," then "You don't want to tell me any about where you're going or why?"

"No."

"All right then. Two weeks. But I . . . ," his voice trailing off.

"Thanks, Elroy."

"It sounded like you were going one way or the other."

"I was."

"Here's an idea. Why don't I do your work and still send you a check every week? Then you wouldn't be inconvenienced any."

"That'd be awfully sweet of you."

"Shit," Elroy said, and turned back to his paperwork. The last thing Jake said to him was "take care of my coupe."

∎

One night as they ate supper at Luella's Jake told her that he planned to leave Jamestown for a while. Sara had gone out and they talked quietly in the kitchen of the house her father had left her, the house where she had grown up. The house with the garage workbench where she had been smashed up. Luella unsurprised sat listening to his speech, and then she questioned him.

"So you found Gippart," she said, Jake nodding, then the same fear coming that she had felt in her lungs when he had been gone three days the previous week. "Where?"

"St. Paul. Works for an insurance company called IncAmPride."

"You're making that name up."

"No. It looks good on the sign outside, on letterheads."

"It's short for what?"

"IncorporatedAmericanPride."

"Guess I prefer Sun State."

"Easier to write out a check, certainly."

"How'd you find him?"

"Private detective. Gave him Gippart's name at quarter to nine a week ago Tuesday, said I wanted to find him. He called the apartment just after five. Said the search didn't take long. I was impressed—he's *good*."

"This detective work in Jamestown?"

"Yes." He told her the name.

"And then you went to St. Paul."

"Yes."

"Saw him."

"Yes."

"And now you're planning exactly what?"

"For now, just to go to St. Paul. I'll figure it out from there."

"You have no plan?"

"No."

"How will you live?"

"I've got money."

"If you need more, ask me."

"Thanks."

"I'll go with."

"No."

"You'll need help."

"If I do it won't be yours."

"Thank *you*."

"I mean I don't want you mixed up in it. It isn't your problem."

Luella wanting to tell him that if it was his problem it was hers too, but pausing and *I'm not going to beg*.

"It'll bother me a lot to be away from you," Jake reaching his hand across the small table and touching her, Luella folding her hand against the rough calloused skin and thinking *cars must love this*.

"When are you leaving?"

"Two weeks."

For a moment she felt like some dutiful little wife, but "Well," she said, leading him out of the kitchen, "I better make sure you're bothered lying in bed by yourself thinking about what happens when you don't sleep alone."

Later Luella woke as if someone had slapped her, in her momentary disorientation looking first at the bedside clock which announced in bloody letters 3:34. She could not recall dreaming, lay still listening. Jake seemed quiet, his breathing regular. But as she dismissed her sudden awakening and began to sink back into sleep Jake cried out with a guttural exclamation and dug an elbow hard into her side. She winced then turned, reaching for his face and half-hollering "Goddamit, Jake." Her hand found his rough cheek and she felt him drenched with a sweat heavy as blood. She ran her fingers along his bare arm and then his chest, the wetness there cold and thickening.

She withdrew her hand and he began to stir. He shouted the same strange sound and threw his elbow again, but Luella moved away far enough so that it missed her. She shook him but he did not wake. She switched on the lamp beside the bed and the light showed Jake's hair matted dark against his forehead and scalp. She slapped him on the side of the face and his eyes opened. He stiffened, sat straight up and glared at her. She saw that he wasn't angry, but afraid.

"Jake, what?" Jake not replying but continuing his stare.

Luella afraid and "Jake! Wake up!" She woke him by slapping his face again.

"What's going on?" he asked.

"You tell me. You cracked me in the ribs, woke me up. Look at you, you're drenched." Jake felt the skin on his face and arms, looked at them as if they weren't his.

"Christ," he muttered.

"Were you dreaming?"

Jake remembering and "Yes."

"What about?" She was fairly certain she knew, but she wanted him to say it.

Jake silent for several seconds and "You don't want to know."

"Yes, I do."

"Then *I* don't want to know."

"Jake."

But he remembered writing of what he had been dreaming for years, dreaming of what he had written—Jane on the stone slab, her missing arm and leg, the man beyond her on the other table. He lay back, curled fetally around his pillow, waited afraid until the two of them faded from his mind. Luella watched, built a wall of two pillows between them because she remembered what she had read in his notebook and *if that's what he dreams God help him.*

The next week Jake took the bus alone, rented a one-bedroom corner apartment in a decaying brick building not far from Gippart's office; from one window he could see part of the IncAmPride building. He bought another notebook, made sketches and diagrams in it as if he were going to break in. He listed phone numbers and the times when he saw Gippart entering or exiting the building. He tried to remember the details of cases he had handled involving insurance companies and believed he would find a way to get at Gippart, who had begun to take the place in Jake's mind formerly occupied by Mr. Jenson and his DeSoto. He began to jot down the details of a plan.

■

Luella almost two weeks without the metal in her leg bed-warmed by Jake's flesh, lonely in a way she had never been. She marveled at how quickly they had grown close, so imperceptibly she'd hardly noticed. But apart from him now *I miss him* and she felt as indecisive as she accused him of being always, knew that in St. Paul he was doing nothing but assuming the routine he had filled in Jamestown, only he had no work.

One evening her daughter found her merely moving her food in circular patterns on her plate and "Jesus, you're like a teenager," Luella staring and not replying.

Sara louder and "I said Jesus, you're like a teenager," this time Luella starting and looking up.

"In what way?"

"You're pouting like somebody asked for his letter sweater back, or whatever you exchanged in those ancient times," Luella thinking of a boy and a backseat and homework unfinished; his hands became Jake's and she was suddenly desperate for his rough-skinned fingers.

After some minutes Sara nearly worried and "Mom?"

"What?" Luella looking across the table with eyes sadder than Sara had ever seen them.

"Why don't you go find him?"

"He wouldn't like that."

"What people like or don't like doesn't usually make up your mind," Luella laughing briefly and "True."

"Go. I'm sick of this hurt sheepdog look. God."

"I don't know where he is."

"Look."

"How?"

"How did he find that guy he was looking for?"

"Private detective."

Sara sarcastic in the way of her mother and "Well, duh, I wonder how I'd find Jake? Oh, maybe I'd go find the same detective."

"What about the store?"

"I could handle it."

"No."

"Yes," Luella silent thinking *I'm sick of work anyway.*

Sara again, more insistent and "Go."

Luella surprising her and "All right."

■

Jake entered an office building opposite IncAmPride and alone rode one of three elevators ten floors to the top. In his previous walking along the streets around his apartment and IncAmPride he had seen people leaning against a rail high up on this other building, peering down at the street below or gazing outward.

The elevator door slid open on a cafeteria, occupied by only a few scattered people in the early afternoon between lunch and coffee breaks. Jake stood a moment looking around, finally spotting a glass door that led to an observation deck that circled the building on three sides. White metal chairs and tables stood along two of these sides, Jake guessing that in milder weather people took their lunches or coffee there, though now small patches of autumn ice spotted the concrete floor and the furniture.

The door strained against a wind he had not felt on the street below, and after it had closed he stood in an icy barrenness. He stepped to the edge, where a concrete wall three feet high stopped him. Twelve inches above this foot-thick wall ran the stanchioned gray rail, supported every eight feet or so by bolted metal supports. He gripped the rail with both hands to steady himself against the cold wind and stared down at IncAmPride, whose building seemed small now from this new vantage.

The longer he stared the farther he leaned his body over the rail, it pressing into the bottom of his ribs. The height made him feel powerful and good, but suddenly, Jane's image came from the dream. It seemed to push him even farther over the rail. Her voice seemed to want him to fly out into the air and he heard, or thought he heard, "What's the point, you bastard, if what little will you had lies ten years back? You can't, or won't, do anything. Why stand here helpless? At least will yourself a little more over the rail and allow gravity to take you." Her sound took his will, and Jake looked straight down, picking out a space on the narrow sidewalk below where he believed he might land. Decorative iron grates filled some of the concrete squares, and he believed he would fall on one if he moved just a little to his left, which he then did, hardly lifting his feet.

He leaned to an angle more acute and loosened his grip on the rail. He felt his upper body levering his feet from the concrete. He focused on the metal grate, but somehow, in his mind, Luella's voice supplanted Jane's and he stopped.

On the sidewalk below he found the grate he had contemplated, imagined himself covering it pulped and bloodied, ashamed that he had not the strength yet to reject the image. Shaken he walked slowly home, where she saved him again: in the hallway he found Luella leaning against his door with several suitcases stacked beside her. "Those private detectives *are* good, aren't they?"

■

Luella left Jake sleeping and walked through a biting breeze three blocks to IncAmPride, the pain in her leg causing her to mumble "cabs are good." The distance seemed like a mile in the cold. During the three days since her coming they had talked without determining any sort of plan. She had always been better at solving tangible problems, those she could *see*, so she had decided without telling Jake to visit Gippart's office. She had not been able to comprehend his lethargy when he told her he had not even been inside IncAmPride. As she approached the tall building, its bright blue neon proclaiming itself against a cloudy sky, she saw two parking ramps close enough to warrant driving next time. At the entrance to the building she paused, inhaled deeply and tried to keep her breathing regular as she passed through the revolving metal door thinking *Lamaze* and smiling; looking back briefly, she saw again that actual childbirth, which had seemed then so excruciating, had been the easy part. Luella noted gleaming brass frames on the turning door, brightly polished green-tinted glass. Inside she found herself on a well-swept granite surface with long maroon carpet runners unmarked by dirt. She checked her watch and found it was just past eight-thirty, for no reason matched her watch-time with that on an ornate clock high on a wall. It had taken her just over fifteen minutes to reach the place where Dan Gippart worked.

She found an open-spaced reception area thick with large padded chairs and sofas similar to those found in emergency rooms. Two people sat waiting, reading newspapers. Along one wall was an opening filled by a counter, again, she thought, much like those she'd seen in hospitals or courthouses. She went to the counter and within seconds a chirpy young woman in a crisp blue suit greeted her, asked if she could be of help, Luella thinking *you could start by not looking quite so perky and cute and efficient on such a damn cold early morning.*

"Could you tell me where I can find Mr. Gippart's office?"

"Certainly, ma'am," Luella thinking *I'm a ma'am now. A partially disabled ma'am.* In her store she felt secure, but out of Jamestown, in this dark-autumned sprawling city, she felt uncertain, somehow less of a person for not being a sturdy blond-haired Scandinavian with staunch, well-formed limbs and teeth

and just the right amount of make-up. The young woman point-
ing and "Take the elevator there to the fifth floor and go left.
You'll see a sign that says 'Claims.' Mr. Gippart's secretary is
Sheila. Ask for her."

"Thanks."

"You're so welcome," Luella thinking *Jesus* and remembering
all the times she had wanted to be just like that young woman.
She did as the woman had instructed and within minutes stood
at the door of Sheila's office humming the sanitized tune from
the elevator's crisp speakers. She took another heavy breath and
stepped inside. Sheila glanced up from her computer touchpad.
"Can I help you?" She was seldom surprised by walk-ins; people who desired to speak with her boss seemed always to call
ahead for an appointment.

"Yes. Is Mr. Olson in?"

"Mr. Olson?"

"Yes."

"I'm afraid you're in the wrong spot. This is Mr. Gippart's
office."

Luella tried to sound confused, knew what Jake would say
about that. "Oh? I was told downstairs to come to the fourth
floor and I'd find him."

"This is the *fifth* floor," Luella noticing the backs of two picture frames hinged together and guessing at least one child. She
checked Sheila's left hand and saw no ring.

Luella smiling and "Oh brother. I knew having teenagers
would be hard, but I didn't know it would wreck my brain."

"If I remember honestly how I behaved at that age, and how
it affected my parents, I'd guess it most definitely will," Sheila
said, returning Luella's smile.

"Five comes after four, right?"

"Yes," then laughing and "I think."

"You have kids?"

"Two. Girls. Ten and twelve," Luella thinking *single*.

Luella trying to put Sheila at ease, lying and "Mine are four-teen, sixteen, eighteen. All girls too."

"If they're like mine you're lucky you can still speak." They laughed.

"Well, at least my boss is nice."

"So is mine," Sheila moving her eyes in a sarcastic roll.

Luella exploring and "Just you in the office here?"

"Yes."

"And you have to do *everything*? Miss all-around?"

Sheila sighing and "Mail, filing, correspondence. You name it. Woman's work."

Luella turning, "I'm sorry to have bothered you."

"That's all right," Luella sensing *maybe a way in, maybe Sheila.*

■

Gippart smiling, emerging from his office and tossing a magazine five feet across to the top of Sheila's hands as she typed, startling her, Sheila turning wordless, Gippart enjoying it and asking "Have you seen this issue?"

Sheila pushed the thick magazine from her keyboard and it fell to the floor cover up. From the floor large tan breasts tried to spill out of a low blue dress. "I don't read *Cosmopolitan* very often," she said.

"You kid me," Gippart said, not bending to retrieve the magazine. "An attractive woman like yourself?" Sheila again not responding, her fear running faster and ahead of her anger and something inside her again affirming the prudence of such an order.

"There's a great article about hemlines," he said. "How they're going up. Way up," Gippart raising his flattened hands slowly from his waist to above his head. She felt him grin though she did not look at him. She clenched her thighs reflexively together as Gippart bent past her, pawed up the magazine and opened it to the article he had mentioned. With a rigid finger he began to point to the photographs.

■

For several minutes Sheila had listened to Lorna talk loudly about her oldest boy, who had called the previous night to tell his parents he was getting divorced, Lorna telling them "A three-time loser now." On each occasion it had been her son who had filed. Lorna seemed more amused than upset. Sheila remembered tirades against her own daughters and hoped that one day she could, in response to Jasmine and Caitlin, achieve the bemused resignation that Lorna possessed. Sheila waited for Lorna to finish so that she might spill her anger about Gippart and his *Cosmopolitan*. She did not see Luella and Jake pass behind her and position themselves at a table close to her back. They faced at an angle away from her, though Luella felt certain Sheila would not remember her from their brief encounter in the office. Finally Lorna finished and Sheila told them of her anger.

"Did he touch you this time?" Darla asked.

"No."

"What then? You're pissed girl."

Sheila, angry, drew a long swallow from her rum drink and "I've been wearing long skirts and dresses like you suggested. He comes out this afternoon like a goddamn skunk out of its hole and tosses a *Cosmopolitan* on my desk. On top of my keyboard. Boobs hanging out from the cover," her hands gesturing out from her own breasts. "Fu—screwed up the letter he'd asked me to get done quickly."

"You may swear, dear," Lorna told her.

"Then he says 'you ought to read that article on hemlines.' He tells me that according to the latest trend, they're going up. Heavy emphasis on *up* like maybe I ought to pull my dress over my head right there. Of course by then I was so hot for him that I stood, bent over the desk and begged for it."

"He's a pig," Darla said, Cindy following with "he's a man, what else can he think about? They measure everything by those puny little flesh things dangling from their crotches."

"Don't excuse him," Darla told her.

"It's no excuse, just the truth."

"How did you respond?"

Sheila now near tears, again angrier with herself than with Gippart and "Not a goddamn thing. In fact—you'll love this—I told him I'd read it. My God."

"That's putting your foot down," Cindy said.

"I just don't know what to do, exactly. Kick him in the balls?" still not telling them that it wasn't anger but fear, something so fundamental it lay beyond words and could not nor need not be articulated; it came inside her with the air whenever she saw or heard him, even now when she spoke of him. That he no longer had to be close for it to happen, that she would probably quit soon even if he never said another word to her.

"Foot nicely flattening out the testicles works for me," Lorna said, then Darla and "Tell him quite calmly that the fashion sense of a professional woman leans toward the conservative, the comfortable. Tell him you use your legs to move around, not to enhance the visual ambience of his working environment." But she had known the confusion and the fear and "Tell him to fuck off, I don't know."

Sheila still shaking and "It just isn't easy when it's your job."

"Speak up before you quit," Cindy said. "Don't you let him run you off like some stray he might cut from the herd," Sheila knowing she could not wait too much longer and knowing as well that if anyone would ever ask her exactly what he had done to frighten her, she would not be able to tell them anything that out of context would seem important.

They talked on in the crowded pub and when time came to find and watch over children and men Sheila told them their drinks were on her because their support gave her hope, though it wasn't true, a thousand like them were nothing against him, thinking *I want to tell you how afraid of him I am, but I could not explain. Fear like a stench no one can smell in the room. Fear like something you breathe and your blood soaks up.* The others walked ahead, Sheila lingering in a line waiting to pay whatever reckoning had been assigned.

Luella and Jake remained, discussing the conversation they had overheard.

■

The president of IncAmPride lifted the phone from his desk, mildly annoyed at the mid-morning intrusion but pleasantly "This is J. William Lofton. How may I help you?"

The voice from the receiver was clear and loud. "Good morning, Mr. Lofton. My name is James Bense, Vice President of Operations at Great Lakes Property and Casualty in Chicago." Lofton recognized the name of one of his firm's competitors.

"Good morning, Mr. Bense."

"I'm calling to tell you about a matter that has come up in our company, one that may—I don't know for sure—affect IncAmPride as well." Bense hesitated, as if unsure about how to proceed.

"Go on," Lofton prompted.

"I'll try to make a long story short. A few months ago one of our agents out in South Dakota called about something that was bothering him. He had received a call from one of his insured's, a Betty Klemke, who asked some questions about a car accident that happened ten years or so ago. The agent looked into the file, and how the claim was handled, and came up with some irregularities."

Since J. William Lofton didn't like them, he asked, "What kind of irregularities."

"Let me get to that in a moment. Anyway, the agent notified our regional office in Denver, and they felt the allegations were important enough to notify the home office. They did so, and we've had an investigator look into it. The long and short of it is this: it seems our company paid out a quarter of a million dollars that it didn't owe."

This information gathered Lofton's full attention and "How so?"

"We've discovered that the other company involved, Sun State, also settled the claim. It appears both companies' files indicate their insureds were at fault."

"Sometimes those involved in accidents are equally at fault."

"Certainly, but when that's the case, you don't pay anything to the other party. In this matter, my company paid the policy limits and Sun State paid $75,000. Each file has a signed release. Something's obviously amiss. We paid out money to a Jacob Warner, but he obviously didn't get any quarter of a million. He works in a body shop in Jamestown, North Dakota, and lives in a cheap apartment."

"How does this affect IncAmPride?"

"The adjuster who handled that claim for Sun State ten years ago, who may or may not be involved in any wrongdoing, works for you."

"In what capacity?"

"I'm not sure, but his name is Dan Gippart. I notified Sun State, and they are conducting their own investigation. The adjuster who represented us was John Gamble."

"And what does he have to say?"

"We have no idea. He quit us a couple of years later, and we can't find him now."

"Can't find him?"

"He seems to have, well, vanished."

"What would you have me do?"

"It certainly isn't my place to tell you that. I'm simply calling to alert you that I believe our investigation, when complete, will show that one or both of the adjusters involved were guilty of some wrongdoing. I don't feel entirely comfortable saying that Dan Gippart isn't to be trusted, but you might want to check him out."

Lofton hesitated, then, "Yes, indeed, I might want to do that. I thank you for your call."

"You're welcome."

■

Tammy Chorske alone in her red car with her gum and music hurtling south on Interstate 494 late in the Friday afternoon traffic, the low sky gray and filling with an intermittent mist. She had been an hour at the Ridgedale Mall, the fourth such place she had shopped, caught up in thick day-after-Thanksgiving crowds which jostled from her whatever sense of time she had previously possessed. She had a date with her latest boyfriend at 6:30 and as she drove, fifteen miles or more from home, her dashboard clock glowed a green and malevolent 5:30, Tammy thinking that she would need at least an hour to prepare for a first date. She patted the box beside her in the other bucket seat, considered the dress inside it and what Tim would think when he saw it sheathing her, proud of herself and filled with self-esteem for shopping until finding the exact right thing. She remembered standing before the mirror at the store, that she had looked damn good, husbands of older women and the women themselves staring.

The blur of cars and pickups and semis flowed south, brisk but not heavy, a mile or so yet before the highway swung east toward Bloomington and Eagan. She swerved the Pontiac in and out of the two lanes, passing when she could. The darkness thickened.

Dr. Jack and Maureen Scott rode patiently with the traffic north along 35E. Jack kept their Mercedes sedan back from the car in front. This Thanksgiving was the first they had spent in the Twin Cities, having moved north from Dallas after Jack's appointment to Pediatrics at a Minneapolis hospital. He had worked almost non-stop since late August, but this long holiday weekend he had arranged to be off, not even on call. They had slept late that morning, then driven out into the sunlight that earlier in the day had brightened the fading yellow and orange November, acclimating themselves to the cold late autumn of Minnesota and telling themselves maybe it wouldn't get much colder than this. They had seen signs for the zoo, had spent a few hours wandering there impressed but had tired of the crowds and left. They took Cedar north to 35E. Unharried for once by duty or time, they decided to drive home, eat something simple and relax in front of the television.

Ahead of Tammy the traffic condensed with the darkness. Someone's horn rousted her from thoughts of the coming night and she at last acknowledged the darkness by pulling on her lights. The right-lane traffic moved bumper-to-bumper well in excess of the fifty-five limit. Now and then a space opened in the left lane and Tammy, without checking her mirror, jerked the Pontiac into it. Then back into the right in anxious weaving. Harder to see in the heavying mist and dark.

Jack Scott realized the Mercedes needed gas, steered off 35E onto Yankee Doodle Road where he turned left and crossed back over 35E, then left on Pilot Knob toward a Holiday station. There were a number of cars at the various islands but he was in no hurry and decided to wait. He smiled at Maureen and touched her leg again.

Tammy Chorske decided to go south on Pilot Knob into Eagan.

Jack Scott finally got a turn at the pumps, then waited to pay. Verifying his credit card took a long time, the attendant telling him it had been like that the whole day because, as everyone knew, the Friday after Thanksgiving was the busiest shopping day of the year. Then Dr. Scott joined the long lines of animated metal slithering east along Yankee Doodle Road. He came to the stoplight at Pilot Knob, waited, and when the light turned green he, trusting as any child he had attended, pressed the accelerator and moved the Mercedes forward.

Tammy, flying south on Pilot Knob and mindful of Tim, never saw the red lenses glaring above the road, may not have known even that it was an intersection she approached. She sailed innocently along the dark concrete, right hand beating against her thigh in time with her never-ending music. Jack Scott turned his eyes through his door's window to face headlights fatally intent on him, like the eyes of some big cat come surprising. The Pontiac's front caught the Scotts' Mercedes exactly between the wheels, centered its pointed grille at the other car's doorpost, just beyond which was Jack Scott's shoulder and head. The Mercedes compressed and folded like a boxer taking an unseen body blow and Jack Scott made a sound similar to that boxer's as his last verbal offering to the world. Tammy, stunned even further as the airbag that would save her filled itself, pressed inexplicably further on the accelerator rather than on the brake, drove the pinioned Mercedes across the intersection into the front of a north-bound car waiting, drove those two backward into another and yet another before halting.

Maureen Scott for several seconds blank but then aware of the door on her side pressing tight against her and forcing her shoulder up beside her head though nothing on her body gave her pain. Her ears ringing from the quick passage of sounds like no other in the world and her veins alternately distending and shrinking at the direction of a heart seized with terror. Against her other side her husband conforming his flesh to hers, perfectly in his seat as they had been moments before only the car now half as wide as then. Her face pressed tight to his, dear lovers skin to skin as if the something that had accomplished this was now laughing as it watched them paired almost dance-like amid the music of hissing fluids and glass fragments running along the highway or floating from the sky, laughing at her pinned to what she loved most and her feeling no pain at all and then, in him, no pulse. Having to wait an hour there coupled macabre as he cooled beside her before hydraulic-driven metal pried loose their living and dead flesh, ashamed at her salvation, astonished and then angered beyond any measurable degree by such a random act of sundering and the truth that the most awful thing imaginable had truly happened. Too old ever to unbelieve it.

■

They understood that alone they were nearly helpless, that they needed help, decided to chance seeking it from Sheila. Luella had heard hints of Sheila's anger at Gippart when they had spoken in Sheila's office, then they had witnessed it far stronger at the bar. They remained hesitant because they did not know her, feared she might turn them down and go to the police. But they knew none of IncAmPride's adjusters, saw no way to get close to one. They felt certain the adjusters hated Gippart as much as anyone, but Sheila was closer to Gippart, could maybe control whatever needed controlling. Friday after work Luella waited for her to spill from IncAmPride's cold stone, as she stood in the windy chill Luella thankful for small cities like Jamestown and her own business. She did not care for St. Paul, its impersonal, tall, dark and wide buildings. Not even the bright planes of shiny glass seemed inviting. And it pleased her when she fully understood that no Gippart required her obeisance, that she knelt before no boss other than her customers.

As Luella's near homesickness occupied her, she nearly missed Sheila spinning from the revolving door and walking quickly past. Luella fell in a step behind her but after a few paces knew she could not catch up and "Sheila, wait," the latter stopping and turning.

Luella saw that Sheila did not recognize her and "I'm sure you don't remember me. I came into your office by accident a couple of weeks ago, looking for Mr. Olson?"

Sheila stared a second then "Oh, sure. I remember," her look questioning, uncertain.

"I apologize for stopping you like this, but I wonder if I could speak with you for a few minutes."

Sheila hesitant and "Well . . . what about?" having heard in Luella's tone something akin to that used by soap or plastic container salesmen.

"Your boss, Dan Gippart. I know some things about him *you* ought to know," Sheila naturally apprehensive but drawn to the words and "I have a few minutes, but then I do need to get home."

They sat in a small coffee shop across from the parking ramp. Luella had led Sheila inside to a round table in the corner where Jake sat. Everything was white tile and enamel, only the floor marred by dirt and sand carried in on snow. They were the only customers.

Luella nodding toward Jake and "This is my friend Jake Warner."

Sheila watched him warily, as they had expected, Jake smiling and "Hi, Sheila."

She managed a timid "Hi" in return.

"Why don't you get us some coffee, Jake?" Jake rising quickly from his chair as if nervous and "Sure."

Luella turning to Sheila and "I know this seems a little mysterious, so let me explain. Jake used to live, years ago, in Mitchell, South Dakota. Dan Gippart worked as a claims adjuster for a small company—Sun State—in Sioux Falls, which is about an hour east of Mitchell." Sheila sat listening, as if still waiting to be asked to buy something. Luella going on and

"Jake's wife had a car accident south of Mitchell. She and two other people were killed," Sheila remembering her husband and his motorcycle.

Jake returned with and distributed three white mugs, stirred clumpy sugar into his and pushed the small tray that held the sweeteners and cream toward the two women, who sat closer together and almost across from him. Only Sheila took cream. Jake remained silent as Luella finished telling of the accident and the phony investigation, the misdirected settlement. Luella went on about Jake, who he had been and the way he had lived. Finally, looking at the table and fingering his cup, he said, "It's important to me to do something about what Gippart did. We're wondering if you could help us."

Sheila had sat impassive as they spoke. She looked now from Luella to Jake, then back and "Help you in what way?" thinking that she wasn't exactly sure what these people wanted.

"I want the money that I should have gotten ten years ago, and I want the people who Dan Gippart works for to know what he did."

Sheila thinking that she didn't want any part of such a thing and "Tell them."

"Would they believe me? I've no proof. Would anyone take the time to investigate something that happened so long ago? And Gippart must have most everybody fooled. It looks like he's doing all right," Sheila "yes" in agreement.

Jake going on, "And the money wouldn't be coming directly to me. Besides, I don't want to do any of this publicly. Gippart scares me."

Sheila nodding but "Get a lawyer. Everybody else does."

Luella answering and "We just don't think we could prove anything," Jake adding something about the statute of limitations.

Sheila wanting to leave and "I just don't know how I could help you, that's all. And how do I know you're not company investigators? I've heard rumors that IncAmPride does that sometimes."

Jake pulling his wallet from his pocket and "Here's my driver's license. Gives my address. That's who I am," Sheila taking
it and matching the dark photograph to the man across from
her. Then Jake holding his hands out in front of her and "I fix
cars for a living." Sheila saw flecks of paint on his skin, the
knuckles scraped in places.

Jake slightly pleading and "We're just people who need help,
Sheila, just a couple of little things."

She had the feeling she ought to believe him, but she glanced
at her watch and "I'm late. My daughters will worry."

Luella with a last urging and "Consider it, Sheila. And this.
Whatever we'd get, you'd get a third. We split it three ways,"
but Sheila silent as she left.

She drove through the dark thinking of how the man she had
married had missed a curve one day and then lay silent for a
month in a coma. How every month the hospital sent her a bill
for one hundred and thirty thousand dollars, the amount over
that which Orie's insurance had been responsible for and which
diminished only minutely each time she put a check in the envelope they so kindly included. She mailed a small amount, as
much as she could afford, the tenth day of every month, each
time remembering her calculation that such an amount would
eventually eradicate the bill sometime after the middle of the
next century. The calculations defeated her, made her life seem
worthless. And made her angry, thinking about savings and loan
presidents who had stolen millions and didn't have to pay a
dime. She didn't know how she could help, but she didn't put
them out of her mind.

■

Two mornings later Jake decided he didn't want to sit idle in the
apartment any longer. He picked up the phone and began to dial
Sheila's number, then realized that he had better not call her at
the office. He waited until after supper, then phoned. He sensed

her continuing reluctance, but, after telling her that he didn't want to pressure her, he asked her one thing: "If a claim comes in where IncAmPride's liability is large and clear, please let me know. I think I could make you a lot of money."

Sheila made no commitment.

■

She kept thinking of the price of getting caught, but also of possessing enough cash to climb free of debt. She thought that if she went to jail she could lose her daughters, weighing their loss against the unending stack of bills on her kitchen table, against Gippart laughing. Of course Jasmine and Caitlin won, but Sheila felt so good when she imagined Gippart and said out loud, "laugh at this you bastard."

Daily she attended carefully to the loss notices, the most recent disasters and heartaches fallen to those for whom her heart had never ached. She promised that if she agreed to do what Jake asked, no one who had suffered already could suffer more by what she did. She would not agree to that.

She found herself coming, one morning, halfway through the latest stack, to "Policyholder—William Chorske. Liability Auto." Reading through what little there was in the file and sitting, pondering, after thirty minutes calling Jake from her phone, explaining: "Our insured's daughter drove through a red light and killed a doctor. He was young, mid-forties, lots of earning potential. There'll be a big check on this one." Sheila thought about some of the checks she had seen pass across her desk, her breath short as she considered what even a third of such sums could do for her. "Our liability seems clear. Claimant had a wife, no children, from what's already in the file they haven't lived here that long so they wouldn't know that many people," Jake thinking of the wife and how he would have to lie to a woman grieving.

Jake said, "Do one thing. Change the phone number on the

loss form. Instead of Maureen Scott's, put ours. From then on you're out of it. Your adjuster will call Luella, who becomes Mrs. Scott. Luella settles quickly, signs a release, gets the money and disappears."

Sheila uncertain and "It can't be that simple, can it?"

"It could be if we're convincing. I become the IncAmPride adjuster and deal with the real Mrs. Scott. Whatever Luella will need to document her claim can be had from her. It'll all blow up eventually, but by then we'll be gone. No one will ever know what you did."

Sheila hesitating and "I'll look at the file a while longer, see if there's anything I've missed. I'll call you after lunch and let you know, give you Maureen Scott's number if it's a go. But I . . . I don't know." Then she put the phone back in the cradle on her desk and *my God*.

The new files done except for Chorske's, Sheila vacillating. But she saw the years stretching ahead of her and pulled a new loss notice from her drawer thinking *I should wear gloves* but then *I would handle it anyway* and watching her hands quiver. She waited until noon when none of the secretaries were in the claim clerical area beyond her office and sat at JoAnn's desk and typed it out and in the box for the claimant's phone number she typed Jake's and then she put the loss form in the middle of the eleven new losses and set them on Gippart's desk. She called Jake and Luella and told them. She prayed.

■

They began it that same day, Jake inhaling the air of a different and temporary life, then dialing and listening anxious to three rings spaced out interminable, beginning to move the phone from his ear, still wondering if he should be using the apartment phone or some other. But then the line opened, a woman's voice, "Yes?"

Jake recalling his old voice and "May I speak with Mrs. Scott, please?"

"This is Mrs. Scott," Jake thinking *I didn't expect so young, a girl's voice.*

Jake using the name Luella had seen on the IncAmPride Claim Department roster and "Mrs. Scott, my name is Brian Meiners. I'm calling to—"

"I'm really not in the mood for a sales pitch," the voice getting older as its words unfolded.

"Oh no, it's not that. I'm with Incorporated American Pride," Jake pausing, then "the automobile liability insurance carriers for the Chorske's, whose daughter was involved in an accident with you and your husband," Jake feeling the connection turn cold and realizing what all such callers must come to know that *I might as well be Tammy. The blame will come to me. I remember that.*

"Yes, I guess you could say she was 'involved,' but I'd call it something else."

"I deeply regret having to contact you under such circumstances, but it is my obligation to identify myself and my company, to inform you that we are handling the matter. I am calling at the request of my immediate superior, Dan Gippart."

Silence.

"The only other thing I wish to do at this time is to convey my deepest sympathies to you. I lost someone in a similar fashion, so I do know at least some measure of the grief you must be experiencing. I am deeply and truly sorry," that not a lie and Maureen Scott hearing that it wasn't and responding "Thank you," Jake thinking *were you listening to him there just before he died? I wasn't.*

"Please let me give you my name and phone number, so when you feel ready to deal with the insurance matters regarding this loss you can call me."

"I appreciate that but you'll need to speak with my attorney. She'll be handling everything."

"I will be most happy to do that. Could you give me her name and number?"

"Susan Burns, with Farnham and Smith. Her number is 293-0532."

"Mrs. Scott, thank you for hearing me out. I will contact Ms. Burns immediately and this matter will be my top priority until it is resolved. I wouldn't think we'd need to prolong this affair, because the liability is clear and it will require only our determination of satisfactory compensation for your loss," Jake thinking *ten years ago someone should have called me, someone should have said I'm sorry.* Then shivering at what he had told her and "Not that any amount of money could be satisfactory, could take the place of a loved one. I am so sorry."

Maureen Scott had known someone would call her, sometime, and that whoever did would be the one she would hate, but Jake's words came honestly to her and she felt little anger. Still, it was all better left to Susan Burns. Maureen Scott wasn't going to need IncAmPride's money, but she wanted someone to have to pay something. Jack's life had been insured for a million dollars, and that money was already on the way. She hoped that at some future time she could forgive Tammy Chorske because she did not wish to go on hating *that stupid goddamn girl.* She wanted sometime to look at teenage girls and not hate them for all their shallow heavy murderous ignorance.

"Your words are much appreciated, but I must ask you to direct all further communication to Susan."

"I will, and if we ever meet I hope it will be under more favorable circumstances" but knowing *you and I now, we could never speak, we could never be anything but widow and killer surrogate, metal having rent the bond between you and me, too.*

He had expected it, prepared for it, but could not reconcile himself to it. He had relearned in a few minutes the nature of a profession he could scarcely believe he had once given himself to wholly but unthinking. How awful it seemed from his present distance—you got involved after loss and loss only and never with a way to help other than with money. After a smashing, money, and even when the people you represented were willing to give the money none of the injured cared for you. He had expected Susan Burns to be difficult, but when she met that expectation he did not like it. He had called and she wasn't available but he left his number after explaining who he was and in thirty minutes she had called back.

The first thing she said was "Brian Meiners, this is going to cost you a lot of money," as if it were *his* wallet fat and responsible.

"I know."

"Dr. Jack Scott was a young man, a brilliant young doctor, would have earned a lot of money in the twenty, twenty-five years he would have worked had not that stupid little ditz of yours killed him," Jake thinking *not mine*.

"I know," Jake said again.

Susan Burns surprised and "You sick today? Usually the insurance people I deal with are a bit more obnoxious. You sound somewhat reasonable. Did I get a wrong number?" Jake thinking *and this is the first time we've spoken.*

"You will find me reasonable," lying and his thinking turning suddenly and *that could have been me in her office. Jake the lawyer taking a call from Maureen Scott and doing the math and figuring a third for me.*

Jake remembering what Sheila had said about consummating the claim quickly and "This shouldn't take us long. Let's figure what he was worth, get it done. Liability's clear. I merely require documentation. Be fair and you won't find me difficult."

"Did you just say the liability's clear? Jesus, where have you been all my life?" Jake thinking *bolting on bumpers,* then Susan Burns asking "What are your limits?" Jake not understanding.

"I'm sorry?"

"I asked what your limits were," Jake comprehending that she wanted the limit of the liability coverage but not having the papers before him, telling her, "Excuse me this one time, but I can't seem to locate the file. I'll have to find it, get back to you."

"You mean you'd tell me?"

"I'm not sure what you mean."

"You'd tell me your policy limits?"

Jake remembering that such divulgence was unheard of back when he had dealt with insurance policies but "Sure, why not?"

"Because I might want all of it."

Jake not wanting to sound too soft and "What you want and what I'll give might not be the same."

"Of course not, but you're the first claims person who's ever said he'd tell me the limits," Jake thinking *to be the old way, a litigator* as if hearing the word for the first time. Then "Well, I can be difficult when the situation demands it, but I see no need here. Maybe that will change. You never know."

"I'll need some time to put our figure together. I'll call you. We'll meet."

Jake lying and "I look forward to it."

Luella expecting it too, though her part required orneriness, difficulty. She discovered she liked it. She had told Jake "I always wanted to be someone other than who I am. Still do," Jake telling her "I wish you were someone else too" in the kind of acknowledging sarcasm their talk had fallen into and then his hands as well denying that he had meant what he had said. They were both in the apartment when Brian Meiners called, Jake leaning his head against hers, listening.

"Is Maureen Scott there?" Luella thinking as Jake had of Maureen Scott that this sounded like a child maybe not even out of high school.

"This is Maureen Scott" Luella told him.

"Mrs. Scott, my name is Brian Meiners, representing IncAmPride, the insurance carriers for the Chorskes."

"About damn time you called," Luella surprised at the intensity of her response which seemed a thing separate from herself.

"I was just assigned this matter today, ma'am," Luella wincing at the word and Jake not caring for Meiners' defensiveness, then Luella with "I would expect when one of your people murders someone you might want to get at it a little quicker. Be the way I'd do it."

Meiners insincere and "I'm sure it is, and I'm sorry for any delay."

"What exactly do you need from me? Pretty damn clear what happened," Jake not expecting Meiners to admit to that as he had done with Susan Burns.

"Well, we're still investigating what happened."

"*Investigating?!*" Jake considering Luella's tone of indignation just right and *she might be damn good at this.*

"I have to know exactly what happened to determine the extent of our liability."

"I can save you a lot of time, then."

"How so?"

"By telling you your liability is one hundred goddamn percent is how so. You ought to know that by now."

"I understand you're upset Mrs. Scott, and have every right to be. I just need to do my job. Do you have a lawyer?"

"What the hell would I need a lawyer for? I've done nothing wrong," Meiners considering the kind of speech he had in just a few years heard far too much of and "I merely thought you might wish to have someone with experience in these matters look out for your interests."

"I think you'll find that I can look after my own interests pretty well, thank you."

"I wasn't implying that you couldn't. But this is a difficult period for you, and you might want to seek the advice of a lawyer, let whoever you choose handle the negotiations."

"I'll consider it. Sorry if I've come on too strong," Luella sniffling into the phone and "it's just that he . . . Jack was the love of my life and now he's gone," Jake thinking *those soap operas*

she's watching and putting his hands out, palm down, trying to
indicate that she should not overact.

Luella nodding and "Anyway, this is not something I wish to
drag out endlessly. I'll probably be returning to Dallas soon. So
let's get this annoyance over with. Do your investigating or
whatever you have to do, but I want to get a settlement as soon
as possible."

"I understand."

"I'm giving you a way to make this easy, so don't screw with
me. Then I *will* get a lawyer."

"I'll get back to you as soon as I can."

After Meiners hung up Jake thinking *he never said he was
sorry. Wouldn't you be sorry that someone died, wouldn't you
say it?* Then *I wonder if I ever did.*

Later Jake beginning to believe that *this might work* and "You
play the aggrieved widow pretty damn well."

"As soon as I realized I was talking to a claims rep, the old
anger came back. Surprised me."

"What old anger?"

"They treated me like shit when I got hurt."

"Who?"

"Anybody that had anything to do with Dad's car. The dealership in Jamestown that sold it to him, the guys from Detroit
who built it. While I was in the hospital a man who farms over
by Devil's Lake called me, told me the same thing had happened
to him with what he bet was the exact same kind of transmission. His was in a pickup. He was out checking some fields, left
the transmission in park and got out to open a gate. He turned
when he heard the truck coming, almost got out of the way but
not quite. It pushed him against the metal gate—one of those big
welded tube ones—which broke open. He held onto the gate as
it swung out of the way. Truck kept going across the field,
wound up in ditch a half mile away. Went through two barb-
wire fences and almost got onto a highway. He wasn't hurt too

bad, some cracked ribs and a big bruise on his thigh, but he told me the car company had had all sorts of problems with that transmission and I should check and see if one of them was in my dad's car. After I got out of the hospital I contacted the dealership and told them what had happened, asked about whether that sort of thing had happened before."

Jake chuckling and "Let me guess, they'd never heard of such a thing."

"Exactly. I talked to the service manager and then the dealership owner, Ralph Thompson. Dad had bought about twelve cars from him over the years. Had they handled my calls well, I wouldn't have pursued it. I was real pleasant about it at first, but they acted like I was some ditzy broad who'd had too much hospital time to think, no dishes or clothes to wash. The service manager started to explain to me what a transmission was, like I was a little girl, like maybe I really hadn't used it correctly, being a girl and all. Like I'd injured myself out of my own stupidity. Ralph was curt, like he had better things to attend to," Luella not exactly happy to be dredging up the unpleasantness.

But Jake wanting to hear it and "You didn't leave the matter there."

"Hell no. I talked to Jim Stevens—he does legal stuff for the store—and he made a couple of calls. He doesn't usually handle that kind of case, more tax and investment stuff. Two days later I get a call from some hotshot legal mind from Detroit, works for the car maker. What an asshole he was, probably like Gippart. No people skills whatever. He starts right in telling how hard it would be to prove my case, all the hoops I'd have to jump through. Didn't say 'sorry about your leg' or 'how you doing now?' Belligerent as hell, and I hadn't even asked him for anything.

"Well, Jim referred me to a lawyer in Fargo."

"Someone in Jamestown would have wanted it."

"Jim thought maybe it would be easier if I went out of town. Sort of like with malpractice, lawyers don't want to sue doctors in their own town. Probably Ralph knows every lawyer in Jamestown, and if the dealership got brought in, then it would be awkward. I could understand that," Jake nodding in agreement.

"We had Dad's car examined, jumped through all the hoops Mr. Shithead from Detroit warned me about, and in the end they cut me a pretty good check. But it was all so cold and impersonal. Nobody being just people. You don't forget that. Hell, still, today, whenever I drive by a dealership I think of Ralph and how he treated me. Haven't spoken to him since. Bastard. And when I see a dark red car I think of the one—the *defective* one—that injured me and then all the rest of it comes back and I get pissed off all over again. It's hard to put that stuff away," Jake thinking *tell me about it*. Luella finishing and "So, if those are the rules, get me a mitt and put me in. IncAmPride will find out this girl can play."

"Meiners, he doesn't know what he's getting into with you."

Luella contemplating what she had said and "It's so strange. *He* didn't hurt me. *He* didn't treat me badly. Yet all this I'm carrying gets transferred to him. It isn't fair. But that's what this arrogance and impersonality breeds. If people would just act like people," Jake nodding but *I think they do*.

"When you got hurt, did you see the car coming?"

"Yes. I had just raised the garage door and turned. Three feet away and moving fast. I never heard it, though."

"You couldn't get out of the way?"

"Oh sure, but I decided to stand there and let it smash me."

"Sorry. Stupid question," Jake thinking *I know what it is to see something big and heavy coming and the helplessness. I know.*

■

Brian Meiners knew he needed to meet with Dan Gippart to discuss the Chorske file requirements. Gippart watched closely all files—big or small—that were handled in their office, and he scrutinized and assented to payments on all losses over ten thousand dollars across the country. IncAmPride did business in all fifty states, the claims flung to every corner of the country as disaster had never known boundaries. But the majority of claims came from the five-state area where most of the company's business was written: the Dakotas, Minnesota, Iowa and Wisconsin. Adjusters handling large losses knew they had lines they could not cross over; they did the legwork, then Gippart handled the negotiations. Meiners could make no promises to Maureen Scott without Gippart's nod.

Meiners, as he waited in Sheila's office, had thought he heard Gippart and someone else speaking, but when he entered Gippart sat alone.

"You talked to Mrs. Scott already, I assume."

"Yes sir." The five adjusters in the office, even fifty-seven-year-old Jim Bauer, feared their superior in the way that Sheila did, knew that he liked being addressed as sir and never failed to apply it; they intuited that Gippart could make more than their business lives a living hell.

"How did she sound?" Meiners telling him "Bitchy."

"You think she'll stink up this thing?"

"At first I did, but then she backed off, sounded like she'd be relieved if we'd get it done quick. She's moving back to Dallas."

"She from there?"

"I assume."

"Don't assume shit, not with a file like this," Gippart considering and wondering how cheap he could buy a doctor. "Get a statement from sweet little Miss Tammy, interview the cops that responded, standard operating procedure. Looks as if we're screwed blue liability-wise, but get something from Tammy we might use to cut our losses."

"Like what?"

"How would I know? See what unfolds in the statement.

What appears to be one thing on the police report becomes something else entirely in person. See if you can chat with her tonight. I don't like being the last to hear," Meiners knowing he would have to drive out to Eagan before returning to White Bear Lake where he lived and that it would be a long night.

In the dining room were Brian Meiners, Tammy Chorske, and her parents, Bill and Rhonda. Meiners was angry because someone had died and all Bill Chorske could talk about was his car. "Can I go ahead and get another one?" he had asked just after Meiners had introduced himself and before they had walked inside.

"Get another what?" Meiners had asked though he knew what Chorske meant.

"Another car, for Chrissake."

"Sure you can," Meiners looking around the expensively furnished house. Chorske managed the actuarial department of the state's largest life insurance company.

"Good. You bring a check?"

"No."

"Why not?"

"I haven't even looked at the car yet," Meiners almost having forgot the smashed Pontiac under the burden of this and too many other files.

Chorske seeming almost proud and "Take my word for it, it's totaled."

"I'll look at it tomorrow, check the value."

"How is my wife supposed to get to work? Tammy to school?"

"I don't know. I'll leave those decisions up to you."

"You guys'll rent me a car right?" Meiner's nose caught a scent that suggested Chorske might recently have taken a drink. Then paging through the policy provisions and "you don't have that coverage."

"My agent told me I was covered for everything."

"You're not."

"Well, he told me that, so that's the way it's got to be."

"You'll need to see him about that."

Chorske sighing large and "So I'm stuck without a car."

"Looks that way," Meiners thinking *why don't you check with your daughter instead of me about your not having wheels?*

"What do you intend to do about it?"

"About what?"

"About me not having a car."

"I don't intend to do anything about it. I'm telling you that you don't have rental coverage. We'll pay you fair market value for your Pontiac, but it'll take a few days. You do what you think best."

Bill Chorske sulked through some further conversation about deductibles as they sat at the brightly polished dining room table, Tammy at one end wearing her cheerleader outfit, Meiners next to her along the tableside. Meiners from his briefcase extracted a small tape recorder and placed it next to the file which lay open before him. Before he could make certain it held a fresh tape Bill Chorske asked "What's that for?"

"I need a statement from Tammy."

"A statement regarding what?" Meiners thinking *the football team's chances this weekend, asshole, what do you think?* but "regarding the accident."

"Then we should have a lawyer."

"Why? I'm not accusing you of anything." Glancing at Tammy and "We play on the same team. I simply need to know what happened."

"Then just ask her. We don't need the tape."

"Company policy requires a statement."

"I don't think so."

"Look, Mr. Chorske, let's not make this any more difficult than it already is. Your policy requires you to cooperate with me in the investigation of any loss."

"We're cooperating, we're just not giving a statement," Meiners knowing that Gippart wouldn't accept not having a statement in the file, then deciding he'd join the crowd and be an asshole, too.

Meiners almost enjoying it with Chorske and "Then you're *not* cooperating, and I will so inform my boss and underwriting tomorrow. They'll be happy to consider your refusal, can add it to the fact that your teenage daughter just had a very serious accident that might cost my company hundreds of thousands of dollars. See what you can do about rustling up some insurance then, see what kind of rates you get quoted."

Chorske backed off, sat thinking, then "All right," Meiners putting a tape in the player and making sure it was rewound. He turned it on and waited five seconds, then "This is Brian Meiners speaking with Tammy Chorske at 7:15 p.m. on December 1, 1995. We are speaking in her home at 372 Pine Boulevard in Eagan, Minnesota, concerning her knowledge of an accident which occurred on November 26 at around 6:00 p.m. Tammy, may I have your full name please?"

Tammy staring off beyond him and "*My* full name?"

"Yes."

"Tamara Tiffany Chorske."

Though he had previously stated her address, Meiners asked "And where do you live?"

"Here."

"For the purposes of the tape, will you state specifically the address of 'here'?" Tammy speaking the numbers and the names. Then Meiners shepherded her through a series of questions concerning where she had been, what she had been driving, what time of day, until Tammy had described haltingly all that she had done since leaving the Ridgedale Mall up to the point where she approached the intersection at Pilot Knob and Yankee Doodle. Then "What is the speed limit on Pilot Knob?"

"I don't know," her father following with "Don't tell him that, damn it."

Meiners identified the voice as Chorske's, asked him to

refrain from speaking until his daughter's statement was finished, then "How fast were you going as you approached the intersection?"

"I'd say about thirty-five," nodding at her father who smiled and nodded back as a coach or director might.

"Thirty-five?"

"About that," Meiners thinking *you made a car half the width it was and smashed it more than a hundred feet down the road and killed a man and you were going thirty-five.*

"There are traffic lights at that intersection?"

"Yup."

"And were the lights red or green as you reached it?"

Bill Chorske nodding at her again and "Green."

"You're sure?"

"Green," Meiners thinking of the police report that listed seven witnesses, all of whom had indicated at the scene that Tammy had run a red light without ever slowing, Meiners wanting to believe that someday she'd remember what she told him and that she would be ashamed, then seeing her clearly and *no, you never will.*

"Was anyone issued a citation as a result of the accident?"

"Yup."

"Who?" Meiners thinking *cheerleading's about the limit for this one.*

"Me."

"The nature of that citation?" Tammy listing the three that she could remember which included failure to obey a traffic signal, reckless driving, and not having in her possession a valid driver's license.

"But just because she didn't have her license with her doesn't mean it was her fault," Chorske said. "I want that understood," Meiners glaring at him.

"Tammy, if I were to ask you what the primary cause of the accident was, what would you say?"

"I'd say it was because it just happened," Meiners thinking *good christ* and "Could you explain that?"

"Well, it's just something that happened that couldn't be helped. It wasn't anybody's fault. The light was green for me and he must have thought it was green too or maybe it was green both ways and we hit together," Tammy clapping her hands and looking around the table, her father nodding.

"So you don't feel responsible for the accident?"

"No way," Meiners halfheartedly concluding his interview, later in the car tired and *just once I'd like to hear someone say "it was my fault because I fucked up and I'm sorry and I'll go on being sorry." Goddamn, just something that happened.*

The next morning Meiners called Mike Corwin, the Assistant State's Attorney deciding what to charge Tammy Chorske with, if anything.

"Maybe this is private, Mr. Corwin, but have you decided on what to do with Tammy Chorske?"

"No."

"What are the options?"

"Anything from negligent homicide to nothing, depending on circumstances. It won't be homicide, because she wasn't drinking and she has no priors. I don't know. Maybe we'll just let the civil courts handle it."

"Have you talked to her?"

"No. Why?"

"Well, just make sure you talk to her before you make a final decision. Get her dad there, too."

"Why?"

"You'll see."

■

"**Who were you,** Jake?"

"Who was I when?"

"Before you were a schmuck working in a body shop."

"Why do you call me that?"

"I feel the need to piss you off sometimes, to see if you're still alive."

Jake pausing, then "It's good you do that, because it's only with you that I feel truly dead," Luella smiling along the edge of him, moving closer and taking his rough fingers and wanting his touch.

"I mean before Jane got . . . was gone. Talk to me."

Jake considering, then plainly "I was a lawyer who made a lot of money. Who thought he could always do and say the right things. You'd a done been impressed."

"And now you associate with Elroy and Tim, talk—whenever you manage a few words—like a hillbilly. You couldn't have been too smart. Nobody stops being a lawyer just because their wife gets killed. Maybe for a little while, but not for good" and *I wonder what he did with all the money.*

"I'm glad she got killed because it gave me an excuse to quit something I didn't like anyway."

"Jake."

"It's true, the part that I didn't care for it."

"I don't believe that."

"I'm unbelievable," deflecting her with a smile.

■

Brian Meiners listing the players in his file: Bill Chorske, Tammy, and Luella, labeling them "asshole," "perky imbecile," and "mouthy bitch," then considering other courses he might sail on his ocean-life because, thinking back on five years with IncAmPride, at least ninety percent of the people he had worked with or handled claims for fit into one of those three categories. He had just ended a conversation with Luella who had summoned a bitch-voiced Maureen almost too convincingly for Jake. Meiners scribbled summary notes onto a yellow legal pad, closed up the thickening manila folder and carried it into Sheila's office asking "He in? Available?"

Sheila rang Gippart and relayed to Meiners, "Five minutes." He sat by her desk, glad to be away from his own. He'd been assigned a new file first thing that morning. IncAmPride wrote liability insurance for the city of Minneapolis, where someone had tried cross-country skiing across Lake Harriet. Two nights before a brief but intense storm had laid five inches of snow over everything but the open water in the center of all the city lakes, and everywhere you looked skiers glided soundlessly across open land. The temperatures had quickly turned bitter, below zero, and the water which hadn't been frozen completely now held a layer of ice thin as cellophane. Then it had snowed another inch and the thin ice held the snow. No more noticeably open water, only a glimmering and inviting white expanse. The Lake Harriet skier had made it about two hundred yards from shore. Now his family was hollering about the city not nailing up any warning signs. In Meiners' file were pictures of such signs, big red letters on white backgrounds, that had been up for two weeks. The signs warned people to stay off the unstable ice. Well, the family decided, it wasn't that there weren't any warning signs, it was that they hadn't been located in exactly the right spots. Meiners, tired of being polite, wanted to call them and ask if they considered the open water in the middle of the lake two days before sign enough and properly placed. Meiners had been told the man was an avid skier, had gone around the lake a couple of times each day the week before he died. He pictured the man heading out on the thin ice, others watching, but avoided wondering what had driven him, what he had been thinking as he set off briskly into the morning light. Meiners had read the obituary: chief press room operator at the *Star Tribune,* master's degree in business, two-year tour in Vietnam, Meiners addressing the dead man and *after all that one day you decided to do something so stupid it cost your life. You just goddamn didn't have to.*

Sheila drew him from his revery, told him Gippart would see

him. He went in and waited for Gippart to acknowledge his presence, which he did after signing several checks.

"You come up with something on Chorske?"

"No."

"What then?"

"Just got off the phone with Mrs. Scott. She doesn't want to talk to me anymore."

"You mean she's got a lawyer?"

"No. She wants to move fast, deal with the head man. She asked who my superior is, I gave her your name. She said she'd call you," Gippart swiveling his chair and leaning back, pondering.

"You do something to piss her off?" Gippart knowing that Meiners hadn't but wanting to keep him on edge.

"Not that I know of."

"You sure?"

"Yes."

"It wouldn't break my heart keeping a lawyer out of it. It's happened before, but then later they start blabbing about the settlement they got and someone tells them it was worth a lot more—and that nosy someone is usually correct—and then they come back whining," Gippart pondering it more and then "Fine, if she calls I'll just handle it. Get a report to me by the end of the day so I'm up to speed. I assume you've got enough to do without that file."

Meiners laughing and "I'm sure I can find something," stopping abruptly as Gippart fixed him with an ugly look and "Why don't you go fucking do it then?" Gippart swiveling away and considering that "Chorske/Scott—Auto Fatality" might be one for Reno ultimately but wary of the risk, that such an unleashing would come too soon after Lori Hanson.

■

The girls entered the house through the front door as they habitually did, the final day of school before Christmas vacation.

They found the usually warm interior cold. Sheila had instructed Jasmine, the oldest, how to operate the thermostat, and after
the girls had shed their jackets and caps and mittens, neatly
pocketing and hanging them by the back door, Jasmine went to
the hallway to check its setting. On the way she stopped to listen but could not hear the furnace fan. She saw that the thermostat was set just above sixty; outside it had not exceeded thirty that afternoon.

Jasmine turning to her sister and "Why would this be set so
low?" Caitlin responding indifferently "I wouldn't know."

"You didn't turn it down this morning?"

"If I did then I'd know, wouldn't I?"

Jasmine screeching cat-like, curling her fingers into claws and
"Just asking."

"Ask an intelligent question, then."

"Bitch."

"Nice talk. I'm sure Mother will approve of your vocabu-
lary."

"Tell her, I don't care."

But Jasmine still puzzled and "Why would she have set it so
low?"

"I told you I wouldn't know."

"You wouldn't know how to get dressed if I didn't show you
every morning. Tomorrow we'll work on the bra again. When I
say the clasp goes on the flat side, I mean in back. I know you
have trouble telling."

Jasmine rotated the thermostat knob up to seventy and
walked away from her sister. Across the hall from the thermostat and down a few steps stood a door opening into a large
walk-in closet the previous owner had built by knocking out the
walls between a small closet and the bathroom. He had expand-
ed the main bedroom and the bath, used part of the old bathroom for a bigger closet. Inside hung summer dresses and other
clothing unsuitable for winter. One wall held five painted pine

shelves affixed to the sheetrock and studs with metal strips and brackets. On the side opposite the clothes rack were stacked cardboard boxes holding Christmas ornaments, Easter and other holiday things. In the space left over, about three feet by three feet, stood Wally Reno.

He did not particularly care if the girls came into the closet and discovered him. What could they do, scream? If so, he would calmly walk from the house and around the corner, get in his car and drive away. He had left the closet door open three or four inches, that narrow view opening away from where they had stood examining the thermostat. He could not see the girls now, could only hear them in the kitchen opening the refrigerator and cabinets. With his intense ears he heard them pouring liquid into glasses, clinking silverware together.

Presently they left the kitchen and passed through the living room and along the hallway, no more than two feet from Reno's shadowed face. He thought that maybe they would go into their bedroom now and change.

He had already prowled about the house and knew the girls shared one bedroom. He knew that Sheila and her daughters lived without a man, though on Sheila's headboard sat a picture of her with a man she had just married. They were smiling, Sheila in a wedding dress and the man in a dark tuxedo. Reno, since his own, had not cared for weddings. On the living room wall, beside last year's school portraits of the girls, hung a picture of the four of them. As Reno had done in Sheila's bedroom, he had opened the drawers of each girl's dresser, slid aside their closet doors. His gloved hands had opened everything that was closed in the basement and kitchen as well. He had been in the garage but not the back yard, which was open to the neighbors. Those shades he had found up he had pulled down, waiting.

Jasmine crossed from bedroom to bathroom wearing only her underwear, holding her goose-bumped arms across her bare

stomach and shivering. He listened to her urinating and flush-
ing, could hear even the hair brush moving through young long
shiny hair. Impassively he watched her cross back.

Dressed in sweatshirts and jeans they passed him again
almost looking into his eyes but Reno's breath and heart rate
steady because neither danger nor sex moved him. He heard
them in the kitchen again, opening and shutting the oven door.
Then into the living room where they turned on the television,
MTV rap coming loud and Reno angered by it, though he
watched it now and then because he liked the black women
dancing.

Reno stood for a long time waiting for something else to
happen, but the girls continued to watch television. Late
afternoon became night and the hallway darkened, the only
light coming from the bathroom, kitchen, and flickering television. He checked his watch: Sheila would be leaving the bar
about now. The girls finally went into the kitchen and Reno
heard the oven door again, cupboards squeaking open and
closed, plates and glasses. He pushed the closet door open and
stepped into the shadowed narrowness where he could smell
chicken cooking. He paused before the thermostat, then
walked calmly through the living room and out the front
door, which he slammed hard enough so the girls could not
help but hear.

In the kitchen they turned to one another, surprised that
their mother was home so soon. They went to greet her but
found the rooms empty but for themselves. Jasmine looked out
the front door and Caitlin parted the curtains covering the
large front window. But darkness mixes well with darkness,
shadow with shadow, and they noted nothing outside. When
Sheila arrived she remarked as they had that it was cold.
Jasmine checked the thermostat, found it set again at exactly
sixty-one degrees, turning to her mother who could not
explain.

■

Luella, while reading the newspaper, noticed a short article indicating that an Eagan teen, Tamara Chorske, had been charged with manslaughter in the traffic death of Dr. Jack Scott.

5

Luella remembered her promise, made a year and a half after her second divorce, that she would never again suffer boredom on a New Year's Eve. Her father had every year organized large parties in their basement family room, a big carpeted rectangle with a well-stocked bar at one end. Luella could easily call up the smell of thick cigarette smoke and the sound of loud, alcohol-flavored conversation; as a little girl she had knelt ignored at the top of the stairs, fearful yet drawn, knowing that after a few hours she would be able to roam as she pleased among all these loud, happy people who would tell her how cute she was. She remembered her father's drinking with regret, but had to admit a New Year's Eve at the Algers had never been dull. She had uttered her anti-dullness promise loudly after the second New Year's Eve she'd spent alone with Sara; they had eaten cheap hot dogs and greasy chips—Sara's favorite meal—had watched television and played games. Sara had been whining about staying up until midnight, Luella finally relenting in order to silence her daughter's voice that had begun to sound like heavy-metal screeching. After all her demanding, at ten-thirty the six-year-old had given out and fallen asleep on the floor in front of the television. Luella had dragged her to her room and hoisted her into bed, then sat alone with the television boring her and nothing to drink but a single can of cheap beer. After she had jealously watched the lighted ball descend on Times Square she whispered to the depressingly silent house, "I will never do this shit again."

She had kept her promise, inviting friends over as her father had or going to bars, one night a year drinking too much and making noise. When the party was at Luella's Sara sat sullenly with a baby-sitter.

Sara had driven down for an uneventful Christmas Eve, had grown so bored with Luella and Jake that at one o'clock on Christmas Day she had left to return to Jamestown. The apartment seemed pleasant enough among the city's bright winter holiday lights; Luella had purchased a miniature fake tree and strung it with some lights and tiny ornaments. They were uneasy about Christmas because they had not spent one together before, so they exchanged cards but nothing else. They wandered the crowded streets and stores but did not buy anything. Luella had been reinvigorated by the holidays, but Jake seemed mildly uneasy, Luella believing his mood a result of doing things again, of living, of being around people.

New Year's Eve came and Luella late in the afternoon "Tell me again our plans for this evening."

Jake reading a car magazine from the stack of them in the living room and "I am, as of this moment, unaware of any."

"What I thought. So we need to make some."

"I hate plans."

"Obviously—look at your life," she laughed. Jake drew a thin smile across his face. "But surely you don't want to sit here tonight, of all nights, and do nothing while the rest of the planet parties?"

"I surely do."

She looked at him with mild concern and "What's wrong, Jake? You seem down."

He drew in a long breath and "Maybe the memories of other Christmases are crowding in on me, and I don't want to acknowledge them right now." Then, pensively, "I just don't want to live in the past anymore, and this time of year makes that difficult."

She talked him into going out for steaks and drinks and

renting a movie. They drove to a restaurant overlooking a small frozen lake and ate quietly, Jake peering contemptuously into the bar at people already wearing brightly colored hats and speeding resolutely toward drunkenness. He saw one man with a metallic-green sequined jacket and told Luella "Never wear colors that would look good on a customized '53 Oldsmobile." After their dinner Jake ordered one grasshopper with two spoons, Luella amused and "You're too extravagant for me, Jake."

"It's what Jane and I used to do."

Luella slightly embarrassed and "I'm sorry."

Jake smiled and "Don't worry about it."

They drove back downtown finally, wandering into a brightly lit video store not far from their apartment. The place, frequented usually by after-workers, was nearly deserted, and Jake and Luella shuffled through aisles of shiny colored boxes above which hung black-on-white genre signs. Every word had an exclamation mark after it.

Luella trying hard to cheer him up and "Too bad they don't have a car section. Some of those neat old Mickey Rooney or Elvis racing movies," Jake laughing and "Speaking of car movies," then approaching the young man at the counter and asking if they had *The California Kid* but the boy had never heard of it and made no effort to check their computerized inventory.

They moved into the *War!* section and stood staring at boxes covered with khaki'd or camouflaged soldiers waving weapons or riding on tanks, explosions and fires raging around them. Jake turned his eyes to the floor as Luella plucked a box from eye-level and "You ever seen this?" Jake not answering.

"Hello, Jake?" Luella pulling on his sleeve and raising his downturned chin with her fingers. "Have—you—seen—this?" She moved her hands in feigned sign language. She was trying again to be funny, but she sensed that his mood had suddenly changed for the worse.

"I would prefer a comedy," he said.

Luella still trying and "We *are* a comedy. A veritable laugh-riot. 'The Car Guy and the Cripple,' starring Jake and Luella." She walked over two aisles to *Comedy!* and returned with a box she thrust before him and "Here, this is us," her finger guiding his eyes and "'A rollicking, rambunctious, comedic free-for-all you won't forget.' We are four stars out of four, Jake, two thumbs up. So, maybe just for something different, what we need is some action, lots of people and things blown up. Blood. Casual but heated sex." Jake turned away from her and "What we don't need is a war movie," Luella remembering suddenly his notebook, the man behind Jane, and wondering.

"I know. Let's rent 'The Three Stooges Meet Elroy At The Body Shop.' Maybe Robin Williams and Billy Crystal in 'Paint and Fenders.'" Her voice grew louder as she spoke, and the boy at the counter raised his head.

She rented a comedy, but a half hour into it she watched puzzled and afraid as he went into the bedroom, at the door Jake turning and "I'm sorry," though he didn't seem to be speaking to her.

She followed him and found him face-up on the bed, staring, Luella thinking *he's come so far, I can't let him go back.*

"I'll be honest, Jake. I've read your notebook, so I know what you dream about. Want to talk? Don't go back to silence." She expected him to be angry when he sat up quickly, but then he stood and stepped to her and put his arms around her. She could feel him fighting tears.

After several minutes Jake calmed and stood back from her. She saw in his eyes a deep sadness. But his voice was firm when he said, "You're right. Let's go back in and I'll tell you."

When they were seated he began. "The man behind Jane is Mark."

"The other name in your notebook. He must be important to you."

"Yes. Mark and I were really good friends through high

school. Went to football and basketball games together, cruised around at night, all the usual stuff. Sometimes we even got crazy and studied together. June, the summer of '68, after graduation, he came to me with his draft notice and asked me what he should do. Late at night, in my car, he was crying, for God's sake, and he turned to me and said 'Jake, what should I do?' I saw he was scared, terrified. I mean, I *knew* that, I *knew* he needed help."

"What did you tell him?"

Jake suddenly almost shouting, his body gone rigid and "Nothing, not a damn thing. I just sat there. I didn't know. I just didn't know."

Luella firmly like a counselor and "How old were you?"

"Eighteen."

"We're all ignorant when we're eighteen, Jake. We think we know, but we don't."

"But I should have said 'Get the hell out, Mark. Go to Canada. Run, to anywhere.' But I didn't."

"You must have said something."

"*No!* Not a sound. I froze. Couldn't speak. We sat there maybe a half hour, neither of us said a word. Finally I just started the car and drove him home. He got out and went up the sidewalk to his house. I haven't spoken to him since."

"What happened to him?"

"He got both legs blown off beneath the knee, that's what goddamn happened. A year after my beautiful fucking silence I read in the paper that he'd been injured."

"And you didn't go see him then?"

Jake's voice breaking and "No."

Luella thinking she shouldn't press him but "Why not, Jake?"

"My voice fails me sometimes. That's why, after Jane died, I quit talking."

"What does Jane have to do with Mark?"

"I'm sorry, Luella, I just can't go there right now. Please."

She rose, moved to the couch where he sat, and held him until she felt his body go limp; his words had been painful to him, she knew, but she believed he had finally begun to forgive himself.

■

Susan Burns paging through a thick sheaf of tax returns and "Jack Scott earned $197,000 last year," Jake's breath altering a moment and *Elroy could fix up the shop for that, be set for life.*

"I'll send you these documents," she told him, but Jake couldn't trust that Sheila would intercept them or even that she would agree to and "I'll come by and pick them up."

"Suit yourself. I'll leave them with my secretary so if I'm not available you can still get them."

"I'll come by this afternoon."

"I've meetings, but ask for me. I'd like to meet you."

"And I you," but thinking *that won't ever happen* and wanting to tell her that she had a pretty voice.

Susan Burns considering the simplicity of the matter between them and "You realize there isn't much to talk about here."

"I guess not."

"Your limit per person is three hundred thousand. Jack Scott earned that in a year and a half, and in ten years he might have been earning it every year as salary, not to mention investments. He had at least twenty good years of employment left," Jake thinking they might just as well have been discussing a washing machine. He had called Sheila to tell her he didn't know anything about the policy, and two days later received in the mail a policy cover sheet listing liability limits and endorsement numbers. Upon reading them he had understood that the liability maximum could eventually cause a problem for the Chorskes. Jake knew the claim was worth a million easy. But that seven hundred thousand would have to be the Chorskes' problem.

"I know."

"You want to bring over a check?"

"You think that would settle it?"

"Perhaps. Once I tell Mrs. Scott the boundaries of what's available, she might just settle for that. She doesn't seem a vindictive person. She's trying hard to forgive. I'll tell her that if she sued she'd be awarded more but might never get it."

"Well, I'll pick up your documentation and try to get authorization as soon as possible."

"Good," Jake thinking of dead men and "I wonder what kind of man he was."

Susan Burns not following the conversation's turn and "Who?"

"Jack Scott."

"Oh. I didn't know him. From what Mrs. Scott tells me he was quite interesting, not that she's told me a lot. They met at the University of Texas after the war and got married just before he interned."

"You mean Vietnam?"

"Yes. He served in the Army but wasn't a grunt, as she put it, had something to do with the medical corps. I don't remember exactly what she said. It's where he really firmed up his interest in medicine, though. Got a couple of medals," Jake apostrophizing *you crossed over oceans and spent two years there and came home and then one Thanksgiving you were crossing an intersection and you didn't come home from that. Christ.*

Jake angry then and belligerently "What a goddamn waste," Susan Burns bewildered by his angry tone. He hung up before she could say anything more. Mid-afternoon he went to her law office and took the enveloped information from her secretary but did not ask for her.

∎

They negotiated by phone as much as they could, Jake calling Susan Burns often enough to maintain cordiality, Luella talking to Gippart three times. To conducting the claim by phone Susan Burns had raised no objection, but Gippart resisted, wanted to meet her face to face, offered to come to the apartment. Luella told him she had moved into the apartment downtown for a time because she could not bear to be in a house she and Jack had bought together and now could not share. When he offered to visit her she had no choice but to agree to see him in his office; they did not want him in the apartment because he might consider it suspicious that someone with her money would live so cheaply in a location that did not suit her wealth.

The day she had gone shopping she had gotten her hair cut short, especially in back where her neck showed. When she had returned to the apartment, before Jake told her about Susan Burns and Jack Scott, she had complained that the stylist had cut it too short, but Jake put his hand on the back of her neck that he had never seen and said he liked it. He found the soft skin there appealing beneath his hand.

She planned a mild disguise, to keep her hair flat against her head, wear large dark glasses and lots of makeup so that later when her hair had grown out long Gippart could not recognize her. Still, there wasn't anything she could do about her walk, Jake telling her "This is half-assed. He'd know you from your limp," but Luella wanting to do it as she had planned and Jake having no choice.

Gippart waiting for Luella, thinking that the claim was too easy, the policy limits way below what anyone would owe. Still, he considered challenging himself to see how cheaply a doctor could be purchased. He sat wondering what Maureen Scott would look like, eager to see the bereaved widow because he liked women in black. When she entered limping and carrying the materials that Jake had gotten from Susan Burns he was disappointed; to him, she didn't look like a doctor's wife. He believed that money rubs off, gives a shine, and Luella wasn't shiny.

Gippart surprised that Meiners had not mentioned any injury to Mrs. Scott and "I didn't realize you had been injured in the accident, Mrs. Scott. Please sit down."

Luella taking a chair and "This is an old injury that I got years ago."

"Automobile accident?"

"I fell from a horse," Gippart wanting to say to her "yeah, life's tough at the stables sometimes," but maintaining his cordial facade with "I'm sorry."

"I get by."

"Still," gesturing with his hands to indicate again he wished it hadn't happened. "It's a pleasure to meet you, and though I've said it on the phone previously, allow me again to convey my deepest sympathies to you for the death of Dr. Scott. I know John Anderson, the hospital administrator, and when I spoke with him—not officially, I assure you, not snooping—he indicated to me that he and everyone who knew Dr. Scott held him in the highest regard," Luella marveling at his charm and *this is what Eve must have felt.*

"I appreciate your kind words."

"Not at all, not at all. It is you who are kind for coming here. I hope you don't feel like I'm pushing you into anything by arranging a meeting so soon."

"I usually let people know when they're pressuring me."

"Certainly. Anyway, I must be honest with you and say that these kinds of cases usually get ugly at some point, quite frequently wind up in court. I hope to avoid that here."

"I do too. I have some documentation here regarding my husband's income. As far as I'm concerned this isn't a matter of determining liability, merely assessing the value of my claim against your . . . I believe you call them 'insureds'?"

"We do indeed. And I must agree. As I've indicated during previous conversations, my investigation tells me our insured was completely at fault. So from my perspective our relationship should be one of reconciling the claim with the policy limits of our insured's contract with us," Luella almost telling him that three hundred thousand was a ridiculously low figure in this case but catching herself *no way would I know that limit.* She, like Jake, feared errors unintentional or otherwise in a world she knew little about. She had received a settlement from Ford for her leg, but that had been reviewed and consummated by an attorney, had taken nearly two years.

"May I look over what you've brought?" Luella handing him the envelope. Gippart spent some minutes scanning the pages, finally looking up and "I see from one of the pages here that a local law firm is involved. It was my understanding you had not retained counsel."

Luella surprised and "I haven't."

"The name of Susan Burns, who I know works for a St. Paul firm I'm familiar with, appears on this page." Luella took it and found Burns' name scribbled in a corner, searched for a way to explain it and "I don't know who that is. Perhaps Jack had her do some tax work. I don't know," thinking *don't act like you need to apologize.*

Gippart glossing over it and "That must be the case."

"I haven't discussed this with a lawyer and I don't plan to if I'm satisfied with our progress."

"Do you sense any reason why I might not be able to satisfy you?"

"If the money you offer isn't enough."

"The usual concern. The only problem I see here—the only *potential* problem—involves our policy limits. As you know, when a person buys insurance their contract with the company sets definite monetary limits regarding how much any one person might collect. Certainly a judgment can be obtained against the insured's themselves, and they would then be responsible for any amount over our limit, but that doesn't usually work out too well. I can tell you our insured makes a good living but far less than the handsome amount earned by your husband each year. He has children. You'd have a difficult time collecting."

"I understand. What are your limits?"

"I don't usually divulge that, but in this case I'll make an exception. Two hundred and fifty thousand," thinking of the two snowmobiles and trailer he had celebrated the holidays with. He would doctor the file so that it showed the limits applied, pocket the difference between what he sent to Mrs. Dr. Scott. It occurred to him that she might laugh at a quarter of a million, and in that instance maybe he'd have to call on Reno. But Gippart was uncertain of using him, because he didn't think anyone would believe she would settle for less. Then again, maybe Reno could convince her that no one else would have to know.

Luella now understanding that what Gippart had done to Jake in South Dakota had no doubt continued, with different files, ever since. "That's awfully low," she said, Gippart looking at the tax returns and nodding "I know. But it's about this simple, Mrs. Scott. Do you want the policy limits or do you want to go to court? You could get a higher judgment, maybe."

"I'd say my chances deserve more than a maybe."

"You're right. A poor choice of words on my part."

Luella wanting to make sure he knew that she wouldn't be easy and "Damn right I'm right," Gippart smiling and *don't push me bitch.*

She asked, and Gippart told her what more he knew about the Chorskes. She pretending to ponder her options and "I'll have to decide. Keep those documents. I'm not one to wait around. I'll make up my mind soon," Gippart thinking *well, we'll all just be here waiting breathlessly for your call!* and "I look forward to hearing from you." He didn't like her and suddenly he was very eager to pocket fifty thousand dollars.

After she had gone he reached for the phone thinking of Reno's number, but he did not make the call.

In the elevator, descending, Luella felt a strange exhilaration and *it's not so bad to be someone else now and then.*

■

More than a week past New Year's and Elroy laboring over an estimate, two different crash manuals spread out on the filthy metal desk to see if one would allow him a longer flat-rate time than the other to replace a grille and headlamp assembly. Elroy found no difference in the time he could bill, so he sat considering bumping up the generic amount he listed under "shop supplies." The outside office door opened slowly, then closed. Elroy finished writing and looked up to find Wally Reno grinning. Elroy, like God, had damned everyone, but he too offered redemption, which came, if it did, after the first words a man spoke; women in his world were not allowed ascension. Elroy judged the sound of a man's voice, became instantly and forever friend or foe, though sometimes it was difficult to tell if you had been saved or damned.

Elroy staring, silent, awaiting with his infinite patience Reno's application.

Reno falsely pleasant and "Looking for an old friend of mine, Jake Warner. Got a week's vacation after New Year's."

Elroy as usual difficult and "Jake does?"

"No, I do."

"Oh," Elroy deciding *the fires of a long hell.*

"He work here?" Elroy not liking Reno nor Jake gone and a stranger looking.

Elroy deciding to be careful and "He sure does. Sit down, sit down," thinking *I should get my gun and shoot this bastard.* Elroy stood and dusted off a chair and Reno sat.

Reno drumming fingers on a knee and "Can I talk to him?"

"Your timing's bad. He's off a couple days."

"Is he now? Doggone, I wanted to see him. I used to know him in Mitchell, haven't talked to him in a long time," pausing. Then, "But he's working regular, is he?"

"Jake? Sure, ol' Jake's regular as they come, can't think of the last time he missed a day. Good ol' Jake."

Reno laughed.

"Where'd you come in from?"

"Wisconsin. On my way to Seattle. Is Jake in town?"

"He's got relatives up north somewhere by the border. Goes up there this time every winter ice fishing."

"I see."

"He might be back by now, but I think he said he had to go over to Valley for something when he got back."

"Valley?"

"Valley City."

"How far's that?"

"Half hour east," Elroy thinking *if you came from Wisconsin you'd know that.* Then "Can you stick around a while? Jake'd want to see you if it's been a long time."

"Fifteen years," Reno so used to making things up that he sometimes experienced difficulty telling what was real from what wasn't. "We talk on the phone now and then, but we haven't actually seen one another for quite a spell."

"I'd suggest you call his house and talk to Sally, but she's probably with him."

"Sally?"

"His wife. You knew he'd gotten married again."

"Sure. I just couldn't remember her name. Never met her."

"Well, too bad you couldn't stay. I'll tell him you came by. What's your name?"

"Tom. Tom Nelson."

"I'll tell him, Tom."

"Do that."

"So long," Elroy wishing he knew where to get hold of Jake.

"Nice to have met you," Reno said, smiling wide.

Reno decided he'd wait until night, then check Jake's apartment again. He had seen no one there the previous night, though a light was on. He waited through the day like a patient, tongue-lolling dog on a back porch. At six he drove to Jake's apartment building, parked where he could see both the front entrance and Jake's apartment windows. At six-twenty a man and a woman in a beat-up pickup drove into the lot, went in the front entrance. A few seconds later Reno saw the lights in Jake's apartment intensify through the dark between the building and his car and shimmer on the crusty snow.

The heavy black rotary phone in Jake's Jamestown apartment rang and Tim Kinneady answered it as his wife stood by. "Warner speaking," but only silence from the other end and Kinneady repeating. Still only silence, so he hung up. Five minutes later another call and Kinneady announcing himself as Jake once again.

This time an answer and "It's Elroy."

"Was he out there?"

"Yes he was," Elroy said.

"Is he gone?"

"I followed him out toward the highway. He stopped to get gas and make a phone call. He's headed east."

Kinneady guessing and "That must have been him calling here. Phone rang but nobody said anything when I answered as Jake. Who do you suppose he is?"

"Don't know. But a scary bastard, and I just hope he doesn't find Jake."

"Boss-man, it's Wally."

"Where you been? Haven't seen you in a couple days."

"Got bored waiting for you to get me work. Took off for a drive."

"Where this time?" Gippart knowing how Reno would disappear three or four times a year. He'd simply get in his car and start driving, most of the time without a clear destination. He'd be gone a week or ten days.

"Your old stomping grounds. Passed through Sioux Falls, said hello to Jack Kindler. Decided to wander over to Mitchell. Jesus, how long did you stand that dump?"

"I didn't actually have to live there."

"Thank God. Went north to Jamestown, looked up your old buddy Jake Warner."

"You talk to him?"

"No, but I saw him, talked to his boss at a really fine body shop," Reno laughing. "He'd been out of town, just got back. I watched him and the wife go into their apartment. I wanted to go in myself and ask him what he thought his life would be like if he hadn't got fucked out of his wife's insurance money."

"Charming. Who was it said you don't know how to have a good time?"

"The governor, I think."

"Well haul your ugly ass back here. We've things to do."

■

J. William Lofton waited in his office as 1:59 moved toward 2:00, the second hand of his desk clock jerking incrementally. His appointment with the private investigator he had hired was scheduled for 2:00. Lofton was seventy-one years old, had been CEO of IncAmPride for twenty-seven years. Before that he had worked the company's various departments and levels, immersing himself in every facet of company business. He had never been employed by any other firm. He had stayed through three name changes; this last one he detested, though Marketing remained adamant that such a name "enabled a more leverageable market positionality." Lofton detested such talk even more. He preferred the old, direct Minnesota Life and Casualty, but aware that since the name change seven years before business had been very good.

The single thing that every IncAmPride employee knew about J. William Lofton was that if you had an appointment with him you had better be on time, punctuality the one standard from which he never deviated. Fellow CEOs considered him among the shrewdest businessmen they had encountered, and they wouldn't have been surprised to see, listed as tenet number one on his handwritten list of how to do business, the simple "punctuality," underlined three times. Second was "tight control of expenditures," third "tenacity." Lofton could twist the word

into a positive, as in "pursue your goals relentlessly," or into
ugliness, as in "when you turn against someone, become the
meanest, orneriest bastard on the planet." Meanness coupled
coldly with power births unpleasant offspring, and J. William
Lofton had made more than his share of enemies.

Lofton's secretary announced Kurt Schwartz as the second
hand wound inside of five seconds before 2:00. J. William did
not rise when Schwartz entered, directed the man he had known
for twenty years to sit and tersely "Mr. Schwartz."

"Mr. Lofton." Kurt Schwartz lowered his thick short body
into a chair. He was ten years Lofton's junior, his hair as short
and gray. He was an ex-Milwaukee policeman who, twenty
years before, had returned to his hometown of St. Paul and
started his own detective agency. He spoke with the dry, tedious,
laconic jargon of law enforcement, and whenever he began a
sentence he gave the impression that it would be a very long
time before he finished it. Lofton had not hired him for speech-
making, but for the inexorable direction of his will; once set in
motion Schwartz would, like fate, move unerringly toward
whatever he had been pointed, and would live forever if such
immortality were required to finish. Because J. William trusted
no one, especially those who worked for him, he employed
Schwartz's three-man agency to investigate the workings of his
employees. Schwartz did not know that once every three years
Lofton hired yet another agency to investigate Schwartz's own
business, even though no such investigation had ever shown the
slightest wavering in conduct. So, whenever Lofton wanted a
department or an individual investigated, he handed over to
Schwartz the master keys for doors, desks, and files, and turned
him loose.

J. William gazing steadily at Schwartz and "Tell me."

Though he had his report with him, Schwartz left it unopened
and "On this occasion you asked me to investigate Claims. I
have concluded that assignment. For a month, every weeknight
from midnight to five a.m., I have searched the records and files

of that department. I began with Clerical. I found nothing out of the ordinary. I believed I might find, as I have found in other businesses, that the records of materials ordered would not match the inventory of materials on hand, as occurred, as you recall, five years ago in Accounting," Lofton nodding. "After my search of records and inventory I turned to the employees themselves. I watched each as she came to work in the morning. I noted what she brought to the office, what she left with. My report"—he hoisted a thick sheaf of papers from his lap— "includes all my notes. I found nothing unusual. I feel safe in saying that claims clerical workers are not pilfering company supplies."

Lofton nodded again, a priest bestowing blessing. He had not expected that Schwartz would tell him otherwise. He sat with Schwartz unmoving, patient, two old men unenamored with speed.

"I occupied a full month investigating the claim representatives. I employed the same procedures with them as with Clerical. I found that they as well exhibit an honesty commensurate with their position and salary. They do not steal. I followed each of them during the day to determine if the time they claimed as company time was in fact occupied with company business, that when they were on IncAmPride time they were engaged with IncAmPride business. With one minor exception, it was."

Lofton raised a single eyebrow, his only movement. The quiet in his small office was absolute. "Detail that exception."

"Mr. Nichols spent almost two hours on a Thursday afternoon bringing his wife home from a hospital stay. She had slipped on ice at a local grocery store and had broken her ankle badly. Mrs. Nichols spent four days in the hospital after surgery. Mr. Nichols took her at 11:05 a.m. from the hospital directly to their home in North St. Paul. I assume that while inside he made certain his wife was satisfactorily situated. He then returned to the office."

"Did he work late that evening?"

"He did. My records show he left the office at 6:34, exactly the two hours and four minutes he had earlier spent not working."

Lofton nodded once more and made a notation on a yellow legal pad. He had met Nichols on two occasions, considered him a bright and competent young man. He would need to be spoken to, perhaps at first a simple reminder of IncAmPride's "Request For Personal Leave" form, daily version. Schwartz sat quietly, knew better than to ask what, if anything, would follow from the information about Nichols he had just communicated.

Lofton finished writing and impassively "Go on."

"I proceeded to the department's management," and then the office's silence fell heavier between them. Lofton had never known Schwartz to hesitate, raised both his eyebrows this time and "Yes?"

Schwartz intoning solemnly "I believe there exists a very serious and expensive problem in Claims management."

■

The car quit two blocks from the apartment, Luella having the presence to direct it grudgingly into an open space along the curb. The ten o'clock traffic ran lightly along the darkened street. She extinguished the lights, switched off the country music that had been quietly filling the interior. She waited a moment then tried the ignition, the engine turning over crisply but not firing. She tried it at length three more times before the battery weakened.

"Better give it a rest," Jake said but Luella, impatient, tried again and the battery failed. The inside of the windows began to fog over. Luella then angry and "that's the second time in a year it's done this. Quality is job one. Shit. No warning lights, nothing. Just quits. Cars are so male."

"What was it last time?"

"A year ago almost exactly, Sara and I out looking at Christmas lights."

"No, I mean what mechanical ill?"

"I don't know. I just called the garage, they came and towed it, sent me the bill."

Jake thinking of Elroy and "The sort of customer mechanics love."

"Are you criticizing me?"

"No, I'm merely suggesting you keep better track of the car's repair history. You'd be more help to the mechanic," Luella angry and *repair history? You and your fucking cars. Fucking cars period. Pains in the* but trying to control her anger.

"I used to keep a record of Sara's office visits, her illnesses and immunizations. Nice thick file so I'd have records for the school and whoever else. Excuse me if I don't have a similarly complete dossier on my car."

"You're excused."

"Well come on, Mr. Car, get out and see what you can do."

"It won't be much." Jake stepped into the cold and moved in front of the Explorer. He waited several seconds then made some kind of motion to Luella. She tried the ignition thinking *he hasn't even opened the hood*. The battery spun the engine three or four times, then reinterred itself. Jake came around to her side and she lowered her window, Jake laughing and "I meant to pop the hood open."

"Maybe you could do that since you're out there."

"You open the hood by pulling the release inside."

Luella thinking *fucking gizmos* and "Where is it?"

"I would assume under the dash to the left, near the parking brake."

"I've never used the parking brake," Jake laughing again. He opened the door, reached along her leg, found the release. The hood sprang open as he pulled. He slid his hand up along her leg, Luella pushing it away and "You have the finest sense of romantic timing, Jake."

Jake hoisted the hood and held it aloft with extended arms as he stared into the dark engine bay. "Try it" he shouted. She did but it wouldn't fire. He slammed the metal down and got back in the car and "I don't smell gas."

"Is that good or bad?"

"I would think bad. You're not flooding it. Seems like it's not getting fuel. Fuel pump maybe."

"You can fix that?"

"No."

"Refresh my memory. You fix cars for a living, right?"

"I do body work and paint, not mechanics."

"There's a difference?"

"I don't get grease on my hands" and "I couldn't even change an alternator belt on this car. Older cars I can do a little, but not the new ones. Too many electronic widjits. If it's the fuel pump I think it's inside the gas tank. On an old Chevy, for instance, the fuel pump is on the engine where you can get at it. Two bolts and a couple of fittings and you're done. Not anymore."

"You talk like some old fart in a nursing home."

"It's just that I don't trust myself with engines and transmissions and brakes. I like fenders, quarter panels, paint."

Luella grabbing the steering wheel as if trying to choke it and "What do you see in these goddamn things, Jake? I mean, really. All they do is break down on you, cost you money. What is it about cars?" Jake not answering but *they are repairable.* Finally he told her, "We'll need to get it towed out of here," checking the street signs and "tonight. Looks like we're in a bus or taxi zone."

■

J. William Lofton in his long silver sedan insulated from those hurrying on the sidewalks to jobs he left beneath him long ago. On the way to his office raging from what Schwartz had told him the day before; he could not abide money unaccounted for, company drafts to persons who don't exist. He kept asking himself how it could be done. Yet he knew exactly how it might have been accomplished, that against dishonesty there is no ultimate defense. He knew perfectly how a phony file could be set up, a check issued so that none would ever question, how to make the paper trail lay as it should. J. William Lofton had years before managed Claims for six months when the manager there had suffered a heart attack and taken that long to recover fully. Lofton had sat at the other man's desk authorizing drafts, approving claim settlements. It made him uncomfortable when he could not place the check in a real person's hand, follow that person to the bank and assure himself the money went where it should have gone. The way to easy fraud came to him not from greed but from an overwhelming desire to prevent it—a false claim form, phony statements, misled authorizations, a forged release, a check gone and cashed. That's what Schwartz had told him, that in routinely checking files he had discovered one where the person to whom the check had been issued did not exist. Schwartz did not have, yet, any idea who was responsible, but Lofton did—Dan Gippart, because only the claim supervisor could manage such massive deception. There were many details to control—communication with the agent named on the loss notice, loss ratio accounting, false statements and paperwork—no, only the head man could pull it off. Maybe he gave a kickback to the agent.

J. William Lofton considered Schwartz's latest report. Once Schwartz had determined that a draft had been issued to a claimant who existed only on paper, Lofton ordered Schwartz to check other closed files. He doggedly checked all claims settled in the previous year, moving faster than usual because it was a crime that offended him as much as it did Lofton. His procedure was simple. He went to the people to whom the checks had been issued. If he found them he knew the claim was valid, and at first he asked no questions beyond "Did you recently settle a claim with IncAmPride Insurance Company?" But for a reason he could not name he had asked one claimant directly how much money they had received and in so doing found a discrepancy between the amount paid out by IncAmPride and the amount received by the claimant. He returned and asked the others; he found a woman who had brought a malpractice claim for the death of her husband, to whom, according to the file, a draft for two hundred thousand dollars had been issued. She had smilingly told Schwartz she had received one hundred and seventy-five thousand dollars and he did not tell her that the release he had seen had been for twenty-five thousand more. He asked if a lawyer had been involved and she told him yes, and that they had paid him ten percent of her settlement, seventeen thousand five hundred. And a young woman whose husband had been killed in an automobile accident had received only two hundred and fifty of the three hundred thousand the draft had been issued for. Again the lawyer had taken his cut from the amount of the claimant's check, not the amount on the release form, Schwartz and Lofton wondering if Gippart was working with the lawyers. In each file the paperwork was letter perfect.

Lofton grew so angry that he drove two blocks past IncAmPride before realizing he hadn't turned into his private space. But he modulated his anger, an emotion which had never served him well. He had faith in Schwartz, who was busy getting statements. The file they would gather documenting charges against Dan Gippart would be letter perfect as well.

But that man Schwartz had seen several times leaving Dan Gippart's office. Who? Improper as hell, the rear entrance. Lofton made a mental note to have Schwartz check all pending claims as well.

■

Jake had been out several hours exploring the city while Luella remained in the apartment unwilling to confront the cold. When he returned in the late afternoon he put a sack on the small kitchen table before removing his heavy jacket, which he hung dutifully in the front closet. The sack surprised Luella because its bright yellow paper did not suggest groceries and she seldom saw Jake buy anything else.

Jake bent and kissed her as he passed her chair, rubbing his hands as if to warm them, his lips cold. He sat on the couch without saying anything about the sack.

Luella wanting to know and "Jake?"

"Yes."

"You've brought home a bag."

"Yes," but without elaboration.

"Well, now that we've established that, perhaps you'd like to divulge the nature of the bag's contents."

Jake shrugging and "Sure. Something I bought."

"Something?"

"Something."

"Can we move to a higher degree of specificity?"

"It's hard to explain. You're welcome to look."

Luella rising from her chair, stepping to the table and "I'm honored." She unfolded the top of the bag and inside found a white box made of thin cardboard. She slid her hands along the sides of the sack, lifted the box out, placed it on the table. It weighed very little and she wondered if he had bought her a present. And when she had opened it and parted the white packing paper inside, she saw a shiny metal surface and guessed a silver plate or bowl, though it didn't exactly look like either.

She lifted the object, set it on a placemat, turned to Jake and "What in hell is this?"

"A hat."

"Not just a hat. A hat made of metal."

"Yes," Luella lifting her hands and raising her eyebrows as if requesting explanation.

Jake uncertain and "It's not a hat that you wear. It's sculpture."

"You bought a hat sculpted out of . . . ?"

"Aluminum."

"Aluminum."

"Yes."

"Why?"

"I imagine because it's easier to work with than steel or some other, harder metal."

"I meant why did you buy it?"

"Because I think . . . it's neat."

"A metal hat is neat?"

"He has a whole ton of stuff that he's sculpted out of aluminum. Shoes, jackets, cars, a motorcycle, aviator glasses, bombs."

"Who's *he*?"

"Guy owns a store about a mile from here. Sells all these things he's made. I was walking along the street, passed it, saw this stuff and went in. He's about sixty, I'd guess, maybe older. He sculpts everything out of metal. He's even made one of those old drop-tank racers you used to see at Bonneville."

"Jake, I have no idea what you're talking about."

"On the salt flats, in Utah," Luella continuing to look puzzled. "The Bonneville Salt Flats. They race there," Jake saying it like she ought to know, that everyone else did. "Straight line, just see how fast you can go. Back in the forties and fifties guys would take old fuel tanks shaped like bombs—they called them drop tanks—and make them into racers because of their aerodynamics. They'd sit inside with the engine."

Luella raising her hand and "I'll take your word for it." Looking again at what she held and "What kind of hat is it?"

"A World War II bomber captain's. Look at the detail."

Luella kept examining it. She had to admit it looked awfully real, like someone had taken an actual hat and bronzed it. The aluminum mimicked the real leather's cracks and wrinkles, the bill's smooth texture, the belt-like band's stitching and buckle. The insignia's wings. The original must have been sewn together, and every stitch had been reproduced. But in no way did it move her, and she did not share his enthusiasm for it.

"He just starts out with a big hunk of aluminum, then works it with some kind of carving tools. Then he polishes it. Something, huh?"

Luella suddenly wanting to laugh, but "Something is about the right word. How much was it?"

Jake lowering his eyes as if ashamed and "Two-fifty."

"You spent two hundred and fifty dollars for an aluminum hat?"

"Yes."

"When did you get so wild with your money?" That Jake would buy something so impulsively raised him up in her estimation.

"I used my credit card."

"I'd forgotten you had one."

"I don't use it but for motel rooms." Jake stood and came to the table, took the hat from her and studied it. She watched his eyes, saw that what he held enthralled him.

"Damn, Jake, I might make a shopper of you yet."

Smiling, his fingers felt the fine crevices in the polished metal and *I bet I could do this*, imagining his coupe sculpted, polished. *Elroy can get aluminum blocks. I bet I could.*

■

Susan Burns sipping lightly from the bubbles edging her champagne and "Some party."

David nodded and "Why couldn't you have gotten hired by a firm with this kind of money?" She knew he was merely goading her and not serious. He had never much cared where she worked as long as she was happy. He taught high school history in Edina where they lived; he earned about a third of what she did. They had discussed their income disparity but once when she asked him if he felt somehow emasculated by it. They had just finished a slow hour of lovemaking and "Did I seem emasculated?" and "no," drawing closer to him.

David stroking her hair and "Yes" in playful sarcasm that kept their relationship fresh, "it galls me beyond measure that you triple what I make. I hate not having to teach summer school or do crop/hail insurance, hate the lake cabin, hate driving the kind of car I want. Not to mention getting to do what I love without having to worry about money," Susan thinking *or children*. They had none because neither wanted them. But Susan was growing older, thought more about it.

Susan, standing in the blatant opulence of an obscenely successful law firm, knew that if she worked hard enough, got the right breaks, she might be able to double her own income by joining such a firm, but that sort of move would exact a price she at the moment refused—longer hours; weekend work; weightier, pressurized cases. And after years of little but law and long hours, when you had earned a slower pace, what would you know how to do? Slow down, relax? No, she had observed how the big time often chewed up her superiors, had built a proper balance between self and career; she and David were happy. She held to his arm and watched the others.

The party combined after-Christmas/retirement/new office occasions. A senior partner with Hartland, Finch, and Kloster, sixty-eight-year-old Larry Finch, had abruptly decided to remove himself from Twin Cities legal machinations during January's last week so that he and his wife could begin their retirement travels, first stop Rio for a month. Hartland, a much larger firm than Susan's, had the week previous relocated to more spacious and elegant quarters in the World Trade Center building in downtown St. Paul, as if the old office of hardwoods and brass fixtures and deep carpets had been somehow inadequate. The party was lavishly catered with expensive champagnes and drinks of every other sort, roast duck, cold salmon, beef and uncountable hors d'oeuvres laid out along the conference room's endless mahogany table, covered for this occasion with an ornate white cloth.

Susan and David had eaten after their 6:30 arrival, trying not
to seem awed by their surroundings, and now mingled casually,
David not much into networking but acquiescing. Susan held
her champagne glass lightly and David palmed a beer in mild
protest of the opulence. Nearly two hundred other guests moved
in and out of brightly lit and ornamented rooms and among the
hollied desks in the clerical area. A huge, silver-icicled Scotch
pine filled the foyer. Members of Susan's firm had been invited
because they had recently collaborated, successfully, in defending a multi-million-dollar malpractice.

They met Tom Pillatski, one of Susan's colleagues, breaking
away from a group of serious men to freshen his drink. As he
met them, Pillatski half-drunkenly smiled and "how's the fallen
woman?"

"Fine," Susan said, "just fine," as Pillatski moved smiling on,
Susan remembering a recent convention where Pillatski's drinking had loosened his tongue too far and hoping he wouldn't
embarrass the firm again.

"Who's the *fallen woman*?" David asked.

"Me."

"I see no scarlet letter," examining her chest and "Why would
he call you that?"

"Because he thinks I fell into that Dr. Scott thing."

"The doctor who got killed."

"Yes."

"You never did tell me how you got that."

Susan laughing and "Pillatski's right. But about damn time I
got something handed to me. The Scotts worked in Dallas for
ten years before moving up here. Their attorney there was
Martin Dodder."

"Your old law school chum."

"Exactly."

"Your old law school lover."

"We were never lovers. Too busy for that."

"Sure."

Susan sighing and "Not that I would have minded."

"Susan."

"You began this line of questioning, *David*."

"I withdraw it. Your old law school *chum*."

"Mrs. Scott called Martin, asked if he knew anyone here who could represent her. He *of course* knows where I am, gave her my name. She called."

"As you say, it's about time something dropped in like that. You work hard, you deserve something easy," Susan thanking and kissing him.

In the conference room, close to the buffet, Dan Gippart stood talking with a senior partner of Hartland, Finch, and Kloster, who represented IncAmPride now and then. As he talked he scanned those entering, as Reno might.

"That's what's so surprising about Chorske/Scott," Susan went on.

"Who's Chorske?"

"The girl who hit the Scotts. The case drops into my lap and—"

"The court must acknowledge that it's a pretty damn nice lap. Maybe *I* could drop into it later."

"Maybe. Dress up in a legal binder and fall from the ceiling above the bed."

"Kinky lawyers."

"Let me finish. The case drops into my lap, no effort at all required, and now the adjuster from Chorske's company has been so . . . so obliging."

"Unusual?"

"You ought to know, you listen to me bitch about difficult people every night."

"What's the claim rep's name?"

"Brian Meiners. I've asked around and the few people who've run across him say he's straight enough but certainly no pushover."

Pillatski wandered past again, turned and came back and "The head of claims at IncAmPride is by the buffet. Maybe you should chat him up about the Scott file," Susan thinking that for once Pillatski was right.

Pillatski wobbly and "You know Gippart?"

"No."

"Come, I'll introduce you."

They found Gippart still in the conference room eating and talking with Lon Hartland, his watered whiskey in a short round glass by the caviar, wetting the white cloth. Pillatski did-n't want to interrupt the two men, told Susan she was on her own. She waited until Hartland moved away to another out-stretched hand, turned to him and "You're Dan Gippart, aren't you?"

Gippart smiling predatorially at the attractive woman before him and "none other."

She extended her hand and "I'm Susan Burns," Gippart tak-ing it and pressing it warmly while noticing the wedding ring on the hand that held the champagne. Gippart smiled as if he knew her, thought he had seen her name recently.

She was about to remind him of the firm she worked for and the client she represented, but as she began Hartland stepped back in to announce a short presentation for his retiring partner. "Don't want to miss that," Gippart said sarcastically. "Join me?"

"I better find my husband," she told him. "I'll catch you after."

"Certainly," watching her precede him through the door and thinking *ass nice as Sheila's.*

But retirement matters went long, tearful or laughing praise-words piling on top of others like junk cars stacked. David watching amused, listening to Finch's nearly drunk colleagues waxing as lawyers wax. Their interminable eloquence regarding Finch, himself barely able to stand, bored Gippart, who stood thinking *what a bunch of pompous pricks.* He had kept an eye on Susan Burns, saw her nearby holding hands with David, thinking *nothing there* and sliding out unnoticed.

■

She woke to find Jake's side of the bed empty, went to the bedroom door and heard him writing. The next day when she looked at the journal she found that he had merely filled in a few more pages with Jane's name. She was angry and *I'm right here Jake, warm and willing. Why can't you let her go?*

■

Late one afternoon he looked across the room to where Luella sat reading and said quietly, "Can I talk to you a minute?"

She looked up and "Jake, you can always talk to me."

He nodded as if thanking her, then, "I told you about Mark, and there's a couple of other things regarding that," in a voice Luella considered too lawyer-like.

"I'm listening, Jake."

"My lottery number came up in '68, too. Got a draft notice about two months after Mark got his. I was still so stupid I didn't even know what it meant, really," his voice rising at last and Luella hearing anger begin to replace his lethargy. "God I was so stupid."

"I doubt you were ever truly stupid, Jake."

"About the war I was. I didn't even understand the obvious, that if you went to war there was a damn good chance you wouldn't come back. *That's* fucking stupid. Nobody told me. The war on television, in the papers, but where I lived it was like . . . like we were insulated somehow, like the war was just a nuisance somewhere else and not real and no one talked about it. Like the snow and cold kept it distant, the peaceful streets. You know what I mean?"

Luella understanding that she needed to for his sake but "No."

Jake sitting straighter and "The war never walked around in our lives, it never sat down next to us. Where I lived, in South Dakota, and when, in the '60s, *there* was a deadly combination. The fighting and the dying were somewhere else and the people doing them were always somebody else. I never saw a soldier, I never saw a casket—where I lived. Like a relative's drinking, everybody just lowered their faces hoping it would stay hidden. Where I lived you did not acknowledge the painful. We all turned away. I never saw anyone with a sign, never heard anyone yelling 'hell no we won't go.' Not where I lived."

"But you got your draft notice?"

"Yes."

"What happened? You said you never served. You go to Canada?"

Jake grimaced but "Please. I was too dumb for that. And far too cowardly. In more ways than one I wouldn't be here now had I run, because that would have shown an awareness of something to run from. No. My dad made an appointment with our fine white-haired family doctor and he asked me questions and filled out a form and I took it with me to the physical and they failed me. Asthma and some cyst on my ass. I didn't even know what the doctor had written. I didn't know it mattered! I just gave the draft board doctor my note and got a 1-Y classification." Jake leaned forward, wrestled his wallet from his back pocket. From the brown cracked leather he took two small papers. He placed his wallet on his knee and held before him one document in each hand.

Luella stood and went to him, lowering herself onto the armrest on his left. In Jake's left hand he held a faded paper the size of a credit card. Luella took it from him. On the rectangle's lower long side was "Selective Service System" and in bolder letters "Registration Certificate." The card was labeled "SSS Form 2." It held his name, Selective Service Number, date and place of birth, the color of his eyes and hair, height and weight. It listed a left-cheek scar under "obvious physical characteristics." It held Jake's signature and that of the local board clerk, whose handwriting she could not translate. And the date: "was duly registered on the 10th day of Jan. 1968," Luella knowing he would have turned eighteen in December of '67. She put her finger to his cheek, ran it along the mild two-inch scar he had never told her about.

"For a lot of boys," he whispered, "this was a death certificate. They opened the mail one day and they were dead." Luella saw his tears forming, but then he said, "No, I just want to get this out. I'm done being guilty about the past. I'll be all right with this."

She returned the card to him, as she did so turning it over and noting bold print along the bottom "For Infomation and Advice, Go To Any Local Board," thinking *good place to go for advice during a war, a fucking draft board.* She took another paper from him, one initially in the same configuration but folding out to twice the size. The top of it read "Selective Service System" and in bigger letters "Notice Of Classification." The paper announced his name and SSN and "Class I-Y." Dated September 27, 1968. On the back the same advice about advice.

Luella wanting to tell him something and "You should be happy you didn't have to go. *I* am, and I'm sure Jane was."

"Going or not going isn't what bothers me."

"Those two alternatives would seem central to the issue, Jake."

"What's central to me is that Vietnam was the single most important thing for millions of people whether they were there or not, and I didn't even begin to understand what it was all about. How important it was. My dad and I never discussed it. The war was simply never mentioned, the kind of mentality that if you didn't acknowledge something it wasn't real. You'd think something on the order of fifty thousand deaths would occupy a pretty big place in your life, make you speak, but it didn't. I see now that that's where I learned my silence."

Luella put her hand on his neck and "Please don't be ashamed that you didn't go."

"I'm trying, but it's difficult. I was lucky, Mark wasn't. I—"
Luella left her hand on his neck, happy that he was continuing
to tell her what had happened to him but *it isn't only Mark, or
not going, or even Jane dying. He will need to speak it all sometime.*

■

Reno in Gippart's office and "You want me to see her?"

Gippart uncertain, pacing, then making a decision and "No.
Too soon," Reno nodding but thinking he'd probably check in
with the doctor's widow anyway. He had come through the rear
door to Gippart's office at five-thirty, and they had talked for
nearly two hours, sitting and drinking. He left now quietly without saying good-bye.

Schwartz had watched him enter Gippart's office, then waited
in his car near the front entrance hoping the man he could not
identify would come out. When he did Schwartz watched him
move away along the sidewalk, quickly left his car and followed.
Pedestrian traffic remained heavy enough so that Schwartz did-
n't worry about being spotted and he worked his way up close
behind Reno who walked the frosty sidewalk leisurely.

Reno located Jake and Luella's building and swung through
the front security door behind someone entering. Schwartz got
his fingers between the heavy door and its metal frame just
before it closed. He found Reno waiting by one of the two elevators, Schwartz knowing Reno wouldn't recognize him from
Adam and walking up next to him. He nodded at Reno and
"Cold out," Reno only glancing with his silent frigid eyes and
Schwartz too immediately disliking him.

In the elevator Reno pressed the illuminated four-button and
when the doors parted Schwartz hung back tying his shoe, then
followed. Ahead Reno stopped at a door and knocked, waiting,
Schwartz moving past and grateful for a corner to turn at the
end of the hall.

Reno, keenly aware of but unmenaced by the old man who had shared the elevator, waited for him to pass and disappear. Had Luella been home he would simply have told her he had the wrong floor. When after a sufficient time no one came to answer his knock he reached into his pocket and pulled out a small metal tool, quickly jimmying the lock and entering the dim apartment so quickly and silently his movements were nearly imperceptible. He stopped inside the door, listening. His heart rate had not altered. He calmly called out "Is anyone here?" then listened to the refrigerator condenser hum.

After passing Reno, Schwartz had rounded the hallway's corner and now stood waiting as well. After a few minutes he passed back along the hallway glancing at the door upon which Reno had knocked. Schwartz had heard a door opening and closing. In a small brass frame a name was printed "M. Scott." As Schwartz descended in the elevator his mind, obsessed with details, brought him recollections from a pending claim he had looked at the day before. Auto accident. Doctor's wife. Dr. Scott? His wife's name Maureen? If he remembered correctly, this building was the address given on the claimant information sheet. He'd go back to IncAmPride that moment and check.

Jake and Luella returned late. He helped her with her coat and hung his beside it inside the closet near the front door on flimsy metal hangers that had stopped swinging only minutes before. On his way through the living room to the kitchen, where he planned to make coffee, Jake shivered. He stood silent and felt the cold and knew it wasn't any residue they had dragged in from the chilled night. He went into the living room without checking with Luella, who stood in the bedroom changing. The thermostat was set exactly on seventy. Jake puzzled and "Is it cold in there?", Luella not answering. He walked to the bedroom door and watched as Luella pulled a sweatshirt over her naked back. "Is it cold in here?" he asked again, but as he entered he could tell that it wasn't. He went back into the living room.

Their apartment had old cast-iron radiators through which a boiler and pump pushed hot water. Tall narrow radiators stood in the kitchen and bathroom but they were turned off because they made the small rooms too warm. Longer, lower ones lay against the walls in the bedroom and living room. Jake methodically checked each, discovering the living room's to be only slightly warm. He found the bedroom's almost too hot to touch. At the cold radiator he tried to turn the round handle on the heavy pipe near the floor, but could not move it. Finally he was able to twist it with a pipe wrench he retrieved from a workroom he had noticed one afternoon in the basement when, bored, he had explored the building. One of those odd things, he guessed, because he could make no sense of the cold radiator. He would check with the apartment manager in the morning.

■

J. William Lofton and Schwartz like statues bracketing a desk, Schwartz laying a folder on the shiny wood and sliding it across to the sternly quiet figure waiting. Lofton taking but not opening it and "A current matter?"

Schwartz nodding and "Auto liability. An IncAmPride insured, or rather his daughter, struck and killed a doctor. Clear case of liability."

Lofton opened the file and Schwartz waited while he paged through the report's initial pages. Lofton puzzled and "It would seem the limits are hardly sufficient. How could the doctor's wife agree to anything less than three hundred thousand?"

"She wouldn't unless she had been told the limits were less. Gippart would ask for authorization for the policy limits, which he could get easily in this case, then pay her what he'd told her was his limit. Pocket the balance. It's that simple."

Lofton removing his metal-rimmed glasses, stroking his fore-head and "I'm tired. Tell me why you believe this file is one where what you've just described will happen."

"The man I told you about, the one who isn't on the payroll but who sees Gippart often, I saw him enter this building two evenings ago. He took the stairs up and went in the rear door to Gippart's office. He stayed two hours. I waited. When he came out I followed him. He walked three blocks to an apartment building. He took the elevator to the fourth floor. He knocked on apartment number 416. Although I did not see him do so, I am convinced he entered that apartment. I passed back along the empty hallway; I heard a door opening just before, not any steps back toward the elevator. On the apartment's door was a small card, temporarily affixed, with M. Scott hand-lettered. I remem-bered the name. I returned here, located the file I remembered, checked the claimant's name and address. I found it to be the same as that on the fourth floor of the apartment building. Odd that a doctor's wife would be living in a very ordinary apartment."

"Is she? The doctor's wife, I mean?"

"I am not one hundred percent certain, but I believe not. I went back today and watched. A man and a woman live there. I do not yet know who they are. My theory is that they are involved with Gippart and the other man in this phony file."

But Lofton seeing the difficulty with Schwartz's assertion and "The other files, the closed ones, they were different. Those claimants were either made up completely, or they were people who for some reason had agreed to accept less than the checks were ultimately issued for. What we have here seems to be both at the same time. Doesn't make sense. If the woman in that apartment is not actually Mrs. Scott, then they aren't dealing with her directly and don't intend to get her to accept less. On the other hand, this is not a file made of whole cloth. This was a real accident," Schwartz nodding.

"You'd better determine who those people are."

"It's being done."

■

Susan Burns and Maureen Scott lunching at the latter's Stillwater home, Burns admiring the furnishings and the view and "This is a lovely spot."

"You know, I didn't care for the cold when it came, but then I'd never lived anywhere that had winters like this. I'm getting used to it, and the snow down through the trees to the river. It's beautiful. Jack would have liked it. He was so excited about his job, excited about this place. He was going to build a big gazebo down the slope a ways. Relax and watch the river, he said, although we both knew he was too busy for that. Planned to build it himself."

Susan Burns reaching across the small table, covering the other woman's hand and "How are you doing? Are you getting support? You shouldn't be alone."

"My sister has been here, and the wives from the hospital have been wonderful. I'm all right."

"I'm sorry to have to contact you regarding this insurance matter so frequently, but I think it can be concluded rather quickly. What it boils down to is two things: either you accept a settlement for the policy limits or you go to court and get a judgment that will no doubt be higher than the limits."

"You indicated the limits were three hundred thousand."

"Yes."

"What could I expect a court to give me?"

"Let me answer that in two parts. The court isn't going to *give* you anything but a judgment. It doesn't have the money, which must come either from the policy holder's insurance or from the policy holder himself. You could expect two, three, four times the limits from a jury or a judge, of which the insurance company would pay its three hundred thousand. The rest of it would have to come from the Chorskes. William Chorske would have a judgment against him, probably for the rest of his life. Also, you have under-insured motorist coverage on your policy, which would kick in at least as much as Chorske's company."

"I can collect from my own company if the guy who killed Jack didn't have enough coverage?"

"Exactly."

"You're suggesting that perhaps I should just take the two settlements and drop it. Conclude it cleanly."

"I'm not necessarily suggesting you do that. I'm just making your options clear."

"If I did that then Tammy Chorske would walk away without some price being exacted from her, or her family," Maureen Scott feeling her anger rise, not liking it but feeling justified and "Maybe I should screw up their lives the way they screwed up mine—forever. Maybe sue them and garnishee his wages forever."

"That's within your options, certainly."

"I want to forgive, to come to what our pastor keeps yapping about—closure—but I keep coming back to the idea that if I don't sue them, if I simply take the insurance money, then Tammy Chorske doesn't pay at all. Nothing. She lets their insurance company handle it and walk away."

"Yes, but she may not just 'walk away,' as you put it. She's responsible for an awful thing she will have to live with for the rest of her life," Maureen Scott wondering if that was enough and "Doesn't she face some serious charges?"

"Yes, but she's so young that the penalties won't be harsh." Then, "If you don't need the money, maybe it's best to end it. Oh, and I've been in touch with the life insurance carrier. We should have that money next week."

"A million dollars." Pausing, then "How can I say such a figure and not be excited? When we were young and struggling we dreamed of wealth." Maureen Scott returned to the IncAmPride claim, laughing and "Odd settlement advice from a lawyer. The bigger the judgment, the more *you'd* get."

"Quite true," Susan Burns thinking of her annual billing and the money she would have brought to the firm.

"You believe the insurance company will simply issue me a check right away?"

"I don't have a commitment as of yet, but my sense is that's the case. There's no room for negotiation here. I'll call them yet today. In fact, if you don't mind, I'll call Brian Meiners right now."

Without saying anything Maureen Scott rose from her chair, left the glassed dining area that overlooked the river, then returned with a cordless phone. Susan Burns located Jake's number from her briefcase and punched the numbers. It rang twice and "Brian Meiners speaking."

"Mr. Meiners, Susan Burns."

"Hello, how are you?"

"Fine. You?"

Jake playing his part well and "Too much work. People make mistakes too often. Big ones."

"And they always will. It's called job security."

"I guess."

"Brian, I'm having lunch with Maureen Scott, and she's just asked me if Chorske's insurance company will commit to issuing a check for the limits. She's deciding what she wants to do. A lawsuit is still very much in the picture."

"Well, we'd certainly rather not see that," Jake thinking *if she sues the whole thing disappears and we will have wasted our time.*

"Nor I."

Jake wanting to forestall any notion of a lawsuit and "Odd that you would call. I was just going to call you. Met with Dan Gippart this morning, received such a commitment from him. I have authorization to settle this matter for the policy limits."

"Excellent. I'll tell her that. I spoke with Dan the other night," Jake's mind going immediately blank. "We didn't get a chance to talk about the claim," Jake coming again to life and "I didn't know Dan and you were acquainted."

"We aren't. I introduced myself at that Finch thing and then the ceremonies started and I lost track of him."

"That's too bad. You'd find him most interesting."

"That's what I hear. Anyway, please understand that this conversation between you and me in no way obligates my client to accept the settlement we've talked about. She's still deciding."

"Understood. I'll wait to hear from you."

■

Luella eager and "We're close, Jake. I could meet one more time with Gippart, sign a release or whatever I need to sign. Give him the account number. He transfers the money."

Jake had called the private investigator in Jamestown, asked if he knew how to set up accounts so money couldn't be traced. John Carson said he didn't but he knew someone who did. Three days later Carson had called back, indicating that, if the money was moved electronically, they could transfer it immediately out of the account he had set up at a bank very near IncAmPride. Once they had transferred it, the money was untraceable. He asked Jake not to pry into the details. He gave them the two account numbers and the number to access the St. Paul bank's phone transaction line. He said it would take only one call once the money had been transferred.

"Easy money," Jake said to Luella.

"Those private investigators are good," Luella not hearing Jake sighing, not seeing him turn away.

■

Gippart had been available and willing to see her the next morning, Luella now seated across from him hoping this would be the last time she'd have to look at him and "Let's just get this done."

"You'll settle this for the limits?"

"Yes," but Gippart then hesitating. Should he have Reno suggest to her that she should consider even less than $250,000 acceptable? She was just a woman without a husband, helpless.

But then *this is so easy, why fight it?* He reached into a drawer and withdrew a release form, bent over it and began writing. When he had finished he pushed it across the desk toward her and "I'll need you to sign this."

Luella pretended to study it closely though she didn't care what it said as long as it had Maureen Scott's name on it and a quarter of a million dollars. She fished a pen from her purse, Gippart asking "You don't want a lawyer to look it over?"

"No."

"It'll take me a few hours to do the paperwork, to get the money approved."

"I thought you were the boss."

"I am, but the boys in accounting kind of like to know when I write checks that big."

"I'm leaving late morning tomorrow. I'll check my account before I go. I'd appreciate it if you'd transfer the money to this account." She handed him a slip of paper with a long string of numbers inked across it. "And believe me, you would appreciate it, too."

"Count on it, Mrs. Scott." Gippart stood and extended his hand, hating the woman who was going to get so many dollars for doing not one goddamn thing and "Once again, I'm sorry for your loss, and I'm pleased that it has not been necessary to draw this out." *Thanks for the fifty thousand, bitch.*

Luella took his cold hand but said nothing, turned and limped away.

■

Maureen Scott waited on the street near the exit from the Eagan high school's lot. After her lunch with Susan Burns she had sat for an hour debating. She wanted the matter concluded, but she wanted what was right, too. As it did Jake, something about the convenience of dollars bothered her. She had after saying good-bye to Susan Burns convinced herself to accept the insurance money and allow the matter to fade like the exhaust fogging from her idling car. But not even thirty minutes later she wavered, became nervous, uneasy. For reasons she could not explain to herself, she drove to the high school. From where she sat in her car she had a clear view of the doors out of which she believed Tammy Chorske would come. She had no idea if Tammy was in the school or not, if she usually left at 3:30 or some other time. She merely waited, a newspaper picture of the girl, paired with Jack, next to her on the seat. Trapped in the car, she had never seen Tammy at the accident scene. She wanted now to see the girl who had killed her husband.

The school buzzer sounded and young people began to flow from the low brick building. She remembered such a scene from her school in Dallas, and it seemed from another lifetime. She watched the flash of earrings in the sun, the ripped jeans, the torn T-shirts baggy and dirty. She watched girls in short tight skirts, in long flowing dresses, both with combat or work boots, and tried to tell herself that it didn't matter what they wore. In the middle of three blond girls Maureen Scott recognized Tammy Chorske, who bounced along with her friends laughing, their blond hair shining breeze-blown in the January sun. The sight of Tammy in her jeans and white athletic shoes and multi-colored ski jacket made Maureen Scott suddenly, surprisingly sick, as if she were on a wild carnival ride gone sour. She watched the girls get in a new blue car, Tammy driving, and as they passed through the exit into the street she saw them laughing still and heard the bass thump of music. She reached to open her door thinking she might have to vomit, but the spasm passed. She followed them as they drove carelessly to the Mall of America. Occasionally a candy wrapper or cigarette would fly from a rolled-down window. She did not follow them into the mall ramp.

Back home she poured an early drink and sat a moment at the breakfast counter, high on a stool. She had taken only two sips from the whiskey before she picked up the cordless phone and dialed.

"Susan Burns speaking."

"Susan, Maureen Scott calling."

"Hi. I didn't expect you to get back to me so soon."

"I've made up my mind. I would like to sue the Chorskes for as much as I possibly can."

"You sound angry. What happened?" Maureen Scott telling her and finally "If there's any way to assure that she will remember as long as I do, then that's what I'll have to do. I owe Jack that. How soon can you prepare the papers?"

"Are you in a big rush?" Susan Burns did not like the way Maureen Scott's voice sounded, ugly and mean, not the same woman from a few hours before.

"An hour would be too long if it could be done otherwise."

"I can have the papers prepared mid-morning tomorrow."

"Whatever it takes. I would greatly appreciate it. Can they be served right away?"

"Yes."

"Wherever that little bitch's father works, find him and give him the papers," almost crying from her anger and revulsion, at the same time Susan Burns chastising herself for believing that for once a file would unfold and conclude smoothly, that one time the too-human capacities for hate and vengeance would not be tapped.

6

At 7:55 a.m. the following morning J. William Lofton leaned toward Kurt Schwartz arms out and palms open Pope-like as if commanding the other man to speak. Schwartz responding and "We will need to act this morning."

"You have enough evidence?"

"Yes."

"You're certain?"

"Yes," then meticulously and repetitiously "Last evening I visited Mrs. Maureen Scott, the widow of Dr. Jack Scott who perished as a result of our insured's negligence. Our insured is William Chorske. Our insured driver is his seventeen-year-old daughter Tammy," Lofton thinking *I know all that* but patient from long exposure to Schwartz's plodding. "I found Mrs. Scott at her Stillwater address at 7:35 p.m. Upon seeing her at her front door I knew immediately that she was not the woman in the apartment three blocks from this building. By this building I mean IncAmPride. I identified myself, explained my purpose in visiting her unannounced, and after some hesitation she invited me in. It was my impression that she was surprised to see anyone from IncAmPride. She seemed quite hostile, angry.

"Inside I risked asking her directly for identification. I hinted at the possibility of problems with her file, then told her I had to be certain with whom I dealt. She resisted, so I went on to inform her that we had been experiencing some difficulties with our claims handling. She finally produced a driver's license, by which I verified that she, not the woman in the apartment, was

Mrs. Maureen Scott. Also, I made note of the fact that she had no pronounced limp, as does the woman from the apartment."

"Do you know yet who those two are?"

Schwartz raising his hand and "I will come to that," Lofton patient.

"I asked her to describe for me the manner in which her claim was being handled. She informed me that a lawyer, Ms. Susan Burns, was in charge of all negotiations. That she and Ms. Burns had lunched that day—yesterday—after which Ms. Burns contacted Brian Meiners and was informed of IncAmPride's intention to settle the loss for the policy limit of two hundred fifty thousand dollars."

Lofton wanting the clarity his life usually offered him, not receiving it and "It is my understanding that Meiners is no longer working on that file, that he did the initial contact and some investigation but that the matter had been turned over to Gippart."

"The file indicates that, yes."

"Then why would her lawyer call Meiners? And why would Meiners tell her we were prepared to settle? And why would he tell her the wrong limits?"

"I do not know. My guess is that Ms. Burns, the lawyer, spoke not with the Brian Meiners in our claims department but with someone else. Perhaps the man in the apartment."

"Why do you suggest that?"

"I have a hunch."

Lofton not caring for profanity but "I don't much give a damn for hunches."

"I am aware of that. Mrs. Scott went on to tell me that she had decided to initiate a lawsuit against our insured. That she intended to seek a judgment well in excess of the policy limit. That Ms. Burns had that afternoon begun preparation of the papers and would be serving them this morning."

"This is a mess."

"I concur, but one we can clean up. I received just a few

minutes ago a call from Mr. Richardson in Accounting. I had indicated to you several days ago that I would like a contact in Accounting. As you recall, you gave me Mr. Richardson's name, then you contacted him yourself and explained who I was. He informs me that Dan Gippart late yesterday requested authorization for $250,000, a sum to be transferred electronically to Maureen Scott's account at the First Guaranty Bank and Trust Company just down the street. Also, for $50,000, to be transferred to an account allegedly held by the law firm representing Mrs. Scott. Gippart told Richardson he would call and let him know when he had the signed release, and then he could transfer the money."

Lofton sat motionless. He folded his hands like a man praying and "It can't be both ways. We can't be preparing to defend a lawsuit on behalf of an insured and at the same time be issuing settlement money. We are either settling or we are being sued."

"I am quite certain we are not settling. I contacted Ms. Burns late last evening, after talking to Mrs. Scott, to confirm what Mrs. Scott had told me. She indicated in no uncertain terms that a lawsuit would be served this morning on William Chorske, at his place of employment. It is an action that lists him and his daughter as co-defendants. And it regards an accident that claimed the life of Dr. Jack Scott."

"Where then is the money going?"

"I would guess that both transfers are going to the people in the apartment. Then to Gippart."

"I don't see the logic in that. Such a procedure would hardly constitute an ideal crime. We'd still have to settle with the real Mrs. Scott. How would Gippart think he could explain that?"

"I don't know, but clearly some sort of fraud *is* apparent, and we ought to initiate action against Mr. Gippart and his accomplices as soon as possible. The fact that he has been involved in the alteration of earlier files that show financial discrepancies, and that he now seems associated with the Chorske/Scott matter, cannot be a coincidence."

"I ask you again, who are the accomplices?"

"There are three, none of whom has been identified at this point: the man and woman in the apartment, and the man who visits Gippart often. I suggest they are all in it together, and that after we have arranged for Mr. Gippart to be taken into custody, we go to the apartment and do the same with whoever is there."

"But surely Gippart knows he'll be found out if this goes through. He will have paid out a large sum of money and still have Mrs. Scott to deal with. I don't understand this."

"Neither do I."

"No money has been transferred as of yet?"

"Richardson has the account numbers, and had set up everything for the transfer before he contacted me. I instructed Mr. Richardson to make no transfer until he had been authorized to do so."

"Did you inform Richardson of our suspicions regarding Gippart?"

"I did not."

"Does he have documentation that Gippart in fact requested the transfer? Is there a clear paper trail?"

"Yes," J. William Lofton leaning back, nodding, believing *there will be an end to thievery in this company. Today.* "When should we move?"

"We must allow matters to develop a while longer. My partners are watching both the front and rear entrances of Gippart's office, and one other man is watching the apartment entrance. What unfolds will dictate our further actions."

■

Bill Chorske took the fourth in a series of phone calls at 9:02 a.m. hoping it wasn't another agent calling to complain about a policy sale being canceled for what the agent considered some petty reason, relieved when "Mr. Chorske, it's Brian Meiners." They had talked several times about the check for Chorske's car and about how the claim was being handled. Chorske had cared more about the car until Meiners told him that Mrs. Scott could sue and that the claim was worth more than the policy limit.

"You mean she'll sue you," Chorske had said.

Meiners stringing Chorske along and "Why would she sue us?"

"You're the insurance company."

Meiners' dislike for Chorske had not diminished and "A correct observation on your part, but she wouldn't—she couldn't—sue us. She'll sue *you*."

Chorske practically yelling but his words shaded with concern, "Why would she sue me?" Meiners shaking his head and *how do they survive being this stupid?*

"Because you're the one who killed her husband."

"*I* didn't. She can't sue me."

"You're the policyholder. Tammy is listed as an insured driver. That makes you liable."

"Well what the hell do I buy insurance for?"

"To pay any judgment against you up to the limit of the policy. To defend you against any legal action," Meiners wanting badly to reach through Chorske's thick fog of arrogance and "Let me spell this out for you. If Mrs. Jack Scott sues you we will defend you in court. If she is awarded a judgment against you, we will pay it up to three hundred thousand dollars. Anything over that is *your* responsibility."

But that had been before Christmas, and now Meiners was calling, almost reluctantly, to give Chorske good news. "Mrs. Scott has decided to settle the claim for the policy limit. My supervisor Dan Gippart obtained a signed release form from her yesterday. We are in the process of getting her the money."

"She's not going to sue?"

"No."

"Oh sweet Jesus that's good news," Meiners thinking *you can go back to being a prick now.*

"That's the only reason I called. I talked to Dan just a bit ago and he told me about the settlement. I knew you'd want to know," Chorske silent and Meiners thinking *you're quite welcome, glad to help out.*

"Well, I guess that's it," Meiners said.

"Not quite" Chorske told him. "That new car I got with the insurance check you gave me, it's not running like it should," pausing as if Meiners was an auto mechanic.

Finally Meiners breaking the silence and "How exactly might that concern me?"

"Well, I'm having some trouble with the dealership and you need to help me out."

Meiners at last losing his patience and "Whose goddamn car is it, mine or yours?"

"What kind of question is that?"

"Just tell me, who owns the car?"

"I do."

"I just thought we should be clear on that. Now, who picked out the car?"

"I did."

"Who paid for it?"

"You."

"No, you did. I gave you money, *you* bought a car with it. If it's a lemon I'm really sorry, but call someone who gives a damn."

"I wouldn't have bought the car if it hadn't been for that accident. That car that got wrecked was a good one."

Meiners yelling "And who wrecked the car?" Chorske silent. "Your daughter. Jesus, Bill, take a pill or something. I hope to hell I never have to deal with you again."

"You won't, you son of a bitch. I'm switching companies. I'll find one that'll give me some decent service. I'm calling the insurance commissioner," Meiners thinking *a dead man, a widow, two smashed cars, now this.* Ripples in a large dead pool.

The last thing Brian Meiners ever said to William Chorske was "Fuck you."

■

He began to understand that the events of this particular day would bend in a direction unfavorable to his well-being when he took what Sheila labeled an urgent phone call and "Dan Gippart speaking."

A voice shouted "Bill Chorske" but nothing else followed.

Gippart waiting and finally "Yes, Mr. Chorske."

"What do you fucking mean yes?" Gippart's mind lowering itself like a cat threatened or stalking.

"I'll tell you one time, Chorske, and one time only—don't you fucking swear at me."

"Fuck you and every other asshole in your building. You and that Meiners piece of shit. You tell me the claim is settled and not a half hour later I'm served with papers. And one of them has a very large number on it, like two million dollars," Gippart hearing Chorske's obvious anger and his hidden fear as well, Chorske adding "You guys think this is funny?"

Gippart missing but one breath and "I would suggest making what you just said a little clearer. Served with what papers?"

Chorske almost blubbering and "A goddamn lawsuit papers is what."

"Suit papers from whom? Regarding what?"

"Mrs. Jack Scott," in an instant Dan Gippart realizing there was something to the Chorske/Scott file he didn't know, something he could not control.

"Who gave you this lawsuit?"

"A damn process server. Walks through my company and into my office and asks if I'm William Chorske. The prick. I tell him yes and the next thing I know I'm looking at a two-million-dollar lawsuit."

"What do the papers say, exactly?"

"They've got my name, her name, Jack Scott's name, Tammy's name and a big fucking two with lots of zeros after it.

And 'wrongful death.' That's about all I need to know. What's the deal? Meiners called me and said you have a signed release from that bitch."

"I do," Gippart pulling it from the file and staring at Maureen Scott's signature.

"Are we on the same page here? You can't have a settled claim and me a lawsuit."

Gippart feeling something he had not ever felt before and "No shit. I'm going to put you on hold and call Mrs. Scott. Hang on" before Chorske could object. He found Luella's number and listened to the phone ring in the apartment.

The ringing startled them as they sat, Jake reading and drinking coffee at the table and Luella watching television. They had received only a dozen or so calls during their stay in the apartment. Jake and Luella had tried to anticipate the unfolding claim's demands, had been the ones to initiate conversations. When they called Sara they did so from a pay phone. Each tried now to imagine what could prompt a call at this stage. Jake knew that Susan Burns would be phoning about a settlement or a lawsuit, but he hadn't felt she would call so soon. Luella could not think why Dan Gippart would call except to tell her something had gone wrong with the check. It could be Sara with an emergency even though Luella had been stern in telling her not to call.

Jake near the phone and "It seems more likely to be Burns," Luella nodding and "You answer it." Jake put the receiver to his ear and "This is Brian Meiners," wondering immediately why he hadn't simply said "hello."

Gippart further confused and "Brian? What are you doing there?" He had seen him no more than ten minutes before, outside his office.

Jake recognizing Gippart's voice and fumbling for an answer, after a second "I'll put Mrs. Scott on," turning to Luella as he covered the phone and whispering "Gippart." Luella understood as quickly as Jake had that he had made a serious mistake.

She took the phone and "Hello, Mr. Gippart," sounding not hard but nearly apologetic.

"What's Meiners doing there?"

"I asked him to come pick up some things here . . . that he, you, didn't have. I called you but your line was busy."

"What things?"

"Paperwork. Some other tax forms I don't need, thought maybe you'd like them in your file," Gippart hearing her changed voice, somehow understanding and *this never was Maureen Scott.*

Gippart drew in a breath and "I have Bill Chorske on the other line. He called about a lawsuit filed by Mrs. Maureen Scott, but I guess you wouldn't know anything about that, would you?" Luella hanging up and feeling like someone in a building collapsing, turning to Jake and "He knows."

"Just because I answered as Brian Meiners?"

"She's filed suit. He said Chorske's on the phone. I signed the release yesterday, Chorske gets sued today. No wonder he called."

"Luella, I may be stating the obvious here, but I think we ought to get the hell out of here as damn fast as we can."

"I wonder if I could still get that money somehow."

"Screw the money," Jake moving quickly.

Wally Reno had been watching talk shows for a couple of hours until he grew bored again and eager for a different kind of amusement. He decided what he would do to fill the rest of the day, dressed, then left his apartment. He was on the stairs one floor down when the phone back on his desk began ringing.

After speaking with a man who wasn't Brian Meiners and with the woman who wasn't Maureen Scott, Gippart had reflexively dialed Reno's number. His sudden new perception of the world caused him to seek company; he did not want to be alone.

When Wally Reno answered, Gippart was going to tell him "I need you now."

But Wally Reno wasn't home.

Though disappointed, Schwartz decided he had waited long enough for the anonymous man to enter the rear door of Gippart's office; he removed the portable phone from his pocket and called the St. Paul police. There he spoke with an old friend, detective Marvin Mills, who collected a colleague and drove through the moderate mid-morning traffic to IncAmPride. Schwartz met them at the main entrance. He had kept Mills apprised of his investigation so needed to say little.

"The other guy didn't show, so there will be only one inside. I'll go in the front of Gippart's office with you, Marv. Hank, I'll show you the rear door. Wait down the hall a ways. The second man, the one I don't know, will go in that door if he shows up."

"What will he look like?"

"Like a man going through a door. You'll know. I haven't seen anyone else come or go from it."

Mills walking quickly with the other two toward the elevator and "If someone does go in that door, don't allow him to leave, Hank," Hank nodding and feeling naturally for his badge and his gun.

"This other guy will be armed?"

Mills not wanting to take chances and "Yes."

On the fifth floor Schwartz positioned Hank thirty feet down the hall from Gippart's door, then he and Mills walked around and entered the outer reception area of IncAmPride's claim department. At the receptionist's desk they stopped, Schwartz very politely to the woman there "Would you call the president's office please?"

The woman not understanding and "The president?"

"Yes, please. J. William Lofton. Quickly." She dialed. Schwartz took the phone from her and "Come down to Claims."

■

Sheila surprised when Lofton led two other men into her office, recognizing the company president at once though she had seen him only a handful of times, and then only briefly. One of the other men she guessed to be a policeman, though she couldn't have said exactly why. Lofton looked at her as if she were some sort of conspirator, Sheila imagining the cold smoothness of handcuffs on her wrists. Then Lofton commanded her, "Please inform Mr. Gippart that I wish to see him." Sheila did so.

Three blocks away, as they packed what little clothing and accumulations they had brought with them or acquired, Jake said to Luella, "'Turning and turning in the widening gyre . . . the center cannot hold . . . things fall apart.' Man, that Irishman knew what he was talking about." The lines gave him an odd solace, for they suggested that if indeed his life were disintegrating fully, so probably was everyone else's. He considered this observation and *why would that give me comfort?*

Luella, baffled, stared at him and "I don't believe we need poetry at this particular moment in time, dearest," Jake laughing at the sarcasm he had become attached to.

"Perhaps I could act out a scene from a play, then."

"Shit."

They had been packing even before Gippart's call; Jake had nearly completed filling his two suitcases and duffel bag before answering and blundering. While Luella moved slowly among her bags, Jake had straightened the kitchen and thrown away everything he could, leaving some few things in the refrigerator, some frozen vegetables and a bottle of ketchup, leaving in the cupboards some boxes of macaroni and cheese, cereal, pancake mix. He had brought with him plates and glasses and silverware, but very little else, and these they had not needed in the furnished apartment; he had deposited them in a cardboard box which he pulled from the closet. When he had returned to the bedroom, still before Gippart's call, he found her pulling the sheets from the bed and folding them so meticulously it appeared the task might take the rest of the week. Jake in a good mood and "Maybe that could go a little slower," Luella nervously responding that "Maybe it could."

They had planned to pack everything and carry it out to the Explorer, wait until ten o'clock exactly, then drive to IncAmPride. Luella would go in quickly, get the check, and they would drive happy into the noon sun. Gippart's call altered their future and Jake, less concerned about the money anyway, moved with a different priority. Luella tried to match his hurried movements, but soon her leg pained her more than usual.

When Sheila announced his boss, Gippart told her to send him right in; Gippart was glad Reno was not with him in the office. Gippart stood as IncAmPride's president and two other men entered his office. Gippart smiling and "Good morning, gentlemen." With expressions no more humorless than those they usually carried, the three men arranged themselves in a standing arc before Gippart's desk, at which he seated himself.

J. William Lofton pointing sternly and "Mr. Gippart, please tell me who the man is who enters this office quite frequently through the rear door."

Gippart not hesitating and "I'm not sure what you mean."

"There's a man who visits you regularly, who enters and leaves through that door," pointing to Gippart's left. "Who is he?"

"Oh, you must mean Frank. He's a good friend."

"A friend."

"Yes."

"No more than that?"

"No," Gippart smiling.

"Mr. Schwartz informs me this friend, Frank, he visits you often," Lofton repeating himself.

"We're *good* friends. Known him for years. Had I realized

seeing him on company time was such a serious matter, I would-
n't have. Sorry," Gippart meeting and holding Lofton's gaze.

"It's a bit more serious than company time, Mr. Gippart.
Several nights ago that man was observed leaving this office and
going to an apartment a few blocks away. An apartment occupied by a woman claiming to be Mrs. Maureen Scott. She is, in
fact, someone else. The woman your friend visited is, I believe,
perpetrating a fraud against my insurance company. Can you
explain your 'friend's' visit?"

Gippart calm and smooth and "You must have him confused
with someone else."

Schwartz stepping forward and "There is no confusion. I followed him every step of the way. I will swear to it," his thick
eyebrows raised in wide-eyed confrontation.

"Swear all you like, but he's got nothing to do with any
fraud."

Lofton humping himself up and "We'll see about that," then
"Can you tell me, Mr. Gippart, why Mrs. Maureen Scott is filing a lawsuit against our insured when we have in our possession a signed release in the amount of two hundred fifty thousand dollars?"

Gippart outwardly relaxed and "Is that what this is about?
Well, then, there certainly is some illegality going on somewhere.
I personally obtained that release, and not more than an hour
ago Bill Chorske, our insured, called to inform me he had been
served papers. I'm as much in the dark about this as you are. I'm
with you—I believe my department is the victim of a very clever
fraud."

Lofton sternly "As to your being in the dark, my first reaction
is to doubt that very much. As to your being a victim, that is not
the case. No check has been delivered, and none will be."

Gippart lowering his head into his hands and "Thank God
for that."

That was the only thing Lofton could agree with and "Yes,"
then "Who are the two people in that apartment?"

"I believed there was only one. Maureen Scott. She told me she had moved there because it was too painful to live in a house so recently occupied by her dead husband. She provided me with tax documentation to support her claim, and I had no reason to believe she was anyone else," Lofton remembering the photocopies from the file that Schwartz had shown him.

"Why did your friend go to that apartment?"

"I'm quite certain he didn't. You have him mixed up with someone else."

"Well, let us assume that what you say is all true. That Frank, as you call him, is indeed only a good friend and not a co-conspirator. That you, Mr. Gippart, are the victim here, and not this company. In the matter of Chorske/Scott, let us assume these things to be true. But . . . I would like an explanation as well about some other matters." He left the room for a moment, picked from Sheila's desk three large files, those that Schwartz had uncovered inconsistencies in. He walked purposefully back into Gippart's office and placed the files before him, spacing them so Gippart could see the names.

When Jake and Luella had six suitcases and three boxes stacked near the front door, the phone rang once more. They allowed it to go on until the answering machine clicked on. Jake had forgotten to pack it, would have left it had it not been activated now. Jake didn't know if it would even work, as they had received no messages on it before. They had not gone out often and had been home to take what few calls came in.

Sheila's voice, which at first they did not recognize, came loud and "I think you guys had better get the hell out. The company president and the police are in Gippart's office. I'm calling from a booth in the lobby downstairs." Sheila watched as Schwartz and Mills moved quickly across the granite floor and out the revolving door. "The police are leaving the building right now, getting in a squad car out front. Oh Christ, how stupid is this? I shouldn't be leaving a message on your machine, should I?

Brilliant. I heard them say they were going to your place. I don't know where you live, but they acted like it wasn't far. Go if you can. If not, see you in jail."

Jake had stood unmoving, listening, unable to move to the machine and talk directly with Sheila. But now he roused himself and moved quickly to disconnect the machine, placed it on top of wet towels in a box. Luella frightened and "We don't have time to take this stuff to the car. What're we going to do?"

Jake opened the door and peered into the hallway. Just before he was going to tell her that he did not know, he spotted the maintenance closet three doors down near the stairs and elevators. He had seen a janitor working out of it twice before. He believed it would hold their things and them. "Grab two suitcases and come," he commanded, Luella stooping to grasp the leather handles. Jake put one small suitcase under his arm and picked two from the floor. They shuffled the length of the hall to the closet door. Jake dropped what he carried and tried to turn the knob. It would not rotate, Luella observing their position in the hall just where whoever was coming would soon find them and "Shit."

Jake put his shoulder to the door and tried to force it in but had no luck. Then he stood back from it and gave one kick with his right leg, near the handle, and the wood splintered away to the inside and the door banged open, colliding first with an upright vacuum cleaner and then with shelves holding rags and bottles of cleaning liquids. Two bottles fell but they were plastic and did not break.

Jake grabbing the nearest suitcase and "Go back and get what you can," Luella limping up the hall. Jake had stacked the five suitcases by the time she returned. He took the box she held and set it on the floor. He grasped Luella by the waist and shoved her into the closet, wedging her between the shelves and the stacked suitcases. There was no doubt in him that they could all fit, but some concern that he could not wedge everything in and still be able to swing the door shut.

Luella with her chest pushed against a thick wood shelf and "Thank God for small breasts," Jake not hearing as he went back for the last boxes and suitcase. They both heard the old elevator motor start turning, Jake imagining the metal cable winding on a drum. There were no lights on the walls to indicate what floor the elevator was on, whether it was going up or down, only two plastic buttons.

In the apartment Jake piled one box on the other, then the small remaining suitcase on top. He bent and hoisted them feeling a twinge in his back. To free his hands for the door he would have to place his burden on the hall floor, then pick it back up. He chose not to do so, leaving the apartment entrance open wide. The suitcase fell against Luella as he dumped the boxes in and she yelled at him. He bent to straighten the stack and then heard the elevator start again. Swinging the top half of his body upward he cracked his forehead on an old metal coathook, among four others, protruding from the plaster wall. He realized he had not heard the elevator quit. Then he was overcome with the notion that he ought to go back to the apartment and check a last time to see if they had removed everything, but Luella pulled him in. He wedged himself against her as he wrestled the door shut. Full darkness covered them, Jake afraid of *the splintered wood on the doorjamb. I hope nothing shows from outside.* A trickle of blood ran into his right eye.

They heard the elevator stop, the doors part. Then motion past the closet door and one man "Down this way three doors." Then two muffled voices talking, then silence, then the voices coming back, ceasing as footsteps hurried by, then nothing. After a minute "Fucking elevators" and the stairway door opening.

They listened to each other breathe. Once the door had swung shut they were not pressed tightly together, but close enough. Jake had one arm up to keep the top suitcase from falling. He laughed and "The grand schemes of men." Spurred by his adrenaline he asked, nearly laughing, "Time for a quick one?" Luella covering her mouth but her laughter coming louder than either she or Jake had expected. Finally "Standing up is my best position," then after several minutes "Think they've gone?"

"I think they're downstairs at the apartment office checking to see if we've left. They'll talk to the old guy who owns the place, then all three of them will be back," Luella bolstered by the seeming confidence of his assertion.

"What if the old man decides to check in here?"

"I think you know the answer to that."

Pretty soon the elevator and "You know if people just take off I've no responsibility for their deposit. I have every right to keep it."

Another voice and "Were they paid up through the end of January?"

"Yes. Rent is due the first . . . ," then the voice trailing off as they must have entered the apartment, Jake telling her "I'll bet the old bastard is checking for damage, making sure we didn't scratch anything." Jake had talked to the sullen, uncooperative old man only once, the day he rented. They otherwise had tried to avoid seeing people, talking to any neighbor. They had succeeded because the building was quiet and private, the apartments rented mostly by people who were gone all day.

"You suppose a neighbor heard us?"

"Would have come out, wouldn't they?"

"Yes."

"You sure?"

"No," Luella grabbing his crotch and "Enough foreplay," the two of them strangely laughing. Soon the voices came back along the hall. Jake waited for them to see the doorjamb broken, but they passed, one no more than a foot away, and soon the elevator took them.

"What now?"

"We wait."

"How long?" Jake answering "I wish I knew. If they think we're gone for good, which the open door and empty apartment suggest, then we could walk out of here any time. If they believe we're still around, they may keep surveillance."

Luella feeling Jake's face and with a tissue from her purse wiping his forehead clean of thickening blood and "They'll ask what kind of car we drive."

"No way to tell if the old man knows, if anyone in the building knows." The apartment had no parking facilities so they had rented space in a ramp across the street, occupied only by monthly renters who were issued a card. Leaving the lot, they slid the card into a scanner and the gate would raise, so there was no one to say "yes a woman with a limp drives the green Explorer on level two." As he stood with her Jake began to wonder if most of what happened to anyone wasn't simply a matter of luck, that very little had anything remotely to do with his desires or anyone's, and that, strangely, gave him hope.

They waited until 1:30, when Luella's leg began to ache badly. Jake massaged it, but that relief did not last long. Jake's back began to hurt. He tried to arrange a seat from the suitcases, but there wasn't enough room. He realized they could stay in the closet no longer, laughing again and "Broken down old people." He did not tell her that he loved her but he kissed her tenderly and held her and then worked his way into the hall as Luella listened. If someone were watching, they might well be somewhere near their apartment door. But no one confronted him.

He took two of the suitcases down the stairs, then went to the main entrance and peered through the narrow window beside the door. Across the street a man sipping coffee sat in an idling car, Jake deciding not to take chances. He found where the building service entrance emptied into the alley. He circled two blocks west, entered the parking ramp from the rear, seemingly holding his breath the entire way. Upon exiting the ramp he had to pass the idling car, but it remained where it was as Jake drove to the corner and turned. He pulled into the alley and stopped under an "Absolutely No Parking" sign, found the suitcases where he had left them. He worried about blocking the alley but six minutes later they exited it, Jake steering through the dim afternoon. A few blocks away he found himself laughing again and "That went to hell in a hurry, didn't it?"

But then he didn't want it to go to hell, and he swung the Explorer around the block and headed back toward IncAmPride, Luella surprised and "Where are you going?"

"I want my damn money."

"Jake, we can't go in there."

"Yes we can."

He located a handicap parking spot near the front entrance of IncAmPride. Luella, having decided she would go to jail with him, got out and trailed him into the building. They ascended to Gippart's floor and found Sheila at her desk, the entire area near Gippart's office empty of people.

Sheila shocked to see them and "What in hell are you doing here?"

Jake firm and "Is there a way we can get the money transferred?"

Sheila, in the rush of events with Gippart and Lofton and the others, had practically forgotten about the money. Now the image of green bills stacked very high returned to her, and she made up her mind.

"I'll go down to Accounting," she said. "I'll tell Richardson that Gippart wanted this sent through. Maybe he'll do it."

Jake admiring her and "You sure? If it's too risky, we can live without the money."

Sheila trembling and "Goddammit, I can't."

■

The afternoon unwound slowly, Sheila edgy at her desk and watching the clock too often for it to move quickly, realizing that Gippart would be gone from his office forever. Though she had hoped for exactly that resolution when she decided to aid Luella and Jake, now it seemed somehow unreal, untrue, that in a morning or two Gippart would be back inside his den, tip his chair back and laugh at someone whose husband had electrocuted himself with a television antenna.

When she had gone down to Accounting, Richardson wasn't there. His secretary said he'd be back in a minute. Sheila told her that Gippart had gotten a release regarding the Chorske/Scott matter and wanted the money transferred as soon as possible. She gave the secretary the file with the release paper-clipped to the top and "I better get back upstairs. If Mr. Richardson comes back soon, show him this, will you? Thanks."

On her break she met Lorna at a nearby coffee shop, told her only about what had happened that morning. When she returned to her desk it seemed the clock on the wall she faced would not move. She eventually made it through the afternoon by focusing on business as usual—she blankly answered the phone, startled every time it rang; faxed and mailed correspondence to branch offices; maintained files. Lofton had not indicated what she should tell anyone calling for Gippart, so she simply announced that he was not available and took messages.

It was her night to meet the others at the bar, but Sheila found herself so drained and unnerved that she desired most the familiar comfort of her own home. She called Darla at 4:00 and told her the news about Gippart and that she planned to go directly home after work.

"You sound like you could use a good stiff drink," Darla told her.

"I'll be fine. I just want to go home, put on some sweats and lie down."

"If you need us, call."

"I will. Thanks."

At the house she surprised Jasmine and Caitlin, who seemed disappointed at her early arrival, Jasmine telling her mom-like "You should have called first."

Sheila laughing and "So you could clear out the boyfriends?"

The girls repulsed at the idea of boyfriends and in unison "Please." Then Sheila explaining "I was just too beat to go out tonight." She smelled nothing cooking and "Did you guys start anything for supper?"

"No. Sorry."

Sheila feeling almost light-headed, celebratory and "That's all right. Let's get a pizza. Anything you want. You call while I change," the girls looking at each other surprised.

"You meet somebody at work today?"

"What do you mean?"

"A man?"

Sheila mimicking them with an exaggerated roll of her eyes and "Please."

"You seem in a really good mood."

"I guess I am. Hard day at work and it feels good to be home. That's all." She left them and went into her bedroom, where she shed her dress and slip. From a drawer she removed a new dark sweatshirt and pants but then decided she wanted something older, softer. She remembered the gray sweats that she had bought the blue to replace—the grays had a hole in one knee, were threadbare at the elbows and covered with small paint and food stains. She had decided at the last moment not to throw them away, had put them in the hall closet.

Wearing only her underwear she went down the hall three steps, pulled open the closet door and switched on the light. She was more than startled but did not scream when she saw Wally Reno smiling at her. He turned, lifted from a shelf an old cowboy hat that Caitlin had used for a school play audition. He calmly placed the hat on his head, hooked his thumbs inside his belt and "Howdy, ma'am. I'm a stranger to these parts."

■

In a phone booth at a truck stop Jake had punched in the numbers from a slip of paper in his wallet. He had checked the balance, an electronic voice informing him dispassionately that he possessed a quarter of a million dollars. Then he followed the voice's instructions and made the transfer.

Now, Jake sitting across from Luella in one of the restaurant's booths and "I think we should just go on. Get the hell out. We got the money."

Luella adamantly "I want to know the rest of what happened to Gippart. And I want to know that Sheila's all right."

After leaving the alley behind their apartment Jake had driven south on the highway, thinking vaguely of catching I-90 west to Sioux Falls and then maybe Mitchell. He did not know what drew him in that direction rather than to the northwest, Jamestown and home. They had not discussed what they planned to do, and when Luella sensed his intentions she made him pull into a busy truck stop. They were hungry anyway in the late afternoon.

Jake arguing mildly and "Look, we're finished here. Let's get the hell out and spend the rest of our lives wondering if someone will ever discover it was us who ripped off IncAmPride. There's no reason for us to stay. We'll call Sheila sometime."

"We'll *drive* to Sheila's. We'll talk to her there," Jake looking at her like she was a fool and "We don't know where she lives."

Luella sensed an unexpected tension between them, which she tried to lighten with "They have this new thing called a phone book. You look up a person's name and the book lists their number and address." Then "Jake, I'd just like to know *today* what went down. And I'd like Sheila to know."

"What if they know about her, what she did? What if she's told them about us? They could be watching her place. It'd be like us driving in, honking the horn and waving—'Here we are! Come arrest us!'"

She couldn't figure out why he wasn't feeling the same high she was from the danger and the money. They talked a while longer, then Jake reluctantly agreed to drive to Sheila's.

They sat drinking coffee until almost four, located Sheila's address, then took the highway back toward St. Paul. "We'll get there early," Luella told him, "see if anyone's watching her house. We'll see what happens when she comes home. We should be able to tell if things are okay."

"This is her night at the bar."

"You're right. Let's go there first." So they returned through thickening late afternoon traffic to St. Paul and reached the bar just past 4:30. They waited fifteen minutes before they saw Darla arrive, then a little longer for Lorna and Cindy. Twenty minutes beyond that they concluded Sheila wasn't coming.

"Why isn't she here?" Luella asked.

Jake apprehensive and "Could be bad."

"Could be."

Now it seemed like it was Jake who wanted to know, that Sheila's perhaps ominous absence had kicked him out of his previous mood. "Let's get out to her place," he said, Luella nodding and following him out into the winter dusk.

It was nearly 6:00 and fully dark before Jake and Luella finally located and drove past Sheila's house the first time, noted a car in the driveway they had to assume was hers. There were three cars parked nearby along the street, but none appeared to be police vehicles or occupied. Jake circled the block, parked along the low curb in front of a house neighboring Sheila's, waited several minutes.

Luella anxious and "What now?"

Jake focused, pointing and "Let's walk along the hedge between her driveway and the neighbor's yard. We'll go into the garage, see if there's a door inside," Luella noting the two-stall garage, its door raised but inside a darkness she could not penetrate. Jake got out of the car, closed his door quietly. He walked around to her side and helped her out, then they stepped along the nearly shoulder-high hedge, Jake asking "You want your wheelchair? You could be a female *Ironside*." Luella whispered that she was fine as they squeezed between the hedge's stiff bare branches and the garage and slipped into the black interior.

They stopped for what seemed like a long time waiting for their eyes to adjust to the dark.

Jake turned to the inside of the garage while Luella peered out along the driveway, watching for anyone who might have seen them. No one came. Jake could see a curtained window at the top of what he guessed to be a door, but the curtains were drawn tightly together and let out only a thin light. Jake took Luella by the arm and walked slowly toward the light. Since it was a few feet above him, he guessed there were stairs, maybe two or three steps up. As he moved slowly he tentatively circled each alternating foot ahead attempting to find anything that might lay on the floor along the line of their movement. They were very near the door when his lead foot lightly bumped a wooden step. Jake knelt and felt up the three steps.

"Stay here," he told Luella, she not as secure after he had released her arm; she had lied to him, for her leg ached badly from having stood so long in the closet.

Jake moved slowly up the stairs, found that the window was eye-level. At one place where the curtains were drawn together there was an opening no more than an eighth-inch wide. He cocked his head and peered through it. The narrow curtain opening revealed what looked like a small entry way just inside the door, Jake guessing the basement stairs lay to the left or right. Beyond the entry was the kitchen, whose overhead light, though he could not see it, must have been on, because the light in the room was quite bright. He could make out a young girl sitting in a chair at a round table. He saw as well that she was naked at least from the waist up. He could not see below the middle of her back because of the chair. He shifted a little, saw that beyond the girl sat Sheila. When the girl shifted Jake blinked twice, surprised that Sheila wore nothing on top either. On the table before them he saw the shiny corner of what appeared to be a board game. In a moment he watched Sheila reach, pick up some dice, and roll them. She looked terrified, Jake knowing immediately *Gippart's pal*.

He stepped down to Luella, put his hands on her shoulders and "Someone's in there with them."

"The cops?"

"I think maybe Gippart's buddy. I see Sheila and one daughter. This may sound a little odd, but they're sitting at the kitchen table, topless, playing a board game."

Luella blinking surprised and "Jesus."

"Go back to the car, find a phone, call 911. We've got her address written on that paper in the glove compartment. Okay?"

Luella trembling but "Okay," wishing she had given in to the salesman and got the car phone option he had so enthusiastically pushed but then *there would be a record.*

Jake insistent and "Go. Now."

He pushed her away, watched her walk as quickly as she could out the door and along the driveway. When he heard the car start he turned back to the steps.

Reno grinning, rolling the dice and "Isn't this special now? *Pachisi* is such a fun game. Always used to play it with my mom when I was a kid. And now here you girls are playing with your mom. Really a nice moment, I'd say." The three women sat silent.

Reno clapping and "Will you look at that? Another six." He leaned forward and moved his playing piece out onto the board. "I'm doing pretty well given the distractions," examining each woman in turn. Pushing the dice toward Caitlin and "Your turn."

Jake put his fingers around the door handle. He turned it with the patience of a man who knew how to sit for hours in nothingness. It was not locked and revolved without noise. He felt for a deadbolt but found none. He drew in a breath and without thinking pushed the door open. He found himself suddenly in the kitchen with three women covering their breasts and one man standing.

Reno, without changing his tone or the expression on his face, said, "Sorry, maximum of four players. Well, go ahead, take my place." He turned calmly and began toward the living room. Jake stepped after him and grabbed his shoulder, spinning him around. Jake balled his right hand into a fist and swung, but Reno ducked cleanly out of the way. Then Reno, with the presence and skill of an accomplished boxer, countered Jake's miss with a right of his own that caught Jake in the belly with ferocious energy. Jake had begun to double over when Reno's left caught him flush on the jaw. The punch sent him reeling into a chair, then onto the carpet. Reno stepped efficiently to him and delivered a kick to Jake's belly, which Jake partially blocked with a forearm. He tried to get up but Reno hit him in the face again. "I said you could take my place," Reno told him, laughing, "no need to get upset." Then he turned and went out the front door.

Sheila running to Jake at the same time yelling at her daughters "Get some clothes on." Bending to Jake and "You all right?"

Jake sensing that despite a tremendous pain in his stomach and on his face he was not seriously hurt and "Yeah, I guess so." Then nearly laughing and "Guess I showed him. Too bad the cops didn't get here in time."

Sheila thinking ahead and "Cops?"

"Luella went to call them."

"They better not find you here, Jake. Too many questions."

Jake realizing that she was right and standing. "Everything all right at the office? You okay?"

"Gippart got fired. No one accused me of anything, so I assume I'm not in trouble. Not yet, at least. They'll be investigating further." Pushing him toward the kitchen door and "you really better go, Jake. Check your account. I think the transfer went through, but I'm not sure. Wait a couple of months, then call."

Jake nodded, staggered down the steps into the garage. Then

he remembered. In the dark he turned to her and "It went through. We transferred it by phone. We got the damn money." He didn't sound that happy. "Thanks, Sheila." He shuffled out beyond the hedge, squatted painfully where the branches were thicker. In no more than a minute a police cruiser drove up and two uniformed officers got out, drew their guns. One went into the garage, one to the front door. From his shadows Jake watched Sheila answer the door. He didn't know what she would tell the police, what she would tell her daughters. He didn't know how the 911 call could be explained. Sheila would just have to say someone must have seen Reno inside with them and called.

He walked through three yards, keeping close to the houses. Just around the corner he saw Luella's car. She didn't see him coming and he startled her when he opened the door. In answer to her look "Police are there. He got away. Beat the shit out of me first." He put a hand to his jaw and "This, goddamit, is what you get believing the past is a frame rail you can straighten. I want no more of it. Drive."

■

Reno driving as if nothing had happened, on his way to IncAmPride to have a laugh with Gippart over what he had been doing at Sheila's. He found the building's front doors still open. It was not yet late and he imagined quite a few people were still working. He felt sure Gippart would still be in his office. He began his usual route up the stairs to the fifth floor.

Kurt Schwartz watched Reno come in, waited a few moments, then began following him up the stairs. When he got to the fifth floor he was well out of breath and had to wait a minute before going into the hallway. He pushed open the door and found Detective Marvin Mills standing by the rear door to Gippart's ex-office.

Mills looked up from the carpet when he heard the door

open, and when he saw it was Schwartz he said, "Haven't seen anybody yet."

Schwartz alarmed and "What do you mean?"

"I mean I haven't seen anybody come through that door."

"But I just followed the man we're waiting for up the stairs."

Mills joined him and they went back down, at each landing opening doors into hallways that showed no trace of Wally Reno.

■

Luella turned her car northwest, toward home, anxious suddenly to be in her own house and feeling triumphant in a way she never had before. She let her mind race into the future; she would remodel the store now, maybe pay for tuition if Sara wanted to go to college. She thought of Sheila paying off at least most of her debts. She turned the radio on and the music fed her euphoria as she tapped her fingers on the steering wheel. Jake sat silent beside her, holding his belly and his jaw, looking into the dark sky beyond the headlights, trying very hard *not* to think of money.

7

They drove northwest along I-94 until they reached Alexandria. They were still at least three hours from Jamestown, and Luella told Jake that she didn't want to ride in the car any longer; that her leg, after all the events of the day, needed something other than a car seat. Jake was exhausted, too, so they checked into a motel just off the highway.

Later, in bed, Jake listened as Luella's breathing slowed and she fell into a deep sleep. He lay awake, staring at the dark ceiling, knowing that when sleep took him he would not be able to avoid the old disaster of his dreams. He had known his defeat ever since Wally Reno had kicked him in the stomach, but had said nothing, not wanting to take the edge from Luella's excitement. He knew that Jane waited for him, that she always would, and that he had no choice but to give in at last. He closed his eyes.

■

She comes soon after. He sits cross-legged on the grass near her grave, and when he looks up from the grass he sees that the granite stones marking the graves are gone, replaced by the now-empty slab tables upon which Jane and Mark had rested. Jake feels a slanting afternoon light, his spine military straight, his calloused and paint-stained hands curled palm-up on jeaned thighs, his posture monk-like, meditative. The grass smells recently cut, a coagulate green all around. He blinks to clear the vague scene and things in front begin to focus. The tables arrange themselves into a long row, just as before.

Then, beyond the tables, a building rises from the field. He cannot tell if its walls are metal, concrete, or brick. A single window marks the one wall that he can see, two or three stories up. Jake stares at the window's shiny black opening.

He feels people coming up from behind, but he cannot turn to see whom. He is afraid when he hears their shuffling steps closing. A bare woman's arm reaches over his shoulder and places a gallon can of gasoline on the grass in front of him. Jake sees the can's shiny red metal diagonally striped yellow, on the stripe red letters, "GASOLINE." The rectangular top glimmers unpainted, as does the thin handle, its edges rolled. A screw-on articulating spout rises from one end.

Jake glances up to the window as if expecting someone, but its dark metal casements frame nothing. He feels as if a million people are watching him through the window.

Jane appears, her body whole, dressed as she was the last time he saw her. She reaches for the can, lifts it from its green cradle. Jake hears the liquid sloshing. Fume-smells come strong. She pops open the small plastic vent cap opposite the spout, raises the can and tilts it above Jake's head. He feels the liquid soaking his hair, running in the crevices behind his ears, layering his face like thin clear lacquer. His eyes remain open. He feels nothing. The can empties and Jane tosses it aside. Jake looks down and sees his shirt and jeans soaked. The fumes intensify.

A large box of wooden matches appears where before the can had rested—Jake notices how the box lies inside the flattened grass rectangular. Jane picks up the box.

Behind her a crowd of vague figures flows out of the window and assembles on the grave-marked grass between him and the building. Tom Mortonson, a boy with half his face missing and his mother. Others like them, to whom Jake had once given comfort with a small piece of paper. Jake sees gasoline running down their faces, too, soaking their clothes. A flowing channel of gas runs eagerly from him to the figures.

Jane removes a match from the box and "Shall I light it, Jake?" He sees it is her but does not recognize her voice.

"I asked you, Jake, whether I should light the match."

Jake cannot speak. He wants to shout "No!" but his mouth seems gone. He raises his right hand to where it should be but feels nothing.

"Jake? Can you not speak?"

She lights the match, moves it toward him and "If I light you, Jake, I light them all. What should I do?"

Jake sits mute, unmoving.

"I'll take that as your answer, Jake." She drops the match into his lap and the whoosh from igniting fuel comes to him just before the flames run up his shirt, then across his face and eyes. Through them he can see the flame running along the channel between him and the others; when it reaches them, it rises in massive conflagration. And beyond them two men laughing down at him and the others ablaze. And Jake not moving, not speaking.

■

He awakes calm and dry, because he knows where he must go to surrender, where it must end. He wakes Luella and they gather the few things they had brought in. Jake tells her he will drive. The only thing he says in the car is that he must go to Mitchell, and from the resolute tone of his voice and the hard glare of his eyes, she knows she has no power to stop him. She shivers when she knows he has changed again, asks him what caused it, then allows anger to consume her when he will not speak of it.

■

Jake beginning toward Jane's marker, three steps from the car turning and "You could hear this too."

Luella had felt his passivity almost fully reemerge as the space between them and Mitchell had shrunk. Halfway there it had intensified, turned malevolent. Her sense of triumph had been replaced by fear and anger as she felt Jake retreating. So her sarcasm came and "I *could?* I feel so *lucky!*"

Jake stopped as if lost, but Luella had already had enough of him and she wanted to end it. She took his hand, shepherding him to the low-mounded grave of the woman long-driven into memory but still too real in his head. They parted and stood each to a side, Luella watching him. He moved his weight foot to foot in the thin layer of crusty snow, his eyes at the ground.

At Jane's grave shafts of sunlight broke through and warmed them slightly, though the wind, with nothing to impede it, moved from the northwest with a mild bitterness.

Luella prompting him with "Well, we're all gathered. Speak to us, Jake." He stood for some moments longer and then lowered himself onto the brown-stiff grass in a small place where the snow was not thick enough to rise above it.

"Don't get up, I'll manage," Luella told him, Jake rising and holding her as she awkwardly bent her legs. Her palms touched the ground flat as she pivoted into a sitting position. The snow crackled as she composed herself, sitting her bad leg folded. She looked at him, softened and "You are not alone," Jake sitting again without looking back at her.

"No doubt about that," Jake told her, putting his hands to his head, "a damn crowd here pointing at me. It got worse after Mark. That summer the POWs came home I watched them gaunt and shrunken and hollow-eyed and saw they too had died from their witness of death working. That they were like cars, partial or total losses, driven a long way and not taken very good care of. That you couldn't count by body bags only. I thought of them for the first time as they returned . . . as they returned . . . I felt them looking, considering *me*, their eyes asking 'why did you let this happen?' I had no answer. Nothing I could say to them could change even slightly what had happened, what I had done."

"Young men dying wasn't your fault, Jake."

"Oh yes it was. Mark. But I only realized it after," Jake clobbering his hands together and "After after after after. Real people took real bullets, filled real caskets. Those who loved them shed real tears. Why did I never hear anyone crying? Too busy being stupid. Only *afterward*, don't you see? Like I had chosen to be brain dead, or that in my ignorance I had chosen not to understand. Still, it wasn't even a choice. For me it was . . . *nothing*. Other people, who were *alive*, understood the horrible mistakes, and if more of us had been like them, the war never would have escalated. They knew what a nightmare it was, what an ungodly horrible Jesus Christ mistake that no one not even God could make right if it continued. But too many of us didn't say a goddamn thing. We let it happen. *I* let it happen" and he began to cry again, Luella thinking *he believes it. All that in St. Paul for nothing.*

"Brother, when I got it, I *got* it. Sometimes I'd be walking along and I'd think about taking another step and triggering a mine and it blowing my legs off. I'd look down at them still whole and think *my legs*, then imagine them gone. Such a thing happened over there ten thousand times while I sat reading books, silent. God. There aren't many things worth your legs, Luella, not many at all. Not unless you choose to offer them up. I'd go outside at night and imagine it raining and me in the jungle in the mud and scared to death. But you see I didn't do that *while* it was raining, *while* people stepped on mines. I did it fucking afterward. It took years for the bombs and bullets to reach *my* brain. And by then a lot of people were past tense. You don't deserve life if you're aware of it only after it's gone by."

"Jake, get to it. What's all this have to do with Jane?"

"After the POWs I started thinking about Mark again. This was six, seven years after I betrayed him. Jane and I would be lying in bed at night, holding each other, making love or just finished. Or just sitting reading. I would wonder what right I had to hold such pleasure, to feel such joy, when people had died, given up their legs. I *still* feel that guilt. It *still* overwhelms me. Touching you gives me such pleasure, Luella, it really does, but then I start thinking again. What right have I to you? What right do any of us have who were silent and survived? None. But I was pretty good at blocking that out, at least until Jane died. Then I blocked out *everything*. I thought I could do it forever."

Luella stretched, put her hand to his shoulder and "Someone dies every minute, Jake, every second. They get killed by cars, shot, starve. You'll go nuts if you sit around thinking how or why you're still here and they're not."

"But goddamn it I could have said no. Jane and I saw Mark in the mall in Sioux Falls, not long before her accident. I looked in his eyes and they asked 'why didn't you tell me?' I just ran. Having seen him was killing me for a few weeks but then I was getting it buried again. She must have thought something was wrong between her and me. Because I refused to speak of it, she had no way of knowing. My fucking silence. She wanted me to go with her to Parkston that last afternoon, but I wouldn't. I told her I wanted to work in the shop. Again, all I had to do was say the right thing, the decent thing, *right then*, and she would have known. And I was going to, that night. *After* she came back. I have no doubt that's what was on her mind driving, the last thing she thought of me." He turned to the head of the grave and said, "I loved you, Jane, and you brought me so much joy. My final words, had I known they would be final, would have been 'I love you.'" And then, as if she were there, "I've never stopped, and I am so sorry for what I didn't say and do," Luella watching his hands come flat on the grass and feeling him yearning to touch her.

"You never talked to her about it," Luella remembering her first husband who would draw silence around himself and mope and never speak to her what was wrong.

"No."

"Why, Jake?"

"Luella, *I don't know*. My shame made me dead inside. I have no explanation, no excuse. All that's left is I didn't."

"You're speaking now, Jake."

"Too late. Always too late. Oh Christ, Luella, too many silences that can't ever be filled, too many people dead" and he wept as hard as she had ever seen a man weep.

When his sobs ebbed she said, "I thought what we did in St. Paul meant something."

"It did, but don't you see it can't last?"

"No, I don't see."

"You can't fix people with money or revenge. I pretended for a few months, like I did when I was a lawyer. 'Here, take this check, you're all right now.' All that was a lie and so is what we did in St. Paul."

"It's not a lie for me, Jake."

She moved to him and held his head in her arms feeling the quiet exhalation of his tears and then he clung to her like a drowning man to salvation thinking *two women holding me. I was and am now blessed*, but he could not receive it because he could not trust his own voice for its failures. They sat twined like a single frozen figure past lunch time, grew colder as frost filled the patchy grass between drifts, Luella finally stiff and hurting in the cold and "I can't sit this way any longer. We have to go, Jake."

Jake numb and "Leave me here."

"No. I'll help you up." She stood awkwardly and reached for him. He lifted his arms weakly, but she took them firmly and raised him. He walked behind her to the car, opened her driver's door and closed it after her. She lowered her window and "Get in the car, Jake," but Jake silent. "Please."

Jake bending to the open window, remembering *all of this happened before the same thing over.*

"We'll drive to Mitchell, get something warm to eat. Come. Now," her eyes scared but Jake still hesitant.

"I need you, Jake. I do. Please." Then Luella angrier than ever at his placing between them something old and lost and "Or rot like your fucking car, Jake. So lay yourself out here and rust." Then trying again and "Cut it away, Jake. Leave it here with the dead. You made mistakes, like everyone else," but knowing her words alone had no power over him. Simply asking another time, "Last chance, Jake. A short walk. You could at least repair that part of it. You could come this time." He did not move.

Luella on the highway approaching Mitchell thinking *I don't need somebody that fucked in the head, I don't. Responsible for everyone else's life. Why not mine?* It began to snow, at first lightly but within a mile heavier, driven by a stronger wind out of the northwest. She pulled into a field approach and *Jesus he can't be that stupid, can he?* She sat a half hour torn between going back to try yet again and going north to Jamestown and forgetting him.

He was not in the cemetery when she went back, Luella wondering if he had gone to Pete and Kathy's but *no, his shame wouldn't allow him there.* She drove back to the highway and turned south toward Vermillion, but she didn't see him and knew that he could not have walked that far in the time since she had driven away from him.

She found him walking along the edge of a gravel road heading east in the direction of Sioux Falls, head bowed, ungloved hands at his side, far enough onto the road that it wouldn't be difficult for someone confused by the thickening snow to make a mistake and run him down. She slowed and *he's going to Mark. Or he just wants to die.* One side of him was coated with snow, it melting in places around his eye and joining the tears. She drove on and turned into the next field approach, then backed out far enough so that he would have to walk around her to go on. She waited. He stopped when the car blocked his march. She got out and stood next to him in snow already three inches deep, but he did not acknowledge her.

"Jake," she said, then after he failed to move she repeated it louder because the wind had increased. She began out of anger to cry herself and then she shoved him with both hands. He toppled onto the slope of the ditch like a corpse two-days stiff. She was going to kick him but he opened his eyes, and in them, through splintered bits of horizontal snow, she saw the last glimmer of his will.

She shuffled two small unsteady steps to his side, bent and took his hand though he had not offered it. She unzipped her coat and put his reddened palm and fingers against her leg where the metal plate joined bone-ends that had once been unable to hold themselves. "My leg, Jake," pressing her hands over his as hard as she could, "my leg." She felt his fingers tighten.

■

Sheila standing at her kitchen sink washing the last of the supper dishes, rinsing and placing them carefully in the drainer to her left, the warm water steaming slightly the window that looked out onto the back yard where the trees had begun to green. She looked at the dead leaves they had not raked the previous fall. She, Jasmine, and Caitlin alternated kitchen duty, so every third night required her to clean up after they had eaten. She tried to give order to their lives by demanding certain deadlines, one of which set supper for no later than six-thirty, clean-up and dishes immediately following. As she cursorily finished she stared out the window grateful that the days were not so dreary now that April had come, the sun longer in the sky and on the trees.

She heard the phone ring as it did ten times a night for her daughters, surprised this time when Jasmine stepped into the kitchen and gave out a disappointed "Mom, it's for you." Sheila knew it wouldn't be a telemarketer; the girls had been trained to screen them, and in their youth they took pleasure in a cheerfully sarcastic "No thank you" and hanging up.

She took the cordless handset and "Sheila Voigt speaking."

"Sheila, it's Luella."

The name and its attendant voice took a moment to register, Sheila managing only "Hi" and then "It's been so long."

Luella's voice wary and "Is it all right to talk?"

"I'm sure it is."

"I debated calling, thinking trouble might have developed on your end." Luella let the end of her sentence hang, as if expecting Sheila to tell her there was or there wasn't.

"No trouble for me."

Luella relieved and "You're still at IncAmPride, then?"

"Yes, same job. Got a great new boss. A woman," Luella hearing a distinct lack of enthusiasm in Sheila's announcement and "You don't seem too thrilled."

"She is, if you don't mind my language, a complete and utter bitch. You could light matches off her. Make ice with her voice. Sometimes I almost wish for the good old days," pausing, then "well, not really. But she is *difficult*."

Luella sensed that she should change the focus of their conversation and "What's become of Gippart?"

"Well, I think I told Jake that night that they fired him. The company president canned him just after I called you guys to warn you."

"Yes, Jake told me."

"It was truly a pleasure to watch him escorted out by two security guys. He didn't look real happy carrying one little box of his personal things. Pathetic. IncAmPride brought charges the next day. Dan Gippart is in legal trouble big-time. I heard that almost half a million dollars is unaccounted for.

They arrested him, he pleaded not guilty, out on bond. I haven't seen him. From what I've heard, they have an awfully strong case against him. There's a good chance he'll see jail time."

"I hope so. But you're okay, nobody suspects you?"

"An investigator came around and asked about the phone number on the loss form, but I just played dumb. Told him that's the way it had come in. He wondered about there not being any agent's signature at the bottom, but I told him I couldn't help him there."

"I'm really happy to hear you're okay. I worried."

"They were after another guy, too, someone they think helped Gippart."

"The police got him?"

"No. He'd come back to IncAmPride about 6:30 looking for Gippart, couldn't get in because they'd changed the locks. IncAmPride's investigator and a cop were waiting. But he just disappeared."

"Jake says he believes that man in your house was the same guy he'd seen with Gippart."

"I thought that, too. I heard voices often in Gippart's office, but I never saw anyone. Still, why would Gippart's partner be in *my* house?"

"I don't know. The guy's obviously a little strange." Luella not wanting to talk anymore about Gippart or Reno and "We're feeling guilty about Mrs. Scott. She's the one who deserves the money. You hear anything?"

"I wouldn't worry. IncAmPride's busy defending Chorske, but obviously when that goes to trial there'll be a big judgment. She'll get hers." Sheila pausing, then eager and "Speaking of money. . . ."

"That's really why I called. How do you want it? Oh, and you get almost half."

Sheila surprised and "Why? That isn't what we agreed to."

"Jake doesn't want his share, but he does want some for the

moron who owns the body shop where he works. Wants us to split the rest." The two women talked for a few minutes making arrangements for Sheila to get her money.

"If you're in town, give me a call," Sheila told her. Then, laughing, "We can meet after work. I know a good spot."

"You still seeing your friends?"

"Yes, I need that support, because my girls worry me. They like *clothes*. And, suddenly, boys. Lord help me."

Luella considering Sara and "Children surprise you—*nicely*—sometimes. They'll be fine. They have a good mom."

Sheila puzzled that Luella hadn't mentioned him and "How is Jake? That man didn't hurt him too bad, did he?" She wondered if Jake and Luella were still together.

"Jake's good. He stays here a lot. Maybe he's stranger than ever—he's into sculpting things out of aluminum. Late at night. Got little metal shavings all over my apartment. Men," thinking *long as he keeps his hands on me. Long as he remembers what can be repaired.*

■

Wally Reno walking late night through a parking lot along the bay in San Diego. He had just parked his car and was making his way toward the outdoor mall. He wanted to resume his habit of following and finding out more about a woman. As he went he inhaled the warm breeze off the water and wondered why he had spent so many years in Minnesota. He watched two young women in short, sleeveless dresses get in a white convertible and believed he wouldn't ever want to leave Southern California. He considered calling Gippart to tell him of the weather, and began singing softly "Oh Danny boy, the pipes, the pipes are calling." *I'm the pipes Danny. Calling.* But then he just shook his head and laughed.

He walked for an hour among the small shops of an outdoor mall but the only unattached women he came across were, he

felt, too plain for him to waste his time on. He returned to his
car and, as usual, disappeared into the night.

■

A serious man in a dark suit found Jake in the lot in front of
Jimtown, bent over an old black Monte Carlo, aligning the
hood. Jake had replaced the entire front clip and painted it, but
something in the gaps between the hood and fenders still didn't
look right.

"Mr. Warner?" the man asked, Jake straightening and
uncomfortable upon seeing the man's hard face.

"Yes?"

"My name is Lawrence Enger, and I represent the Great Lakes
Property and Casualty insurance company."

Jake did not recognize the name, and said so.

"Well," the man continued, "I didn't expect you would. We
insured the Jensons, the old couple who had an accident with
your wife."

"Oh yes," Jake finally shaking his hand.

"I'll come right to the point, Mr. Warner. Do you recognize
this?" From a file he had been holding in his left hand he withdrew a sheet of paper and gave it to Jake, who saw that it was
a signed release from 1985, and that it had his name at the bottom.

"No, I don't. What's this all about?" and *reminds me of when
Siverson walked in here.*

"That is a release form. I take it you never signed such a
thing?"

"Of course not. The accident was my wife's fault. Why would
I sign a release?"

Lawrence Enger revealed to Jake the astounding information
that his wife had not really been at fault, that the adjusters and
the sheriff in Mitchell had falsified documents and forged Jake's

signature, had perpetrated a huge fraud against not only Great Lakes but against Jake's carrier as well. Jake acted appropriately dumbfounded and *Luella would say that isn't much of a stretch for me.*

Mr. Enger indicated that Great Lakes was reopening the file, and that if Jake wished to pursue a claim, the company would respond. Jake said he would.

■

Three weeks gone since the metal plate in Luella's leg, and the screws that held it, had been removed. They walked slowly now along the hallway of the outpatient clinic, time for the stitches to come out. Only in the past couple of days had she allowed Jake to place his hand along the zippered incision, Jake brushing only slightly the reddened skin and "I sort of miss it."

"Thanks for mentioning it now. Maybe I can have him put it back in."

They had been given the plate and its screws and when Jake saw them he thought *Phillips head. The other no good*, remembering times working on cars when a straight-bladed screwdriver had slipped and marred the surrounding metal.

Sara had been managing the store so well, and it looked so good, that profits were way up. Luella marveled at the way she had taken to the responsibility during remodeling, as if she were making the store her own. Luella had said more than once, "Christ, the customers like her better than they ever did me," Jake telling her "Doesn't surprise me."

He thought of the six-holed plate and "I still don't understand why the doctor wouldn't let me unscrew it."

"You're jealous because he's got a bigger drill," Jake laughing and "You know there are other unnatural substances you can put in your body. Like *silicone*."

Luella taking his hands and placing them on her breasts and "You don't like these?"

"Yes. Tonight?"

"Be patient."

"Easy for you to say. You don't have to lie next to such a gorgeous body every night."

"True."

They came to an incline built for wheelchairs. They had not brought Luella's because she had resolved to use it less, Jake taking her arm and "Can I help you?"

"I can do it," but holding to him anyway.

"Can I watch?"

"Jake, you'll do anything to see a naked woman, won't you?"

"If it's you, yes."

"No, you can't watch."

"Tomorrow night, you think?" the two of them working slowly up the long ramp.

■

Jake dreamed often of Jane and of the bodies down the long line behind her, but as time passed the dream changed, and she and the table on which she lay became no longer flesh and stone. Now, as Jake approaches, light glistens from their surfaces as it might from polished metal, not chrome, maybe aluminum or magnesium. Jake stops his advance next to her, watches for a time, reaches his hands to touch her. He slides his fingers beneath beneath her, lifts, her weight too insubstantial for steel or iron. Aluminum alloy, he is certain, from the touch. He finds its hard surface, though polished, malleable; the metal-flesh gives, though more reluctantly than human flesh. Polished bone and flesh-ends, pooled blood. The living alloy aging, brittling. Jane's body growing whole again, not skinned in metal but solid through. With each successive dream her skin's metallic sheen brightens, takes light from Jake's fearful shame. He wakes without waking Luella, imagines a time the flesh gone solid hard, Jane a sculpture, art.

Allowing her in that way to die, allowing himself enough innocence to be set free. Remembering suddenly that he did not see
Mark in the dream at all.

The blue notebook oxidizes in his toolbox.

■

Tammy Chorske stood in the ditch along Pilot Knob Road, not
far from where she had killed Jack Scott. She had been walking
along slowly, picking up litter. She had been at it for seven
hours; she felt tired and dirty and didn't like the way she
smelled. She had been sentenced to two hundred hours of com-
munity service, the first part of which involved spending eight
hours each Saturday and Sunday cleaning up the roadsides,
beginning in May. She knew that two days equalled sixteen
hours, but she couldn't quite determine if that would require
every weekend throughout the summer. She felt she was being
treated very badly.

She heard laughter from the road. When she looked she saw
four of her girlfriends fly past in a small white convertible, their
hair flying in the wind. Tammy began to cry.

■

In Jamestown spring came quick and wet and muddy, the
plowed and drifted snow melting rapidly and running. Rain fell
often and pooled in low spots in city yards and country fields
where dried corn stalks stubbled the fallow furrows. But it was
warm and sunny too and if the rain stopped and the fields dried
the growing season promised to be fine.

On a dry late-April day Tom Gifford drove his Chevy past
the new-signed JimTown Automobile Restoration Specialists.
He hadn't been by in months and the old Quonset's new shingles and metal siding surprised him. He saw that the building
was being enlarged to the west. He had been on the street
beside Jimtown a few times over the winter and each time he

slowed and glanced through the slatted fence and saw Jake's coupe resting, settling itself seemingly further into the ground even though the ground was frozen. Once after an early January blizzard he had seen a mammoth drift that began in the middle of the fenced yard and rose elliptical to the apex of the Quonset's roof. The drift bisected the coupe so that only the pointed hood and grille shone in front. At the rear, only the pitted trunk handle and the last foot or so of the trunk lid itself. Gifford took consolation in the cold knowing the car wouldn't rust but cursed Jake when he considered what the snow would do when the sun liquefied it. He had shaken his head at the inexcusable wastefulness and driven on.

In November Gifford had begun reading two area car-marketing publications, one out of Sioux Falls and the other from Fargo, their flimsy newspaper pages filled with grainy photographs and brief descriptions; they gave him a good idea of the market. He familiarized himself with the kinds of cars available and their prices and had as a Christmas gift bought a white '62 Chevy hardtop with a 409 engine and Muncie four-speed transmission. He had paid forty-five hundred dollars for it, but considered that sum well spent. The car's owner lived in Sioux Falls, had towed the car up from Arizona where it had been with one owner since new. The dry desert air hadn't rusted it and all the sheetmetal skin except the passenger rocker panel was straight. Gifford buffed out the paint one Saturday, and the chrome was good enough to leave. Arizona heat had cracked and faded the interior, but he had already purchased a replacement kit and would probably install it his next weekend off. Gifford put on new radial tires and drove it fast, though not often. It wasn't a car to drive in salty winters or wet springs. A summer car to be pampered.

Gifford had believed he wanted an older car like Jake's coupe, but when he saw the '62's picture he remembered a young man from his hometown who drove a red hardtop with exactly the same engine. The year was '63 or '64, and the young man who with his drawn-back black hair looked left over from the fifties would take bets on the car. He didn't race, simply laid a fifty-dollar bill on the dash up by the windshield and bet anyone they couldn't reach forward and grab it while he accelerated. If they could, they could keep it. If not, they owed him ten. Gifford had never heard of him losing.

Gifford now in second gear slowly by Jimtown and turning his head fenceward and Jake's coupe gone, Gifford believing that somebody had finally offered him enough money so that Jake could not resist letting it go. He downshifted and pulled to the curb, then circled the block to JimTown's entrance. He pulled into the driveway and saw the lot had been newly asphalted. He left the Chevy near the street so that no one would park near it. When he walked into the office he found Elroy at his desk figuring an estimate. Elroy didn't look up.

"Can I talk to Jake?"

Since Reno, Elroy hadn't liked anyone asking specifically for Jake. Gifford saw Elroy's hesitation and "I'm Tom Gifford, I was in last summer asking Jake about his coupe. I manage the Western Inn." He nearly added "downtown" but refrained. Elroy in recognition softened and "Yeah, he's out in the shop."

"I can just go out there?"

"Sure, why not? Nothing wrong with you, is there?" Gifford sensing what Jake had sensed years before and smiling and "Not unless you ask my wife," Elroy grunting and "When I see her tonight."

Gifford walked through the door, saw Jake in a far corner bent over the side of a dark green van that had been smashed in front. Gifford walked to him and "Hi, Jake. Don't know if you remember me. Tom Gifford. I asked about your coupe last summer."

Jake straightening and "I remember. How you doing?" Gifford thinking that he looked thinner.

"Fine. You?"

"Good," the kind of conversations North Dakotans often have difficulty going beyond.

"I see your coupe's gone from out back. You sell it?"

"No," Jake nodding toward the other end of the shop where Gifford had not yet looked and "It's over there." They began walking, Gifford wanting to talk but Kinneady air-wrenching two bumper bolts and the racket echoing from the walls and curved ceiling. Jake gave him the finger but Kinneady, smiling, did not acknowledge it.

In a dim corner the coupe lay in pieces, the fenders resting against the south wall and the hood and trunk lid upright next to them. Gifford didn't see the doors. The engine and running boards had been removed as well, so it was just the windowless body still mounted on the frame. All the suspension pieces were gone as well, four jackstands supporting the frame at the corners. Gifford didn't think the car looked so good in pieces but pleased and "You're working on it."

"I'm working on it."

"I didn't think you ever would. You didn't seem too enthusiastic last summer."

"That was then, so on and so forth. A lot of work and time, and I'm not as young as I used to be."

"If you're going to do it right."

"I plan to."

"Elroy letting you work on it here, inside. Amazing."

"I was going to take it home, had it trailered up and he comes out and asks me where I'm going. I tell him. He offers to let me have this corner. Of course, it had to be the one where there's no lights. We used to keep parts and toolboxes here. Elroy will sometimes give, but not everything you want."

"I don't know him that well, but from what I've seen I'd have to agree."

Jake pointing to a temporary light stand with a big reflector cone and "I'll rig up some better lights and it'll be fine."

Gifford leaned inside the coupe's interior which had been

stripped bare except for the dashboard. From one of its knobs he saw two silver chains hanging, each holding larger, solid pieces of metal. He did not ask Jake about them. He examined the metal floor, wanting to suggest "I told you so" with "This is going to take a hell of a lot of work." Rust had eaten away below the doors and in front of the seat mounts. In back the trunk floor had holes the size of baseballs. Gifford pushed at one of the rusty areas and his finger went through, flakes of oxidized metal falling to the concrete.

"Sorry."

Jake laughing and "I wouldn't worry too much about that. I've got a good replacement floor lined up. Going to cut out the old, weld the new one in," Gifford nodding. He noted that the rest of the body's metal seemed as sound and straight as he had estimated it to be the previous summer. He guessed that once the floor was replaced the rest of the bodywork shouldn't be too bad.

"You going straight restoration?"

"That was my plan, as I think I told you, but now I don't know. Kind of thinking about a hot rod."

"What color?"

"I always thought black, but maybe red. If I go black, then maybe flames and louvers," Gifford smiling wider as he remembered such a flamed black car roaring up the night streets not far from where he grew up.

"Flatheads are back in," he told Jake.

"That's what I hear. But I'm getting these strange feelings lately, like it ought to be something huge with a blower on it. Big Chevy, maybe a hemi. Big and noisy."

"That'd be a long way from original. What's brought all this on?"

Jake pausing, then "I've changed."

"Well good luck. If you don't mind I'll stop by once in a while, see how you're doing."

"Don't mind at all. I can't work but nights a few hours, Saturdays. I don't want to ignore Luella."

"Women," Gifford muttered, chuckling, "they can trouble a man," Jake thinking *indeed, both dead and living*, and grateful to them both.

"Come outside a minute, see the Chevy I bought." Jake followed him out and admired the car, it bringing memories to him too, a low white one with six exhaust pipes exiting below the rear bumper. Gifford popped open and raised the hood and when Jake looked at the engine he wondered if one like it could fit under his coupe's hood and between its fenders. Gifford climbed inside and started it, the 409 idling roughly as they talked of old memories tied to cars and speed and the smell of gasoline.

As Jake admired the car he noticed the rear bumper in particular, the chrome thick unpitted, Jake marveling at what endures. On the driver's side he noticed a faded sticker—"America, love it or leave it"—and grinned wide.

Gifford saw him looking at the sticker and "I should get that off there. Kind of messes things up."

"I guess."

"What works to get it off?"

"Bug and tar remover. Some good chrome polish, it'll look new. Amazing."

Then Jake mentioned Elroy and excused himself, went back inside where for a moment he joined the tenuous flesh of his hands to the metal he believed might hold him together long enough thinking *low in front, red wheels trim-ringed and hub-capped, flames flowing orange to red over the hood and fenders. How the world will look through this window frame when I finish, the world beyond the curves and chrome, forward.* He picked up a wrench where he had left it, ran his hand across a front fender's curve and *we must live or die by steel.* He imagined *the shine of black paint on its faded surface.* But then he

reminded himself that the floor came first and *the long restora-*
tive lessons of metal. The replacement floor comes in tomorrow.
Then the cutting away, the fitting, the joining with heat and light
too strong to watch unaided. Into one new thing. Pausing, bow-
ing and *this metal in tribute to our flesh,* and finally *the dead*
restored by living hands. Luella.